# THE BUCK STOPS HERE

## MINDY STARNS
## CLARK

## HARVEST HOUSE PUBLISHERS

### EUGENE, OREGON

Scripture quotations are taken from the HOLY BIBLE, NEW INTERNATIONAL VERSION®. NIV®. Copyright © 1973, 1978, 1984 by the International Bible Society. Used by permission of Zondervan. All rights reserved, and from the King James Version of the Bible.

The author is represented by MacGregor Literary.

*Cover by Dugan Design Group, Bloomington, Minnesota*

*Cover photo © RandFaris / Corbis Premium RF / Alamy*

**THE BUCK STOPS HERE**

Copyright © 2004 by Mindy Starns Clark
Published by Harvest House Publishers
Eugene, Oregon 97402
www.harvesthousepublishers.com

ISBN 978-0-7369-2960-8 (pbk.)
ISBN 978-0-7369-4173-0 (eBook)

The Library of Congress has cataloged the edition as follows:

Library of Congress Cataloging-in-Publication Data
Clark, Mindy Starns.
    The buck stops here / Mindy Starns Clark.
        p. cm.—(Million dollar mysteries ; bk. 5)
    ISBN 0-7369-1294-0 (pbk.)
    1. Nonprofit organizations—Fiction. 2. Women detectives—Fiction. 3. Widows—Fiction. I. Title.
PS3603.L366B83 2004
813'.54—dc22                                                                2004008061

**Printed in the United States of America**

12  13  14  15  16  17  18  19  20 / LB-SK / 10  9  8  7  6  5  4  3  2  1

This book is dedicated to my late father,
Robert M. Starns, M.D.,
who blessed me with a lifetime of
unconditional love and unwavering support.

**Mindy Starns Clark** is the award-winning author of 17 books, both fiction and nonfiction, including the number one bestselling *The Amish Midwife*, with Leslie Gould, and the perennial favorite *The House That Cleans Itself*. A former stand-up comedian, Mindy is also a popular playwright and inspirational speaker. She lives with her husband and two daughters near Valley Forge, Pennsylvania.

# Acknowledgments

A giant "thank you" goes to all who helped me in the course of writing this book, including John Clark, Emily Clark, Lauren Clark, Theresa Curry of the Myositis Foundation, Karl Enters, Jim Filo, Linda Filo, Kay Justus, Steve Laube, Kim Moore, June Ann Murphy, Stacy Peters, Carolyn Shields, David Starns, Jackie Starns, Robert Bruce Thompson, Tracy Tucker, Ken Weber, Shari Weber, Barbara Wedehase of the National MPS Society, and Frank Wiemann. Also, thanks to the brilliant minds at Sisters in Crime, MMA, DorothyL, and Chi Libris—particularly my colleagues James Scott Bell and Randall Ingermanson, who allowed me to draw on their considerable expertise.

Special thanks to the families of Ricky Weber and Erin Peters, for honestly sharing with me their struggles in dealing with rare disorders.

Congratulations to Heidi Gollub, winner of the Name-the-Charity contest, for creating the name Family HEARTS.

*Bear with each other and forgive whatever
grievances you may have against one another.
Forgive as the Lord forgave you. And over all these
virtues, put on love, which binds them all
together in perfect unity.*

COLOSSIANS 3:13-14

# *One*

Someone was following me. Again.

I spotted the vehicle about three car lengths behind me, a familiar silver Buick that had appeared and disappeared in my rearview mirror a number of times in the last few days. The surveillance was being conducted by more than one person, and though they tried to hide the fact they were trailing me by alternating different vehicles from day to day, there was something uniform about the way they came and went, the way they hovered back in traffic, took the same turns, got off at the same exits. They were at it again. Whoever they were, I was growing tired of them.

They had latched on early today, less than three miles after I started out from my home on Maryland's Eastern Shore. By the time I reached the top of my rural peninsula and the town of Osprey Cove, I could see the car a few lengths behind. Despite its presence, I knew I had carried this burden by myself long enough. My nerves were shot. I was caught in an incredibly confusing and disturbing situation, and it was time to talk with someone about it.

I had been thinking for several days about what to do, about whom I could bring into my confidence and simply use as a sounding board. The one person who kept springing to mind was my pastor. This wasn't exactly a situation that I could discuss with just anyone, but because Pastor George was bound by confidentiality rules of the clergy-parishioner relationship, he would have to keep everything I told him to himself. He was also a wise and godly man.

Despite my near-constant tail, I decided to head there now. I didn't have an appointment with him, nor did I use my telephone to call ahead; for all I knew, my phones were tapped as well. Better to catch everyone off guard and go for what looked like a casual visit to my church.

On the way I stopped at the grocery store and bought some staples: salt, sugar, and flour. I hoped these would provide a visual explanation for why I was going into church at ten o'clock on a Monday morning. Not that I cared for my own sake, but if I had misread the situation, I certainly didn't want to put my pastor in any danger. At the checkout I asked for a box instead of bags, and as I walked to my car, I made sure that the items I was carrying were sticking out of the shallow box and plainly visible.

Up the street, the church parking lot was nearly empty, but I pulled in beside the cars that were there and unloaded the box of groceries. The front door was locked, so I made my way around the side of the building, casually glancing around as I did so. I didn't see my tracker at the moment, but that didn't mean it wasn't there.

My church was a lovely old building at the end of a lane and looked like something out of a storybook with its tall, white steeple. The best thing about the facility, to me at least, was that it was located directly on a bluff overlooking the water. Last year we had put in a "prayer garden" on the most scenic spot, and I sometimes came and strolled there, reading the Bible verses that were inscribed in stone, taking in the view, and praying. On this beautiful May morning, the garden looked quiet and peaceful—despite the turmoil that reigned in my heart.

The side door was open, so I went inside and made my way to the office, showing the groceries to the secretary there.

"I noticed we were running low on sugar," I said. "I was just at the store, so I thought I might stock us up a little."

"Oh, how nice," she said, standing up and following me to the kitchen. "That's great, Callie." She was in my Ladies' Circle group, and I let her chatter on about an upcoming event as I walked to the kitchen and unloaded the supplies into industrial-sized cabinets.

"Is Pastor George in?" I asked when she paused for air.

"He's in his study," she replied. "Do you need to see him?"

I finished my task and tossed the box into the recycle bin.

"If he's free," I replied, trying to sound nonchalant. Fortunately, the phone was ringing when she and I got back to the office, so while she answered it, I took the liberty of walking up the short hallway to the pastor's office myself. He was at his desk, deeply engrossed in the newspaper.

"Hi, George. How's it going?" I said, waving from the doorway.

"Callie Webber!" he said, glancing up at me. "What's a seven-letter word for 'vanquish'?"

"Um…conquer?"

He counted off the letters and smiled.

"That's it. Thanks. Can't start my week without the Monday morning crossword."

Without being asked, I stepped into his office and shut the door. And though I kept the same casual smile on my face, my words were quite serious.

"I need to talk to you, George," I said. "It's a matter of great urgency. Can you give me a few minutes?"

"I—of course," he said, standing. He was quite tall, with brown eyes behind old-fashioned, rectangular glasses. He gestured toward the chair opposite his desk. "You know you can come here anytime, Callie."

The blinds were open over a broad window next to his desk. Fortunately, the angle of the morning sun allowed us to see out but not those on the outside to see in. I sat, repositioning my chair slightly for the maximum-possible view of the road.

"I just need someone to talk to."

"Lots of folks come to me for a little counseling," he said as he sat back down and put away the crossword. "There's no need to be embarrassed."

I focused my gaze away from the window and onto his kind face. Though he and I had never spent much time one-on-one, I had seen his impressive background on his resumé when the church called him two years before, and I knew he was a devout man of God, both from his actions day to day and from the wise words he spoke from the pulpit every Sunday.

"I'm not embarrassed, George," I said. "I just have a complicated problem and need some advice. I also need this entire conversation to be totally confidential—without question, without compromise. No offense."

He did not seem offended.

"I never divulge a confidence," he told me earnestly, "though I assume you know that under certain situations I'm not only free but actually obligated—"

"I'm not planning on harming myself or anyone else, if that's what you mean."

"Very well, then. How can I help you today?"

I scooted back a bit farther in my chair. How could he help me? After all I had done to get here, I found myself faltering. Where should I even start?

"Maybe we should narrow things down a bit first," he said gently, sensing my hesitation. "Let's begin with a word of prayer." We bowed our heads and he said a brief prayer, asking for God's wisdom and peace in this moment. "Now," he said, leaning back slightly in his chair, "tell me what's on your mind."

I placed my hands on my knees and tried to gather my thoughts.

"It's a long story," I began finally, forcing myself to focus. "I'll try to make it quick. As you probably know, four years ago my husband, Bryan, was killed in a boating accident."

"Yes, I had heard that. I'm sorry."

"We were water-skiing on the Appomattox River in Virginia, and Bryan was hit by a drunken speedboat driver named James Sparks. Sparks was caught and charged with manslaughter. He pled guilty and was sentenced to sixteen years in prison—a stiff sentence, but apparently the man had a prior history of driving under the influence."

George nodded thoughtfully.

"Bryan and I were…" I faltered, wondering how to make my point. "We had a solid marriage, George. A great marriage. When he died, I very nearly thought I would die too." I didn't add that in the early days, I really didn't want to survive without him. But I did, of course. I had no choice but to go on with my life. "About a year after Bryan died," I continued, "I was offered an unusual job with a company I had never heard of—a nonprofit organization, actually, called the J.O.S.H.U.A. Foundation. I wasn't really looking for work—and I wouldn't even have entertained the offer except that it came to me through one of my dearest friends, a man I consider my mentor, a private investigator named Eli Gold."

"I'm familiar with your work, Callie. I've always been very impressed with you and the foundation."

"Thank you, George. Anyway, I have known Eli all of my life and I trust him implicitly. When he told me about this job offer, I let him persuade me to take it, even though I had never heard of the foundation, I couldn't find any information about it, and the man who was at the helm was a complete mystery to me."

"You accepted a position acting on the advice of a wise and trusted friend," he said. "Nothing wrong with that."

"Yes," I replied. "Exactly. Except now I'm starting to wonder if Eli really is a trusted friend. I'm starting to question everything I know about him and myself—and about the man who founded the J.O.S.H.U.A. Foundation. Right now, it seems as though I can't trust anyone."

The room was so silent I could hear the second hand on his watch.

"That's a scary feeling," he said finally, "to think that you can't trust."

A sound escaped my lips that started as a laugh but came out sounding more like a bark.

"I'm not paranoid, if that's what you're implying. Things have happened, George. Concrete, tangible things."

"I'm listening."

In my agitation, I wanted to stand and pace, but I didn't. Instead, I focused my attention on a soothing sculpture on the corner of his desk. It was an abstract piece, a deeply sanded and polished hunk of wood in a free-form shape. I reached out to touch it, running my fingers along its smooth edge.

"As you probably know, I'm a very curious person by nature. And the longer I worked for the foundation, the more intrigued I became about its founder. We never met in person, at least not at first. In the beginning, I didn't even know his full name—he just told me to call him 'Tom.' He explained he was a very private person, and if I wanted to work for him, I would have to respect that privacy. Which I did."

"Did you have much contact?"

"Well, we spoke on the phone and e-mailed one another frequently, but otherwise he was very hands off. He has a primary business out in California, where he lives. The foundation in D.C. is a side thing for him."

"Tell me again your official title at the foundation?"

"I'm the director of research," I said, "and my job has been the perfect mix of my two professions. Basically, I investigate nonprofit organizations that have applied to our foundation for grants. Using my investigative skills and my legal background, I verify their integrity and suitability for grants."

"Must be fascinating and rewarding work."

"It is," I said, looking out at the sunny May morning. "It's everything I ever wanted in a career. Especially when a case is closed satisfactorily and I get to present the recipients with a big grant. That's the best part."

I closed my eyes, wishing this were easier. The closer I came to spelling out what had happened, the more real it all felt.

"Last fall," I continued finally, "I realized to my great astonishment that I was starting to have some feelings for Tom. We still hadn't met in person, but our phone relationship had become very important to me. From the things he said over the phone, the interest seemed mutual." I swallowed hard. "When we finally met and then spent a bit of time together, I knew without a doubt that I was falling in love with him. The same thing was happening for him as well. With Tom, I really thought I could begin a new chapter in my life. I thought we had a future together."

"Why do I sense a fly in the ointment?"

"Bigger than a fly," I replied. "More like a Cessna. Or perhaps even a jumbo jet."

Outside, I noticed the silver Buick moving slowly down the street.

"The thing is," I said, feeling a sudden sense of urgency, "even though we had acknowledged our feelings and our relationship, Tom still wanted a lot of things about his life to remain private. It was as though he had secrets from me. He also alluded frequently to feelings of regret and the need for forgiveness, but I never understood what he was talking about. A few weeks ago, I decided I had had enough of all his secrecy. I did a little investigating, and I learned, much to my surprise, that Tom is a code breaker for the National Security Agency. To complicate matters, I also learned that my mentor, Eli, had been an NSA agent as well, years ago when he was younger."

"Wow."

"Then ten days ago, I overheard a conversation between Tom and Eli at the hospital. My world fell apart at that moment."

"The hospital?"

"Eli was…having some medical problems." I didn't elaborate, thinking there was no need to cloud the issue with the fact that Eli had landed in the hospital after having been shot by a sniper. Tom and I had investigated Eli's shooting and solved that mystery. "Tom and Eli were talking in Eli's hospital room. I came in and overheard them, but they didn't realize I was there because of a privacy curtain in the way."

"And what did you overhear?" George asked, leaning forward.

I closed my eyes, remembering the conversation as if it had happened ten minutes ago, not ten days.

*"I want to marry her, Eli!" Tom exclaimed.*

*"So ask her and be done with it," Eli replied. "It's that simple."*

"It's not that simple. She has to know. I have to tell her."

"You said it yourself, you can't. The NSA has tied your hands."

"But if I don't tell her, Eli, the secret will always be there between us. Even now, every time she looks at me with those trusting eyes, it just tears me apart. James may be the one behind bars, but all of our lives irrevocably were changed that day. Callie has the right to know the truth."

Piece by piece, I tried to relay that overheard conversation to my pastor. When I was finished, George squinted his eyes.

"What did Tom want to tell you?"

"I don't know. There's some secret, a big secret, that stands between us. Something that has to do with the NSA and—I'm very afraid—with my late husband."

# Two

George sat back, picked up a pencil, and began tapping it lightly on his desk.

"Your late husband?" he asked finally. "Did he work for the NSA also?"

"No! Bryan was an architect for a private firm in Virginia."

"Did Bryan know Tom?"

"Not as far as I know. I never even heard of Tom Bennett until months after Bryan had died."

George sat back and rested the pencil against his chin, looking as confused as I felt.

"The only 'James' I know is James Sparks," I said, "the drunken boat driver who killed my husband. He is definitely behind bars. And my life was irrevocably changed the day he killed my husband. But what that has to do with Tom, I have absolutely no idea."

My words sat in the quiet between us. Finally, George cleared his throat and spoke.

"James is a fairly common name. Maybe you've gone off on some tangent that doesn't even exist."

I shook my head vehemently.

"You had to have been there," I said. "Somehow, I just know that's who he was talking about. In my gut, I know."

"Did you confront Tom about what you had overheard? Did you ask him what was going on?"

I nodded, my heart pounding as furiously as it had at that moment.

"I stepped into the room and told them I had overheard what they were saying and that I wanted to know what the secret was. Tom just looked at me and said, 'I'm sorry, Callie. You can't ever know.' Then he left. I haven't seen him since."

"He disappeared?"

"Well, not exactly. He left this note with one of the nurses."

I reached into my pocket, pulled out a folded piece of paper, and handed it to him. I had read it so many times I had it memorized.

"'Callie,'" George read, "'I'm sorry. I love you, but this can never be. Please forgive me. Tom.'" He looked at me, his eyes wide.

"With the note was some money," I said. "According to the nurse, Tom said it was for taxi fare to the airport and a plane ticket home. I left later that day. I've been back here ever since."

"Didn't you talk to Eli to try to find out what was going on?"

"Yes, of course. But Eli was even more closedmouthed than Tom had been. He became very weepy, and he kept talking about forgiveness and love and how God calls us to *His* standard of forgiveness, not our own. I was so confused, so hurt, and so angry that I finally gave up and left. As I said, that was ten days ago."

"And you haven't heard from Tom since?"

"Only indirectly. He benched me."

"Benched you?"

"At work. He sent word to the office manager that I wouldn't be getting new cases anytime soon. Instead, he wanted me to spend my time putting together a summary of all of the cases I've handled since the foundation opened in a presentation form. I just finished putting them all together in PowerPoint yesterday."

"Interesting. Have you tried to contact him?"

"A few times, but all I get is his voice mail. I've been doing what he asked me to do at work, but otherwise I feel like I'm in limbo."

I gestured out of the window at the silver car, which was now parked in a shady spot down the street. I explained I was also being tailed now, and that I had a gut feeling it was the NSA.

"But why?" he asked, leaning forward to see where I was indicating.

"Who knows? I think they're just keeping tabs on me. But worse than everything is the uncertainty about my relationship with Tom. It can't end here, like this. It just can't."

He nodded.

"You feel helpless."

"Of course I do," I snapped. Then, realizing how I sounded, I softened my tone just a bit. "George, I love Tom. I don't want to lose him, but I don't even know what it is that stands between us."

"It seems to me there are some big issues at stake here."

"That's why I'm so confused. Is anything real? Is anything truly the way I thought it was? Am I some kind of an idiot, some fool who fell for the first nice guy who came along, not realizing that he was somehow involved in the death of my husband? Then I start thinking, what about my husband? Was he involved in all this too? Did Bryan have things he had to keep from me, secrets I knew nothing about? How far back does this go?"

George sat there quietly, letting my words fly.

"What should I do?" I whispered finally, the question floating to the floor between us.

George took off his glasses and polished them on his shirt pensively, not speaking until he had finished and placed them carefully back on his nose. I had seen him make the same gesture in church board meetings, and I knew it was his way of composing his thoughts.

"I see now why you needed to talk to someone, Callie. Rest assured that your secrets are safe with me."

"Thank you, George. Can you help me? Can you give me some advice?"

He took a deep breath and exhaled slowly.

"Well, from a purely practical standpoint," he said, "it seems to me that at the very least Tom owes you a conversation. There may be secrets that by law he needs to keep, but he has no right to expect his budding relationship with you to simply die on the vine without some sort of explanation."

"I agree."

"Assuming that Tom does work for the NSA, maybe you just need to present your questions to him in a way that he might be able to answer without breaking any rules. 'Did you know my husband Bryan?' 'Are you somehow connected with the man who killed him?' Maybe Tom's hands really are tied due to security reasons, but if you approach him in the right way, perhaps you can get the basic answers that you need in order to make some decisions. Given what you have told me about him and his feelings for you, I'm sure he doesn't enjoy leaving you hanging."

"But if he won't answer my calls, how can I ask him anything?"

He shrugged.

"Only you know that, Callie. You're a very resourceful woman. Why haven't you found a way yet?"

I thought about that, going over the past ten days in my mind. Maybe I had been so frightened and confused that I hadn't been thinking clearly.

"You think I should seek him out? Hop on a plane to California and show up on his doorstep and force him to talk with me, face-to-face?"

He looked at me with interest.

"Your words, not mine."

This time I couldn't resist the urge to stand and pace.

"Why haven't I done that already?" I asked, my navy pumps making soft thuds against the carpet as I walked. "I'm not the kind of person who just sits back and takes what comes without a fight."

"Maybe you're scared of what you'll learn. Maybe it's safer to not know."

"Of course it's safer not to know!" I cried. "But I can't go on like this. I can't live in limbo!"

My words echoed in the quiet room. George didn't respond, and in the silence, I understood that I had no choice. I needed answers.

And I knew God would give me the strength to handle them when the time came.

Returning to the chair, I took my seat, feeling a sudden calm settle over me. I would act. I wouldn't just sit back and allow the situation to control me any longer.

"Don't be too quick to assume the relationship is over, Callie," George said gently. "True love and prayer can overcome an awful lot of obstacles."

Tears filled my eyes.

"I'll go to him," I whispered, reaching out for the box of tissues near me on the desk. "If I show up, Tom will have no choice but to talk to me. He owes me that much."

George nodded, waiting as I blew my nose and wiped away my tears. The answer was so simple! I felt relieved and also a little stupid. Show up at Tom's door and force him to talk to me. Make my questions simple. Do not leave until I have some answers.

Of course.

"Thank you," I said finally, pulling myself back together. As I did, it felt as if some of the weight I had brought into his office was now off my shoulders. "I guess I just needed a sounding board. I'm so glad I came here this morning."

"May I leave you with one thought as you go?" he asked.

I nodded.

"Ephesians 4:15: 'Speaking the truth in love, we will in all things grow up in him who is the Head, that is, Christ.' Just something to keep in mind, Callie."

He was right. Speak the truth in love. That was exactly what I needed to do, and what I needed for Tom to do. It was within my power to attempt to force a confrontation where I could ask Tom questions and get some answers. I would frame my questions in such a way that perhaps he could answer at least some of them. He owed me this.

By the time I thanked George and left his office, I didn't care if I was being watched or not. I went out into the prayer garden and sat on a bench by the sea with a pen and a pad of paper. My brain was too full, my mood too urgent to do anything other than sit there and write down the questions I was going to ask Tom. Within ten minutes my list nearly covered the page. Once it was finished, I sat and looked out at the water and wondered why I had tolerated Tom's obsessive demands for privacy all of these years.

Eli. Eli was the reason, of course. I trusted Eli with my life, and he was the one who told me that Tom was a good guy, on the up-and-up, and I could trust him without reservation. I had taken Eli at his word, but now that push had come to shove, Eli wasn't giving me any explanation nor any good reason for the conversation I had overheard at the hospital between him and Tom. Because Eli was still recovering from his gunshot wound, I hadn't pressed it, but I was still dismayed that this mentor of mine, whom I loved and trusted so much, could keep such secrets from me. It completely shook my trust in him and made me question our entire relationship.

I patted the pocket where I kept my cell phone and thought about calling him and giving him one more chance to tell me what I needed to know. But then I thought about my last call to him, intercepted by his wife, Stella, who kindly asked me to give him a little space.

"He's very tormented right now," she had said to me several nights ago, "and worried about you and Tom. But he needs to focus on getting better. Please don't keep stirring this up, Callie, at least not until he's feeling a little stronger."

Despite my anger and frustration with Eli, I was concerned about his health. I decided not to call. Instead, I concentrated on forming tangible plans for confronting Tom face-to-face about all that had transpired between us. I had planned to go into the office today, as I had every day for the last week, but now I realized I would do better just to head home. There, I could go online and make flight reservations, pack, deliver my dog to the sitter, and head to the airport. Considering the time difference, I could be at Tom's door in California before the day was over. My heart pounded at the thought.

I put away my list, returned to my car, and pulled out my cell phone. I needed to call the office and tell my friend and coworker Harriet that I was going out of town for a few days. Harriet knew nothing of what had transpired between Tom and me, of course, though she certainly had a sense that something was wrong. She had pushed and prodded every way that she knew for details, but I had merely told her that Tom and I had sort of "broken up" and that I didn't feel like talking about it. Though she respected my privacy, I knew it had bothered her to see me so quiet and withdrawn. The last week at the office had been a bit strained, to say the least. It would probably be better for all concerned if I took off in pursuit of my confrontation as soon as possible.

When I turned on the phone, I was surprised to see that I had six messages. They were all from the same number, the J.O.S.H.U.A. Foundation. I called back.

"J.O.S.H.U.A. Foundation," our receptionist, Margaret, announced. When she heard my voice, she nearly started yelling into the phone.

"Callie! Where are you? We've been trying to reach you all morning!"

"I'm sorry," I told her. "I forgot to turn on my phone."

"Well, hold on a minute," she said. "Let me put you through to Harriet."

I heard a click and then, almost immediately, the voice of Harriet.

"Oh, Callie, I'm so glad you called," she said, sounding breathless and excited. "You'll never guess what message was waiting for us this morning."

"What?" I asked, butterflies suddenly flitting around inside my stomach. "Who?"

"It was Tom. He's coming here today. He wants to meet with you at five o'clock!"

# Three

By the time I reached the office, it was nearly one o'clock. That gave me four hours to prepare, which really meant four hours to pace and worry.

I parked in a paid lot several blocks from the office, and then I walked along Embassy Row until I reached the nondescript door with the small brass plate that said "J.O.S.H.U.A. Foundation." Another of Tom's secrets, I didn't know what the "J.O.S.H.U.A." stood for—and the few times I had asked, I had been told that it was personal, something I could never know.

Pushing open the door, I stepped inside to see Margaret standing near her desk, a bottle of furniture polish in hand. Margaret was always obsessively neat, but now with Tom's imminent arrival, the place was positively gleaming.

"Oh, Callie, you scared me!" she said in her nasal voice. "I thought you were him."

She bustled toward my office, and I followed along behind.

"I was waiting till you got here to dust your office. May I?"

Without waiting for my assent, she swung open my door, turned on the light, and went to work on my desk with the spray polish. I hesitated and then took a detour into the conference room, glad that Harriet hadn't seen me come into the building yet. I really just wanted some peace and quiet where I could pull my thoughts together.

Tom was coming here. Today. At five o'clock.

I didn't know why, but my gut feeling was that he was coming to fire me, close down the foundation, and end our personal relationship permanently. Just thinking about it caused nerves to clench into a ball in the pit of my stomach.

"Please, God, no," I whispered, pulling out a chair to sit at the wide table.

I bowed my head and prayed, not really forming words at first but simply letting my fear and concerns wash through me.

"I don't know what any of this is about or what I'm supposed to do," I whispered finally, "but I put it in Your hands."

Margaret came into the room just as I was opening my eyes.

"There," she said busily, spraying the table in front of me, not even noticing that I was simply sitting there. "Your office is sparkly and shiny. Once I've done this room, I'm finished."

"The place looks great, Margaret."

"Thanks! I'm just so excited. How about me? Do you think I look okay?"

I forced myself to focus in on the woman in front of me. In her mid-forties, Margaret had salt-and-pepper hair in a short bowl cut, her features girlish despite the fine age lines around her eyes and mouth. She was wearing a simple dark brown suit with a white blouse and a Peter Pan collar.

"You look lovely, as always," I said, meaning it. Margaret was a sweetheart, sturdy and sensible and the perfect upbeat presence for the foundation's front office.

"Harriet ran home to change into some nicer clothes, but she should be back soon."

As if on cue, we both turned to see Harriet in the doorway. She was wearing a vivid green suit, her bright cheeks nearly as red as her hair. Her left hand was held up at her shoulder, her fingers hooked through the top of a hanging bag.

"No!" she exclaimed, hurrying into the room. "No, no, no, no, no!"

She came up to me and grabbed my hand.

"It's all wrong. You're coming with me."

"What—"

"No objections. Let's go. I'll call Antonio on the way and he can fit you in."

I let her lead me to the door, trying to place the name, when I realized that Antonio was Harriet's hairdresser. I dug my heels into the ground, forcing her to stop.

"What are you doing?" I demanded. "I'm not going anywhere."

"Darlin', you look worse than a blue tick hunting for a hound dog. Your hair's all flat, your eyes are puffy, and you don't have on a speck of makeup."

"So what?" I asked, offended.

"So you're gonna see Tom in four hours. Do you really want him to find you looking like this? You've been moping around for a week, but now that he's on his way, you've just got to get it together. Haven't I taught you anything?"

Margaret had followed along behind as we went up the hall.

"At least your outfit looks nice today, Callie," she chimed in tentatively. "Of course, your outfits always look nice."

"Thank you, Margaret."

Harriet tugged on my hand, and I resisted until Margaret intervened.

"Harriet, let Callie go," she said. "If she doesn't mind looking like that when she sees Tom, then that's her choice."

Her backhanded defense of my position was a bit startling.

"Do I really look that bad?" I asked.

Harriet and Margaret exchanged glances, and then they both nodded at me. I took a deep breath and exhaled.

"Don't either of you find this whole situation a little demeaning?" I asked. "I mean, we learn that the big boss is coming into the office during working hours—for the first time after being in business for three years—and instead of preparing presentations or double-checking our numbers, we're running around acting like a bunch of giggling girls. Cleaning the office. Getting our hair done. Changing our clothes. What are we doing?"

They both considered my question.

"Maybe it's because we do such a good job all the time, whether he's here or not," Margaret finally ventured. "Our presentations and our numbers are already in perfect shape. That leaves us a little free time to prepare, is all. I don't see anything wrong with it."

Harriet nodded in agreement. They both stood there looking at me so plaintively that finally all I could do was groan.

"Fine," I said. "Call Antonio. Just give me ten minutes first."

"Good. I'll wait by the front desk," Harriet said.

I left Margaret there in the hall and returned to my office, shutting the door behind me. In a way, they were right. I needed to face this meeting with Tom with confidence, not feeling self-conscious because I had wiped all of my makeup off with this morning's cry.

I powered up my laptop and quickly ran through the presentation I had prepared. If this presentation was what Tom was coming to see, then he would definitely be wowed. I had done a good job assembling a comprehensive history of the agency's charitable works, even if I did say so myself.

Once I felt confident that all was as ready as it was going to be, I grabbed my purse and went out to the main area. Harriet was biting her nails, and she fussed at me that she would have to get a quick manicure repair while we were there.

The salon was only a few blocks away, so we set off on foot as I decidedly ignored the thought of whether I was being tailed at the moment or not. As we walked I braced myself for a barrage of questions from Harriet, but she was oddly silent. Finally, when we were less than a block away from our destination, I couldn't stand it anymore.

"You're so quiet," I said to her. "What are you thinking?"

She sighed.

"I'm just wishing that things were different," she said. "I've been waiting three years to meet the man on the other end of that telephone line. Now I'm finally getting that chance, but instead of it being a happy occasion, it's full of tension. Do you think Tom is coming here to…to shut us down?"

Once again, my heart quickened at the thought.

"Why do you say that?" I asked evasively.

"I don't know. I keep running different possibilities through my mind. Something about this meeting just doesn't feel right."

We turned the corner, and with a start, I looked up to my left. The J.O.S.H.U.A. Foundation kept an apartment across from the Watergate in the exclusive Halston Court building, and I suddenly realized that that's probably where Tom would be staying tonight. In fact, if he had flown into town early, there was a chance he was already there. The thought made my heart race.

"Here we go," Harriet said, opening a door to our right. We stepped into the salon and were immediately swept up into the energy and confusion of the place. Harriet had arranged for me to have a manicure, hairstyle, makeup, and a massage. Leave it to her to pamper me when I wouldn't have considered pampering myself. I tried to object, but before I knew it I was face down on a table in a darkened room with soft music and candles and a woman kneading beautifully into the small of my back.

By the time my massage was over, I felt like a new person. As the stylist worked me over, I tried to center myself, thinking calm thoughts and practicing deep breathing. Finally, as I sat for my manicure, I looked out of the front window and at the Halston Court across the street. The apartment was on the tenth floor, and I tried counting the windows, up and then over, to find the correct apartment. At this time of day, I couldn't see inside, of course, but I stared hard at those windows, wishing I could just march up there and confront Tom in private.

We had a meeting scheduled at the office, however, so I would play this the way he wanted to. My list of questions was ready, and I was determined to achieve my objective, which was to get some tangible answers.

By the time we were back in the office, I felt much better, and my hair and makeup and nails were simply meticulous. I hadn't needed a cut or color, just a wash and style, but I loved the way they had blown it out, giving me a look that was stylish and sleek. Harriet had been right; at least I would face Tom with confidence.

She and I were in her office, going over some last-minute items, when we both heard voices in the front of the small building. We looked at each other, knowing it was five o'clock. I felt as though the breath had suddenly been sucked from my lungs.

"You are a talented, intelligent woman," Harriet whispered sharply. "Any man on this planet would be lucky to have you. You remember that."

I tried to regain my composure, standing when Margaret appeared in Harriet's doorway.

"Callie, Harriet, we have some visitors," Margaret said smoothly, though the vivid blush on her cheeks gave away her excitement. "They're in the conference room if you'd like to step in and say hello."

"Visitors?" I asked. "Plural?"

Margaret discreetly held up two fingers in front of her and then motioned with her head toward the conference room. Harriet and I rose and went to meet them.

"Is there any lipstick on my teeth?" she whispered as we went, baring her teeth at me in a wide grimace.

"No, you're fine."

I let her walk into the conference room ahead of me, watching as two men stepped forward to shake our hands. One was a man of about 60 with silver-white hair and an air of quiet calm. He introduced himself to Harriet and shook her hand.

The other was Tom.

Our eyes met and held, communicating a thousand emotions in one instant: heartbreak, fear, pain, joy. Why did our love have to be so complicated?

"Callie," Tom said softly, nodding, and just hearing my name on his lips made me want to both slap his face and throw myself into his arms. Instead, I stepped forward and held out a hand, which he took and held.

"This is Kimball Peterson," he said to me, gesturing toward the silver-haired man. "One of my lawyers."

My pulse surged. A lawyer? Tom had brought along a lawyer?

I pulled my hand from Tom's and then shook the lawyer's hand, though I had to force myself to make eye contact.

"You know Harriet," I said to Tom, gesturing toward my red-headed friend.

Tom stepped forward, taking Harriet's hand in both of his and giving her his warmest smile.

"We've never met in person," he said, "but I feel as though I've known you for years."

Harriet seemed speechless, and I nearly smiled as I looked on. I had warned her that Tom was handsome, but I think nothing could have prepared her for meeting him in person. There was something about him beyond his dark good looks, beyond the tall and muscular physique. Tom was a *presence*, generating something intangible in the air around him—something welcoming and approachable and sexy and exciting. I could see that his appeal had hit her full force.

"Th-the pleasure's all mine," she said finally. "I've been waitin' to meet you in person for a long time."

"You are exactly as Callie described you," he said.

"You aren't even close to—" Harriet stopped herself, clearing her throat. "Well, Callie said you were handsome," she added. "But that's kinda like saying the Grand Canyon is big."

Everyone laughed, even me, and I was grateful that Harriet was able to break the ice. Tom and Harriet chatted for a moment about the foundation, with him complimenting her work and her always-positive attitude.

"Shoot," she said, "I'm just lucky to have a job I love. Helping Callie give away your money is a real hoot."

"Well, you are definitely an asset here, and I'm glad we were able to meet in person," Tom said, still talking to Harriet. "But don't let us hold you up. Margaret either. Kimball and I will be meeting with Callie for quite a while. Please don't feel that you need to stick around."

Harriet glanced at me, and I nodded my head.

"It's fine," I said, my voice lost somewhere down in my throat. "You can go home."

"Actually," she declared to the two men, "Margaret and I are going to dinner at the Red Rooster."

"We are?" Margaret said from the hall.

"So we'll just be around the block if you need us," Harriet added, looking pointedly at me and then hustling out of the room. I could hear fervent whispers out in the corridor.

Tom and I looked at each other until the whispers had faded away.

"Something tells me she doesn't trust us," he said.

"She's a good friend," I replied. "She's being protective, I think."

He did not reply.

"This is a nice conference room," the lawyer said, ignoring the tension and moving toward the table. "Why don't we make ourselves comfortable?"

"Where's Ms. Nelson?" Tom asked him.

"She'll be along in a minute," Kimball replied.

"Callie," Tom asked, "were you able to put together a presentation about the foundation?"

Heart pounding, I nodded. So this was it. Tom wasn't closing the foundation down, he was merely closing *me* down by replacing me with some woman named Nelson.

"May we see the presentation now?" Tom asked.

"Why don't we cut to the chase, Tom?" I demanded suddenly, trying to remember the resolve I had felt that morning in George's office. "What's really going on here?"

Tom glanced at Kimball and then back at me.

"Just bear with us," he said. "You'll understand in a little while."

"Are you firing me?"

Tom's head jerked back as if I had punched him.

"Firing you? Of course not. What gave you that idea?"

"You've got your lawyer and you've got some woman coming in. I assume she's my replacement."

A silence settled between us, and then Tom moved closer. I thought he was going to hug me, but instead he simply moved his lips next to my ear and spoke. The feel of his breath on my skin was like an electric current jolting straight through my body.

"Carole Anne Nelson is an NSA agent," he whispered. "She's coming here to sweep the room for bugs."

# Four

"This is the Greater Nashville Honor Guard," I said, moving to the next image. On the screen flashed a photo of about 30 older men posed in front of a big American flag on the back steps of their veterans' hall. The woman hadn't yet shown up to sweep for bugs, so we were proceeding with the presentation while we waited, pretending as if nothing were going on here other than a simple business meeting.

"These guys provide honor guard services for all funerals of veterans in their area. They play 'Taps,' give a twenty-one gun salute, the whole thing. It's quite beautiful."

I moved to another image, showing about ten of those men standing at attention in a cemetery in the pouring rain, one of them with a bugle raised to his lips. This photo I had snapped myself, from a distance, and though the exposure was a bit dark, I thought it captured the somber mood of the occasion.

"In their grant request, they asked for money for additional bugles and bugle lessons. We gave them five thousand dollars toward that end."

The next image appeared, a glossy ad from a car company.

"They also requested better transportation to the various funerals they serve, so we bought them this new twelve-passenger van."

Kimball grunted appreciably, the first sound he had made since the presentation started.

"These men were so sweet and grateful," I continued. "They sent a few photos with their thank-you note."

I moved smoothly through the next ten or so images, snapshots the men had taken of themselves on board the van. Once they had decent transportation, they had expanded their services and now, besides performing honor guard duties at funerals, they also drove all over the southeast giving free patriotic presentations in elementary schools. Their smiles were so wide, you could feel their delight coming through the pictures.

"And that was the grant we gave the Greater Nashville Honor Guard," I said, clicking to a new screen showing the figures. "Total value, about thirty-five thousand dollars."

I moved on to the next charity, and then the next, describing each one in turn, including the focus of their operation, and how we were able to help them. Moving chronologically through time, I came upon the last big grant I had given out by myself to a group called MORE. At the helm of that group were the parents of my late husband. Tom had allowed me to give a whopping million-dollar grant to the charity the Webbers had created in Bryan's honor.

As I looked at photos on the screen of the MORE facility, the people, and the clients they served, I felt my eyes welling up with tears. Had that million-dollar grant been guilt money? Had Tom thought he could pay off the debt he owed the Webbers with dollars? Somehow, he was involved in the death of their son. Did he really think that any amount of money could make that up to them?

The final grant was one that Tom and I had given out together a few weeks ago, a small amount to a friend of his who was raising money to send inner-city children to summer camps. I had culled a few images from their website in order to include them in the presentation.

"And this was the grant we gave to Kamps for Kids," I said, blinking away my tears as I clicked to a new screen showing the figures. "Total value, almost fourteen thousand dollars."

I clicked to the final screen, the one that summarized everything, showing the total amount of grants we had given out since we first started. Truly, the figure was stunning: Since opening our doors three years ago, the J.O.S.H.U.A. Foundation had given away 57 grants totaling almost 16 million dollars.

Incredible. I didn't know why Tom had asked me to pull all of my work together into this one single presentation, but I was so glad he had. Seeing all we had accomplished since we started was truly a humbling thing.

"Thank you, Callie," he said as I turned off the projector light. "Not only was that an excellent presentation, but the work it represents is commendable."

"It's your money, Tom," I said, as I always did. "Giving it away is the easy part."

I turned around to flip on the lights, surprised to see a woman standing there in the room, leaning against the doorframe.

"Oh!" I said, blinking in the sudden brightness. "You startled me."

She stepped into the room and thrust out a hand. She was tall and striking, with spiky blond hair that made her seem even taller.

"Carole Anne Nelson," she said. "Glad to meet you."

"Carole Anne," Tom said, rising and coming around the table. "Thanks for coming."

"I didn't want to interrupt your little slide show there," she said. "It looked like you were almost done."

She reached into the hall for two suitcases and then brought them over to the table and opened them up. Inside was the equipment she would be using to sweep the room for bugs.

"This could take a while," she announced as she assembled one of the pieces. "If you want to move into another room, I'll call you when I'm finished."

Tom glanced at his lawyer.

"I'll stay here with Ms. Nelson," Kimball said. "You two can go on ahead."

My pulse surged as we stepped out. Tom pointed toward his office down at the end of the hall, so we went there.

His office was fairly large but modestly decorated, with a simple desk and chair at one end and a couch and coffee table at the other. It was also so rarely used that it felt stuffy when we stepped inside. Fortunately, it was at the end of the building and had two big windows along the back wall. We worked to get them open, feeling the warm May breeze sweep into the room as soon as we did.

"I don't know why you won't take this end unit for your office," he said, gesturing for me to have a seat on the couch. "It's so much bigger than yours, and it has these windows. You've got nothing but a wall."

I sat on the couch, thinking how absurd the moment was. With all that was going on, we were conversing about who used which office as if it were the most natural thing in the world.

"I'm rarely here," I said finally. "I don't need much."

"I'm here less than you are," he said. "So I need even less."

He hesitated before sitting, and I could feel his mind working. Should he sit next to me? Pull out his desk chair from behind the desk and roll it over here? Finally, he lowered himself onto the wooden coffee table, facing me, the front of his knees barely an inch from mine. He leaned forward, elbows on his knees, catching me in the intense gaze of his eyes that I knew so well.

"So how are you doing, Callie?" he asked me in a soft voice.

I just stared at him, wondering where to begin. How was I doing? How did he *think* I was doing?

"It takes a lot of nerve to sit there and ask me that question," I said after a moment, surprised by the anger I could hear in my own voice. *Speak the truth in love,* I reminded myself. *Speak the truth in love.*

"You're right," he said. "I'm lucky you're even willing to meet with me."

"I'll do whatever I need to do to get some answers," I said. "I mean, it isn't all that common for a man to say he wants to marry you and then abandon you in the space of a few minutes."

He nodded, and in his eyes I could see pain and grief. I had to remember that he was hurting too.

"What's this about, Tom?" I implored, leaning forward. Our faces were mere inches from each other, and I had to resist the urge to fall into his arms. I missed him so badly!

"We'll talk when she's finished," he said, gesturing toward the door, meaning the agent who was sweeping for bugs. I nodded.

Sitting there, his eyes studied my face as if he were memorizing it. Unable to stand his scrutiny, I closed my eyes.

"I miss you so much," I whispered.

"Callie, can I hold you? Please?"

While my mind said no, my head nodded yes. Tom moved onto the couch and pulled me into his arms, burying his face against the top of my head.

"I love you," he whispered, kissing my hair, my face as his lips sought mine. I loved him too. I knew that despite everything, I always would.

When the knock came at the door, it jarred us from some other place, some other time. Tom pulled away, cleared his throat, and told whoever it was that we would be out in just a minute.

"Agent Nelson's all finished," we heard Kimball say. "We can get started."

We stood, smoothing our clothes and hair. What on earth had possessed me—after all that had happened—to sit there on the couch, kissing Tom? Had I gone utterly insane?

He turned to me and ran a hand over my hair, smoothing it down.

"You have some lipstick on you," I said softly, reaching up to wipe a smudge from his lower lip. He caught my wrist and kissed it, and then he pulled me into a long, fierce hug.

Finally, we returned together to the conference room, where Kimball and the agent were chatting. As we stepped inside, she approached us with a handheld tool, a personal sweeper, and examined us each in turn.

"Okay, that about wraps it up," she said when she was finished, slipping the unit back into its case. "You're all clear."

"Any problems with the room?" Tom asked.

"Nope. Clean as a whistle."

"Very good."

Kimball saw her out while Tom and I sat at the table. He took the end spot, so I sat to his left. When Kimball returned, he closed the door and took the place at Tom's right.

Lifting his briefcase onto the table, Kimball rooted through it for a moment and then took out a plain manila file. He shut the case and set the file on top of it.

"Callie Webber," he said, reaching into his front pocket for a pair of glasses. "Thank you for meeting with us today. Well, tonight, I guess I should say."

He took his time unfolding his glasses and putting them on. Though my heart was hammering away in my chest, I remained silent.

"I'm sure you want to know what's going on," he continued, "so I'm going to cut right to the chase."

He opened the file, tilting it toward himself so that I couldn't see inside. After flipping several pages, he paused.

"Here it is," he said, pulling off his glasses and fixing his gaze on me. "I'm sure you've heard of a confidentiality agreement."

I nodded, wondering if they would ask me to sign one.

"Often, a company will make you sign such an agreement as a condition of employment. Being in technology, Tom has signed more than his share over the years. There are a lot of secrets to be kept in the computer business."

"I'm sure there are," I said. I glanced at Tom, but his eyes were fixed on some distant point across the room.

"Six years and six months ago, Tom signed a confidentiality contract with the National Security Agency. Two years later, he signed an addendum to that contract. The fact that I can even tell you that such a contract exists required special permission from the agency and necessitated my presence at this meeting."

"I understand," I said, though I didn't, really.

"In business," he continued, "these contracts are often enforced with fines—sometimes heavy fines. You talk, you pay."

"Yes, I've heard that."

"In Tom's case, however, the contracts are not just enforced with fines."

"They're not?"

I looked at Tom and then back at Kimball. The lawyer was putting on his glasses again, and he skimmed the page in front of him.

"Pursuant to section five, paragraph four," he read, "violation of the confidential nature of this agreement subjects agent to fines not exceeding five hundred thousand dollars and imprisonment not exceeding ten years."

He put the paper down and pulled off his glasses.

"Imprisonment not exceeding ten years," he said. "That means that Tom Bennett risks up to ten years in prison if he breathes even one word to you about the facts restricted by this document."

I sat back in my chair, my mind spinning.

Ten years in prison…for telling me a few secrets?

"Callie," Tom said, reaching for my hand. "What you overheard in the hospital in Florida were things that should never have been said. I can't take them back, but I also can't ever tell you what we were talking about."

I pulled my hand away from his grasp.

"But Eli knew things—"

"Eli ferreted some stuff out on his own a long time ago. I never confirmed or denied what he learned, but he found enough outside sources to gain a full understanding of the facts anyway. Because he was former NSA himself, I felt free to talk with him that day at the hospital, though I really shouldn't have."

"Tom, was the 'James' you spoke of James Sparks?"

Tom looked back at me, helpless.

"I'm sorry," he said. "I can't answer that question."

I stared at both men, thoroughly confused. Had they really gone to all of this trouble in order to tell me...nothing?

"You said I have the right to know the truth."

"You do have the right to know the truth," he replied. "But I can't be the one to give it to you. Believe me, I've tried. I've pulled every string, spoken to every legal expert at my disposal, exhausted every option I have. My hands are tied."

"So what does this mean?" I asked, afraid to hear the answer. "Is there someone else I can talk to? Kimball?"

The lawyer shook his head.

"Tom sought my counsel on this matter, and I'm sorry to say that I also have exhausted every avenue available to us. He is under a strict gag order. That's the long and short of it."

"I'm so confused," I said, appealing to Tom. "You know you can trust me. Why can't you tell me these things you think I have a right to know? Why, in the privacy between the two of us, can't you say what's going on?"

"Because I signed a contract," he said simply. "Because I gave my word."

I shook my head, closing my eyes.

"No one would ever know," I said, shame coursing through my veins even as I uttered the words. "I wouldn't tell."

"You can't know that," he replied simply. "You can't know what you might do with this particular knowledge."

My heart pounded in anger, frustration—and fear. Just what sort of information did he have?

"I'm so sorry, Callie."

I looked down at my hands in my lap. His apology was not sufficient. "So who's been following me for the last ten days?" I demanded. "Am I under some sort of round-the-clock NSA surveillance?"

"Actually, that's the FBI," Tom said. "The NSA isn't allowed to do domestic surveillance. The FBI sometimes works on their behalf."

"But why?"

"Just to keep tabs on you. Just to make sure you stayed local until some decisions were made about how much, if anything, I would be allowed to tell you. You can't know how sorry I am that this is the final, official word on things."

The final word? *Not very likely.*

I thought of Pastor George and what he might tell me to do at this moment, and then I remembered my list of questions.

"Hold on," I said, reaching into my pocket. "I'm going to ask you some questions. You're going to answer the ones that you can."

Neither man responded as I pulled out the list of questions I had scribbled in the prayer garden. Hands shaking, I read the first one.

"Tom, did you know Bryan?"

Tom looked surprised by my question.

"No. Gosh, Callie. No."

I swallowed hard.

"Was my husband's death an accident?"

"As far as I know, yes," he said earnestly.

"Was Bryan…" I felt myself faltering. "Was Bryan involved with the NSA in some way?"

"Not to my knowledge."

"Prior to his death, was Bryan involved with James Sparks in some way?"

"Not to my knowledge."

"Is there anything I didn't know about my husband?" I asked, hating the words even as I said them. "I mean—you know what I mean."

Tom clasped his hands together on the table.

"Callie, let me say something. Bryan was simply in the wrong place at the wrong time. He was an innocent victim of a terrible accident. He had no ties with the agency and his death was not intentional."

"And there's nothing else that connected him to you?"

Tom hesitated, looking at the lawyer and then back at me.

"Not prior to his death, no," he said.

Not prior to his death. I thought about that, about all of the unspoken implications. If Tom and Bryan were not connected *prior* to Bryan's death, then they must have been connected *after* his death. For the life of me, I couldn't guess what that meant.

I tried a different approach.

"Tom, do you know James Sparks, the man who killed my husband?"

Tom didn't reply, so I looked up at him. Clearly, there was anguish on his face.

"Yes," he whispered.

Our eyes held. My instincts had been right. James Sparks was the man Tom had spoken of in the hospital, when he said *James may be the one behind bars, but all of our lives irrevocably were changed that day.*

"How did you meet him?"

"Um...we were introduced."

"How long have you known him?"

"About ten years."

"What was your connection with James Sparks at the time of Bryan's death?"

"I'm afraid I can't answer that question."

"Do you still keep in contact with him?"

"I'm afraid I can't answer that question."

I let out a frustrated breath.

"What about me?" I asked. "How is it that you came to offer me a job?"

"I'm afraid I can't—"

I held up a hand to stop him, a cold shudder coursing through me.

"It's no coincidence that I work for you, is it?" I asked. "My position here, with this foundation, was it somehow...engineered?"

"It's not that simple," Tom said. "I...I created this foundation with you in mind, yes."

"With me in mind? What does that mean?"

"I knew I wanted to hire you. I knew you were the right person for the job."

"A job you sought me out for," I said. "Even before you hired me, you knew who I was, you knew all about my husband's death, and in fact you knew the man who killed him."

"Yes."

I could feel my face burning with anger.

"What about our relationship, Tom? Our personal relationship? Was that preordained too?"

Tom surprised me by standing and going to the door and opening it. At first he didn't answer my question. Then he said, "Kimball, could you excuse us for a minute?"

"I don't think—"

"Please, just for a minute."

Without reply, the lawyer put the file back into the briefcase and stood.

"I'll be in the hall," he said.

# Five

I listened as the door shut with a soft thud, leaving Tom and me alone in the room.

"Do you remember Wendell Smythe?" he asked me suddenly. "My friend in Pennsylvania?"

I thought back to last September, nine months ago, when Tom sent me to deliver a grant to a friend of his in Philadelphia. When I showed up with the check, I found the man dead on the floor behind his desk. As a favor to Tom, once Wendell's death was classified as a homicide, I investigated and found his killer.

"Yes, of course."

"Do you remember when you went to his funeral? How much it upset you?"

I nodded. I could remember the whole thing vividly. Wendell's widow, Marion, had arranged for a singer to perform the hymn "It Is Well" at the gravesite. Still grieving for my own late husband, it had been difficult for me to handle the funeral, but when that song began, I simply lost it. I sobbed my way through most of the service, crying not for Wendell's survivors, whom I hardly knew, but for myself and my own loss, my own pain. It wasn't until later that I learned Tom had also been at that funeral. He hadn't identified himself or told me hello, he said later, because it didn't seem like the right time. Though at that point we had become good friends through our phone conversations, we continued with only a long-distance relationship for some months more. He had left that day without ever telling me he was there.

"Something happened to me at that funeral," he said, sitting down in his chair.

"Something happened?"

"I fell in love with you," he said. "I didn't expect it. I didn't want it. But at that point you and I were already such good phone friends. When I saw you in person, everything changed. But then I saw you crying so hard, and I knew this could never be."

"Why not?"

"Because there was too much between us, too much that you couldn't know."

I turned my face up toward the ceiling, wishing I could just reach down Tom's throat and pull the truth out.

"Then why did you come to see me at my home two months later?" I demanded. "Why did you come to me again when I was in North Carolina and sweep me off my feet?"

"I couldn't help myself, Callie. I fought it long and hard, but a part of me just wouldn't let go. I thought if we could give our relationship a chance, maybe none of this other stuff would matter."

"But it does matter."

"Yes, it does. In my heart, I always knew it would."

"And so that's the end of it. Of us."

He leaned forward onto the palms of his hands.

"It doesn't have to be."

"Tom, you are somehow connected with the death of my husband. Am I simply supposed to forget that, to go on through life without ever knowing what that connection was or what you had to do with it?"

"I said I couldn't personally tell you the facts about Bryan's death. I didn't say you couldn't learn them some other way."

I sat back, thoroughly confused, trying to understand what he was saying. He looked toward the door and then back at me, an imploring expression on his face.

"You want me to investigate," I whispered suddenly, sounding as stunned as I felt. "You can't tell me what's going on yourself, so you want me to figure it out on my own."

He was silent, but I could almost detect a slight nod of his head.

"That's what you're implying, isn't it?" I pressed. "You think I can learn the truth some other way."

Again, he did not speak, but I could tell from his expression that I was correct.

"You overestimate my abilities, Tom," I protested softly, glancing toward the door. "I can't go up against the NSA."

"Maybe you don't have to," he said. "Sometimes there's more than one way to get at the facts. Eli did it. I think you can too."

I simply stared at him, flummoxed. After all these years of asking me to respect his privacy, now he *wanted* me to investigate him? In my entire life, I had never undertaken a full investigation simply on behalf of myself. Could I do it? Could I treat this like any other investigation and get down to the facts of the matter?

More importantly, if I did, what would happen then?

"Tom, if I knew the truth, the whole truth, about Bryan's death," I said, faltering, "would you and I have a future together? Could we go on, as a couple?"

He took a deep breath and slowly let it out.

"I don't know, Callie," he said finally. "I just don't know. But at least with all of the facts out in the open, we could make that decision together."

Without another word, he rose and went to the door, letting the lawyer back into the room. The meeting ended soon after that. There wasn't much more to say, really, so Tom offered to wait while I put away the projector and gathered my things. Kimball stayed with us the whole time, and I had a feeling he was starting to have his doubts about Tom's ability to keep silent in this matter. Maybe the man hadn't realized how much love was there between us until he saw it firsthand. What he didn't understand was that Tom truly was a man of his word. If he had promised not to talk, he wouldn't talk. It was as simple as that, whether the threat of a prison sentence hovered in the balance or not.

We all stepped outside into the darkness, and with a surge of guilt I realized that Harriet and Margaret were still probably cooling their heels over at the Red Rooster, waiting to make sure I was okay. I locked the door to the foundation office and then allowed the two men to walk me to my car. As we went I used my cell phone to call Harriet; I told her that all was well and that she really could go home now. She could tell by my voice that I wasn't alone, and she made me promise to call her later and fill her in. Little did she know, there was absolutely nothing from our meeting that I would be able to tell her about.

"So how long are you in town?" I asked Tom once I hung up the phone. Considering the situation, my question sounded rather inane.

"I'm not," he replied. "Soon as we leave here, I'm heading to the airport and back to California."

"Tonight?"

He shrugged.

"I've got lots going on."

The three of us walked through the quiet streets, the two men escorting me cautiously despite the fact that we were in a relatively safe section of D.C. Just as Tom had assured me, I did not see any signs of a tail.

"Tom, why did you have me put together that presentation about the foundation? Was it for Kimball?"

"No," he said, "I just wanted a summary, something showing what we have accomplished. What we can accomplish. Together."

So that was it. Tom had thought if I spent my time assembling a report that summarized our efforts, it would somehow sway me to look past our current problems and at the bigger picture. In a way, his plan had worked. As I considered our future as a couple, I also had to question my future with the foundation, and I felt a profound regret at the possibility that my job there might have to come to an end.

As I thought about my job, I wondered what my next step should be.

Could I really pursue this case? And if I did, should I take a leave of absence while doing so? We reached the lot where I had parked my car, and as if in answer to my question, Tom produced a manila envelope from his briefcase and held it out to me.

"What's this?" I asked, taking it from him.

"Your next charity. I'd like you to look into it."

Hoping this was his way of passing along some clues, I took a glance inside despite being under Kimball's watchful eye. Sadly, it was just another charity investigation. My heart sank. Did he really think we could go on as before, business as usual? "Tom, I don't—"

"Please?" he said. "I just thought it might help to have a new case to work on. Keep your mind off of things." His eyes were trained on mine, but I looked away.

"At this point, I'm not sure what I'm going to do about anything."

"I understand."

I took my keys from my purse and clicked the button that would unlock my car. Tom reached inside, pulled the parking tag from my dashboard, and turned to Kimball.

"We'll be right back," Tom said, and then he took my elbow and led me toward the payment booth. As we walked toward it, I felt his hand slip into my jacket pocket, leaving a weight behind.

"I'm giving you a special cell phone," he whispered. "Try not to contact me, but if you have to, that's the phone to use."

I nodded, not quite understanding, though I assumed it had some sort of scrambler on it. At the booth I let Tom pay my parking fee, knowing that arguing with him was pointless.

As he walked me back to my car, he thanked me for meeting with me. I didn't reply, not sure enough of myself or how I felt at the moment. Mostly, I was angry and confused. And scared. But when it came time to part, I was reluctant to let him go without speaking my mind just a little further.

"Tom, do you know how much pain you've caused me in the last ten days?"

Kimball was standing behind my car, but as we approached he moved away from it toward the sidewalk.

"I know," Tom said. "I know."

"You left me there, Tom. You left me stranded in the hospital," I said. "You didn't explain, didn't even say goodbye. You were just gone."

"I was confused. I had to think."

"And what has all this thinking done for you?"

He glanced over toward the lawyer, who was waiting at a discreet distance. Then Tom turned his eyes back to me, the expression on his face intense. It was time to say goodbye.

"I love you, Callie," he said, taking my hands in his. "But I've done everything I can. The ball's in your court now."

He leaned in to kiss me, but I tilted my face downward so, instead, he gently placed his lips against my forehead.

I closed my eyes. Underneath all of the anger and pain in my heart there remained one solid, steadfast thing that could not be extinguished no matter what had recently transpired or what had happened in the past: my love for him.

The only question that remained now was how hard I might have to fight for it.

# Six

Almost without thinking, I made the choice not to go home. I called Harriet's machine at her house and left a message not to be worried but that I was heading out of town on a new investigation—implying, of course, that it was a charity investigation. I said I would be in touch. After that, I called my neighbor and frequent dogsitter, Lindsey, and asked her to pick up my dog, Sal, and take good care of her for me. Then I followed the signs to I-95 south, set my cruise control, and sped forward toward my past.

The night was dark, with clouds covering a half moon and the stars. I drove into the darkness, the city receding behind me, the black folding around me like velvet. My mind was a blur, a confused swirl of emotions. Though this sudden departure wasn't the most logical way to proceed, I knew I couldn't simply go home to my little cottage on the Chesapeake. I needed to move forward, to *do* something. Two hours down the road, I crossed into Richmond, feeling the weight of this decision bearing down on me. After a quick rest stop, I continued onward. If there was anyone tailing me now, I sure didn't see them.

It was after midnight by the time I reached Melville, Virginia, so I took an exit that was lined with motels. I pulled into the first decent-looking one I could find, went inside, and got a room. I asked for some basic toiletries, and the clerk gave me a free toothbrush, shampoo, hand lotion, and a shower cap.

Once I was in my room, I again had to admit how dumb it had been to go off half-cocked like this and make this trip without any preparation. I had no extra clothes, no makeup, and nothing to sleep in. Still, after the tense day and the long drive, I was exhausted. I used the flimsy little toothbrush to clean my teeth, got undressed, and climbed under the sheets. I was asleep almost before my head hit the pillow.

I dreamed of water—smooth, black, glassy water—the black slowly turning to red, the red of Bryan's blood. In my dream, his body was dead but his face was still moving, his lips screaming a silent yell. When I woke up, I was covered in sweat.

I sat up, heart pounding. This was a dream I hadn't had in over a year. According to the clock, it was nearly 4:00 A.M., far too early to get up and face the day. I climbed from the bed, turned on the noisy air conditioner, got back under the covers, and forced myself back to sleep. When I opened my eyes again, it was morning and the room was freezing.

There was a complimentary breakfast buffet in the lobby when I went to check out, so I ate first, taking an empty table by the window and reading a newspaper that someone else had left behind. Mostly, I just flipped through the pages looking at pictures, my mind far too full to take in anything beyond that. At 9:30 I filled a plastic cup with coffee, took care of things at the front desk, and then went outside and got in my car.

First things first, I wanted to get out of my suit. Pulling from the parking lot I drove up the road until I found a discount store. Once inside, I hit several departments, filling my cart with toiletries, some comfortable-looking clothes, sneakers, and some basic office supplies. I also selected a pair of binoculars and a camera, a good digital one, and put everything on my credit card. Before leaving the store, I ducked into the bathroom and changed into a shirt and jeans I had just bought, clippling off the tags as soon as I was sure they fit.

I was much more comfortable by the time I got back in the car. At the nearest gas station I filled up my tank and bought a county map. Though I had a specific destination in mind and could have used my GPS, it was helpful to see the big picture.

Staring at the map, it struck me how normal it was, with simple lines crisscrossing the paper and a squiggle of blue for the river. I plotted my course and then took back roads out of town, catching glimpses of the water through the trees as I drove. Somehow, I hadn't thought I'd ever come here again.

About a half hour later, when I reached the town of Riverside, Virginia, a surge of emotion overtook me. Something about it seemed so familiar and yet so foreign all at the same time. It was almost as though the town were two places to me: Before the accident, it had been a cozy little borough where we visited a souvenir shop and strolled to an ice cream parlor and asked for directions to the campground. After the accident, however, it had become merely the site of the police station and the hospital and the morgue where my husband's dead body was processed.

Now it certainly seemed as if life had continued along here as usual. I drove through tree-lined streets, noting little shops, wide planters filled with petunias, and a small group of senior citizens standing near a bridge, taking a photo.

I passed through town and out the other side, driving on about two miles before I began looking for the turn. I missed it the first time, realizing that I had overshot it when I reached the intersection with the highway. I made a U-turn in the middle of the empty road and tried again, finally spotting the break in the trees and the little sign for the campground. The blacktop soon turned to gravel as I drove toward the river, trees hanging so low in some places that their leaves brushed the top of my car. When I pulled up to the little hut at the entrance to the campground, a woman in a tank top and cutoffs emerged and slowly ambled to my window.

"Camping or day use?" she drawled, looking bored as she smacked her gum.

"Day use," I said. "Just for an hour or so, really."

"Still have to pay the full day fee, even if you only stay a little while."

"Fine. How much?"

"Six dollars."

I pulled out singles from my purse and handed them to her.

"Have a good time," she said, stepping away from the car.

My heart was pounding as I followed the winding one-way drive past the picnic area and the boat launch and on into the camping area. Among about 30 numbered spots, only a few were taken; a Tuesday early in the month of May wasn't exactly high-use season for Virginia campgrounds. Beyond the main area was a small spur with the five best spots, isolated little plots among the trees right along the river. Ours had been number 22, a shaded stretch of grass with a picnic table, a fire pit, and a little dock where we tied up the boat. Fortunately, for now the whole section was empty.

I parked the car and got out, my shoes crunching on gravel. I shut the door and walked to the picnic table, inhaling the distinctive scent of Virginia woods.

Camping. Bryan and I had come here almost four years ago for a simple camping trip, along with my brother and a few friends. We had taken up three spots—the girls in one tent, the guys in another, and Bryan and me in ours. As the only married people in the group, Bryan and I were always sort of "parental" figures—making everyone quiet down after dark, handling most of the food preparation. The boat was my brother Michael's, new to him though he had bought it used, a Sea Ray with an inboard motor that seated all eight of us. When we started doing some water-skiing, however, we took turns going out on the boat in groups of three so it wouldn't be weighed down with all of us. When it was our turn, the three that went out were Michael, Bryan, and me.

Now I stepped past the fire pit, black with the ashes of past fires. I wondered if somewhere down deep in the ground, inside the circle, were *our* ashes—still there, the remains of the fire we had enjoyed on Bryan's last night alive. We roasted hot dogs and marsh-mallows and sang stupid songs and then played Pictionary until it was quite late. The next morning Bryan had gotten up first and made scrambled eggs, bacon, and fire-cooked toast for everybody. When I emerged from the tent in shorts and a sweatshirt, I found him setting everything out on the picnic table, and I had wrapped my arms around him in the cool Virginia morning and told him that I loved him. I would always be grateful I had thought to tell him that I loved him that morning. More than that, I would go back in my mind, again and again, to the way he put his arms around me, kissed the top of my head, and said "I love *you*, Callie," back to me.

Gingerly now I tiptoed among the roots of a weeping willow tree, making my way to the little dock. I walked to the end of the boards and then sat cross-legged, hands on my knees, looking out at the beauty of the water. And it was beautiful here, despite all that had happened, despite the cost it had exacted from me. We had never been to this river before that trip, but it was only a three-hour drive from home and my friend Judi had seen it on the internet and thought it looked nice. She wrote me a letter over a year later, saying she still lost sleep over the fact that this place, this location, had been her idea.

A bird flew out from a nearby bush, startling me. As I watched it take to the sky, I forced myself to go back to that day, to the events that led to my husband's death. It had all been so normal, so run-of-the-mill. We had boarded the boat and taken turns, Bryan driving as Michael skied, then Michael driving as I skied, with Bryan as the spotter. I remembered a moment when I was gliding over the water, handle firm in my grip, legs taut and strong, a moment when I had a surge of pure elation, a flash of extreme happiness.

When my legs grew tired, I had given the signal and Michael slowed. Letting go of the rope, I angled down into the water, and by the time they had turned around to come and get me, I had removed the skis and was waiting to trade places with Bryan.

"Why don't you take it a little further up river," he had said to Michael as he lowered himself into the water. "I want to see what's beyond that bridge."

Soon we were off, Michael at the wheel, me facing backward to keep an eye on Bryan, and Bryan at the end of the rope on the water skis. He didn't have very good form—my brother and I were both much more graceful skiers—but there was something so energetic and daring in his technique that he was really fun to watch. He loved to jump the wake and speed forward way out to the side, and this river was so wide in spots that he was able to do that quite a bit. When we neared the bridge, Michael had to slow way down but Bryan kept up, hanging onto the rope directly behind the boat as we went under and then picked up speed again.

Beyond the bridge, the river narrowed a bit—a little at first, and then a lot. We had spent the morning going up and down the same piece of shoreline in front of the camp, so it was fun to see a different part for a change. Behind us Bryan was having a blast, jumping the wake and then jumping back in again. We were taking a wide curve when a sudden jolt made him lose his balance and drop the rope, spilling into the river.

"He's down," I called to Michael over the roar of the engine, and immediately he pulled back the throttle so that he could slow down and turn around.

The river was narrow at the bend, and Michael had to be careful not to get too close to the sides as he made a 180 on the water. It took a little bit longer than usual, and in the distance, I watched my husband to see if he was ready to stop or if he wanted to ski some more. I saw him holding the skis in his hands rather than putting them back on his feet, a sure sign he was tired and ready to quit. As we completed our turn, we heard the roar of a very loud engine that sounded as though it was coming our way. Then suddenly it was there, rounding the corner, a long, pointed cigarette boat, flying across the top of the waves at 50-plus miles an hour.

The driver never saw Bryan in the water, never even realized that there was a swimmer in his path. In a moment that was seared into my brain like a firebrand, I could still see how it was right before impact: the sun was warm and the sound was loud and the air smelled like suntan lotion and outboard motor exhaust and Bryan had not a moment to get out of the way.

The sound of his death was like the sound of fiberglass hitting lumber, and I remember thinking it was the sound of the skis being struck by the motor, that Bryan must have simply left them there on the surface and then ducked way down under the water, somehow propelling himself to the bottom of the river until the speedboat had passed. But an instant later the speedboat was gone, the skis were still intact, floating on the water, and Bryan was face down a good 40 feet away, the dark water turning red all around him.

"Oh, oh no," Michael had cried, pulling our boat up even with Bryan's body and then jumping overboard to lift him onto the steps. Between the two of us, we were able to drag him on board, and suddenly there were other boats around, someone yelling, someone else taking off after the speedboat.

I sat on the floor of Michael's Sea Ray and cradled my husband in my arms. He was bleeding everywhere, which at the time I knew meant that at least he was still alive, at least his heart was still pumping. But his heart didn't pump for very long. He died in my arms of massive blood loss and internal injuries. They told me later that I screamed nonstop for half an hour.

I didn't remember that. I remembered pretending it hadn't happened, pretending that I had rewound my watch and taken time backward. Just a few minutes would have been enough to alter the entire sequence of events. When the ambulance came, they had to pry me off my dead husband. Hours later I realized I was still clutching strands of his hair in my hand.

There wasn't much after his death that I remembered. Somehow, time continued to progress: the man in the speedboat was caught, the police came, the ambulance took Bryan's body away. I think we stayed locally for a day or two, our families racing there to take charge of the situation and take care of me. My father cried, unashamed, great streaming tears down his weathered cheeks like twin rivers of sorrow. Someone gave me some pills that helped me sleep. Somehow, eventually, I ended up back in our little house in Blacksburg. I didn't have a lucid thought for at least a week.

The funeral was private, just the family, despite the fact that the whole town wanted to come. Two days later, however, Bryan's family arranged a memorial service at the church, where I was put into a receiving line like a bride at a reception. At one point, my mother had to usher me out because I started laughing and couldn't stop. I had a vague recollection of what was funny, something someone said about God taking Bryan home because He "needed another angel up in heaven." People were so ignorant in their attempts to soothe me that I wanted to kill them.

Michael was beside himself with sorrow and guilt, despite the fact that there was nothing for him to feel guilty about. It had happened, a horrible, horrifying sequence of events that was over practically as soon as it began. It was no one's fault. Bryan was dead, and it was no one's fault.

Correction. It was one man's fault, one man named James Sparks who had been at the wheel of that cigarette boat. But now I knew better. Now there was another person to consider. In some way, Tom was involved with Bryan's death as well. The thought made me physically ill.

# Seven

As I sat on the dock, looking out at the water and remembering the day my husband died, I realized that, in a way, it felt good to be here, to reconnect with this place now that I had several years' perspective. As Tom had said, *James may be the one behind bars, but all of our lives were irrevocably changed that day.*

My life *had* been changed irrevocably, in an instant. I had everything and then I had nothing. I was left with a void that would never completely be filled, no matter how much I might go on with my life or even love again. Bryan was dead and gone.

I closed my eyes and prayed out loud, thanking God that through it all He had been there to fill that void. His love had kept me sane in the midst of insanity. His steadfast assurance that He would bear my grief saved me from grieving all alone.

Some people, I knew, experienced a tragedy like mine and turned from God, concluding simply that He did not exist. I don't know why, but that had never happened for me. I spent a long time angry with God, yes, but I never felt He wasn't there. His presence was far too real to me for that.

A song came to mind, an old hymn, and with my eyes still closed I sang it softly, my voice echoing on the water.

*Our broken hearts have left us sad and lonely,*
*but Jesus comes to dwell Himself within.*

Opening my eyes, I stood up and held out my hands, knowing there was no one around to see or hear as I sang the chorus in an act of worship.

*When Jesus comes the tempter's power is broken.*
*When Jesus comes the tears are washed away.*
*He takes the gloom and fills the life with glory.*
*For all is changed when Jesus comes to stay.*

"Amen," I whispered. Then, wiping away my tears, I turned around and walked back to my car.

I drove out of the campground as slowly as I had driven into it, catching one last glimpse of the river as I steered through the trees. Back at the highway, I turned right, heading toward Riverside. In my heart I was determined to learn the truths I needed to know.

When I got back to town, I went in search of a library, certain they would have archives for the local newspapers. Fortunately, there was a good-sized facility downtown, and I parked and went inside, preparing my heart for the brutal truths I was about to encounter.

The library hadn't put their collections online, but shortly I unearthed a whole week's worth of stories on microfilm. The first headline was on the front page and said "Tourist Dies in Boating Accident on Appomattox River." The article was fairly concise, the word "tragic" jumping out from the page in several places. Yes, it was tragic. The photo that was front and center was a distant shot of the water, with an ambulance parked beside it and several paramedics pushing Bryan's lifeless, blanketed body inside. There were several smaller photos also, including one black-and-white shot of me as the "victim's wife," standing on the shore, my bathing suit and shorts covered in what I realized now was blood. I stared at the picture for a long time, at the dazed expression on my face, at the dark stains that marked my clothes, my hands, my legs. I had a sudden memory of Michael making me go in the water to rinse off. At the time I had been so out of it that I hadn't even understood what he meant. Now I knew.

The article concluded with a paragraph about Sparks:

> The driver of the speedboat was arrested less than a mile from the scene when he stopped at the Docksider Grill, allegedly unaware that he had struck Webber in the water. The suspect, as yet unnamed, was taken into custody and is being held without bail.

Feeling oddly detached from the stories in front of me, I went to the next day's paper, which also had an article on the front page, this time with a photo of the speedboat being impounded by the police as evidence. "Speedboat Killer Tests Positive for Intoxicants" claimed the headline, though the paper didn't say whether those intoxicants were drugs or alcohol or both. There also wasn't any information about where he had been staying in the area, though it was clear he had been the only person on board the boat at the time. A local resident, Harry Stickles, had witnessed the accident from his own motorboat and had pursued the speedboat to the Docksider Grill.

"That fellow had no idea what he done," Stickles was quoted as saying. "When we caught him at the dock, he was absolutely shocked."

I didn't know until reading the article that Sparks had been taken under citizen's arrest until the police could get there. A photo at the bottom of the page showed him being carted off in handcuffs by an policeman identified as Officer Darnell Robinson. Strangely, I felt a wave a pity for Sparks, who thought he'd been out for a little boat ride, only to learn he had just committed a hit-and-run.

My pity didn't last long. In the next day's paper, the test results had been released: The driver's name was James Sparks, and his blood alcohol level was listed as 1.2, way beyond the legal limit for any kind of driving. His mug shot was featured prominently, next to a photograph of Bryan, with the caption: "Sparks Held for Manslaughter; Architect's Life Cut Short in Hit-and-Run."

Bryan's photo was a professional head shot that had been taken for a company brochure the year before. In the picture he looked studious and handsome, brown hair cut short, his wire-rimmed glasses adding just the right intellectual touch. The article had apparently been written with information supplied by one of Bryan's brothers, who was quoted as saying, "Bryan was a very special guy. He will be greatly missed by all who knew him."

That was the last article that earned the front page. There were other mentions inside later issues of the paper, but the whole thing eventually became less about the specific incident and more about the perils of drinking and boat driving. When it had degenerated into mere statistics, I concluded my search. As neither the killer nor the victim were locals, there didn't seem to be any further follow-up articles.

At least I had some names. I returned the tapes, signed out at the reference desk, and wandered from the library, my notebook and pen in hand, pausing at a pay phone near the front door to look in the local phone book. I found a phone number for a man named Harrison Stickles on Oakmont Road and copied it down. I also noted the address of the police station.

By the time I got back into the car, I realized I was starving. I found a small restaurant up the street and went inside, ordering tea, vegetable soup, and a grilled cheese sandwich, all comfort foods. As I waited, I scribbled thoughts in my notebook, scary thoughts that made me vaguely nauseous.

*Tom feels guilty about Bryan's death,* I wrote. *Culpable. Why? Did he drive the boat? Supply the boat? Supply the alcohol?* I was reaching, I knew, but there had to be some reason why Tom blamed himself.

If Tom knew James Sparks, there were many ways he might have somehow been involved in Bryan's death. I just needed to learn where the gaps were—what Sparks had been doing in the area, who he was with, if it was his boat. I knew that cigarette boats cost a fortune, and that frightened me. Certainly, Tom had a fortune to spend on a big fancy boat if he wanted to.

By the time the food was put in front of me, my appetite had waned a bit. Still, I sipped at the tea and picked at the sandwich. I needed to keep going, and I wouldn't last long without eating.

Once I finished and paid the bill, I called Harrison Stickles from the car, feeling a rush of relief when he confirmed that, yes, he was the same Harry Stickles who had helped out with that hit-and-run boating accident a few years back.

"Who wants to know?" he drawled. "You a reporter or something?"

He sounded eager, as though he missed the attention the whole incident had brought him. I said that no, I was the widow of the man who had been killed that day.

"Oh, I'm so sorry," he said. "I didn't realize. What can I do for you?"

"To be honest," I replied, not being honest at all, "I was passing through the area and I realized I never really thanked you for your help that day. I just wanted to give you a call and let you know how much I appreciated your efforts."

He sounded touched, like a sweet old guy who would have done his civic duty either way, but it was nice to be acknowledged.

"I did what any good citizen would do," he told me. "When I saw that boat plow into that guy—uh, I'm sorry, into your husband—I didn't even think. I just took off behind him."

"You followed him all the way to the Docksider Grill?"

"It weren't too far. Maybe a mile at the most."

"So he was never out of your sight the whole time?"

This was the question I didn't want to ask, terrified that perhaps Sparks hadn't been the one at the wheel that day at all but had somehow made a quick switch with Tom.

"Never out of my sight," Harry said. "He wasn't getting away from me no way, no how."

"And there was never any moment where you didn't see him?" I pressed. I had to be sure.

"Nope. Lemme tell ya how it was," Harry said, his voice warming to the tale. "My son and I was down at the river that day, trying out the new five-point seven-liter MerCruiser we put in our ski boat. When you folks came by, we had just put her in the water, and J.T. was parking the car. I was sitting there idling the boat when I heard that big sucker come roaring 'round the corner. I saw what was gonna happen, and sure enough it did. Pardon me, but the sound that boat made smacking into your husband's body still gives me nightmares."

I swallowed hard, thinking, *Me too.*

"Anyway, I didn't even wait for J.T. I just slammed down the throttle and took off. I wasn't sure how far I'd have to go, but then pretty soon the guy starts slowing down like nothing's going on. He pulls into the Docksider and ties up. By the time I got out of my boat, he was walking up the dock."

"What happened then?"

"Well, I was a wrestler in high school," Harry said, "so I used some of my moves to get him down. He wasn't nothing but a little guy anyway. I pinned him to the dock and held him there till we started drawing a crowd. A buddy of mine owns the Docksider, and I hollered for him to call the police, that we had ourselves a hit-and-run boat driver."

"So if it hadn't been for you," I said, "he would've gotten away."

"If it hadn't been for me," he said, "I don't think that boy would've even known what he done. I said to him, 'Didn't you even hear that big thwack? Didn't you feel it?' He says, 'I just thought I clipped a little driftwood.'"

So it really *wasn't* Tom who killed my husband, which had been my greatest fear. I breathed a deep, long sigh of relief.

"You know, I was gonna testify and everything," Harry said. "But then that fella pleaded guilty and they ended up not having a trial."

"Have you ever heard anything about him since?" I asked.

"Nah. It's old news now. He got a pretty stiff sentence from what I recall—though of course you know that. I 'magine he's locked up tight over at the state penitentiary."

"I imagine so."

We talked a moment longer, but I had already learned what I needed to know. I thanked the man again and hung up, glad at least that I had been able to acknowledge the good he had done.

I started up the car and drove to the police station, finding it tucked away on a little side street. It was a cute building, red brick with white trim and an American flag flying out front. I found parking at a meter down the block, and then I walked back toward the station, wishing I had kept my suit on after all. Somehow, I knew jeans wouldn't make quite the same impression.

I'm not sure what made me glance back over my shoulder as I turned to take the wide white steps to the main entrance. But look back I did, and I caught a glimpse of someone, a man, suddenly ducking into a doorway. I wouldn't have thought twice about it, except for the fact that he hadn't made his move until I turned my head. Feeling a deep sense of foreboding, I proceeded into the building. At least I would be safe inside a police station.

At the front counter, I asked for Officer Darnell Robinson. A man pointed toward a fellow sitting at a desk not too far behind him.

"Darnell!" he called. "Somebody here to see you."

The man looked up, the same officer I recognized from the newspaper photo. He stood and waved me over.

"Can I help you?" he asked, looking as though he'd rather not help me. Mostly, he just looked tired.

"Officer Robinson?" I said. "I wonder if I could talk to you for a moment."

"Sure," he said, gesturing toward the chair that sat alongside his desk. "I'm off in about ten minutes, but I can help you if it's quick. What can I do for you?"

"My name is Callie Webber," I said. "You probably don't remember me, but my husband was killed here in town about four years ago."

"Killed?"

"In a hit-and-run boating accident on the river. You were the arresting officer."

His eyes widened and then filled with understanding. He nodded, leaning back a bit in his chair.

"Of course," he said. "Mrs. Webber. You and your husband were water-skiing at the time."

"Yes."

"I remember it very well."

He looked at me, so I continued.

"I'm back in town for the first time since it happened," I said, "and I'm really just trying to piece together the facts of the case. I wonder if you could fill in some blanks for me, things that weren't in the newspapers."

"I can try. There were a lot of us involved in the case at first. I'm not sure I'll be able to tell you everything you want to know."

"Mainly I was just wondering about James Sparks, the man who killed my husband. I want information. Does he live around here, or had he come on vacation? Whose boat was he driving that day? Was it his? And so on."

"James Sparks," he said, thinking. "Yeah, he was staying up the river, not too far from where the accident happened. A fancy rental home. The boat came with the house, I believe."

"Do you know if he was staying there alone?" I asked.

The officer shook his head.

"I don't rightly remember," he said, "but it's a big place, four or five bedrooms. Goes for a couple hundred a night. Most folks don't pay that much just to stay by themselves."

"Does the name 'Tom Bennett' mean anything to you? Do you know if he was also staying there at that time?"

"No, I'm sorry. The name doesn't ring a bell."

"Do you have the address of the house, or maybe the name of the rental company that handled it?"

"The house is out on Randall Road, the last one just after it dead ends. I could check the file to find out who manages the property. The information might be in there."

"I would appreciate it."

He stood and went into another room, and while he was gone I opened up my notebook and skimmed through what I had written, trying to remember what other questions I wanted to ask. Before I could think of anything else, Officer Robinson was back at his desk, looking confused.

"I'm sorry, but there's nothing there," he said.

"Excuse me?"

"The file on James Sparks," he said. "It's missing."

The officer tried to be as helpful as he could, but there was no record of James Sparks—on paper or in the computer.

"Somebody goofed somewhere," he said finally, staring at the computer screen. "I can put a request out. Maybe his file's been pulled and is sitting on somebody's desk."

He gestured around the room, and I guessed I was supposed to take into consideration the number of desks that were there.

"What should I do?" I asked.

He pulled a business card out of his top drawer and handed it to me.

"Give me a call here tomorrow after one. I'll see if I can find the file before then."

"Okay," I said hesitantly. Something about this felt very wrong.

I reached in my bag and pulled out one of my J.O.S.H.U.A. Foundation business cards. I scribbled my cell phone number on the back and then handed the card to him.

"If you find something sooner, could you call me?" I asked.

"Sure," he said, looking at the card. "What's the 'J.O.S.H.U.A.' stand for?"

"I wish I knew," I said.

# Eight

Back out on the street, I looked cautiously around before walking toward my car. It was broad daylight and I was near a police station, but still I felt apprehensive, remembering the man I thought was following me earlier.

Still, I made it to my car with no incident and without seeing a single passerby on the road. As I started it up and pulled out, I made sure no one was following me, adding several odd switch-backs just to be certain. There was no one there. It must have been a coincidence.

Once I felt confident that I was all alone on the road, I pulled into a nearby parking lot to study the county map. I found Randall Road and then traced with my finger the way to get there from here. I would need to cross the river and come at it from the other side.

I followed the route I had worked out, trying to calculate how much more daylight I had left. By the time I turned onto Randall Road, I figured that the sun would probably set in about an hour. That should be plenty of time for what I needed to do.

As I drove I thought of what Officer Robinson had told me when I asked for the address of the rental house where James Sparks had been staying at the time of the accident.

*The house is out on Randall Road, the last one just after it dead-ends,* he had said, so I stayed on the road as it followed the river, and after about five miles it finally looked as if there were an end in sight. When I followed a slight rise and could see far behind me in the rearview mirror, I was glad to confirm that mine was the only car on this road.

Randall Road petered out in a heavily wooded spot with one lone driveway shooting out from the end like a spur. Ignoring the "Private Property" signs, I turned into the driveway beside a mailbox marked "4839 Randall Road," pulling past the screen of trees to see a big riverfront home, the lawn wide and expansive, the house itself pretty but not ostentatious. On the other side, of course, lay the river, wide and dark and slow moving.

There were no cars here, and the place looked empty, closed up tight. Still, I drove all the way up to the house, got out, and went to the door. I knocked and rang the bell several times, but no one came. I tried peeking through the windows, but there were no lights on inside, so I couldn't see much. What I did see looked like a typical upscale vacation rental—wide fireplace, sturdy furniture, muted tones.

I walked around the house and noticed a graceful porch fronting the river, with a walkway leading down to a dock and an over-the-water shed. I followed the walkway to that shed, peeking inside and then catching my breath at the sight of the red cigarette boat docked there. Was it the same boat, the one that had struck Bryan and killed him? I stared hard at the waterline, near the front, but I couldn't see any dents or marks. Of course, the accident had happened several years ago. With a nice boat like that, any damage caused by striking Bryan's body would have been repaired by now.

From my vantage point, I looked out at the river, trying to calculate how far this was from the scene of the accident. From what I could tell, it wasn't far at all, maybe a quarter of a mile, just enough for the boat to pick up some speed.

Frustrated, I headed back up the walk, taking the steps onto the front porch. There were no curtains on these windows, and I could see a little better. The place was nice inside, with a large kitchen and a table with seating for ten near the windows.

There was something on the kitchen counter, a sort of brochure that was propped up, with the word "Welcome" printed on it. I couldn't make out what else the thing said, so I quickly ran to the car, dug out the binoculars I had bought earlier, and came back for a better look.

"Welcome!" the top line said in large red letters, and then in smaller letters the next line said, "We hope your stay is a pleasant one. Please read the following information."

There was a bulleted list of rules about things like trash disposal and recycling, and information on where different items could be found, such as "Local maps in top right drawer of credenza." At the bottom was a small logo, with the words "Chalfont Vacation Homes, Richmond, Virginia."

Back in the car, I was frustrated to see that my cell phone couldn't get service. I started up and drove back the way I had come. I finally got service once I was on the highway, so I pulled over into an abandoned gas station, left the car running, and dialed information for Chalfont Vacation Homes in Richmond. They connected me right away, and when a woman answered, I asked for the agent who handled 4839 Randall Road. After a moment, a woman picked up, identifying herself as "Misty."

"How can I help you today?" she asked cheerily.

"My name is Callie Webber," I said, "and I'm a private investigator. I need to ask you a few questions about a rental property you handle at 4839 Randall Road, near Riverside."

"Yes? Is there a problem with the house?"

"No, ma'am," I said. "This is regarding an incident that happened several years ago. An accidental death involving a man who was staying at that house at the time."

"He died in the house?"

I pinched the area between my eyes.

"No, the man was staying in the house. The death happened nearby. On the river."

"Oh. Okay. What do you need to know?"

I tried to make my voice sound nonchalant, though I knew that what I was asking for was probably against the rules for her to give.

"I need the name that the house was registered under at that time." I gave her the date; she repeated it back to me and then asked me to hold on.

While I waited, I tried to decide what I would do once I heard the inevitable, that the house had been rented under the name "Tom Bennett." I had nearly convinced myself that this was the case, that Tom felt responsible for Bryan's death because he had coordinated the vacation that had brought his friend James Sparks to the house, to the river. That wouldn't explain all of the weirdness, all of the secrecy, behind my meeting with Tom and the lawyer, but at least it would give him a tangible claim for guilt—and a starting place for me to begin finding forgiveness.

"Miss Webber?" Misty said.

"Mrs. Yes?"

"I'm sorry, but this is odd. I can't tell you who rented the house that week."

"I know it's probably against the rules, but it's just a simple request that would save me an enormous amount of—"

"No, you don't understand. If you're an investigator, I don't mind telling you what you need to know. But that week isn't in the files."

"What do you mean?" I asked, feeling the skin prickle along my neck.

"I checked the paper file and the computer. The house was occupied on that date, but under the place where it tells you the name and the address of the person who rented it, it's been deleted."

"Deleted?"

"Deleted in the computer. And in the paper files, that page is missing. I'm sorry I can't help you."

First the police file, now the real estate file. My mind raced.

"I wonder if you could tell me the agent who would've handled the rental."

"Gosh, we're a big place. It could've been anybody."

"But at the time there was a tragic death, an accident on the river. The speedboat that rents with the house ran into someone in the water and killed him. The boat was impounded by the police and all of that. Surely someone there would remember."

"Wow. I wasn't here then. Hold on. Let me see if Trudy knows."

This time I was on hold for so long I was afraid my cell phone battery might die. While I waited, I nervously cleaned out the little basket that sat between the two front seats of my SUV.

"Hello? Maybe I can help you," a different woman said finally, coming onto the line. "I remember all that. It was real sad. Just tragic."

"Yes."

"Our insurance company handled the situation with the widow's lawyers."

"Who handled the matter on your end, in your office?"

"I did. Man, what a brouhaha we had with that boat afterward. It was impounded by the police, you see, and we had to get it back and then get it repaired. We lost a lot of money in the meantime."

I held my tongue, thinking, *Some of us lost a lot more than money.*

"See, the boat is a big draw for that house," she continued, oblivious. "A lot of people rent the house just to get the free boat that comes with it. I mean, we say it's free, but they don't understand that we build the cost of the boat into the rental price, if you know what I mean. Anyway, the police impounded the boat and kept it for a couple weeks. The folks that had the rental during those weeks were furious. We finally had to rent another speedboat for their use just to shut them up. It was terrible. What a pain in the neck."

"A pain in the neck?" I said, feeling a sudden rage. "A man *died*." Certainly, she could hear the anger in my voice, because when she spoke again, she was much more subdued.

"Yes, well, anyway," she said, "once we finally got the boat back from the police, we weren't really involved anymore. Though I think our insurance company did end up giving a big settlement to the widow."

I hesitated, knowing that I was the widow in question and that, yes, the settlement had been satisfactory.

"Well," I said, trying to regain my composure, "I really just need the name of the person who was renting the house when the accident happened."

"Yeah, Misty gave me the file. That information doesn't seem to be in here. Huh. That's weird. It's like somebody came along and just plucked that page right out of the file."

"But you handled the rental. Don't you remember who it was?"

"No, I'm sorry, I don't. They rented the place sight unseen over the phone. After the accident we turned everything over to our insurance company."

"How about Tom Bennett?" I pressed. "Does that name ring a bell?"

"No, I'm sorry, hon. I handle so many rentals. Unless they're a repeat customer, I'm not going to remember their name."

"And you don't remember *anything* about the rental?"

"No, but I'll tell you this. When the accident happened, I was really surprised."

"Why?"

"Because I do remember that the renters weren't even interested in the boat. They called here wanting a place with privacy. That's the most private rental we have, you know, way off at the end of that dead-end road. Even though it's one of our more expensive properties, they took it. I don't think we ever even talked about the fact that it came with a boat. I guess they figured that out on their own."

"I guess so."

I asked her a few more questions about their company's billing and contractual procedures, trying to find some way to learn the identity of the person who rented the house.

"What about payment?" I asked. "Could I track the rental payment somehow and find the name that way?"

"Probably not. I mean, I suppose you could go through old deposit slips or something, but we handle a lot of properties. You wouldn't have any way of knowing which payment went with which property unless you pulled all the files of all the properties and cross referenced them with each other, eliminating the ones you do know. It would probably take you a week just to figure it out, if you even could."

"I understand," I said, exhaling slowing. "One last try. Misty said there was a computer file that was deleted also. Would there be a history to the record? Some way to pull up what had been there before?"

"It's just a simple database," she said. "Far as I know, all you can see is what's on the screen in front of you."

There wasn't much else she could tell me, so finally I thanked her for her help and concluded the call. Then I pulled out onto the road, not even sure where to turn next.

# Nine

My cell phone died as I got back into town. The sun had set, and I realized I didn't even have a place to stay for the night. Feeling a little lost, I checked into the Holiday Inn along the main drag. As I carried my things to my room in plastic shopping bags, I decided I would need to pick up some inexpensive luggage very soon.

Once I was organized in the room, including plugging my cell phone into the charger, I used the motel phone to call my old Virginia law firm, the place where I was employed at the time of Bryan's death. My boss back then, Preston Gulliford, had kept an eye on the legalities surrounding Bryan's death for me right up until the day Sparks pleaded guilty and was sent to prison for manslaughter. I thought Preston might be just the person to contact now.

Leaning back against the headboard, I propped a pad of paper on my knees for taking notes. If Preston was the same workaholic he used to be, he would still be at the office, just settling in for a few more hours of work. Sure enough, I used the company directory to get his extension, and a moment later he answered the phone himself.

"Preston Gulliford."

"Preston? This is Callie Webber. How are you?"

"Callie Webber?" he cried. "Talk about a voice from the past! How are you, dear?"

We talked for a while, catching up, and I found myself feeling oddly nostalgic for the time I spent working at the law firm. There was no comparison to my job with the J.O.S.H.U.A. Foundation, of course, but I had always liked the firm and its partners, and Preston had been my favorite of all. An older, fatherly-type fellow, we were already friends when I learned that his hobby was making hand-hewn canoes. He and his wife had invited Bryan and me to dinner a few times, and we always ended up out back in Preston's fancy workshop, talking wood buoyancy and water displacement.

"So what can I do for you tonight?" he asked. "I'm sure you didn't call just to catch up."

"No, Preston. If you have a minute, I actually need to ask you some things about my husband's death. You handled all of that for me at the time, but some new issues have come up, and I'm hoping you might have some answers."

"Well, sure, Callie. I'll do my best."

"First of all, I need to know if the name 'Tom Bennett' means anything to you."

"Tom Bennett. I don't think so. Should it?"

"I'm just wondering if his name ever came up during that time. He would've been connected with James Sparks in some way."

"Hmm. I don't recall, but I could check the file. Why don't you hold on and I'll see if I can find it."

The whole time I was holding, I expected him to come back to the phone and tell me the file was missing. Instead, when he returned, I could hear him flipping pages.

"You said Tom Bennett?"

"Yes."

"I don't see anything here…"

His voice trailed off as he continued to page through the file. Finally, he spoke again.

"Nope," he said. "Sorry. No one in here by that name."

"Okay," I replied. "Then let's move on. I'm wondering if you can tell me where Sparks ended up. I know he got manslaughter, but I don't even know—"

"He's at the state penitentiary, down near Surry. He got sixteen years, so even if that gets cut in half with good behavior, he'd still be in there now."

"Good. Okay, that's what I needed to know."

"You're not thinking of filing suit against him, are you, Callie? Because the statute of limitations—"

"No," I said, "no suits. It's just information I'm after now. What do we know of Sparks?"

I knew my question sounded stupid, but I had never asked much about the man, instead leaving Preston to handle all of the legal matters on my behalf. I think I wanted to keep Sparks at arm's length, sort of a nameless, faceless entity. It was easier to blame him that way.

"Let's see, I'll tell you what's in my notes here." Again, I could hear pages being flipped in the background. "This is from a deposition we had with him. He says he was born and raised in Atlanta, Georgia...went to Georgia State, worked after that as a sales associate..."

"Where?"

"Looks like a place called Silmar Systems in Atlanta. Had numerous DUIs, pled guilty to manslaughter, and got sixteen years. That's about all I know of the man personally."

"What was he doing in Virginia when Bryan was killed?"

"According to him, vacation. Staying at that big house with some friends."

"Did we ever get any information on the friends?"

"Not that I can recall. I do remember thinking that they had sure made themselves scarce after the accident. From what I remember, police weren't even sure who Sparks was for the first twenty-four hours. He wouldn't say a word, and no one else showed up to help him out."

"You mean he wouldn't tell the police his name?"

"Everyone has the right to remain silent, Callie. They finally ID'd him from fingerprints."

"I guess with his prior record of DUIs, he couldn't remain anonymous for long."

"Guess not."

My mind was working, trying to think of any other questions I might have before we concluded our call.

"Is there anything else you remember from that time, anything at all that seemed out of the ordinary?" I asked.

"Well, looking back, I do remember being quite surprised with the speed and the amount of the settlement from the insurance company."

"Bryan's life insurance?"

"No, the Realtor's insurance. From the complaint we filed."

"Tell me about it."

I wrote "Realtor's insurance" in block letters on my pad.

"On your behalf, we filed a complaint against the Realtor who handled that piece of vacation property," Preston said, "alleging negligence in allowing a boat like that to be rented without proper provision. It's one thing to rent someone a boat, but putting somebody behind the wheel of a craft like that one should require special training. It's just too powerful of a machine, and it was way out of the league of the poor kid who ended up—well, who ended up accidentally killing someone."

I felt a surge of some emotion I couldn't identify. Somehow, I had never considered James Sparks to be a "poor kid."

"So what happened with the complaint?" I asked.

"You know how those things go. We sent it out, 'We allege this, we allege that, blah, blah, blah,' expecting everything to be denied, which would end up giving us a jury trial and a long court battle. Instead, we got an answer back within two days, offering to settle for the full amount as long as we released them permanently from any further liability."

"And that's the five hundred thousand that's in trust?"

"Yes, minus the firm's costs, of course. You ended up with four ninety and some change."

"What was the name of the insurance company?"

"Virginia Mutual, out of Richmond. Looks like we dealt with a man named Burkett. Lance Burkett."

I wrote down the information and then thanked Preston for his help. I was glad I had called, and I told him so.

"Oh, anytime, dear. It's been a pleasure talking with you. Hey, you're not looking to move back to the area by any chance, are you? Because you know there's always room for you here."

"No, I'm quite settled where I am," I said. "But thanks for the offer."

"We don't get workers of your caliber anymore, Callie. Good grief, this latest batch all dresses like the lawyers on TV, with short skirts and stringy hair and everything. The other day I even spotted a belly button. It's crazy."

I laughed, knowing a lot could change in a few years' time.

We concluded our call, and after I hung up the phone, I felt the silence of the room closing in on me. Needing to do something, I put my pen and paper aside, plugged in my laptop, and went online.

Using several of the databases I subscribed to for my job with the foundation, I looked up Silmar Systems of Atlanta, Georgia, James Sparks' former employer. They were almost impossible to find until I went back several years prior to Bryan's death, when the company went belly-up. That didn't make much sense. Why would James have claimed to work at a place that didn't even exist at that time?

I wrote down the names of Silmar's registered agent, and then I tracked down the home telephone number of one of the members of the board.

I looked at my watch as I dialed, feeling bad for calling someone at 9:30 at night. The man was home, however, and I seized the opportunity to ask him if he could give me any information about a former employee, a Mr. James Sparks. He didn't remember anyone working there by that name, but he did provide me with contact information for the former office manager, who had been with the company from beginning to end and knew everyone.

Fortunately, I was able to reach the office manager as well. Unfortunately, he had never heard of anyone named James Sparks.

"So you don't know when Sparks might have worked there?" I asked.

"No, you're not hearing me," the man said. "No one named James Sparks ever worked there."

He was irritable and insistent, so I let it go and asked about the name Tom Bennett.

"Strike two," the man said. "Never heard of him either."

By the time I hung up the phone, I was thoroughly confused. Had Sparks faked his past? This information had been provided to my law firm by James himself during a deposition. Was it possible that none of it was really true? Had he perjured himself?

Heart pounding, I used one of my online databases to access Georgia State's alumni records. I had to take a guess at the year of his graduation, based on his age, but he wasn't listed there. I decided to look forward and backward ten years in each direction. It was slow and tedious work, but in the end I had to conclude that James Sparks had not graduated from Georgia State, nor did I see any evidence that he had ever matriculated there at all.

What on earth was going on?

# Ten

The first thing the next morning, after checking out of the hotel, I drove all the way to the Richmond office of Virginia Mutual and asked to see Lance Burkett. I had questions about the quick and simple insurance settlement they had paid to me on behalf of the Realtor, and I hoped he would be the man to answer those questions.

Once he had the file in front of him, he reacquainted himself with the case.

"I remember this..." he mumbled to himself as he flipped through the pages. "Oh, yeah, I remember..."

He was a warm and friendly guy but extremely short, and it felt odd to be sitting across from him and looking down. I thought if I were him, I might build myself a little platform behind the desk to put me at an eye level with everyone else.

"Just between you and me," he said, his voice low, "this was one of the most surprising cases I've ever handled."

"Really?" I asked, leaning forward. "Tell me about it."

"Well, we got your firm's complaint—no big surprise—and I was in the middle of drafting a denial when I got word that we would not be contesting the complaint after all. The settlement would be paid in full, through us but funded by an outside third party."

My pulse quickened.

"An outside third party?" I asked, feeling in my gut that it must've been Tom. "Who?"

"Uncle Sam," Lance whispered. "The U.S. government."

I sat back, utterly perplexed.

"The government?" I asked. "The five hundred thousand dollars I was given as a settlement was paid by the U.S. *government?* Why?"

"Don't know, don't ask, don't tell," he said. "It was just a relief to pay your claim without having to go through a lengthy court battle. I'm always happy when we can settle out of court, especially early on in a case before we've already taken up resources and…"

His voice droned on but I tuned him out, thinking instead about the implications here. If the government paid the insurance claim, then James Sparks might have been working for the government at that time. Was it possible?

"Mr. Burkett, what do you know about James Sparks personally?" I asked. "The man who was driving the boat?"

"Oh," he said, surprised by my question. "Nothing. We represent the Realtor. And, by the way, you'll be happy to know that they did institute some new protections on that boat once the settlement was reached."

"Protections?"

"Safety precautions. Now whoever rents it gets a one-hour orientation of the boat by the Realtor and they have to sign off on a whole checklist of…"

Again, his little voice droned on and I tuned him out. He seemed eager to chat, but I had to pursue this new knowledge. My settlement was paid by the government. Did that mean that Sparks had been an employee of the NSA as well? Had he been one of Tom's coworkers?

I thanked the man for his help and managed to extricate myself from his office. Back on the interstate, I headed south once again, toward Riverside. I needed to pay another visit to the police station there.

As I drove, I had a bit of trouble with my cruise control. The button was acting funny and wouldn't kick in, which caused me to slow down and then speed back up several times. Finally, I realized that I had accidentally turned the switch to "off." Once I put it to "on," I accelerated to the speed I wanted to go and then set it there.

It was then that I noticed a blue sedan about two car lengths behind me. Everyone else who had been behind me was now in front of me, thanks to my cruise control problem. But the sedan had stayed back, always keeping a few cars between us. As one who knew how to tail someone myself, it made me suspicious. As I thought about it, I began to grow angry. Tom had told me the FBI wouldn't be tailing me anymore. Now here they were, back at it again. Good grief.

I took the Melville exit and wasn't surprised to see the sedan take it as well. From there, I had about a 30-minute drive on a highway that would take me to the town of Riverside. Melville and Riverside were both congested areas, but in between the two towns lay many miles of nothing but farmland—miles where no one would be around to see if something were to happen. I would have to lose the tail before leaving Melville.

I drove slowly, my mind racing, trying to think of some way to do this. I was pretty good at losing a tail, but this town wasn't exactly the most complex when it came to traffic lights or one-way streets. Finally, I tried to think of what Eli had taught me, that a forward chase didn't always have to move forward. I decided to do his "switch and brake" maneuver.

First, I got in the left lane of traffic and waited until the sedan was also in the left lane with two cars between us. When the light turned green, I moved forward. Then, suddenly, as soon as I saw a break in the right lane, I pulled to the right, put on my flashers, and simply stopped my car in the middle of the road. Though my maneuver earned the honks of the cars behind me, it forced the sedan to pass me by. As it did, I looked hard at the driver. He was a young man with black hair and a goatee, his features bland, his eyes pointing straight forward at the road. My stomach did an odd flip-flop as I got the feeling he wasn't FBI after all. I faltered, a chill passing through me.

Then I decided to turn the tables on him. Flicking off my flashers, I pulled ahead, glued myself to *his* bumper, and followed him.

"All right, buddy," I said angrily as we drove. "Let's see how you like it."

I wasn't surprised when he made a U-turn. I followed suit, making sure that he saw me in his rearview mirror. I had a feeling he was going back to the interstate, and, sure enough, as we approached the overpass, he turned onto the northbound entrance lane. I watched to make sure he went all the way up the ramp, and then I quickly made another U-turn and headed off toward Riverside. As Harriet would say, I needed to get while the getting was good!

I sped quickly through the country, reaching Riverside in record time. Once there, I drove straight to the police station, found an available parking spot a few doors down from it, and hurriedly went inside.

Officer Darnell Robinson was at his desk, and he looked up and saw me before I could even ask for him. I had come here to talk to him, but the look on his face was so odd that I hesitated. As I looked at him, he widened his eyes and then tilted his head toward the door I had just come in. Then, to my surprise, he discreetly raised one hand to his ear, thumb and pinky sticking out, in the universal symbol for "telephone."

"Help you?" the man at the desk asked, oblivious to the entire exchange, his attention focused on a newspaper sports page in front of him.

"I, um, I just wondered if I need a permit to have a garage sale," I said, flustered.

"You'll have to ask at the township building," he said, "up on Pecan Street, next to the library."

"Thank you," I said. Giving a sharp glance to Officer Robinson, I turned and left, going back to my car. Once there, I pulled out his card and dialed his number on my cell phone.

"You know where Park Lane meets Woodland?" he asked, without even saying hello.

"I can find it," I said.

"I'll meet you there in ten minutes."

Heart pounding, I started up my car and sat studying my map for a moment. The meeting point wasn't very far away, and I used a zigzag of back streets to get there.

I found myself facing a small neighborhood park. I pulled to a stop in one of the parking places and sat with my engine running. On the other side of the park was a lone mother, trying to handle an active toddler and a big dog, a Lab. Finally she got the toddler into a swing and then let the dog roam free as she pushed the swing. I kept my eyes open, but I never saw the blue sedan.

A few minutes later, a police cruiser pulled up next to my car. As I watched, Officer Robinson got out and climbed into mine.

"Thanks," he said. "I thought this might be better."

"Of course," I replied. "Should I drive us somewhere?"

"No, I think we're okay here. This won't take long."

"What's going on?"

"I don't know," he said, shaking his head. "Something's definitely fishy."

I listened as he described his morning. First thing, he was called into his captain's office and asked why he had put out a request for the file on James Sparks.

"I explained that the victim's widow had been in asking questions, but that I couldn't really help much until I got a look at the file. He told me the file was no longer available to our office and I was to drop the matter."

"Drop the matter? What about me?"

"I was directed to tell you that no further information is available at this time."

"But—"

"Listen, the more I thought about it, the more I remembered about the whole thing. I figured if I can't check any of the details out in the file, at least I can tell you what I recall. There were some strange things about that case. Definitely some strange things."

"Like what?" I asked, eyes wide.

"Like the man I arrested. James Sparks. He never said a word to me from the moment I got there till we had him locked up in the jail. Wouldn't give his name, his address, nothing. Woulda thought he was a mute, 'cept he used his one phone call to talk to somebody. I ran his prints myself and came back with nothing."

"Nothing?"

"Well, there was information there, but it was restricted."

"Restricted?"

"Like, he had a record, but we weren't allowed to access it. I've seen that once or twice before. There's usually some legal reason their facts are protected, at least until we go through the proper channels—jump through a few hoops, you know—to get at them."

"So did you go through those channels?"

"No. Here's what's weird: I didn't have to. The next day, he still wasn't talking, so my boss told me to run the prints one more time the regular way. Lo and behold, this time I got a full, unrestricted record on the guy—name, age, social. He'd been arrested for driving under the influence more than ten times in the past. Later that day we got back his blood work, which showed an intoxication level of one point two."

"That's a lot."

"Yeah, especially considering that when I arrested that man, he wasn't even drunk."

"What?" I asked, my heart pounding.

"He didn't smell like alcohol, he wasn't weaving around, he didn't display any of the characteristics we look for. Only reason they took blood is because it's mandatory in vehicular homicides. I barely even glanced at the lab report when it came back in, so when I saw one point two, I nearly flipped."

"Did you talk to anyone about it?"

"Nah, I was working double shifts back then, trying to pay off my car note. I just remember thinking, you never know. You never know."

"So what happened after that?"

He shrugged.

"I didn't have any other involvement," he said. "I fielded a few calls from the press, but otherwise I went on to other things. I'm sorry I can't tell you more than that. But I hope at least this much is a help to you, whatever you need the information for."

I nodded, thinking about the kind officer sitting next to me, wondering what motivated him to speak to me despite the edict of his boss to cut me off.

"Why did you tell me all of this?" I asked finally, wondering how I could repay this debt.

He exhaled slowly.

"Because I remember you," he said, his eyes sad as he gazed off across the park. "I responded to the scene of the accident first, before they called me over to the Docksider. I heard you screaming. I watched you clinging to your husband's dead body, even as the paramedics were trying to pull him away from you."

"I don't remember much about that day," I admitted softly.

"That's funny," he replied. "Because I've never been able to forget it."

# Eleven

I was in a daze once the officer left, my mind reeling.

James Sparks hadn't been drunk after all? Surely, that couldn't be true. I looked in my notes for the phone number of Harry Stickles, the man who had chased down the speedboat in his own boat and then tackled James Sparks on the dock.

His wife said he was out in the yard, working on the car, and that he would have to call me back. I told her it was urgent, so she asked me to hold on and then set the phone down with a clunk. I listened as she yelled for her husband. After about two full minutes, it sounded as though he had come inside.

"Don't get grease on the phone," she said in the background.

"I won't," he said irritably. Then he spoke into the phone. "Hello?"

"Mr. Stickles," I said, "this is Callie Webber again, the one who called about the boating accident. I'm sorry to bother you, but I just have one more question for you."

"Oh, it's no bother," he replied. "But call me Harry, please."

"Sure," I said. "Harry. I just wanted your impression of James Sparks that day you caught him at the Docksider."

"My impression?"

"About his...about him being so drunk. His blood alcohol level was very high. I'm sure he must've been pretty out of control?"

"Naw, on the contrary," he said. "He was upset at first, but then he got real quiet. I was surprised when the paper said he'd been drunk at the time. Sure didn't seem drunk to me."

"Did you smell alcohol on him?"

"Not that I noticed, but then again, I had already had one beer myself, so maybe I wouldn't have smelled it anyway."

"I see."

"He sure wasn't out of his head, though. I mean, I know drunks. I've seen my share around here, that's for sure."

He cracked up laughing, his laugh finally turning to a cough. I waited for the spell to be over before I spoke again.

"So you would say he definitely did not seem drunk at the time?"

"That is correct. He did not seem drunk at the time, though I guess he might've been. Some folks is quiet drunks, you know. Takes all kinds."

I thanked him for his help and concluded the call, knowing what I had to do next. The time had come to see Sparks in person. I didn't feel that I had any other choice.

After stopping in a convenience store for a small fruit salad in a cup, I drove back to Melville and then hit the interstate once again and headed south toward the state prison in Surry.

I had a little trouble finding it once I got there, because the road to the prison wasn't well marked. Still, that came as no real surprise. Most counties didn't exactly like to advertise the locations of places that brought down property values.

Finally, I found a small, brown sign that simply said "Virginia State Prison, Next Right." I turned and followed a long road that wound through deserted farmland, finally reaching a checkpoint with a guard and a tall barbed-wire-topped fence branching out on both sides. Large signs warned that both my vehicle and I were now subject to full search.

"May I help you?" the guard asked as I pulled to a stop.

"I'm here to see a prisoner," I said.

"Are you on his list?" he asked.

"Excuse me?"

"Prisoners have a list of approved visitors. Are you on his list?"

"Oh, yes," I lied.

The guard eyed me suspiciously.

"What's his name and your name?" he asked. "I'll take a look."

"He's James Sparks," I said, feeling my face turn red. "My name is Callie Webber."

He stepped into the booth, the rail remaining in the down and locked position. Up ahead, I could see two guard towers flanking the roadway, each with an armed and uniformed officer inside.

"How're you spelling that?" he asked me finally. "His name, I mean."

"S-P-A-R-K-S," I said. "James."

He went back to his computer but finally came back out, shaking his head.

"I'm sorry, but there's no one here by that name. Have you ever visited him here before?"

"No," I whispered, feeling my lunch rise in my throat. James Sparks wasn't even here.

*What was going on?*

"I'm sorry, but is there someone I could talk to, please? The man is supposed to be here serving a sixteen-year sentence for manslaughter."

He went back into the booth and then came back out and handed me a preprinted sheet of paper. On it were listed several websites and telephone numbers, with the heading "Prisoner Locator Services."

"Chances are he got reassigned to another prison," he said, his demeanor a little kinder now. "You just call them numbers or go to them websites and type in his name. You'll find him."

"Thank you," I said numbly.

Then I backed up the way he indicated and drove out of there.

I headed back to the town of Surry and once again sought out a library. I couldn't find one, so instead I went to a nearby coffee shop where a small sign in the window read "free wi-fi." I parked at an empty meter just outside the shop and went inside.

I ordered tea and took the paper cup to an empty table, facing my back to the wall and pulling out my laptop.

The connection was good and I was online soon. Fortunately, there weren't many other customers in the shop so the tables around me were empty. I was glad to be left to myself as I sipped my tea and searched for information.

Heart pounding, I went to the first website on the list and typed in Sparks' name. He wasn't listed in that system, so I moved along to the next. I ended up working my way through all of the state prisons in Virginia, North Carolina, Maryland, and Delaware, all to no avail. Sparks' name simply didn't register.

Finally, I came to the last resource on the list, the Federal Prison Locator System. I entered the name "Sparks, James," expecting another dead end. Instead, it responded with a prison name and address: FCI Berwick, Tobacco Road, Box 1001, Berwick, Georgia. It listed phone and fax numbers and then, under "Security Level," it said "Minimum/Male."

James Sparks was currently incarcerated in a minimum security men's federal prison in Berwick, Georgia. Or at least that's what the computer said. But that made no sense to me. Considering his crime, he should be in a state prison in Virginia, not a federal prison in Georgia—and especially not one that was minimum security!

I logged off, put my laptop away, tossed out my empty cup before visiting the restroom, and returned to my car. Once I was in the driver's seat, I pulled out my cell phone. It took phone calls to several different branches of the correctional system, but finally I was able to confirm that yes, indeed, one James Sparks was currently incarcerated at the Berwick Federal Correctional Institution in Berwick, Georgia. Of course, there was a chance that this was a different James Sparks, but since they wouldn't tell me the nature of his conviction over the phone, the only way I could know for certain was to go there and see him in person. As to why he was there and not where he was supposed to be, I didn't have a clue. The best I could assume was that he was a former NSA agent and that somehow, upon his arrest, special provisions had been made.

Remembering the guard at the gate of the Virginia State Prison, I asked about visiting restrictions for Berwick. Much to my surprise, even though Sparks was at a minimum security facility, I would still have to be on a list of approved visitors in order to get in to see him.

The woman who was helping me said that the process for putting my name on a prisoner's visitor list involved submitting an application which would take at least a month to process.

"A month!" I cried.

"Yes, ma'am," she replied. "All this information is on our website. He would've made up his list of visitors when he was first incarcerated, and then everyone on his list would've all put in applications and gotten background checks. The only way he can add your name now is if you had a relationship with him prior to his incarceration."

The more she talked, the more hopeless my situation appeared to be. I had no idea it would be so difficult to get a face-to-face meeting with the man who had killed my husband.

"What about special approval from the warden?" I asked, grasping for straws.

"Put it this way," she said, not unkindly. "Unless you're clergy or a lawyer, you're really out of luck."

A lawyer. Of course. I could get in to see him as a lawyer!

Thanking her for her help, I opened up my computer one more time and went back to the bureau of prison's website. I scanned the rules for attorney visits to federal prisons. From what I could see, the process was fairly straightforward and merely required that I make arrangements ahead of time with the warden.

Once I was done with that, I brought a map of Georgia, again needing the big picture of things.

I also bought some bottled water for what was going to be a long drive. Then I sat in my car and plotted out my course. I would take 95 north to 85 south to 185 south, breaking off to local roads at Columbus, Georgia. Calculating my time, I had a feeling the drive would take around 12 hours. Briefly, I considered heading to the nearest airport and flying there instead, but somehow it just seemed easier to drive than to manage airport parking, flight schedules, and rental cars. It was already after 3:00 P.M., so I figured I could drive halfway, spend the night somewhere in South Carolina, and go the rest of the way in the morning. Saying a quick prayer, I dialed the number of the warden to make my appointment.

In the swirl of confusion surrounding this case and my eagerness to get answers, I had forgotten one fact that now confronted me head on, that tomorrow I would see my husband's killer, face-to-face, for the very first time.

# Twelve

~

I suppose I should have been better prepared for what I would see once I reached my destination. Unlike the Virginia state prison I had tried to visit the day before, this place had no Fort Knox-like check-in point, no barbed-wire-topped fence, no armed officers looming above the place in guard towers.

Instead, this facility looked like some sort of industrial farm, with an entry point no more secure than what you might find in a gated neighborhood.

The woman in the booth didn't even come outside but merely slid open her window and asked if she could help me. I had the insane urge to ask for fries and a Coke.

"I'm here to see a prisoner," I said. "I have an appointment."

I hadn't been able to sleep last night and had gotten back on the road by 5:00 this morning. Now it was 11:30 A.M., and I was in a part of Georgia that was so empty, it gave new meaning to the term "rural." Though the surrounding countryside was very beautiful, it had felt odd to drive through miles and miles of nothing but woods with only the occasional pecan farm for relief.

The woman asked for my driver's license, and then she checked it against a list on a clipboard.

"Your appointment's not till one o'clock," she said.

"I know. I'm sorry. It took less time to get here than I expected."

She made a phone call, hung up, and told me that I could go on in and wait in the common room.

"But the men are out working in the field right now," she added. "They won't be back until twelve."

"That's fine. I don't mind waiting."

She pointed to the building I would need, handed back my driver's license, and raised the gate so I could pass through. I drove ahead and to the right, parking in a "Visitor" spot near the door. Once inside, I faced a window plastered with a list of "Visiting Rules," which I skimmed while I waited for the man behind the window to get off the phone. According to this list, the prisoners could have paperback books but no hardbacks, and all food items would be x-rayed. I wondered if anyone ever tried to slip a file in a cake anymore.

"May I help you?" the man asked, hanging up the phone.

"I'm here to see a prisoner," I said, pulling out my driver's license as the sign directed. I dropped it into a little drawer, which the man slid toward himself on the other side of the glass.

"Callie Webber?" he said, reading from the license. "Is this your correct address?"

I waited as he logged me into the computer, and I gave Sparks' name when asked whom I was here to visit.

"James Sparks," the man repeated, typing on the keyboard. "Since this is an attorney visit, you do have the right to request a private conference room, you know."

"Private?" I asked, pulse surging. Despite the need for privacy, I didn't think I wanted to be completely alone with the man who had killed my husband.

"You might not need it," he added. "It's not a visiting day, so you'll probably have plenty of privacy in the common room."

"That will be fine, I'm sure," I said.

"Okay, go through the door to your left. You get your license back on the way out."

*Just like when you rent a canoe,* I thought absurdly as I followed his directions.

The door buzzed and I stepped through to find the same man coming around the desk to process me. He took my purse and put it into a small locker, had me sign my name on a piece of paper next to the locker number, and then he asked me to step through a metal detector.

"All right, you have a nice visit," he said, gesturing toward another door. I opened it to find a large, industrial-looking room with tables and chairs and a row of vending machines along one wall.

All along I had imagined speaking to Sparks on a phone and looking at him through thick Plexiglas. Instead, I realized, he would be right here in the room with me, with nothing between us but a table. I guess that was how minimum security worked, especially when it was an attorney visit.

The room was empty, and I chose a spot in a corner and sat, my hands folded in my lap. I was glad to have a bit of time before he came because my heart was pounding away in my chest like a jack-hammer.

Closing my eyes, I thought back to the months following Bryan's death, when the legal system ground along in its quest for justice against James Sparks. Though I had given depositions and visited with attorneys and followed the progress of the man's case through legal channels, there had never come a point where Sparks and I were in the same place at the same time. I had seen newspaper pictures of him, of course, and a few film clips on TV. I could have even gone to his preliminary hearing if I had wanted to, but there was no reason for me to be there, so I chose not to go. In the end he pled guilty, and we were spared the agony of a trial. Today, for the first time, I would look into his eyes—the eyes of the man who killed my husband.

*Oh, God,* I prayed silently, *I need You right now like I have never needed You before. Calm my heart. Guard my tongue. Give me strength. Help me to remember that I have forgiven this man.*

When my prayer was over, I thought back to the day I learned that Sparks' sentence had been handed down. Procuring justice for my dead husband had been my driving force since the accident, and when I learned that, indeed, justice had been served, my heart was filled with a mix of relief and great desperation. Once I knew that Sparks would pay for what he had done, I was left with no focus for my hurt, no target for my rage.

My pastor had been trying to counsel me about forgiveness, but I had turned a deaf ear until that point. Once Sparks was sentenced, I knew it was time to hand the whole matter over to God.

According to what I understood, "forgiveness" of the unforgivable didn't mean retribution nor restitution nor reconciliation. It simply meant that I let go of my claim toward the anger and hurt, no matter how justified. In forgiving, I would grant a pass, so to speak, releasing this man to my heavenly Father, who alone was in a position to judge.

It hadn't been easy, but there came a point late one night where I knelt on the floor in the middle of my silent, empty living room, sobbing, repeating a prayer over and over: "Forgive us our trespasses as we forgive those who have trespassed against us. Forgive us our trespasses as we forgive those who have trespassed against us."

Somehow, the healing hand of God had touched my soul and let those words soak into my heart. The next morning, I got up feeling as though a weight had been lifted just a tiny bit from the core of my being. I decided then to move away, to leave behind the home my husband and I had shared and start a new life in a completely different place, out on the shores of Chesapeake Bay. Despite making the move, it ended up being many more months before I recovered from the dark depression that enshrouded me. But at least I had given forgiveness. That much was done and over with. Today would be a test of how genuine my heart had really been.

I looked up at the sound of voices to see two guards coming in from the visitor processing area. They didn't even glance my way but instead bought some drinks from the soda machine and exited through a door on the other side of the room. Soon, the door they had gone through opened up again, and this time a different guard entered, escorting a man dressed all in khaki, the prison uniform. It was James Sparks. I recognized him from his pictures.

I stood. Sparks saw me and then took a step back in reaction.

"Hello, James," I said loudly. "Thank you for agreeing to meet with me."

The guard positioned himself near the door, hands folded in front of him. Slowly, Sparks walked toward me, a suspicious squint on his face.

"I know who you are," he said in a slow Southern drawl. "When they said your name I wasn't sure if it would be you, but it is. I recognize you from the newspapers."

"Yes," I said, feeling suddenly tongue-tied. The man across from me was about my age, with sandy blond hair and dark brown eyes. He wore glasses, which he pushed nervously into place.

"What do you want?" he demanded.

I gestured to the table between us.

"Why don't we sit down?" I said, feeling oddly detached from my voice. I took a seat and then watched as he pulled out a chair on the other side of the table and perched on the very edge.

"What do you want?" he repeated.

"I want to talk to you," I said, sounding much calmer than I felt. "I've been trying to piece some things together, and I have questions I think only you can answer."

"What questions?"

He looked ready to bolt, and I tried to gather my wits about me. I was quaking on the inside, as the situation had really thrown me for a loop.

"First of all, why are you here, in this prison? I thought you were in a state penitentiary in Virginia."

"Long story and none of your business. Why did you *come* here?"

He grew agitated, bouncing his knees up and down frantically.

"How do you know Tom Bennett?" I asked.

"What do you mean, how do I know Tom Bennett? He's my brother-in-law."

If he had punched me in the stomach, my reaction wouldn't have been more profound.

"Your brother-in-law?" I managed to gasp.

"Yeah, my wife's brother. Well, ex-wife."

My mind reeled. Tom's sister had been married to James Sparks? Everything in me yearned to stand up right there and start screaming. Instead, I forced myself to remain calm.

"How was Tom connected to my husband's death?"

"What?"

"Tom. Was he there in that house on vacation with you? Did he rent the house, the boat? What was his connection?"

"I'm not telling you that."

"You killed my husband, James. Is a little information too much for me to ask?"

Sparks turned pale and his breathing grew ragged. He started digging frantically in his pocket. He produced a small yellow asthma inhaler, which he immediately put to his mouth, squirting it out and inhaling deeply. Once he caught his breath, he surprised me by reaching out with his other hand and gripping me tightly on the wrist.

"Don't come here asking questions like this," he rasped sharply. "That time is over. Done."

The guard called out a warning and James let go of me.

"You were wrong to come here," he whispered. "You've got to go."

He stood, and as he did I could feel a sort of blackness closing in on me. He had to tell me more—I would make him tell me more!

"Are you allowed to make phone calls from here?" I demanded, wishing they hadn't taken my purse, wishing I had a business card to hand him.

"Collect," he said suspiciously.

"Then please call me," I implored him. "I need some answers."

He started to walk away, and I called out my cell phone number after him.

"Please," I called. "Write it down."

He stopped and looked at me.

"I don't have to write it down," he said derisively. "I have a head for numbers."

# Thirteen

Somehow, I was able to find the mental resources to make the next logical move. Tucking my emotions carefully away for the moment, I forced myself to breathe normally and decide on a rational course of action. Rather than leaving the prison straightaway, I claimed my purse and license and asked the man at the window how I might be able to meet with the warden. Perhaps he would be able to give me a little background information on Sparks—not to mention explain to me why a man who was supposed to be doing hard time in a state prison in Virginia was sitting in a cushy minimum security prison in Georgia. I wasn't sure if I had a right to any of that information, but I should—as an attorney, as an interested party, and as the widow of the man Sparks killed.

While I waited, the fellow behind the glass made a few phone calls, and then he told me the warden could see me in about an hour, if I felt like hanging around.

"Where should I wait?" I asked.

"You can go on over there," he said. "Out that door and then the third trailer on your left."

I did as he said, passing two large temporary aluminum structures—what I assumed the man had been referring to as "trailers."

Sure enough, the sign on the third one said "Warden." I knocked on the door and then stepped inside.

"Yeah?" a man asked from behind a desk. He was also in khakis, and I realized that perhaps he was a trustee, doing a little secretarial work.

"I'm here to see the warden," I said. "He agreed to meet with me in about an hour."

"Yeah, he's busy right now," he said. "You wanna wait here till he gets back?"

"If I may."

"Suit yourself," he said, gesturing toward two chairs that were in a corner, with a small end table between them. On the table was a tacky ceramic lamp and a small pile of magazines.

I sat, forcing myself to flip through the magazines, not surprised at the titles: *Field & Stream, American Hunter, Car and Driver.* The man returned to what he had been doing, typing slowly on a keyboard and staring at a computer screen in front of him. He seemed frustrated, and between grunts and curses, he would say, "Pardon me, ma'am." Then he would curse again.

Knowing I needed to stay focused, I tried flipping through one of the magazines, but the words and pictures blurred together on the page. What was I going to do with what I had learned? If I answered no other questions in this investigation, one thing was astoundingly clear: I could never, ever trust Tom Bennett again.

"You know anything about Microsoft Word?" the man asked suddenly.

I looked up, surprised that he was talking to me.

"A little," I said. "Problem?"

"Yeah. I don't know what I clicked on, but all of a sudden these dots and symbols popped up on the page."

"Can I take a look?"

"Yeah."

I walked to the desk and leaned forward, knowing immediately what the problem was, that he had accidentally turned on the function that showed spaces between words and carriage returns. I showed him how to turn it back off, and when he did everything disappeared from the screen except his words. From what I saw of the text, it looked to be a requisition letter, something about frozen peas for the cafeteria.

"You smell nice," he said suddenly, his voice husky.

I backed away, aware that the two of us were alone.

"Thank you," I replied curtly.

"I'm sorry, I don't mean to be forward," he said. "We just don't have a lot of sweet-smelling women around here."

He was blushing, and for some reason I didn't take him as much of a threat. Balding and stocky, I had a feeling he was a white collar criminal, probably convicted of insider trading or something. This was minimum security, after all.

"May I ask you a question?" I asked, going back to my chair and thinking I just might use my "appeal" to this guy to my advantage.

"Sure," he said, focusing on me and giving me what I'm sure he thought was a charming smile.

"Do you know James Sparks?"

"Who, Crunch? Yeah. He's a decent fellow."

"Crunch?"

"That's his nickname. He's some kind of math whiz, a number cruncher. We call him Crunch."

"A math whiz?"

"Yeah, he's always talking about 'algorithms' and stuff like that. Way over my head. He's a computer geek.

"Wow," I said. "Is that what James—uh, Crunch—did before he went to prison?" I asked. "Computer work?"

The man shrugged and turned his attention back to the screen. I think I offended him by using the word "prison."

"I dunno," he said. "Crunch doesn't talk about his life on the outside."

"Where's he from?" I asked, crossing my legs. I could see the man watching me from the corner of his eye.

"Not too far from here," he said finally, warming up to me again. "Albany."

"Albany, Georgia?"

"Yeah, I believe so. His mother comes to see him every Sunday, always brings homemade bread and a big tub of soup."

Just then, the phone rang. He answered it, spoke for a moment, and hung up.

"That was the warden," he announced. "Said it looks like he's gonna be a good bit longer than he thought. You can wait if you want, though."

I felt a sudden surge of claustrophobia. I knew that I wouldn't wait, that I needed to get out of there.

"That's okay," I told him, standing. "I'll call him later. In the meantime, I need the address and phone number for James' mother."

The man shook his head.

"Sorry," he said. "That's confidential. No can do."

"It's just that I'm on my way to Albany now. Sure would save me some time if you could get it for me."

"Look, I couldn't help you even if I wanted to. I don't know where they keep that kind of thing."

I hesitated.

"Between you and me, then," I said, giving him a wink. "Any ideas about how I might be able to find the woman? You think she's in the phone book?"

"No telling," he replied. "I know she works as a waitress."

"You happen to know the name of the restaurant?"

"Huh…" he seemed lost in thought. "Sorry. It's always printed on the side of the soup container, but I can't remember. Something with ivy leaves trailing off…"

"How about her first name? Do you know that?"

"I think it's Tildy. Trudy. I don't know. She looks a lot like her son, small and blond, but without the glasses. Most of the guys just call her Miz Sparks."

I thought about giving him my card and asking the warden to phone me when he got in. I decided against it, however, realizing that this fellow might take it upon himself to keep my number and start calling me himself. If I couldn't turn anything up with James' mother, I could always call the warden later.

Back in the car, I drove slowly out of the prison and then used the GPS to find my way to Albany. The highway was weather worn with dips in the blacktop that made a steady whooshing sound against my tires. As I drove, the sound turned to words: *Brother-in-law. Brother-in-law.* James Sparks was Tom's brother-in-law.

I wouldn't let myself think, wouldn't let myself go crazy just yet. There was simply too much to do.

# Fourteen

By the time I reached Albany, it was nearly two o'clock. I found a motel right off the highway, and I went inside and looked in the telephone book, first for a listing for Sparks, and then for a restaurant with either "Ivy" in the title or ivy in its ad logo. I struck out on all counts.

Desperate, I paused at the front desk, where two young women were sitting on stools, chatting with each other. They were both pretty in a "Georgia peach" sort of way, with perfect skin and highly stylized hair, one a blonde, the other a redhead. They wore the uniform of the motel chain, matching navy suits with floral-printed scarves.

"Can I help you?" the blonde asked cheerily, hopping off her stool.

"I'm trying to locate a restaurant," I said. "I don't remember the name of it, but their sign has vines in it, like ivy? Does that ring a bell?"

"Oh, yeah," the blonde said, prettily squinting her eyes at her friend. "What is that place called? We went there after the Country All-Stars concert."

"The Porch?"

"The Back Porch," the blonde corrected. "Yeah, it's off Dawson Road over by the Phoebe Northwest building."

She pulled out paper and a pen and drew a map of how to get there. Thanking her profusely, I nearly ran to my car. Following the little map, I made my way across town, passing some lovely neighborhoods and a number of strip malls and then the big medical building they had told me to watch for. Sure enough, just past the medical building, on the left, was a sign that said "The Back Porch," its letters entwined with ivy.

I parked and went inside, hoping the restaurant would still be serving lunch this late. The place was quiet and empty, with only a few diners. Still, a man greeted me cheerily, grabbed a menu, and said, "One?" I nodded mutely.

He led me to a table by the window, nicely set with a spray of fresh flowers in the center. Had the situation not been so fraught with tension, I might actually have enjoyed dining there.

I practically held my breath until the waitress came, but she was in her twenties, far too young to be Sparks' mother. She took my drink order, and then I scanned the menu, wondering how to work this. When she came back with my tea, I placed my order for a salad and sandwich and then handed her back the menu, nonchalantly asking my question.

"There's another waitress here, small and blonde…"

"Who, Mary Jean?"

"No…"

"Tilly?"

"Yes," I said, pulse surging. "Is she here now?"

"No, I'm sorry, it's her day off." Seeing the crestfallen look on my face, she added, "She might be coming in, though. It's payday, so she'll probably stop by for her check so she can get it over to the bank."

I asked if there was any way I could leave a message with Tilly's paycheck.

"Sure," she replied, so I borrowed her pen and an order slip and wrote out *Tilly, please call me. This is in regard to your son, James.* I hesitated, deciding not to write my name. She would probably recognize

"Callie Webber," and I didn't want to give her the advantage of knowing who I was before we talked. Instead, I wrote *A friend* and then, under that, my cell phone number.

I handed the note to the waitress, who pocketed it and then told me my food would be out soon.

When she came back just a few minutes later with my salad, she said, "I put your message in with her paycheck. She'll probably get it before five."

"Thank you."

"So you know James?"

I hesitated, surprised not that the girl had read the note, but that she wasn't even trying to hide that fact.

"Yes."

"She's so proud of that boy. But I think he kind of takes advantage of her, don't you?"

"In what way?"

"She's always doing for him, going to see him, bringing him food every Sunday. I say, why does she always have to go to him? I don't care how big and important he is, why can't he come see her once in a while? That house of hers is practically falling down, but all it would take for him is a couple weekends of work to get it fixed back up. You know, clean out the rain gutters, fix the screen door, things like that. But no, he's too busy. Can't even come over and give the place a coat of paint. I say, shame on him."

I looked down at my salad, understanding that Tilly's coworkers had no idea her son was a prisoner in jail. Either that or I had the wrong person. But I didn't think so. I think she had created a whole false life just to keep his true circumstances a secret. For some reason, I felt a surge of protectiveness toward the woman.

"Sometimes family lets us down," I said simply.

The girl could see I wasn't going to gossip with her about Tilly. With a shrug she turned and walked away, back to the kitchen.

Numbly, I ate my salad, wondering what I would say to James' mother when she called. *If* she called. In the meantime I was hungry, and when my sandwich came, I ate almost every bite.

When the waitress brought the check, I asked if Tilly had shown up yet.

"No, but the bank doesn't close for another two hours. She'll probably be in."

When I left the restaurant, I double-checked my cell phone to make sure the battery was good. I pulled out of the nearly empty parking lot, drove a few blocks, and then turned around to come back to the parking lot of the big medical building next door to the restaurant.

Three feet of grass and a row of scraggly bushes were the only barriers between the two parking lots, but I knew I would be much less conspicuous on this side, where there were more cars. I pulled in next to a navy Honda and parked, glad that I could see the restaurant clearly. I wasn't sure how long I would have to wait, but if my waitress was correct, Tilly Sparks would show up at some point in the next two hours.

I settled back against the seat, holding a map in front of me so I wouldn't look too conspicuous just sitting there. The car was warm, and after a while I rolled down the windows, relishing the light afternoon breeze that swept inside. A car pulled up on the other side of me, a low red Mitsubishi, and a woman climbed out, a professional-looking brunette dressed in navy pants and a white lab coat. Pocketing her keys, she gave me a friendly nod and then walked briskly toward the building.

An hour later, I was still waiting for a glimpse of Tilly when the brunette came back. She noticed me and paused, leaning down to look in from the passenger's window.

"Hey," she said warmly. "You need some help?"

"Excuse me?"

"The map. Are you lost?"

"Oh, no," I said, and from the corner of my eye I could see a car turning into the restaurant. "I'm waiting for someone. I was just reading the map to kill time."

"You've been waiting quite a while," she said, flipping through her car keys to find the right one. "If you need to use a phone or anything, just go inside that door there. Tell them Patricia sent you."

"Thanks," I said. "I will."

She got in her car and left just in time for me to see a short blonde woman bound up the back steps of the restaurant. I started my car as soon as she went inside, hoping this was indeed Tilly and not the other short blonde, Mary Jean.

A few minutes later, she came back out with much less bounce to her step now. I could see a white envelope clutched in her hand, and she went straight to her car without even glancing around.

She turned left onto the main road and I followed suit, riding close at first and then putting a few cars between us when we reached some traffic. She surprised me by turning into a bank, but I kept going and pulled over into a donut shop soon after.

From there, I followed her across town, praying out loud into the car as I went. My prayers were twofold: first, that she would be willing to talk to me, and second, that, if so, our conversation would be fruitful.

Eventually, my pursuit led me onto a bridge over a wide, teeming river. Once on the other side, I realized we had entered a visibly poorer section of town. When she turned onto a side street, I went straight, hoping that if I doubled back in a few minutes I would be able to locate her car.

Sure enough, I found it parked in front of a ramshackle yellow house. I drove past to the end of the block, pulling to a stop in a convenience store parking lot.

My intention was to sit and wait there for the phone call, but the longer I waited, the more uncomfortable I grew. The neighborhood wasn't the best, and my SUV stuck out like a sore thumb, garnering curious looks from pedestrians. The last thing I wanted was to draw attention to myself, so I decided to relocate.

I had seen a pretty little riverside park just prior to crossing the bridge, so I drove back over into the main part of town and went back there. I found a shady spot to park and turned off the engine. The phone rang about ten minutes later.

"Hello?" I said, praying that Tilly was on the other end of the line.

"Hello?" a woman's voice said tentatively.

"Yes."

"You left a note? It said from a friend?"

"Yes."

"How do you know my son?"

She sounded frightened and confused and even a little bit angry.

"Is this Tilly?" I asked, wanting to make sure before I told her.

"Of course."

"This is Callie Webber. My husband was the one—my husband, Bryan Webber was—"

Somehow, I faltered, unable to think of how to say it, not wanting to blurt out "your son killed my husband." In my hesitation, she filled the void.

"I know that name. Your husband is the one who got hurt in the boating accident?"

"Yes," I said, wanting to say, *not hurt, killed*, but I held my tongue.

"What do you want?" she asked, sounding more confused than anything.

"I'm in town," I told her, "and I wondered if I could talk to you. Face-to-face."

"You wanna talk to me?"

"Yes. It won't take long. Maybe ten, fifteen minutes?"

She was quiet for a moment.

"I don't see why," she said finally.

"Please?" I asked. "I could come to your house, if you'd like."

"No," she replied finally. "I'll come to you. Where are you?"

I described the park, and she said she could be there in a few minutes.

While I waited, I got out of the car and wandered over to a nearby picnic table. I sat facing the water, my back to the parking lot, wishing that none of this were necessary, that today could have been a simple day like any other. The further I went into this investigation, the further I went from Tom. Deep in my heart, I had a feeling that with every new fact I unturned, things were only going to get worse.

I glanced at my watch, counting the minutes until she would get here. Finally, I spotted her car coming over the bridge, and I followed it with my eyes as it turned into the parking lot and pulled to a stop next to mine.

She got out of the car. Tilly Sparks was short and blonde, as described, and she did look like her son. But where he was wary and suspicious, she seemed merely tired and beaten down. She walked over to me. I stood, and after an awkward moment stepped forward and extended my hand to her.

"Callie Webber," I said, shaking her hand. "Thank you for coming."

# Fifteen

"James was the result of a one-night stand," Tilly said, "but it wasn't like it sounds."

We were sitting at the picnic table, the river bubbling in front of us, our conversation going much better than I ever could have expected. My fervent prayers must have been answered, because Tilly had warmed up to me almost from the moment I shook her hand. I had a feeling she kept so much of her son's story to herself that it was a relief to talk about it with someone, even if that someone was the wife of her son's victim.

"I had had a crush on Jimmy Shepherd for two years, ever since we were assigned as lab partners in the tenth grade," she continued. "All my friends thought he was a nerd, but I knew how smart he was. None of my family ever went to college, you see, but Jimmy was gonna go to some Ivy League school and find a cure for cancer or something. I used to dream about being an Ivy League wife."

As I listened to her tale, I couldn't help compare her present situation with how her life might have turned out had her wishes come true.

"It's an old story, but graduation night we ended up next to each other at the bonfire. Jimmy hadn't ever been with a girl, see, and I thought maybe if I was his first, he would fall in love with me. We did it in his daddy's car, parked not too far from here. Three months later, I realized I was pregnant and he was off to college without a word."

"What did you do?"

"Jimmy wouldn't return my calls, so I went to see his daddy. He gave me a check for five thousand dollars and told me never to contact his family again."

"Did you take it?"

"Yeah, I did," she said. "I figured it was the most I was gonna get. I think he expected me to use some of the money for an abortion or something, but I would never do that. I named the baby James, after his daddy. I'm sure that didn't go over too well at the Shepherds' house."

She rolled her eyes wryly, and I was struck with the sudden, surprising notion that I actually liked this woman.

"You raised James yourself?"

"I sure did," she said proudly, "with a lot of help from my mama. I got a job nights tending bar so I could be home with James during the day. 'Course, that didn't leave much time for sleep, but I was young, what did I know? When he started first grade, I switched to being a waitress at a coffeehouse. That way I could get up early and work all day and get home right when he got off the school bus. Nowadays, of course, I work over at the restaurant, doing all different shifts, whatever they need. Ain't nobody home waitin' for me anyway."

"It must be hard keeping the fact that James is in prison a secret."

Her face turned red.

"It's nobody's business."

"I can see not wanting to tell your coworkers, but what about your closest friends?"

She shook her head no.

"How about your church, Tilly? Do you have a church?"

"I go once in a while over to the Church of the Way. The pastor knows, but nobody else."

"You know, people might not be as shocked as you think. It's the duty of the church body to love you through something like this. To step in and help you when you're all alone."

"I'm pretty self-sufficient," she said. "Always have been."

I nodded, knowing I could see a lot of me in her. I, too, struggled with the burden and blessing of being self-sufficient. For now, I needed to steer the conversation back to the past.

"That must've been a hard life," I said. "As a single mom."

"James was a good boy," she replied, shrugging, "smart as a whip, just like his daddy. James taught himself to read when he was only three, so soon as I realized he had some brains, I planted some big seeds in his head. Told him he could use his mind to take him places I had only dreamed of going. Maybe I made him dream a little too much."

She looked out at the water, and I could see pain in the lines on her face.

"What do you mean?" I asked, reaching for a leaf that had dropped from the overhanging limb onto the table.

"I built him up, made him expect too much. Told him he was smart enough to become anything he wanted. That made him impatient. Nothing ever happened fast enough for James. He graduated high school two years early, got through college in just three—and that was with a double major."

I asked where he went to college, and she said MIT—not Georgia State, as he had lied about in his deposition.

"There were some lean years in there, you know, and I think he was really just in a hurry to make some money. For a long time, he said, 'Mama, I'm gonna be a millionaire by the time I'm twenty-five.'" She shook her head sadly. "I never knew how much he hated growing up so poor until the FBI arrested him the first time and what he done all came out."

I tried not to let a sudden burst of emotion show on my face.

"Wait, back up," I said, my voice calm, my fingers breaking the leaf into pieces and letting them fly away in the breeze. "When they arrested him the *first* time? What had he done, exactly?"

She glanced at me sharply.

"You don't know 'bout all that?" she asked, and I had a feeling she was sorry she had brought it up.

"I don't know the details," I hedged.

"Well," she said, exhaling slowly, "he was working down in New Orleans at a start-up company that had something to do with computers. He created a secret code or something; I never could quite understand it. But the folks he worked with were all supersmart, just like him. Together they made something really important—some kind of computer thing that was gonna change the world."

I swallowed hard, knowing that Tom must have been one of the "folks" he worked with.

"Everything seemed to be going right for James. He got married, she got pregnant, they had twins."

At this she choked up, and I was glad for the distraction. My heart pounded. The twins she spoke of were Tom's nieces, his sister's children, the flesh and blood that connected him forever to the man who killed my husband. How could Tom have spoken to me so many times about the twins, all the while knowing they were the daughters of my husband's killer?

Tilly took a tissue from her pocket and tended to her tears.

"Those kids were my heart," she whispered. "I miss them so bad."

I looked at her.

"Don't you see them?"

"No," she said, folding the tissue in her hands. "Not since the divorce. When Beth broke things off with James, she broke off with me too."

"That's not right," I said.

"That's how it is, though," she replied.

"So James doesn't have a relationship with his own children?"

"Not hardly," she laughed bitterly. "Pretty soon after the divorce was final, he got arrested by the FBI."

"For what?" I asked.

"For 'violating U.S. export restrictions,' they said. The FBI accused James and his friends of selling their secret code to a restricted country—Iraq, Iran—one of them places. I didn't believe it till he told me himself that it was true. He got convicted and sentenced to five years. A traitor to his country."

"What about his friends?" I asked. "His coworkers."

"Well, they was all investigated, of course, but James had done it by himself. Got paid five million dollars and had to give it all up. He says now that was one million for every year of his sentence."

I tried to comprehend all that she was telling me, each answer giving rise to new questions.

"What happened then?" I asked. "Did he have to serve all five years?"

She looked at me, her face growing suddenly hard.

"You know what happened then," she said.

I shook my head, wishing I could take notes, wishing I could put a timeline down on paper to keep all of these facts straight. But I didn't want to spook her, so I worked hard to keep it all straight in my mind.

"He had the boating accident," she said simply.

"After he got out of prison?"

She shook her head.

"I don't know," she said. "He was *in* prison, supposedly, up at Keeplerville. I went to see him once a month for three years. Things were always the same. He was doing okay, he was hanging tough, he was counting the days till he would get out and he could start over again. He wanted a fresh chance."

"So where did the accident come in?" I asked. There were now three different prisons involved—Virginia State Penitentiary, where I thought he had been incarcerated following Bryan's death; Berwick Federal Correctional Institution in Berwick, Georgia, where he actually had been incarcerated following Bryan's death; and now Keeplerville Federal Prison, where he had been incarcerated *before* Bryan's death! It made no sense.

"Where did the accident come in? I don't know!" she exclaimed, though her sudden anger wasn't necessarily directed at me. "I haven't understood a thing since, I'll tell you that, and he won't talk about any of it."

"What do you mean?"

"I mean, I don't know what he was doin' in Virginia, I don't know why he was driving a big fancy boat, I don't know how he ended up killing your husband. Here I thought he was locked up in prison, and the next thing I know I see his face on the news. They said he killed a man while drunk and driving a boat. I thought they made a mistake, put the wrong guy's picture with another man's story. Then I found out it was true. I 'bout had a heart attack."

I put my hands on my knees, my head spinning.

"I don't understand," I said.

"Try being me," she said, making fists with her hands. "I think my boy's in prison, and then I find out he's been in a horrible accident and killed somebody. He won't tell me what's going on, and every single thing I read in the papers is a lie. They got his whole life wrong. Wrong college, wrong job, not a word about the FBI or the prison sentence."

"And the DUIs in his record?"

"No such thing. James don't even drink!"

"Did he ever live or work in Atlanta?"

"No way. It was all lies."

Something caught my attention, from the corner of my eye. I looked up to see a blue sedan driving slowly past. My hair stood up along the back of my neck.

"What is it?" Tilly asked, turning to look.

"Nothing," I said. "I just thought I recognized someone."

The car turned the corner and drove away. Before I could react further, she spoke again.

"When I saw all these lies in the newspaper about my son, I wanted to clear them up. But then James said, 'Quiet, Mama. If you love me, you'll just let it be.' I wasn't gonna shut up, no how, but then they gave him sixteen more years—sixteen years!—and all I could think was, please God let him be close enough to me that I could go and see him once in a while. I think they put him in over at Berwick just to keep me quiet. Now I go once a week and try not to think about the fact that he might not be free for years."

Tilly's tears were flowing freely at this point, and I couldn't help but be moved. The woman and I were on opposite sides of the same tragic incident, one horrifying day that changed many lives—and ended one.

We sat in silence for a while, the river's gurgle unable to calm my raw nerves. Coming here had answered some questions, but it had created many more. I wondered if I would ever make it to the bottom of this confusing labyrinth of secrecy. More than that, I wondered if I would be the same person now that I had heard the other side of the story.

"Why did you come here?" she asked finally, her words echoing those of her son earlier. I didn't know what to tell her, didn't know how to answer. I didn't want to lie, but I also couldn't speak the truth.

"Like you," I said, "I have questions about that time. I thought maybe you could help me get some answers."

She was about to reply when my cell phone rang. I saw that it was the prison, so I asked Tilly to excuse me as I answered.

The call was collect from James Sparks, so I accepted the charges.

"Yes?" I tried to keep my voice steady and my expression blank even as my heart was pounding wildly in my chest.

"Can you come back and see me tomorrow?" he asked. "I'm ready to answer your questions."

# Sixteen

I didn't tell Tilly it was her son on the phone. I simply agreed to come, set the time for noon, disconnected the call, and then wrapped up my conversation with her. Between seeing the blue sedan and hearing from James, I was feeling thoroughly rattled and eager to be on my way.

In the end, my encounter with Tilly left me feeling sad, confused, and yet in some way a little bit healed. I think it was the same for her. As we said goodbye, for some reason we hugged, and the hug was spontaneous and genuine.

After I left there, I stopped off at a home improvement store, bought a $1000 gift certificate, and delivered it to the pastor at the Church of the Way. I told him it was to be an anonymous gift to Tilly Sparks, and that my hope was that a group of parishioners might band together, use the money for supplies, and donate the labor to fix up Tilly's house. The man seemed astounded and grateful. Apparently, Tilly's situation weighed heavily on his heart, but until now he hadn't really been able to think of a way to reach her.

After that I drove across town and got a room at the same motel I had stopped in earlier. I brought in everything I might need for the night from my car, and then I double-locked the motel room door and slid the table up against it as an extra safety measure. As I did, I kept trying to figure out how the blue sedan could have possibly caught up with me here in Albany. Was it just a coincidence that the same color and model of car had driven slowly past us today? If not, then obviously whoever that driver was, he wasn't working alone but as some sort of tag team. If so, though, who were the other members of that team? I had been on the lookout constantly, and I had never spotted any other vehicle doing anything even remotely suspicious.

For now, I would have to table that question. It looked as though all that was left for me to do was to pass the time until noon tomorrow when I would get to see James Sparks again and learn the truths that had thus far been hidden from me.

I watched television for a while, flipping channels with the remote, but I clicked it off when I couldn't stand the noise anymore. I wondered absently how my dog was faring without me and how angry Harriet might be that I hadn't yet checked in with her. It struck me that there wasn't a soul on earth who knew where I was right now, with the possible exception of whoever was tailing me in the blue sedan. And though I kept going to the shaded window and peeking outside, I didn't see any signs of anyone observing me.

I sat back on the bed and stared at the phone, wanting to call Tom, thinking about calling my mom, knowing I ought to call Harriet. I did nothing but sit there and stare. Finally, a surge of pure loneliness pierced my heart, and before I knew it, I had doubled over from the pain.

It hurt so bad! I clutched my pillow and closed my eyes, tears suddenly flowing down my cheeks. Up until today I had held out hope for my relationship with Tom—despite the fact that he had abandoned me in Florida, despite the fact that he had something to do with the death of my husband. At this point, none of that mattered. His sister had been James Sparks' wife. His nieces were James Sparks' *children!*

I sobbed, rocking back and forth, deep, heaving sobs that left me breathless and gasping. I wasn't crying for Bryan, really—that wound had been healing for a while. I was crying for Tom, for all the dreams I had allowed myself to have about our future. I was crying for myself, that I could have been so utterly and completely deceived.

Bryan had been a good man, a good husband, but everything he was had died that day in that river. Truly, a big part of me had died as well. At that time, I knew one thing for certain; I would never love anyone that way again.

But then, eventually, there was Tom. Our relationship had grown slowly and steadily, for a long time in friendship and then, much later, in love. I thought it was love.

I didn't know it was a complete and utter lie.

Still crying, I leaned over onto the bed and held my pillow tightly to my chest, curling into a fetal position. As I had cried over Bryan's death so many times, I now cried over the death of my relationship with Tom. In my mind, the two men's faces blurred together, two men, both gone from me in their own way. I fell asleep, finally, the bedside lamp still on, my eyes swollen shut from crying.

I slept for nearly eight hours, waking a little before 4:00 A.M.

I sat up in the bed, my head pounding, my nose completely stopped up. Knowing I wouldn't be able to get back to sleep, I climbed under the spray of a hot shower, the water soothing away the tension in my neck.

I hadn't cried like that since last fall, I realized. Surely, there would come a day when there were no more tears left, when my memories brought me only a dull sadness.

Right now, the pain was as sharp as glass. Saddest of all was the realization that the entire focus of this investigation had now shifted—and something in my heart had frozen into solid ice. This was no longer about learning the truths so I could move forward in my relationship with Tom.

Tom had betrayed me.

No, now this investigation had one single purpose: to learn the truth about Bryan's death, for Bryan's sake. If I did one thing with what I was about to learn, I would make sure that every single person involved in the death of my husband received full justice for the life they had taken away.

# Seventeen

~

Clipping the tags from the last of my new clothes, I got dressed and went out into the predawn darkness in search of breakfast. A new boldness had taken hold of me, and I almost welcomed an encounter with the blue sedan, but it was nowhere in sight.

I found a nearby coffee shop that was open 24 hours, so I bought a newspaper and took a seat by the window and ordered my usual breakfast of poached eggs, whole wheat toast, and hot tea. On second thought, I had the waitress bring me a plate of blueberry waffles and coffee instead. Somehow, today I just couldn't face the routine.

The paper didn't really hold my interest, other than to remind me that while my world was falling apart, everywhere else life was rolling along, business as usual. I was finished with breakfast before 6:00, and the sun was just starting to appear along the horizon as I came back out to my car. I couldn't believe I would have to wait six hours before I could see James Sparks. Of course, driving there and getting inside would use up almost an hour, but otherwise the morning stretched before me like an eternity.

I returned to the motel, determined to use part of that time to get myself organized and answer my e-mail. As I opened my laptop, I decided to start by creating a database for this case, as I always did. Certainly, I needed to sort out the facts I had gleaned thus far.

Most puzzling to me, I thought as I began entering data, was what Tilly Sparks had said to me about James' personal history. The man had worked with a group of computer experts, created a product, and then sold it to a country that was prohibited by the U.S. government. This caused an FBI investigation and eventually a conviction for violating export restrictions. He had acted alone, earning five million dollars for the secret trade. Unfortunately for him, not only did he have to give up the five million dollars upon his conviction, but he was also sentenced to five years in Keeplerville Federal Prison.

From there, he must have somehow earned an early release—and not told his mother—because the next thing she knew he had gone to Virginia, stayed in a vacation home, and accidentally killed my husband with a speedboat. After that, bogus facts about James hit the newspapers, and a falsified criminal record appeared on the police computers, tied in with his fingerprints. Everyone involved with the death on my end had been told that James Sparks was a drunk driver who was given 16 years for manslaughter. Now, however, I had learned that he had no history of drunk driving and he wasn't at Virginia State Penitentiary as we had been told, but was instead at a male minimum security federal facility located within an hour of his hometown. When his mother had questioned him about the odd facts and incorrect information that the media was presenting, he had told her simply to keep quiet.

There was something big going on, and though I didn't want to believe it, my mind kept flashing "Government cover-up! Government cover-up!" like a billboard.

I wasn't one for conspiracy theories. I wasn't one to suspect the hallowed halls of the FBI or the NSA of nefarious activities. Certainly, I knew there were questionable decisions made at all levels of government from time to time—not to mention rogue agents like the man I had dealt with last fall in a case that involved the

Immigration and Naturalization Service. But by and large I trusted the entities who watched out for our nation's security. I really didn't want to believe they had somehow buried the real facts of this case among a bunch of lies.

Still, there were records missing. Falsified information had shown up on the police computers. Someone somewhere was playing fast and loose with the facts.

As I finished inputting everything I knew, I simply sat and stared at the puzzle in front of me, knowing there was a single glimmer of hope: Maybe today James Sparks would tell me all that I needed to know, and my investigation would be over.

Giving up for the time being, I closed out the database and then went online and scanned through my e-mail, cringing at the number of urgent notes that had piled up from Harriet. I read them all, variations on the same theme of "Are you okay?" "Where are you?" and "What's going on?"

I wrote her back a heartfelt apology, telling her I would understand if she was furious with me. I said I was sorry that the conversation at the meeting had been confidential and I couldn't tell her about it, but that the foundation was not in danger of being closed down, and that I was traveling for personal matters, not J.O.S.H.U.A. business. I ended by saying it might be a while longer before I could get in touch again but not to worry about me, that I was fine.

Once I had answered all important mail and deleted the junk, I signed off and decided to clear out my briefcase. Inside was a manila envelope, and as I picked it up, I remembered that it was my next assignment for the foundation, the one Tom had handed me as we were saying goodbye. Now I opened it with a heavy heart, knowing there was probably no future for me at the foundation. I doubted I could work any longer for a man who had so deceived me. Still, I pulled out the contents of the envelope and set everything down on the table in front of me.

On top was the cover sheet detailing the charity's name, address, and phone number, its function, and the amount Tom was hoping to donate. In this case, the amount was $50,000 to a place called

Family HEARTS. Under the cover sheet was a brochure, and I skimmed through it, trying to get a feel for their mission. Apparently, the place served as a sort of nationwide support network for families of children who had rare diseases and disorders.

"It's hard enough to see your child suffer," one parent was quoted as saying, "harder still when no one has even heard of the condition that is causing their suffering."

I had never thought about it, but I imagined that to be true. At least with juvenile diabetes or muscular dystrophy, there was a certain knowledge level in the general public. But the kids in this brochure suffered from conditions I had never heard of: mucopolysaccharide disorder, hyperinsulinism, juvenile dermatomyositis.

Under the brochure was more standard paperwork: an audit report, the mission statement, minutes from a year's worth of board meetings.

I didn't see a grant application, which was odd, because it was kind of hard to approve a grant when I didn't even know what they wanted the money for. It wasn't until I reached the last page that I caught my breath. Under the title of "Contact Information" was a list of names of the board of directors and, below that, contact information for the staff and volunteers. One of the volunteers was named Beth Sparks.

James Sparks' wife.

Tom's sister.

Holding my breath, I reviewed the page again, and this time two other names also jumped out at me: Irene Bennett and Veronica Wilson. Irene, Tom's mother, was on the board of directors, and Veronica was the director of the program. Whether this was the same Veronica who had been Tom's high school sweetheart and one-time fiancée, I wasn't sure. I had never learned her last name— but Veronica wasn't all that common of a first name. I had a feeling that it was, indeed, her. I turned back to the cover sheet, surprised that I hadn't even noticed where the charity was located: New Orleans, Louisiana.

Tom's hometown.

I closed my eyes and tried to recall Tom's demeanor when he handed me this file. At the time I had been so preoccupied with all that had happened at the meeting that I hadn't really paid much attention. Now I thought back, realizing that there had been something in his face, something odd as he gave it over to me. "I'd like you to look into it," he had said. When I protested, he repeated himself. *I'd like you to look into it.*

I glanced at my watch. It was nearly 8:00 A.M., which made it almost 5:00 A.M. in California, far too early to call. Still, at this point, I didn't care if I woke Tom up or not. I dialed his number but hung up halfway through, remembering suddenly the cell phone he had slipped into my pocket just four days before, after our meeting at the foundation. *If you have to call me, that's the phone to use,* he had said. I had stashed it in my briefcase once I took off on my long drive to Virginia. Now I dug it from the pocket of the case where I had shoved it, turned it on, and studied it.

It was the size of a regular cell phone but seemed a little heavier somehow, the mouthpiece thicker. I turned it on and fooled with the buttons a bit. On the stored numbers screen was only one name, Tom Bennett, followed by a number I didn't recognize. I pushed the buttons to dial that number, and after about six rings, Tom answered, his voice sounding freshly roused from sleep.

"It's Callie. I have a question for you."

I could hear rustling, and I pictured him sitting up in bed, rubbing his eyes, trying to get his wits about him.

"What time is it?" he asked.

"I need to know about this file," I said, ignoring his question. "This charity."

"Are you alone?"

"Yes, I'm calling on the phone you gave me. I assume that makes this conversation secure?"

"Yes. Yeah," he said softly. "Okay, Callie. What do you want to know?"

"Was this charity somehow related to the death of my husband?"

"Family HEARTS?"

"Yes. I see the address. I see the people involved. What am I supposed to do with this information?"

He was quiet for a long moment.

"You understand that I'm not at liberty to explain, really."

"Tell me what you can," I replied.

"I thought it…I figured it might be a good way to give you access to…certain people. That's all. I hoped it would serve you well as a *concurrent* investigation, if you know what I mean."

"This charity has nothing to do with me or you or Bryan?"

"No, absolutely not. Family HEARTS is a good group. No connection. I really would like to give them a donation."

"You expect me to run a charity investigation as though nothing else is even going on?"

"I just thought you needed a way to get there, a reason to be there. There are people connected with the charity you need to meet."

"Who, Tom? Like your mother?" I asked. "Your *sister*?"

He was quiet for a moment.

"So you know."

"Yes, I know. Why would I want anything to do with any of these people? For that matter, why would I want anything ever to do with you again?"

I was so angry! I closed my eyes, my fists clenched, about to hang up. It had been a mistake to call.

"I know you're angry, Callie," he said. "And you have every right to be. Just don't…don't give up on us yet."

I held my breath, fighting back tears.

"When this is all over," he continued, "then you can walk away if you still want to. For now, please. I'm begging you. Keep your focus. There's more to learn."

"I'll try," I whispered, the only words I could manage to say. Then I hung up the phone, not telling him that I would be learning everything in just a few short hours, when I went face-to-face again with James Sparks. After that, I knew what I would do: return to D.C., hand in my resignation to Harriet, and then go home and make some decisions about the rest of my life.

I paced for a while, knowing I needed to go out somewhere, to do something physical to work off some steam. I really wanted to go canoeing, but I decided the best I might be able to do was catch a swim in the motel pool.

I kept a gym bag in my car with a swimsuit and towel inside. I went out and retrieved it. Officially, the pool didn't open until 10:00 A.M., but it was well hidden from the front desk, behind a row of rooms, and I doubted anyone would stop me as long as I wasn't making much noise.

Towel in hand, I worked my way over to the pool area and then slipped into the chilly water, going immediately into laps. After a while I warmed up, my muscles working hard to propel me across the water. I blanked out my mind, counting the short laps with each stroke: "Nine, nine, nine, nine, nine, nine, nine, nine, nine, nine, nine, nine, flip, ten, ten, ten, ten, ten, ten, ten, ten, ten, ten, ten, ten, flip…" In that manner I pushed forward, back and forth, counting like a mantra, until I reached one hundred. Then I turned over onto my back, chest heaving for breath, heart pounding, paddling more slowly back and forth as my muscles cooled down.

It was going to be a sunny day, and I squinted up at the sky as I paddled, peering at the fluffy white clouds that drifted past. All of this felt like a nightmare. The only problem was, I didn't think I would be waking up any time soon.

Back in the room, I took my second shower of the day, but this time I took care afterward to style my hair and put on some makeup. I don't know why I was fixing myself up to see James Sparks, other than I wanted the confidence and self-possession that looking my best always seemed to bring me. I dressed in my suit, the same suit I had worn several times now in a row. It was the only really nice thing I had with me, and though it was time to get it to the dry cleaner, I thought it could go one more round if it needed to.

When I was completely dressed, I packed my meager belongings in their plastic bags, propped them by the door, and then I sat on the side of the bed for a moment, knowing I needed to go to the Lord in prayer.

I didn't want to. I was a little mad at God right then, and I really didn't feel like talking to Him any more than I felt like talking to Tom. Still, I knew I was about to head into an incredibly difficult moment. I needed to be right with God, and that started with a willing and compliant heart.

Unable to pray, I reached into the bedside table drawer, thinking that at the very least I could read a verse or two from the Bible. I had recently given away my travel Bible to a friend, but the Gideons, God bless them, had placed a Bible in this motel room as usual. It opened to 1 Corinthians 13, verse 12:

> For now we see through a glass, darkly; but then face to face; now I know in part; but then I shall know even as also I am known.

I closed the Bible, a sudden rush of emotion catching me off guard. Taken out of context, maybe God was trying to tell me something. He wanted me to persevere, to keeping working forward until I could "know fully" everything there was to know.

"Be with me, God," I prayed, the only prayer I was able to utter. Then I put the Bible back in the drawer, picked up my things, and went to the car.

# Eighteen

I was sitting in the same chair as the day before, waiting for Sparks, when he came through the door. This time he didn't hesitate but walked right over to me. He looked horrible, and I wondered if he had slept at all last night. His hair was a disheveled mess, and there were deep circles under his eyes. As he sat across from me, a guard positioned himself just out of earshot, arms hanging loosely at his sides.

"Thanks for coming," Sparks muttered, his manner much calmer today.

Before I could reply, several other women came into the room from the visitor processing area. As they took seats at different tables, I realized that it must be a visiting day, and these ladies were here to see prisoners. I leaned toward Sparks, lowering my voice.

"By law," I said, "we can request a private conference room, if we want."

"Doesn't matter. I don't care who hears me."

"But I want to know the circumstances of my husband's death."

"Then I'm going to tell you a little story," he replied. "About a group called 'The Cipher Five.'"

He sat up straight then, looking around the room and seeming to gather strength in front of my eyes. My heart pounded, and I felt as though I were standing on the edge of a precipice, about to jump off.

"The Cipher Five?" I asked softly.

"This was back in the late nineties," James continued, his voice a little louder than I would have liked. "Like the name says, there were five of us. We were a team. We were working in secret, doing things with code that Diffie and Rivest had only dreamed of."

He paused for effect, taking out his asthma inhaler and giving himself a squirt.

"Diffie and Rivest?" I asked, trying to tune out the noise that was building around us. Though there were no other prisoners in the room yet, a few more visitors drifted in and, again, I wondered if we should ask for a private room.

"The pantheons in the field!" he said, exhaling a medicinal smell as he tucked the inhaler back into his pocket. "Haven't you heard of Diffie, Hellman, and Merkle? Rivest, Shamir, and Adelman?"

"James, you've lost me."

"*Encryption*," he said. "We were taking it all to the next level. The Cipher Five broke the door wide open, man. No one will ever know how significant our work was."

A noise erupted across the room and I jumped, looking to see that an empty soda can had been accidentally knocked from a table. My nerves were at the breaking point.

"So who were the Cipher Five again?" I asked, trying to remember the names. "Diffie, Rivest..."

"No, no, no," he scolded, the arrogance I had seen the day before suddenly returning to his features. "All those people, all those guys, they were before us. They laid the groundwork. Our group came *after*."

There was an odd expression on his face, and I tried to decide what his overriding emotion was at the moment. I wasn't sure, but as he spoke I thought I detected anger—and an odd sort of defiance, though whom he was defying, I didn't know.

"Okay, let me get this straight," I said. "In a long line of very significant encryption experts, you were part of a group of five people who also made important contributions to the field."

"Correct."

"So who were the people in your group?" I asked. "Who were the Cipher Five?"

"Me, my wife Beth, her brother, Tom, Phillip Wilson, and Armand Velette," he replied, counting off on his fingers. "All five geniuses, in our own way. We all brought something good to the table."

"When was this again?"

"Back in the late nineties. Most of us were fresh out of college or grad school. Tom hired us to implement his ideas."

"He *hired* you?"

"Yeah. He got a business loan and put together a little computer company. We were his employees."

"How did he find you?"

"I went to MIT with his sister, Beth. She recommended me, and then when we started working together, she and I ended up falling in love and getting married. But that's another story."

Suddenly, the inner door opened and a group of inmates spilled into the room, followed by two guards who placed themselves along the perimeter. The prisoners were all dressed in khakis, just like Sparks, and many of them greeted their visitors with hugs and kisses, something I knew was allowed in minimum security.

I closed my eyes, trying to refocus on our own conversation.

"So Tom Bennett was your boss, but he was also one of the five," I said slowly.

"Yes, of course," James replied. "We worked together for a year and half and were finally ready to release in March of ninety-nine."

"Release?" I asked, not following much of what he was saying.

"Our *encryption program*," he said, obviously frustrated with my stupidity. "Everybody knew it was better than what was already out there, that it could've made us a fortune. But Tom had to follow the rules, had to do everything by the book. His way was taking too long. Is it any wonder some of us ended up courting the T-Seven?"

"Courting the T-Seven?" I asked, and it struck me that Sparks' thought processes were about as confused and jumbled and nonsequential as the computer code he probably wrote.

"You never heard of the T-Seven?" he asked, his lip curled in a sneer.

"No, I've never heard of it. What is it?"

He used both hands to hold up seven fingers, wiggling each finger as he spoke.

"What *was* it, you mean. Cuba, Iran, Iraq, Libya, North Korea, Sudan, and Syria. The T-Seven. Also known as the Terrorist Seven."

"I see," I whispered, remembering that his mother had spoken of this, that James had been convicted for selling a computer program to a restricted country.

"Our team may have started with five, but with all of the… issues…we had to deal with, folks started dropping out. There were three of us for a while, then just two. There are still two. Despite what everyone thinks, I have never acted alone."

His eyes were intense, and he held my gaze for a long time. I wasn't sure what he was trying to tell me, but I knew it was important.

"Are you talking about Tom?" I asked. "Are the two of you still some kind of team?"

He laughed.

"Me and Mr. Goody Two-Shoes? I don't think so. He was the first one to pull out. He abandoned all of us and headed off to do his own thing. Ended up filthy rich, while we never saw another penny from the work we did—officially, at least."

I clenched my hands in frustration.

"James, you are confusing me. What are you trying to say?"

"That I have never acted alone."

"In the boat?" I asked, grasping at straws. "You weren't alone in the boat?"

He rolled his eyes, exasperated.

"I'm not talking about the boat," he said loudly. "I'm talking about the sale to the T-Seven! I wasn't acting alone."

Suddenly, I wondered if he *wanted* to be overheard; if, for some reason, he was eager to carry on this conversation in such a public place. I glanced up at the guard who had come into the room with him, and I realized that the man had moved much closer to us and was well within hearing range of our conversation.

"Unfortunately," James continued loudly before I could say anything, "we got busted. Or maybe I should say, *I* got busted. I was the one the FBI caught on tape. When they investigated, I said I acted alone, but I didn't. It wasn't only me. I even have proof—"

Looking back, it's hard to describe what happened next. I saw the guard make some movement, and then, almost instantly, an argument erupted across the room, with a woman suddenly slapping the face of a man. She stood and yelled, and the other two guards who were manning the room all rushed to step in before any more violence occurred. One of them grabbed her hands and held them behind her back while the other collared the man and led him back to the door. This, in turn, seemed to rile up everyone in the room, and for a moment I panicked, realizing that I was, after all, in the presence of a bunch of prisoners—even if this was minimum security. The guard nearest to us put his hand on Sparks' shoulder and whispered something in his ear. Finally, once the man and the woman had both been removed from the premises, the din seemed to die back down. I looked over at Sparks, and much to my surprise, he was standing up. He looked at me and smiled, a grin that spread his mouth but did not reach his eyes. Still, he seemed genuinely happy, as if he had achieved some sort of goal.

"Sorry, Mrs. Webber," Sparks said, holding out his hands. "I guess I have to end the story there."

I shot up out of my chair.

"End it?" I cried. "I want to know what happened. I want to know what you were doing when you killed my husband."

He merely shook his head and let the guard escort him away.

"Sorry," Sparks called out, over his shoulder. "This meeting is adjourned. Don't come back."

# Nineteen

Sparks had used me. I wasn't sure how or why, but I was convinced that our entire conversation in the common room had been some sort of performance. He had been manipulating something. When I left there and got in my car, I felt utterly exploited.

I thought about speaking to the warden, but I didn't think he could shed light on anything—not to mention that I didn't want to call attention to myself just now. There had been some sort of interplay there between Sparks and the guard. I had to figure out what it was.

While my memory was still fresh, I needed to write down everything I could remember from our conversation. I sat in my car in the prison parking lot, pulled out a pen and some paper, and jotted down everything I could remember. My notes were free association, a jumbled mess of names and facts.

*The Cipher Five*

*Diffie and Rivest*

*"Me, my wife Beth, her brother, Tom, Phillip Wilson, and Armand Velette. All five geniuses. All brought something good to the table."*

*"Tom had to follow the rules, had to do everything by the book."*

*"Courting the T-Seven"*

*"The team started with five, but then there were three of us, then just two. There are still two. I have never acted alone."*

*"I was the one the FBI caught on tape. But it wasn't only me. I even have proof."*

I sat with pen in hand, thinking that was when the little fight erupted. I closed my eyes, picturing it, remembering the movement of the guard just before it happened, and then the way he put a hand on Sparks' shoulder and leaned over to whisper to him. Had that whole ruckus been engineered?

Once the fight began, my conversation had ended. With a gasp, I got it: Sparks was warning the guard, *I have proof*. After Sparks forced his hand, the argument served as a diversion and had probably given the guard a chance to communicate something with Sparks while I was looking the other way.

If that were true, then it led to another question: Could the guard have somehow been involved with this team, this Cipher Five? More likely, the guard was working for one of them now, perhaps as a messenger, protecting whoever the other person Sparks was referring to when he said, *Despite what everyone thinks, I have never acted alone.*

I looked at my notes, concentrating. The team started with five, then there were three, then just two. What did that mean? In what capacity did the team still exist? Were they still writing encryption programs? I knew Sparks wouldn't be allowed to do such a thing in prison. Certainly, Tom was still involved with computer encryption, though now in the employ of the U.S. government. What of the others? I reread my notes. What of Beth Sparks, Phillip Wilson, and Armand Velette? Was one of them the second person to whom Sparks was referring?

I studied their names, wondering if Phillip Wilson was related to Veronica Wilson, the woman at the helm of Family HEARTS, the New Orleans charity Tom wanted me to investigate. He must be, I decided, which was one more reason that Tom wanted me to go there.

I heard voices and glanced up to see the main door open and the visitors that had been in the common room now filing outside. Most of them got in cars, though a few walked past the security gate to a covered bench near the main road. I realized that it was a bus stop, that some of these people had had to take a bus here in order to get in a visit.

My pulse surged when I saw that there was already one person sitting there: the woman who had started the fight. Though the guards had escorted her out of the building right away, she was still stuck here, waiting for the bus.

I needed to talk to her.

Fortunately, it wasn't hard to tail a bus. When it pulled up about ten minutes later, I started my car and followed it down the road, allowing a big distance between me and it. Not that anyone would be looking, but I didn't want to take any chances.

The bus went to the town of Dawson first, making several stops along the main street. Then it drove on toward Americus. I stayed behind all the way and watched as it made a few stops in town there. The woman I was waiting for finally got off at a stop near a grocery store, her vivid purple shirt making her easy to spot. I pulled into the grocery store parking lot, dug some cash out of my purse and shoved it into my pocket, and then took off after her on foot.

She was walking toward a row of run-down houses when I caught up with her. I called out and she turned, a look of irritation on her face at the sight of my navy suit and pumps.

"Excuse me," I said. "I need to talk to you."

"What do you want?" she asked, though it came out sounding like "Whachoo wont?"

"I was at the prison today and I saw you there. I just need to know something about that fight you had."

She turned and started walking again.

"Why is that your business?"

"It's not, really," I said. "I just need to know if that was a real argument or if you had it on purpose."

"On purpose?"

"Like, did someone tell you to get into a fight just then?"

She crossed her arms over her chest and kept walking.

"Why would I tell you that?" she asked finally.

"I'll pay you," I answered.

That actually got her to stop walking.

"How much?" she demanded.

My mind raced.

"That depends," I said. "How much were you paid to have the fight?"

"Twenty dollars," she said, not even realizing what she had done, that she had already admitted the truth about what I wanted to know.

"Twenty dollars," I replied, nodding. "Okay, I'll give you thirty to tell me all about it."

"Make it fifty and you got a deal."

I acted as if I were thinking it over, but in truth I would've willingly paid ten times that for the right information.

"Fine, fifty," I said, reaching into my pocket to get the money.

"Not here, not here," she said quickly. "It looks funny. Next thing you'll know, we'll get busted for a drug deal or something."

"Where, then?"

She glanced around, waved at a friend who was sitting on a nearby porch, and led me in that direction.

"Hey, Miz Cora," she said loudly, taking the three stone steps that led up to the covered porch. "You making beans for dinner?"

The old woman was sitting on a rickety metal chair, snapping the ends from fresh green beans and dropping them in a pot.

"Looks like it, don't it?" the woman replied.

She didn't seem surprised by the addition of two new people to her porch. We sat in the remaining chairs, and from there I could look back down the hill and see my car sitting in the grocery store parking lot. My friend grabbed a big pile of the unsnapped beans and surprised me by putting them in my lap.

"Miz Cora's practically deaf and half blind," the girl said to me softly. "Jus' hand back some of them beans to me along with the money."

I did as she asked, discreetly reaching into my pocket and counting off two twenties and a ten. I wadded them up with the beans, handed them back to her, and watched as she smoothly extracted and pocketed the cash.

"It's getting hot, huh?" my friend yelled to the old woman.

"Yeah, it's a big pot," the lady replied.

My friend turned back toward me and spoke softly.

"Okay, here's what happened," she said. "Last night I got a call from Les Watts, one of the guards at the prison."

We both snapped beans and dropped them into the pot as we talked.

"Did you know him?" I asked.

"Sorta. Enough to say hey. We went to the same high school. I see him whenever I go out to the prison to visit my husband. Anyway, he called me to ask if I could go for a visit today. I was thinking about it anyway, so I said sure. Then he said he would pay me twenty dollars if we would 'cause a disturbance.' So I'm like, what you mean a disturbance and he say, you know, like a fight or something. Just make some noise. He said, go ahead and have your visit, but if I take off my hat and scratch my head, you start hollering about something. If I don't give you that signal, don't worry about it. I'll give you twenty dollars either way."

I digested this information, tossing a bean with a worm hole into the trash bag. Glancing down the hill, I spotted a blue sedan just turning into the lot where I had parked my car. It passed my vehicle and then parked far down at the end of the next row, where I wouldn't even have seen it if I hadn't been looking.

I tried to focus on the conversation at hand.

"Why did you think he wanted you to do that?" I asked.

"So he could win a bet."

"A bet?"

"He said they been having lotsa arguments at visiting time, and the guards all have a bet going. He said one more fight in the common room today and he would win the bet."

I glanced at the old woman, who really did seem oblivious to our conversation.

"You believed him?" I asked.

"I believed he was gonna pay me twenty dollars," she said. "What do I care what his reason is?"

I thought about that, snapping the last of my beans.

"Does this Les guy live in town?" I asked.

She shrugged.

"You gonna tell him what I tol' you?"

"No," I said. "I promise. But I sure would like to know where he lives."

She shrugged.

"Somewhere over to the other side of the bridge. I ain't sure where."

"Do you have a phone number for him?"

"No, but he's supposed to meet me later at the Brown Door to give me my money. He couldn't chance being seen paying me at the prison."

"What time?"

"Four-thirty. You not gonna come there, are you? He'll get mad if he finds out I tol' somebody the bet was rigged."

"Don't worry," I said, dropping the last bean into the pot. "I won't tell him if you don't."

# Twenty

The very next order of business was to ditch the blue sedan once and for all. I didn't want the driver to see where I was, so after the young woman and I parted ways, I crossed the street, cut across an empty lot, and then slipped into the grocery store parking lot the back way. The loading bay was empty but the door was open, so I went inside, finding myself in the food storage area. There was a hallway to one side, so I made my way through there, accidentally coming upon a group of teenage employees taking a break.

"I'm sorry," I said, trying not to look too flustered. "I had to use the restroom and I got myself all turned around."

A girl pointed the way into the store, and the next thing I knew I was in the meat department. Smoothing my clothes, I grabbed a few items at random and walked to the checkout. I paid the cashier and went to my car. Before I had even started the engine, I could see the blue sedan pulling out of the parking lot and onto the main road. I tried to catch up, but I got stuck behind a big truck and finally lost sight of it.

A thought had occurred to me earlier, when I was sitting on that porch with the green beans, but I needed to go somewhere to check out my theory. I drove around town a bit and finally pulled over at a gas station, parking in such a way that the rear of my car was protected by the building and a tall fence. I pretended to put air in my tires, kneeling down so that I could see the underside of my vehicle. It didn't take long to find that my theory was correct: A tracking device had been affixed to my car.

Heart pounding, I went into the station to borrow a screwdriver; then I came back out and tried, as discreetly as I could, to pry the device loose. It popped off fairly easily into my hand, and I pocketed it and returned the screwdriver.

Back in the car, I studied the device, a small black metal object about an inch in diameter. It had been affixed to the inside rear bumper with a sticky pad, and I was surprised that it hadn't fallen off in all of my driving.

I felt a bit ashamed of myself as I looked at it, feeling I should have figured this out sooner. There never had been two cars tag-teaming me. There was only the one, and when I wasn't in sight, the driver was keeping track of me with this device.

Now that I knew, I had several choices. The easiest, of course, was simply to put the device on some other vehicle and let it drive away. That wouldn't solve the bigger problem, however, which was to find out who this fellow was working for. That seemed to me to be the more important issue, and one worth pursuing.

I still had an hour and a half before the prison guard was to meet the woman at the Brown Door and give her the $20 payoff. Using that time wisely, I drove to a dollar store and bought 15 helium balloons, some duct tape, and a baseball bat. Then I crammed the balloons in the car and headed out of town, watching the passing scenery for a usable location. Finally I spotted one, a field off to my right with no fencing and an old abandoned barn on the premises. I drove onto the grass and across the field, coming to a stop behind the barn.

Quickly, I got out and ran to the back of my SUV, flipping it open and pulling out all 15 balloons by their strings. I taped the tracking device to the balloon strings, and then I held my breath and let the whole thing go. Much to my relief, the little device was light enough, and the balloons whisked it away into the sky almost instantly.

Without pausing I grabbed the baseball bat, opened the other four doors of the vehicle as wide as they would go, and then crept inside the barn, careful not to leave any footprints in the dirt.

The building was dark inside, but enough slats were missing from the walls that I could see to move around. Trying not to think about rats and snakes and spiders, I situated myself where I could peek through some holes in the front, my view of the highway clear. Sure enough, soon the blue sedan came barreling up the roadway, and then it slowed as it neared the field.

I almost smiled, trying to picture the confusion of the man inside. After all, what did it mean when a tracking device showed that the car had flown up into the sky?

The sedan passed the field twice. On the third try, it drove slowly along and then pulled over to the side of the road.

From where I looked, I could see that my car had left tire tracks in the grass, leading around to the back of the barn. I watched as the guy got out of the sedan and then made his way via a more circuitous route. Trying to conceal himself along the tree line, he ran around the far side of the barn. As he got closer, he darted almost directly toward my car.

I had left the keys in the ignition, and the alert was dinging loudly, over and over, drawing him near. Holding my breath, I watched through the missing slats as he walked to my car and carefully peeked inside.

In that instant, his back to me, I stepped from the barn. Holding one hand at each end of the bat, I whipped it over his head and then jerked him backward against me, the wood pressed tightly against his neck. Afraid he might have a gun, I didn't stop there. I twisted to one side, lurching so that we fell to the ground, my knee against the small of his back.

"Freeze!" I said, catching my breath.

He didn't move, his hands splayed out beside him, though he was gasping for air.

"I'll let you breathe," I said, "if you don't move."

I let go of one side of the bat, and he started choking and coughing as I reached down and frisked him. From what I could tell, he wasn't armed.

"All right," I said, sitting up, my knee still against his back, the baseball bat clutched firmly in both hands, ready to swing. "Who are you and why are you following me?"

"You could've killed me," he gasped, reaching for his throat.

"I still could," I said. "Now who are you and why are you following me?"

He didn't reply, and so I stood, swinging back with the bat as if I were going to bash him in the head. He didn't know that I wouldn't do it, that it was all a bluff. In terror, he rolled over and held up both hands to protect himself, screaming.

"Ten seconds!" I warned.

"Okay, okay!" he said, holding out both hands. Finally, I relaxed my posture enough to let him speak.

"Yeah, I was following you," he said, breathing heavily. "Don't hurt me, okay? I'll tell you what you need to know."

"Who are you working for?" I demanded, knowing for certain now that he wasn't FBI. He had been too sloppy for that.

"A guy," he said. "He paid me to follow you."

"What guy?" I demanded. "Who?"

"I don't have a name. He just hired me to tail you. He gave me a receiver for a tracking device."

"When did he hire you?"

"Monday night. He said I could have the job if I could start right away."

"How did he find you?"

"In the Richmond phone book. I'm a private investigator. I have a big ad."

"A big ad?"

"Yeah," he said, reaching up to smooth out his hair. " 'If you think he's cheatin', our price can't be beaten.' "

"What?"

"That's my slogan. I do a lot of divorce cases. Though this is the first one where I got to use a tracking device."

I put down the bat. This was just too confusing to maintain my threatening stance.

"Look, I'm a PI too," I said. "Why don't you tell me all about it?"

He sat up, brushing the dust from his clothes.

"Fine," he said, trying to gain his composure. "Okay. Some guy called my after-hours phone number late Monday night and said he had a tracking device with a ten-mile range that he needed me to use to follow somebody. Apparently someone else was lined up to do this job out of D.C., but you took off sooner than anyone expected. So this guy paid me to pick up your trail in Melville, follow your car, and report back to him. That's all."

"Did you see this man in person?"

"Yeah, I drove down and met him in Melville. He gave me a cash deposit and taught me how to use the monitor. You were staying at a motel. I've been following you since then."

I tried to process all that he was telling me. Obviously, my quick departure from Washington, D.C., had taken someone by surprise. They had tailed me as far as Melville and then improvised on the road, hiring this dolt to continue to tail me on their behalf.

"Can you give me a physical description of the man who hired you?" I asked, reaching out to help him to his feet.

"Sure," he said, taking my hand. "Tall. Dark hair. Good-looking."

"Age?"

"Early thirties, about the same as you. I thought he was your husband."

"My husband?"

"Yeah, that's how I took it," he said. "He told me to follow you and to watch out for you. He seemed concerned that you might be in some kind of danger. I wasn't supposed to make myself known unless you needed help out of a tight spot."

And there we had it. It sounded to me that this man had been hired by Tom. I pulled a photo of the two of us from my wallet and showed it to him. He took one look and nodded.

"Yep, that's him."

"Let me ask you a question," I said. "Are you by any chance licensed to investigate in any of the states I have led you through?"

He looked down at the ground sheepishly.

"Not really," he said.

"Then let's do each other a favor," I told him. "You go on back home to Richmond, and I won't report what you've done to the authorities."

# Twenty-One

Moving fast, I was able to reach the Brown Door by 4:20, just ten minutes before the prison guard was supposed to meet the woman and give her the $20 payoff for having an argument in the common room. The Brown Door was a ramshackle-looking bar and restaurant about a mile out of Americus. There was a hardware store directly across the street, so I parked there and hunched down low in my seat, fixing my rearview mirror so that I could see behind me. Luckily for me, neither he nor she seemed to have shown up yet.

As I waited, I thought about Tom, picturing the scenario of the tracking device from his point of view. In my mind I replayed our entire encounter at the J.O.S.H.U.A. Foundation the other evening, and then I gasped as I realized when he had put the device on my car: Tom's lawyer, Kimball, must have done it when Tom took my elbow and led me over to the payment booth to pay for my parking. I closed my eyes and tried to picture Kimball's actions as Tom and I were walking back toward the car. He had been behind it, and then he moved away once we drew near. Now I understood why.

Tom probably had some fancy, expensive PI lined up to follow the tracking device from my home the next day. But then I surprised them all by leaving town immediately! I guess he'd had no choice but to follow me himself, and when I finally stopped for the night, he scrambled for a replacement. It was just his bad luck that the local Richmond PI he had pulled into service wasn't all that good.

Now that I knew everything, I felt I ought to call and fuss at Tom, giving him a piece of my mind. But I didn't, because while I should have found his actions invasive and infuriating, in a way, I found them kind of endearing. Despite everything, he wanted to keep track of me. To protect me. He was worried about me.

Soon, a battered brown truck pulled into the parking lot and a man got out, and I put all thoughts of Tom aside for the time being. I thought I recognized the man as the guard, though out of his uniform and in jeans and a T-shirt, it was a little hard to tell. He was slightly paunchy, and his lined face seemed familiar as he sat on his back bumper and lit up a cigarette.

After a few minutes, another car pulled into the parking lot, a low-riding Mustang with the woman I had talked to earlier seated on the passenger's side. The man walked to that car and leaned over the passenger's window. I watched as the guard pulled something out of his pocket and handed it in through the window, and then he stood up straight and rapped his hand on the hood of the car. From there, the Mustang sped off and the man walked on into the restaurant. The payoff was complete.

I wasn't sure how to proceed. A part of me wanted to go inside and confront him. Still, something about that didn't seem wise or safe. I decided instead to take a closer look at his truck.

Fortunately, the restaurant didn't have any windows along this side of the building, so as long as the man stayed in there, I would be okay. I parked right next to the truck and tried the door handle, but it was locked. Putting my hands on each side of my face, I peeked inside, hoping to see something that might have the man's address on it. The interior of the car was a mess, but mostly with fast-food containers and old newspapers. I didn't see anything with an address. I did notice, however, that the window behind the cab of the truck was open.

My heart pounding, I turned and looked in every direction to make sure there wasn't anyone watching me. Then I kicked off my shoes, hoisted myself into the truck bed, squeezed my upper body through the back window, and unlocked the passenger-side door. Climbing out of the cab, I opened the door and then opened the glove compartment and quickly rifled through the papers inside. Sure enough, I found a proof of insurance card with a name and address on it: Les Watts, 179 Weyford Lane, Americus, Georgia. I memorized the address before putting everything back the way I had found it. I locked the door, grabbed my shoes, and got out of there.

My heart was still racing five minutes later as I stood in line at a convenience store to buy a bottle of hand sanitizer and a pair of rubber gloves. What I had done, breaking into that man's car and digging in his glove compartment, was illegal. Now I was about to find his house and take it one step further. The fact that this was wrong, wrong, wrong didn't really matter at the moment. I felt emboldened by anger, justified by all of the roadblocks that had thus far been put in my way in the course of this investigation—not to mention the fact that my adrenaline was still in high gear from my encounter by the barn.

I entered the guy's address in my GPS and then drove back past the Brown Door on my way to his house. His truck was still there in the parking lot, though now there were about ten more cars and trucks parked around it. Hopefully, this was his after-work hangout, and he would be staying for a good while.

His ranch-style house was on a tree-lined street in a neighborhood of modest homes. The only people around were at the end of the block, a family barbecuing in their backyard. Otherwise, things seemed deserted for a Friday afternoon. My mind racing, I tried to think of some way that I could get into his house without attracting attention. I finally decided to park a few blocks over and then make like a neighborhood jogger. At least that way if someone saw me, they wouldn't be able to call in my license plate or identify my vehicle.

I pulled shorts and a short-sleeved shirt from my gym bag and changed in a smelly gas station restroom. Then I parked my car in a parking lot nearby, shoved the gloves in my pocket, and took off running.

When I reached Weyford Lane, I slowed a bit and tried to look nonchalant as I jogged down the street. I reached number 179 and then veered off naturally, as if I might be cutting through his backyard to get to the street behind his. I jogged up the driveway and into the carport, quite relieved to see once I got there that the place was completely private, hidden from the houses surrounding it by all manner of overgrown bushes and trees. The only line of sight was from the house directly across the street, but with no cars in the driveway and no lights on, it appeared to be empty.

Heart pounding, I knocked on the side door, just to make sure no one was home here. When I got no answer, I pulled on the rubber gloves and tried the doorknob, and then I went around back and pushed on each of the windows. The place was locked up tight. I peeked inside where I could, but I couldn't see anything other than the vague outline of furniture. I was just trying to decide whether or not I should dare check the front door and front windows when I heard his car in the driveway.

Quickly, I ducked down and ran toward the far side of the house, hoping he would have no reason to come around that way. I pulled off the gloves and shoved them into my pocket, pressing myself flat against the side of the building, grateful beyond belief that I had been unsuccessful in my attempts to get inside!

I listened for the house door to open and close before I chanced running away, but instead, after a moment, I heard the sound of the truck pulling back out of the driveway. I dared to peek around front, and I was surprised and relieved to see that it wasn't the brown pickup after all—it was a Federal Express truck.

Catching my breath, I waited until the vehicle drove away and then decided that was just too close of a call; I needed to get out of there. The chances of finding some kind of relevant evidence inside the house were not great enough to risk this crazy scheme of breaking and entering.

I doubled back behind the house, hoping to go out the way I had come in, along the driveway. In the carport, I saw the FedEx envelope propped against the door, resting on a black rubber mat I hadn't noticed before. I hesitated, wondering if there might be a key hidden under the mat. I decided to peek, knowing it would be smarter just to leave, but I was unable to stop myself. After all, was it still breaking and entering if the guy was dumb enough to leave a key out where I could find it?

I peeled back the mat and found nothing but dirt. It was just as well, I told myself as I laid the mat back down. I shouldn't be doing this anyway.

It was then, however, that the return address on the FedEx envelope caught my eye, and I gasped. I didn't recognize the name or the street, but the city it had come from was New Orleans, Louisiana.

My heart in my throat, I impulsively grabbed the envelope. I don't know what possessed me, but I folded it in half and shoved it up under my shirt, holding it in place with my left arm. Then I took off running. As my steps pounded on the pavement, one thought raced through my head: *Callie, you just committed a federal offense!*

Once I was safely back in the car, I simply started driving. I must have driven ten miles before I finally had the nerve to pull over and take a look at the envelope again. Ironically, the empty parking lot where I chose to make my stop was beside a church. I ignored the big, illuminated cross on the sign and guiltily proceeded with what I was doing.

The sun was setting, but there was still enough daylight to see without turning on an interior light. For a long while, I just sat there holding the envelope, knowing it might not be too late to turn back. I could drive to the man's house and simply toss this thing toward the door and no one would ever know I had run away with it. But the address on the front kept screaming at me. *New Orleans. New Orleans.* This had to have something to do with Sparks.

I looked off in the distance, trying to think back to my first semester of criminal law. From what I could recall, though stealing the U.S. mail was a federal offense, taking a package that had been delivered by a privately owned company was more along the lines of simple theft. If so, then my going into a carport and taking a FedEx envelope had been about on par with going into a carport and stealing a rake or a bicycle. Though it was still theft, I thought I could live with that a little more easily.

Teeth gritted, I opened it as carefully as I could and looked inside. There was no note or anything, just a wad of paper towels. I pulled out the wad and unwrapped it to reveal…a small yellow asthma inhaler.

An asthma inhaler?

I turned the thing around in my hands, trying to see if it was real. It certainly looked real, and I almost gave it a squirt just to check. Something stopped me, however, and with a start I realized that this was the exact same brand of inhaler that Sparks used. What did this mean?

I wasn't sure, but I had a feeling that this was bad, very bad. I could only come up with two possible explanations: Sparks was a drug addict who snuck his fixes into prison via a "doctored" asthma inhaler, or Sparks was about to become a victim of something much more sinister. Either way I was making a bit of a leap here, but I had a feeling that whatever was inside this inhaler was not what it was supposed to be.

# Twenty-Two

Using the secure phone Tom had given me, I dialed the number of Paul Tyson, a young man I hired from time to time whenever I needed help of a particular nature. Officially, Paul was a "computer research consultant"; unofficially, he was a hacker, and he had ways of digging up information I could never seem to get anywhere else. I kept him on a retainer, and he simply charged me by the hour for any work that he did. Paul lived in Seattle, so I knew the timing of my call was good, that he would probably be sitting at his computer, available to answer some questions for me as usual.

Sure enough, he picked up the phone on the first ring. I identified myself and said I was calling from a scrambled cell phone.

"Oh, goody," he replied. "That must mean this is a big one. What's up?"

"A couple of things," I said, wrapping the inhaler in the paper towels and sticking it back in the envelope. "I have a substance I need analyzed, and I'm wondering if by any chance you know anyone who could do it."

He chuckled.

"Now why would you be asking me that particular question, Callie? You're the PI. Don't you have resources like that?"

"Yes," I said, "but this one's different. I need—"

"Let me guess," he interrupted. "You need someone who's maybe not quite as legit as usual. Am I correct?"

"Something like that."

"What is it, illegal drugs?"

"I'm not sure. But I probably shouldn't have it in my possession, and I definitely don't want any findings reported."

"Gotcha. All right, let me take a look."

I could hear him typing into the computer, whispering softly to himself as he did.

"Okay," he said finally. "Here you go. I got a fellow in Arlington who might be able to help. He's—"

"I'm not at home," I said. "In fact, I'm down in Georgia."

"Georgia? I don't know anybody in Georgia. Can't you mail it?"

"I'd rather hand deliver, if I can."

"Sorry," he said. "I'm afraid I can't help you."

"I don't mind driving a ways," I said, acknowledging in my mind for the first time the inevitable trip that was before me. "In fact, I'm on my way to Louisiana. How about Alabama, Mississippi…"

"Let me think. Hold on."

I heard more typing and then he spoke.

"I don't know if this will do you any good or not. There is a guy in Louisiana that I work for sometimes. He's not a chemist by any means, but sometimes somebody knows somebody who knows somebody, if you know what I mean. I can call him for you, see if he can meet up with you somewhere in the area."

"That would be great, Paul," I replied. "Can you get back to me on it?"

"Give me a day or two. Sometimes he's hard to reach. What else can I do for you?"

"Just answer some questions, if you don't mind."

"Sure. Fire away."

"It's about encryption, cryptography, that sort of thing."

"Then you're talking to the right guy."

I reached for the paper I had scribbled my notes on this afternoon after my visit at the prison with Sparks. Reading from that list, and then adding more from memory, I told Paul all of the names Sparks had thrown out at me today.

"Can you tell me who these people are?" I asked.

Paul helped to straighten the jumble in my mind, giving me a sort of nutshell history of computer encryption. He said that each of those people was well known in the computer world. Some were mathematicians, some programmers, but all of them had made a great contribution to the field of encryption in one way or another. Paul said that Diffie was "the world's first cypherpunk," a man who actually predicted the information superhighway and the digital revolution long before the internet even existed. After him came Ronald Rivest and his pioneering work with "asymmetric ciphers," and later someone named Zimmerman introduced "the world's first secure computer encryption program." Though I didn't understand most of what he was saying, I finally at least got what Sparks had been trying to tell me earlier: A lot of mathematical geniuses had worked hard to pave the way for complete computer security.

My ears perked up as soon as Paul started talking about another one of those geniuses, a brilliant cryptologic mathematician named Tom Bennett. According to Paul, Tom was an expert in "number theory, abstract algebra, and logic and set theory." Apparently, back in the '90s, thinking he might have solved several significant encryption holdbacks such as "key generation," Bennett had rounded up a team of four other people and hired them to implement his solutions.

"The group called themselves the 'Cipher Five,'" Paul said. "And by the time they were finished they had created a masterpiece. Even now, all these years later, it's still the program of choice for secure computer encryption. Amazingly, it almost didn't see the light of day."

"What do you mean?"

Paul went on to tell me how the Cipher Five created their unbreakable encryption program, but that once it was finished,

Tom decided not to release it to the general public after all. Instead, Paul said, Tom destroyed the program and disbanded the company.

"But why?"

"Something to do with ethics. It never has quite made sense to me."

He went on to say that one of the members of the group, James Sparks, had apparently kept a secret copy of the program for himself, because about a year after the company was disbanded, Sparks was arrested for selling it to a restricted country. There was a big FBI investigation, and he ended up getting convicted and going to prison. Eventually, the program leaked out over the internet anyway, and nowadays computer geeks passed it around all the time.

"Can you tell me," I said, "other than Tom Bennett, what were the functions of the different members of the team? I mean, how did they contribute to the program overall?"

"Well, let me see. From what I recall, James Sparks and Armand Velette were software designers, both of them experts in optimizing code for speed—which was a real plus back then, because in the early nineties, CPUs were kind of slow, and encryption is a numerically intensive activity."

"Okay."

"Phillip Wilson, I don't know. He probably either dealt with networking issues or database stuff. Oh, yeah, the user-interface specialist was Sparks' wife, Beth. She did a bang-up job."

"What's that?"

"The user-interface specialist is the person who takes a program and makes it user-friendly, writing the part of the program that everyone sees. That person doesn't have to know a lot about cryptology, but they have to be an expert in human interfaces. She was good."

"I see," I said, understanding that computer skills definitely ran in that family. "So what happened with everyone once the group broke up?"

"Well, Sparks went to prison, of course. Tom Bennett formed a new company and got rich off the internet. I don't know about the rest. They all sort of faded into the woodwork."

My pulse quickened as a police cruiser drove by, but it didn't slow down and the cop inside did not look my way. Feeling nervous, and certain I had gleaned all of the information I could get from Paul Tyson, I concluded our call. Before hanging up he promised to get back to me with a resource for analyzing the substance that was in my possession.

I sat there for a few minutes and thought about the things I knew that Paul didn't. First of all, I knew that after the encryption company folded, not only had Tom formed a new company and grown rich from the internet, he had also passed the management of that company over to someone else and now spent most of his time in the employ of the NSA, breaking codes for the U.S. government.

Also, I knew that even though James Sparks was the only member of the team convicted of the crime of selling the program to a T-Seven country, he hadn't been the only one involved in the sale—at least not according to what he told me today. Now he was claiming that someone else was involved—and that whoever that other person was, for some reason Sparks had decided to protect them. I wasn't sure what his motivations in that might have been, but that was one of the things I needed to go to New Orleans to find out.

Still, my departure would leave some unfinished business in Georgia. I made a call to my friend and colleague Gordo Koski, a private investigator in Akron, Ohio. Gordo and I traded work from time to time, though the last job I had thrown his way had ended up very nearly getting him killed. This time, as I dialed his number, I hoped I wouldn't be putting him in similar danger. I got his answering machine, so I left a quick message.

"Gordo, it's Callie Webber," I said, giving him my cell phone number. "Call me back. I've got a job for you, if you're interested. It would involve a little trip, down to the deep South."

After I hung up, I made one last call directly to Tom's voice mail. I wasn't sure if he had heard from the PI I caught tailing me today, but whether he had or not, I needed to add my two cents. When the phone beeped so that I could leave a message, I spoke quickly.

"It's me," I said. "I just wanted to let you know that I sent your Richmond PI home today with his tail between his legs. When you have someone track me, Tom, I suggest you don't just pick him out of a phone book. Next time, don't send a boy to do a man's job."

# Twenty-Three

By my calculations, the drive to New Orleans was going to take about nine or ten hours. I was exhausted, but I decided to start immediately, even though it would soon be dark. I thought I might drive as far as I could and then go the rest of the way in the morning.

I made it as far as Mobile, Alabama, before I finally had to admit I was nearly asleep at the wheel. I found a motel along the interstate, spent the night, and headed out the next morning around nine.

As I drove, I had a sudden flash of confusion, and I realized that I wasn't even sure what day it was. I thought back, counting off, and finally decided it was Saturday. It had been a busy week, and yet in a way I felt as though I had accomplished nothing.

Gordo finally called me back as I was crossing into Mississippi, and I explained to him as simply as I could that I wanted to hire him to go to Americus, Georgia, and make friends with a man there, a prison guard named Les Watts. I also wanted him to start immediately, like yesterday.

"I think Watts is working for someone on the side," I said, "and I want to know who. I need you to get close to him, to see what you can find out about his 'second' job. Look especially for any sort of connections with anyone in Louisiana."

Gordo was between jobs and eager to get the work, but he also seemed a bit skeptical that he could accomplish what I wanted.

"I know the South, Callie," he said. "Especially small-town South. How am I supposed to fit in there and make a friend right away? In some places in the South, you can live there for twenty years and still be considered a newcomer."

"You know how it's done, Gordo. Watch him a bit first. Find some common ground. Maybe he belongs to a lodge and you could be a lodge brother in from out of town on business. Maybe he's in a weekly poker game and you can finagle your way in through someone else. I just need to know what he's up to. If you have…other ways…of finding out what he's doing without making friends with him, then have at it. I just need my information."

Gordo always teased me about my odd marriage between godly principles and the job of private investigating. Though a PI should have a code of ethics, he always said, the best ones are not always truthful—or legal. Thankfully, he didn't tease me now, though he did fall silent for a moment.

"For you to even suggest something illegal," he told me, "must mean that you need this information really bad."

I didn't even think about all the moral lines I had crossed in the last 24 hours. I only knew that this information was crucial to my investigation, even if he had to do bugging or wiretapping to get it.

"Really bad, Gordo," I said finally. "Do what you have to, just don't tell me about it."

I gave him all of the information he would need to get started, and when we had concluded our call, I dialed Tom in California. Though I was reluctant to talk with him, I had some questions about the people in Louisiana that only he could answer.

I was feeling bitter as I dialed his number, but once I heard his voice on the phone, something inside of me seemed to shift just a little. He sounded tired and burdened. A part of me wanted to reach across the miles and just hold on to him. We needed comfort from each other.

"I'm headed to New Orleans," I said, trying to keep my voice even. "So I need to ask you some questions."

"Of course," he replied. "Before you do, though, let me apologize about the tracking device and the private investigator. I was worried about you, Callie. I know that doesn't excuse my actions, but I couldn't think of any other way to keep an eye on things."

"What about Kimball?" I asked. "Does he know I'm investigating?"

"No, just the opposite. He thinks I wanted the device on there to make sure you *didn't* do anything rash, like head off to Georgia to find Sparks."

"Well, now that I've found Sparks," I said, "can you tell me the real sentence he's serving? Obviously, the sixteen-year sentence wasn't really for drunk driving."

Tom was silent for a moment.

"I'm sorry, Callie. I can't tell you."

I cleared my throat, watching the road ahead as we talked.

"Let's try another one then. What does your family know about the J.O.S.H.U.A. Foundation? I don't want to tell them anything I shouldn't."

"They know the foundation exists," he said, "though they probably don't realize the scope of our donations. In fact, if it's okay with you, I'll call and let them know you're on your way and that you're coming to investigate Family HEARTS for a grant."

"Yes, please do."

"I'll call as soon as we hang up. What else do you need to know?"

"How about James Sparks?" I asked, swallowing hard. "I mean, I understand the connection there, that he was married to your sister, that he's—" I choked up a bit as I spoke, "the father of your nieces. But what do they know about him as far as Bryan's death goes?"

"To be honest, they don't know a thing about that. Beth thinks James finished up his original prison sentence years ago. She has no idea he's in prison now—or, if she does, she's never said a word about it to me."

"Do they not talk at all?"

"No. James and Beth have nothing to do with each other anymore."

"Is he in contact with the kids?"

"No. He wasn't much of a father when they were married, and after the divorce he pretty much washed his hands of Beth and the children."

"That's so sad," I said, thinking of James' mother, Tilly, and her desire to reconnect with her grandchildren.

"Beth knows he went to prison for violating export restrictions, of course," he continued. "But I never told her or my mother about what happened in Virginia. It didn't seem to make the news in Louisiana, so I left it alone. I figured it was up to James to contact Beth and tell her, if he so chose. As far as I know, he never did."

"So they don't know where or why he's in prison?"

"Not to my knowledge."

"I assume, then, that they don't know who I am, or what my connection is?"

"No, not at all."

"How about us?" I asked, wondering why I had never thought to ask that particular question before. "What have you told your mother and your sister about you and me?"

"Nothing. I've never told them anything."

If Tom wasn't close to his family, his admission might not have hurt my feelings. As it was, however, it felt as though he had stuck a knife through my heart.

"You have to understand," he said, obviously sensing my hurt, "the situation between you and me has always been complicated. I thought it was best not to mention it until we knew…until we understood where we were headed."

"I used to think I understood," I whispered, remembering just a short while ago that Tom implied he had every intention of putting a ring on my finger. He had even given me a necklace, a gold chain, to wear around my neck—a place to hold my other wedding ring, the one I had received when I married Bryan.

"I know this hurts you, Callie," he said softly. "And I'm sorry. But you have to put yourself in my shoes. I knew things you didn't. Wanting something to happen and seeing it happen are two different things."

"What does that mean?"

"That just because I *want* to marry you doesn't mean I will be able to. As you have found already, there are a lot of things that remain between us. Nothing is certain until you understand the whole truth of the matter."

"I'm trying," I said, surprised by the tears that suddenly filled my eyes. The angry resolve I had felt when I learned that Tom was Sparks' ex-brother-in-law seemed at the moment to have lost its significance.

"Put it this way," he said finally. "I would love nothing more than to call my mother right now and tell her that my future wife is coming to town. But you know and I know that we're not there yet. Depending on what you decide, Callie, we may never be."

# Twenty-Four

The road was a comfort, in a way, endless miles of nothing but gray asphalt lined with wide expanses of green grass and tall, thick trees. For many miles I let my mind simply go blank, pushing the hurt and the confusion to some place inside myself, someplace hidden and tucked away. I was good at that. My past had taught me that I could postpone heartache simply by aiming my focus elsewhere. Of course, what I really needed to do was pray, but God felt very far away. And while consciously I knew that the space between me and God was *my* doing, a bigger part of me felt that He had let me down just when I needed Him the most. If I had to take matters in my own hands to get this case solved, I would, I decided, even if my tactics fell outside the bounds of my own usual rules and practices.

I eventually heard back from Tom. He had spoken to the people at Family HEARTS and made all of the arrangements for my charity investigation. He had also talked to his mother, and she had invited me to join the family for lunch the next day, after church. According to Tom, they all thought I was merely a valued employee and nothing else. I would be given full access to the charity, and the goal was to present them with a small grant for facility improvements when I was finished, if they checked out. Tom was confident that they would. He also felt confident that this investigation would give me access to several of the people I would need to meet for the purposes of my main investigation.

"What about Veronica Wilson?" I asked him, thinking of the director of the agency. "Is she your former fiancée?"

"Yes, she's the same Veronica I was engaged to for a while. But we're just old friends now. She married a buddy of mine, Phillip Wilson."

"Phillip Wilson," I said, nodding to myself. "One of the Cipher Five."

Tom seemed a little taken aback.

"You really have made progress in your investigation," he said. "I didn't realize you knew about that."

He moved the conversation toward hotel arrangements. Though his mother was currently living across the lake from New Orleans in an area known as the North Shore, the charity itself was in New Orleans proper, so he thought it would be best if I stayed there.

"I took the liberty of making a reservation for you at a place right down in the French Quarter. They know me there, so you should be well taken care of."

I had no doubt that was true. Tom seemed to "know" someone just about everywhere I went. He gave me directions to the hotel, and then we concluded our call. After I hung up, the car felt empty, lonely, and silent.

I continued driving, and as I neared Gulfport, Mississippi, I started seeing signs for a factory outlet mall. When I got there, I took the exit, bought a late lunch, and did some shopping. Having left all of my clothes and belongings back home, I felt justified in purchasing what I thought I would need for about a week's worth of investigating in New Orleans—including some new suits and several pairs of shoes. My final stop in the mall was a luggage store, where I bought a rolling suitcase and a hanging bag. In the parking lot, I stood beside my car, clipped the tags from the new luggage, and loaded everything up so that when I reached my hotel I would be able to go right in without fumbling for all of my belongings.

After about another hour on the road, the terrain began to change, with the land getting flatter and the trees growing more gnarled. At one point, the low, flat road suddenly raised up onto a bridge, and from the view at the top, I felt as though I were in some sort of alien landscape. The horizon stretched as far as the eye could see, pure swamp in every direction.

The closer I got to New Orleans, the more lush and overgrown everything was, the tree limbs practically dripping with moss and vines. It was beautiful in an odd, wild sort of way, and I had a feeling that if the people who lived here all packed up and moved away tomorrow, it wouldn't be long before the foliage simply took over, covering all traces of the inroads that civilization had made.

The interstate finally led me out over open water and then to the other side of the bridge, where a long canal was lined with what looked like a string of fishing camps. I continued forward, the tall buildings of the city slowly appearing in the distance. Eventually, I found myself in a densely populated area, wide and flat and complicated. It took a good 20 minutes and a few wrong turns, but I made my way to the French Quarter. There, the streets were narrow and lined with beautiful old pastel-hued buildings, most of them embellished with fancy curlicues of black wrought iron. Window boxes overflowed with flowers, balconies lined upper floors, and people milled along sidewalks as if they had all the time in the world to get where they were going, despite the fact that it was 10:15 at night.

As it turned out, the hotel I sought was on a one-way street going in the other direction, so I overshot it a bit and then came back at it, putting on my blinker as I reached the valet parking. The service was friendly and efficient, and soon I was at the front desk, asking for the key to my room.

"Yes, Mrs. Webber, we've been expecting you," the man behind the counter told me, his manner completely obsequious. He refused my credit card, insisting that everything was already taken care of. "And please don't hesitate to ask for *anything*," he added. "Mr.

Bennett was very insistent that we accommodate whatever needs might arise."

I was too tired to fight or even protest. If Tom wanted to pay, let him pay.

The bell captain took my bags and escorted me from the ornate lobby into a large inner courtyard filled with greenery, fountains, and subtle, artfully placed lighting. The building itself was fairly new, the man explained, but designed in the old New Orleans style. I thought it was incredible, with rich, textured brick walls, a cobblestone walkway, and a pool and Jacuzzi tucked away among the foliage. My room was at the very end of the walkway, with its own outdoor sitting area. The bell captain unlocked double French doors and then turned on the light inside to reveal accommodations that seemed the very height of luxury. The room was gorgeous, with high ceilings, antique furniture, and what looked like an authentic oriental rug on the floor.

"This is the La Salle Suite," he said, turning on several lamps as he walked through. "We have one other suite as large and elegant as this, but Mr. Bennett was quite insistent that you be given this one. He said you would like the name."

I smiled in spite of myself. La Salle was an explorer who had once traveled a journey of about 3000 miles by canoe. As a canoer myself, I thought so highly of what he had done that I named my dog after him.

The man led me past a wet bar and the bathroom and then down a short hallway to the bedroom. It was as beautifully appointed as the sitting room had been, with a thick brocade bedspread on a giant four-poster bed. Framed on the wall over the bed was a silkscreen of a Louisiana swamp, with a lone canoer paddling through the water at sunset. Gorgeous.

We walked back into the other room as the man told me about the amenities of the hotel, as well as surrounding tourist attractions.

"Oh, and that's from Mr. Bennett," he said, gesturing toward a huge basket of fruit on the counter.

After he left—refusing any tip—I read the card that had come with the fruit basket. It said, *May you love my city as much as I love you. Tom.*

Feeling incredibly sad, I helped myself to an apple and then wandered through the rooms again, taking in my surroundings. The place was beautiful, that was for certain.

Before I turned in for the night, I carefully hung up all of my new clothes, laying out what I would need for the next day. In one afternoon I was going to meet Tom's mother, his ex-fiancée, and his sister, who also happened to be the wife of the man who killed my husband. If I could, I would have rather put on a suit of armor.

I skipped my prayers and went to bed with a heavy heart, dreading whatever surprises the next day would bring.

# Twenty-Five

The next morning, though it was as difficult to find my way out of the French Quarter as it had been to make my way in, I finally located the interstate, headed east, and took a different way across the lake this time, over the Causeway, one of the longest bridges in the world. It wasn't high like the bridge that crossed the Chesapeake Bay near my home, but it was beautiful nevertheless, and the water it crossed over was grayish blue and choppy. I watched New Orleans disappear in my rearview mirror, and then I drove along for a number of miles before I could see the far shoreline materialize ahead of me. I experienced an odd, disconnected feeling being between land masses with neither one visible, and that feeling turned to one of relief as I drove from the bridge and onto solid land again.

I drove past majestic oaks dripping with moss, beautiful old homes on huge lots, and what seemed like a new strip mall every other block. I reached the church in time for the service and was rewarded with a visiting youth group doing an unusual and highly percussive version of "Footsteps of Jesus." The sermon was of the same title, and I squirmed in my seat a bit as the minister spoke about following the narrow and often difficult path that Jesus had laid out for us. Sometimes it was easier *not* to think about where our footsteps might be going.

After church I was met with a number of friendly greetings as I tried to pick out Tom's mother in the crowd. I finally spotted her outside, waiting near the stone bench where Tom had told me to meet her. She was tall and attractive, her hair a blondish-white and swept into a French twist on the back of her head. She wore a light green dress and carried a cream purse that matched her shoes. In her right hand she held a cane, and I was reminded that she was still recovering from last fall's stroke.

"Mrs. Bennett?" I said, walking toward her.

Her face broke into a lovely smile, and the resemblance to her son was so strong that it actually made me ache. *How I wished he were here with me!*

"You must be Mrs. Webber," she said excitedly, reaching out to shake my hand. She spoke with a gentle Southern drawl that was oddly soothing.

"Call me Callie, please."

"And I'm Irene," she replied. "It's such a pleasure to meet you. My daughter Beth should be along in a minute. She went to get her girls out of Children's Church."

I felt a twinge of nerves at the thought of meeting the girls. Would they resemble their father?

"I wish I had known you'd be coming to church," Irene said. "You could've sat with us."

"It was a last-minute decision," I said. "I wasn't sure if I would get here in time."

We made small talk, discussing the sermon and the visiting youth group who had provided the special music. Then we were interrupted by a child who ran to Irene and began tugging on her hand.

"Grandma, come on," she said. "You have to sign up to do cookies for the spring picnic."

The girl was about eight years old, with blond hair and freckles. Irene introduced the child as her granddaughter, Leah, and though she had manners enough to pause in her mission and say hello, she was soon busy again trying to drag Irene off to a sign-up table.

"You go ahead," I said. "I'll just wait here on this bench."

I sat down and watched as the two of them went inside, the grandmother with the slightly impaired gait and the child with the boundless energy of an eight-year-old. Sure enough, Leah looked a lot like her father, with the same tiny stature and blond hair. Still, she was a cute little thing; soon, perhaps, I would be able to look at her and see just her, rather than him.

Another girl of about the same age approached, though this one had darker hair and a fuller face. The woman with her was about my age, and I realized she must be Beth, Tom's sister. Though she wasn't unattractive, she was dressed plainly and wore no makeup, and her hair hung straight to her shoulders from a center part. She seemed vaguely "computer geeky," and I found her shyness ironic. According to Paul Tyson, Beth's specialty was designing human interfaces on the computer—and yet she didn't seem to know how to interface in person at all.

"Hi, I'm Beth Sparks," she said, her eyes glancing at me and then darting away. "Are you from Tom's foundation?"

"Yes, I'm Callie Webber. How do you do?"

"Fine, thank you. This is my daughter Madeline. Maddie."

"Hello, Maddie," I said, taking in her cherub face. "I just met Leah."

"We're twins," the girl said in reply. "People usually don't believe us when we say we're twins, because we're fraternal, not identical."

"I can see that."

"Maddie, Mrs. Webber works for your Uncle Tommy," Beth said.

At that, the child's entire face lit up.

"He's my favorite uncle in the whole world," she declared.

"He's your *only* uncle," her mother reminded her softly.

"Oh, that's true," the girl said laughing.

Irene and Leah rejoined us at that point, and Irene suggested I follow them to the restaurant, which was in a neighboring town. I did just that, enjoying the lush scenery as we went. Though a part of me was dreading every single moment of the rest of this day, another part of me was embracing it. At last I was in the company of Tom's family. In another reality, where nothing had gone wrong, these people might have become my people as well.

We entered a town called Madisonville and then drove over a short drawbridge, turning right just on the far side of the river. After several blocks, we pulled into the crowded parking lot of a restaurant.

"I'm glad we called ahead," Irene said to Beth as we walked inside. "It's packed today."

The two girls walked in first, Leah nearly bouncing and Maddie much more sedate. The hostess led us to our table, which was right by the window and looked out at the river. It offered seating for eight, and Irene announced that the Wilsons would be joining us. Though I would have much preferred dining without anyone else along, I knew I might as well get to know the whole bunch of them at once.

Irene insisted that I take the seat nearest the window, so I did, admiring the incredible view. The river was dark and lazy, lined on both sides with unusual trees dripping with moss.

"Is that the Mississippi River?" I asked, and everyone surprised me by laughing.

"That's the Tchefuncte," Irene said, pronouncing it Chu-func-tuh. "The Mississippi is just a little bit bigger than that."

"The Mississippi River is brown and disgusting," Leah announced.

"With giant boats in it," Maddie added.

We studied the menu while we waited for the rest of our party. I didn't know much about the cuisine of the area, and the menu offered a confusing array of blackened seafood, jambalaya, and crawfish. Irene was explaining the difference between étouffée and gumbo when a couple with a small child approached us.

We stood as I met Phillip Wilson, his wife Veronica, and their four-year-old son, Tucker. Though we made polite conversation, all I could think about was that Veronica wasn't just pretty, she was drop-dead gorgeous. She looked a little like the Veronica in the

Archie comics, all sleek black hair and red pouty lips. Much to my surprise, I wasn't happy about that at all.

"We're so thrilled Tommy's finally going to give Family HEARTS some more money," she said as she helped her son into his chair. "And just in time for our big fundraiser too."

*Tommy?* She called him *Tommy?*

"Provided the approval process goes well," I said. "Did you say *more* money? Has he donated before?"

"Oh, of course," Veronica replied. "He gave us the seed money to get started. But this will be his first donation since then."

The waiter appeared at our table and we placed our drink orders, the three kids piping up simultaneously to ask for Shirley Temples. Everyone at the table, in fact, exhibited such easy familiarity that I had a feeling they dined out together frequently. Even Beth dropped some of her shyness and loosened up. I commented that the children seemed to get along well.

"Oh, we've all known each other forever," Veronica said. "My family grew up next door to their family. Miz Irene was like a second mama to me."

"You grew up around here somewhere?"

"No, over in the city. Beth and the kids moved out here last year."

"Thanks to my brother's generosity in getting us a house," Beth said softly.

"It's a lovely home," Irene added. "I had a stroke last fall, so I've been staying with them since then."

"We want Grandma to always live with us forever," Leah proclaimed.

"We moved her in so that I could help her," Beth said, glancing at her mother, "but now she's a tremendous help to me. I don't know what we'd do without her."

"Well, it's not like I'm moving out tomorrow," Irene said to Beth. To me she added, "My house in the city is still closed up, though I do have a woman in to dust and vacuum once a month."

I was disappointed, as I had hoped to visit Irene in the home where Tom grew up, just to get a glimpse of his past.

"How about you, Phillip?" I asked, pulling him into the conversation. "When did you come into the picture?"

"Not until graduate school, actually," he said, dabbing at his mouth with a napkin. As beautiful as his wife was, he was not similarly attractive. His pale cheeks bore the scars of what must have been some really bad teenage acne; he also had small eyes, close together, and a rather bulbous nose. He did, however, have that "power" thing going for him, which I knew some women found very attractive. Between his elegantly cut suit and his aristocratic air, I could see how a woman like Veronica could be drawn to him. "Beth and I worked together on a few projects, and then I made friends with Tom, and then through them I met Veronica."

He flashed a smile toward his wife, but she was too busy helping Tucker with his napkin to notice.

"I understand you and Tom worked together?"

"And Beth," Phillip added, nodding. "All three of us. Well, there were five of us actually, but that was a long time ago. A lifetime ago."

This time when he flashed Veronica a look, she caught it.

"So, Callie," she said, obviously changing the subject. "Tell us about yourself. You live in Washington, D.C.?"

I let her guide the conversation, providing answers to her questions without really giving up a lot of information. I was eager to bring the conversation back around to the past, but they seemed just as determined to keep it in the present.

Talk turned to their organization, Family HEARTS, and its mission of providing hope and support to families of children with rare diseases. They spoke glowingly about the group and its mission, describing for me the plight of such families, their isolation and confusion and devastation.

"We provide a lot of different services," Veronica said, "but our most important function, by far, is to connect people with other people. Sometimes these families feel like they are the only souls on the planet going through something like this. It helps to bring them into the fold, to connect them with others who are going through the exact same thing."

The way she talked, I could envision a vast, nationwide network of love and support and guidance. Suddenly, I was eager to take on this charity investigation for its own sake.

"What's your involvement with the organization, Beth?" I asked, remembering that she was listed on the contact sheet as a volunteer.

She glanced at Maddie and then back at me.

"Well, first as a client," she said. "Then as a volunteer. Phillip and I run the computer network. I also maintain the website and do other computer-related functions for them."

"A client?" I asked, confused.

"I have JDMS," Maddie announced.

"JDMS?"

"Juvenile dermatomyositis. Only one in a million kids have it."

My pulse surged. Maddie had a rare disease? Tom had never said anything about that.

Beth went on to describe Maddie's disorder, an autoimmune disease that caused her body to attack its own healthy tissue, particularly in the muscles. They were obviously comfortable talking about it in front of the child, who seemed very matter-of-fact about the whole thing, but I decided to bring it up again later when we were alone and I could ask more pointed questions.

"She was diagnosed when she was in kindergarten," Beth continued. "For a long time, we struggled all on our own. Then Veronica got involved, and she was such a godsend for me that eventually I talked her into helping others the same way. About a year later, Family HEARTS was born. With Tom's financial help, they were eventually able to take it nationwide."

"And the word 'HEARTS' stands for..."

"Help, Encouragement, Advocacy, Resources, Treatments, and Services," Veronica said. "It's kind of hard to explain everything that we do, but you'll learn more when you come into the office."

We made arrangements for me to do that first thing in the morning. I asked Irene about her involvement there, but she said she was simply on the board of directors and not involved with the day-to-day activities.

"But it's a top-notch group," she said, smiling proudly at those of us assembled around the table. "Tom couldn't find a better organization to support with his money."

"Well, I look forward to conducting a full investigation," I said, raising my glass. "Here's to a successful grant process."

"Hear, hear!" Phillip cried.

One by one, we all clinked glasses, the mood around the table jubilant. For a while, at least, I forgot that the Family HEARTS investigation was the very least of my concerns, but merely a tool to get to know the people around the table.

# Twenty-Six

My cell phone rang as the waiter was serving dessert, a decadent plate of pecan pie topped with caramel sauce. I glanced at the screen and recognized the number as that of my computer hacker in Seattle. I excused myself from the table, stepped outside onto the deck, and answered the call. As I did, the full reality of the situation came slamming down on me once again.

"Callie," Paul said. "I was just about to hang up."

"What's happening?"

"I got somebody for you."

It took a moment for my mind to catch up, to remember that he had been looking for someone local who could analyze the mysterious asthma inhaler I had stolen from the carport of the prison guard in Georgia.

"In New Orleans?"

"Sort of," he said. "This guy lives about an hour away in a town called Hammond. He's a student at a college there."

"Okay."

"I just talked to him. He said if you can bring it over today, he'll get to it this week."

I stepped toward the rail, surprised that no one else was out here enjoying the warm May sunshine.

"Is he safe?" I asked softly, certain that Paul would know what I meant.

"Yes," he replied. "He's done some work for my buddy. Very reliable, very discreet. Also very expensive."

"How much?"

"Five hundred dollars. Plus fifty to the friend who made the connection, and fifty to me."

I let out a low whistle but, in the end, I agreed to the asking price. After all, what choice did I have? I jotted down the guy's information and thanked Paul for his help. As soon as we hung up, I called the fellow and reconfirmed the information and the address, telling him I would probably be heading out in a half hour at the most.

Back inside, I apologized for the interruption and then retook my place at the table. Suddenly, I realized I had lost my appetite for dessert. I took a bite and then pushed the plate away.

"Don't you like the pie?" Irene asked me after a while.

"It's wonderful, but I'm quite full," I said. "I'll take it in a doggie bag."

"Good idea. I'm sure your suite has a refrigerator."

"Suite, huh?" Veronica asked. "So which of Tommy's hotels did he put you up in?"

"Excuse me?"

"Your hotel. I assume Tommy put you in one of the ones he owns. So which is it? Place de Coeur? Hotel St. Jacques? The Marquis?"

"Tom owns all of those?" I asked, finally understanding what he meant when he said *They know me* at the place I was staying. No wonder they were all so solicitous—I was a special guest of the owner! "I'm at the Place de Coeur."

The twins wanted to go out on the deck, and so I excused myself and walked out with them. We brought a leftover roll and they took turns tearing off tiny pieces and throwing them into the water.

"Gators live in there," Leah said. "Sometimes they'll come if you feed them."

"They won't come for bread," Maddie corrected. "They'd rather have a big rotten chicken or something gross like that."

"Or marshmallows," Leah added. "Sometimes they like to eat marshmallows."

I looked out at the beautiful, peaceful river and tried to imagine alligators in it. Just then, a pleasure boat rode past, the family on board in bathing suits and T-shirts.

"There aren't really alligators in this river, are there?" I asked the twins. "I mean, people go swimming here and everything."

"Oh, sure," Leah said. "The gators won't bother you. They're lazy."

"They're cold-blooded," Maddie corrected. "If you ever see them, they're hardly moving at all."

"Do people ever get bitten?" I asked, shuddering at the thought of coming face-to-face with an alligator, even if it was lazy.

"Just stay away from their nests," Leah told me sagely. "They'll leave you alone unless you threaten their young."

"Or if you bump into one accidentally," Maddie added. "Then it might snap your arm off!"

They went on to tell me about a school trip they had taken recently to a local alligator and turtle farm. The animals were sorted by age and size, with the cutest little baby alligators kept in tiny ponds—and the biggest, nastiest, oldest ones in big, fenced-in pits.

The other adults joined us at that point, my alligator lesson concluded for the day. In the water all manner of fish had surrounded the bread crumbs we had tossed in and were fighting over them, which created a swirl of turbulence. Phillip held his son up against the rail so that he could see, and Tucker kept pointing at the water and saying "Fishies! Fishies!" He was an adorable boy, with big eyes and his mother's full lips.

Once the fish were gone, we all strolled around the side of the building to the parking lot and said our farewells. We had already made plans for the next day, with my formal introduction to Family HEARTS scheduled for first thing in the morning. For now, though Irene invited me back to her house for coffee, I begged off, saying I had some errands I needed to run.

In the car I thought about what a pleasant meal that had been, despite my flares of jealousy toward Veronica. She wasn't that bad, I had to admit, just beautiful. And I also liked Beth, despite her shyness, as well as Irene. Had things worked out differently for me and Tom, this might have been the second time in my life that I married into a family I could really embrace as my own.

The GPS sent me west on the interstate about twenty miles until I reached the Hammond exit. After turning right, I passed a big shopping center and continued all the way into town. I spotted a charming little train station ahead on the right, and then made several quick turns that put me onto the campus of Southeastern Louisiana University.

We were meeting at a place called the "Friendship Oak." I passed several campus buildings and then followed a wide curve lined with parking places. I pulled into a spot that sat in the shade of some tall trees, thinking this had to be one of the prettier college campuses I had seen. The terrain was very flat, but the trees were huge and the buildings quite gracious.

Though there was no sign, it wasn't hard to recognize the Friendship Oak. It was a gigantic oak tree that sat in the center of the circle, its branches so huge and heavy that in many places they grew all the way down to the ground and then back up again. Thick green leaves formed a canopy overhead, and moss hung down from every limb. In the center, around the massive trunk, was a wide, curved bench. Sitting on the bench was a young man of about 20. I walked over to him and spoke softly.

"Hi, are you Hydro?" I asked, thinking of the code name Paul had told me to use.

"Yep," he replied. "You the Pink Panther?"

Paul had thought he was being funny by giving us these names, but neither one of us was smiling now.

"Yes."

"Good. Whatcha got?"

I chose to sit on the bench, my back to the tree. I didn't like doing business this way, but until I knew what substance the inhaler contained, I didn't see that I had much choice.

"Just to reiterate," I said softly, "this will be done quickly and anonymously, is that correct?"

"Absolutely. I won't tell anybody if you won't."

The kid seemed so young, with purple streaks in his hair and a tiny gold loop in his eyebrow. I thought he looked more like a skater boy than a chemist, but I held my tongue and reached into the FedEx envelope to pull out the inhaler.

"That's albuterol," he said smartly. "My roommate uses one of those."

"I have reason to believe the chemical inside has been altered in some way," I said. "I'd like to know how."

I handed him the inhaler, and he turned it around in his hand.

"It could even be lethal," I added, "so be careful."

He let a low whistle.

"Lethal, huh? Like pure nicotine or something? Cool. There's a clever way to off somebody."

"It could also be something a little more benign, but not legal."

"Like crack cocaine?"

"Who knows? I just want it analyzed as quickly as possible. Of course, there's always a chance that it's just an asthma inhaler, but I doubt it."

"I'll need a deposit," he said, handing the inhaler to me. I slid it back into the envelope, which already contained the money.

"There's two hundred and fifty dollars cash in there," I said. "You'll get the rest when the job is done."

I handed the whole package to him, and he took it gingerly.

"Well, nice doing business with ya," he said, standing. "I'll be in touch."

He reached under the bench and pulled out a skateboard, carried it to the sidewalk, stepped on, and took off. I sat there for a bit longer, trying to enjoy the view of the gorgeous tree. Finally, I returned to my car feeling dirty, somehow, as if I needed to find a place to wash my hands.

# Twenty-Seven

The drive back to New Orleans took about an hour, and I went a different way, this time on a long, elevated road that carried me over the Louisiana swamps and provided an incredible glimpse of swamp life below.

There were modest houses in and among the muck and mire of the swamp, some of them built on stilts and some planted directly on tiny pieces of solid land. In front of almost every house there floated a boat or two, and a few homes actually had a little piece of yard, in which I could see a clothesline or a tiny garden. I didn't know if these were year-round homes or simply fishing camps. Either way, they offered one of the most exotic views I had witnessed in a long time. I was tempted to get off of the elevated road and find some way to paddle a canoe through these "neighborhoods." But then I thought of the alligators that might also be there, and I decided against it.

Once I was back in the city, I set about tracking the origin of the FedEx envelope that had been sent from New Orleans to Albany, Georgia. I had torn off the label before giving the package to "Hydro," and I held it in my hand now as I drove toward the address. It had been sent from a place called "Fat City Parcel Service," which seemed like a strange name until I looked online and realized that the section of town where it was located was called Fat City. I found the place easily enough, but it was closed. Leaving the small strip mall, I drove on toward the French Quarter, determined to come back the next day as soon as I could slip away from my charity investigation.

Back at the hotel, I knew it was time to do a little digging online about Family HEARTS. Just because my focus was rather fragmented was no excuse for giving the investigation short shrift. First, I changed into comfortable clothes and grabbed a bottle of water and a banana, and then I spread out at the large table in my suite, settling into this phase of my program investigation.

Before I started, though, I wanted to see what kind of info I could find online. After numerous Google searches, my best luck came from a local news station that had uploaded many of its old reports from the past ten years. I ended up finding seven different videos related to the Cipher Five and watching them one after the other.

The first video showed James Sparks being taken away by the FBI in handcuffs. According to the report, he had been charged with selling a computer encryption program to a terrorist group known as al-Sharif.

"What remains to be determined," the reporter said into the camera, "is whether Sparks acted alone or if other employees who worked on the encryption program were also involved in the sale."

Each subsequent video featured a report tracking the highlights of the investigation. In the end, the other members of the Cipher Five were exonerated and Sparks alone was found guilty. In the final clip, Sparks was sentenced to five years in prison, which he would serve out at Keeplerville Federal Prison in Keeplerville, Georgia.

Watching the news footage gave me nothing I hadn't already learned elsewhere. Still, seeing the filmed reports helped me to put it all into chronological perspective. Photos of the six members of the terrorist group that had bought the program from Sparks were also repeatedly shown, and at one point I clicked on pause just to get a good look at them. According to the report, all were still at large, and two of them were on the FBI's most wanted list. I stared into their dark, empty eyes, wondering what damage they had wrought using that encryption program since. No wonder Tom's guilt wrapped around him like a vise.

My plan was to conduct a normal charity investigation of Family HEARTS—and thereby gain access to people who might be able to give me answers and insight about the Cipher Five, James Sparks, and the secrets of Tom's past. I knew that if I was persistent I would work some questions into what seemed like innocuous conversations. On a piece of paper, I scribbled down the kinds of questions I would try to ask all of them:

*What was your function with the Cipher Five?*
*Were you surprised by what James Sparks did?*
*Do you still have contact with Sparks?*
*How did the FBI investigation impact your life?*

With their answers, I would listen to see if there were any discrepancies, observe their reactions about James Sparks, and search for specifics that might lead me down the path to the real truth about the past.

Once I was finished, I forced myself to change mental gears and get ready to focus on Family HEARTS. Whenever I investigated a charity, I always used a ten-point list that I had devised in my time on the job. I pulled up that list now and loaded its different elements into a database. In my opinion, I knew that a good nonprofit should meet the following criteria: It should serve a worthwhile cause; adequately fulfill its mission statement, showing fruits for its labors; plan and spend wisely; pay salaries and benefits on a par with nonprofit industry standards; follow standards of responsible and ethical fundraising; have an independent board that accepts responsibility for activities; be well rated by outside reporting sources; have a good reputation among its peers; believe in full financial disclosure; and have its books audited annually by an independent auditor and receive a clean audit opinion.

I hadn't been given a lot of literature about the place, but I would work with what I had. I read the brochure, which outlined the functions that Family HEARTS performed. And though I scribbled a few notes in the margins—questions I would ask tomorrow—I felt fairly confident that this group did, indeed, serve a worthwhile cause. According to the brochure, they had provided some form of service to nearly 18,000 families last year alone.

Apparently, families of children with rare diseases were referred to this group by hospitals, doctors, internet searches, and other organizations. Analyzing the ways in which they then fulfilled their mission statement was easy, since it was broken down along the lines of the HEARTS acronym.

They offered *Help* in a lot of different ways, but primarily by coordinating online or in-person support groups for the families. They also helped to match the disorder with the appropriate medical organization. For example, according to the literature, a child with JDMS—which I remembered was Maddie's disorder—would be connected to the Myositis Foundation, who could then offer more specific information and support.

They provided *Encouragement* in very personal ways: sending notes, making calls, and offering a weekly prayer time. Interestingly, they also offered a "free internet weeding" service, and I made a note to ask about that.

They served as *Advocates*, lobbying to make public places more accessible to the handicapped and interpreting the rights of the disabled. They would also intervene on a more personal level, working to settle confusions or misunderstandings between patients and their doctors or insurance companies.

They provided a number of *Resources*, connecting those who had needs with those who could fulfill those needs. For example, the brochure said, they could locate special care equipment stores, search for state funds for particular disorders, recommend respite care groups, track down organizations like Visiting Nurses or the Make-A-Wish Foundation, and even find local volunteers who would be willing to help out the families with such things as rides or meals. They had an extensive website as well, which included

disability-friendly vacation spots and listings for the top physicians
in the country for particular disorders.

They could help with *Treatments* by pointing patients toward
the correct doctors, receiving and distributing information about
new treatments and drug trials, advising about activities that may or
may not be appropriate for the patient in question, and keeping a
keen eye turned toward fraud in the field of drug development,
drug testing, and medical care.

They offered two different *Services* that, to me, seemed invaluable:
A daily hotline for families to call for instant emotional support
and prayer, and a weekly "Ask the Doctor" segment on their website,
where questions of general interest about the different disorders
were posted, along with the corresponding answers, collected by
Family HEARTS from different experts in the field.

If all of this were true, I realized, this really was an amazing
group. And what an unusual niche to have found, the families of children with rare disorders.

Tomorrow, I would see how all of these claims actually translated
into action. I didn't have enough financial information just now to
draw any conclusions about their spending, salaries, fundraising, or
auditing activities. Still, I could eliminate two of my criteria simply
by going online and seeing if they were well rated by outside
reporting sources and if they had a good reputation among their
peers.

I worked online for several hours, starting with different
charity-ranking sources, such as Guidestar and the Better Business
Bureau, and then moving along into peer review sites and the nonprofit watchdog site Charity Watch. Everything looked good, and in
the end I dashed off a few e-mail inquiries to some contacts of
mine, asking for confidential comments about the effectiveness and
reputation of Family HEARTS.

By the time I was finished, it was nearly 9:00 P.M. How the day
had flown by! I was feeling hungry, and though I was tempted to
order room service, I also wanted to get a breath of fresh air. I
changed into jeans and a light sweater and then strolled past the
quiet pool and Jacuzzi, the flowing fountains and discreet lights,

and into the elegant lobby. I asked a man at the front desk if there might be anything open at this hour where I could get a bite to eat, and he just laughed.

"This is N'awlins, *cher*," he said in a strange accent. "De party's just gettin' started!"

He described several places within walking distance, insisting that I would be safe alone on the streets at this hour as long as I didn't deviate from the main areas. He gave me the names of the streets to use as my boundaries.

"If ain't nobody on it, don'tchou go down it neither," he said. "If dey people dere, you okay."

I took him at his word, surprised to realize when I stepped outside that there was noise and commotion in every direction. Nothing specific seemed to be going on, just the sights and sounds of a busy night in a tourist-heavy area. I strolled a few blocks to my right, passing restaurants with lines out the door, the delicious aromas emanating from inside simply indescribable. The crowd began to seem a little louder, a little drunker, the farther I went, so I turned around and headed in the other direction, past my hotel and into the area known as Jackson Square.

Jackson Square was some sort of small park, flanked on three sides by beautiful old historical buildings, including a magnificent church called the St. Louis Cathedral. The paved areas between the buildings and the park were for pedestrians only, and there were little clusters of artists sprinkled all along the walkway, most of them painting portraits for sitting tourists. A lone saxophone player had set up near the church, and as he played a soulful blues tune, passersby dropped coins in his open saxophone case.

I dug in my pocket and found a dollar coin, a Susan B. Anthony. I tossed it into his case and then continued on my way. Following the scent of something incredible, I finally found myself in front of an open-air coffee shop called the Café du Monde. I walked inside and sat at a table, surprised to see once I was there that it wasn't really a full restaurant. The menu primarily focused on something called "beignets," but before I even had to ask what that was, the people at the table next to me were served, and I understood. They looked like little square fried pastries topped with generous heapings of confectioners' sugar. When the waitress finished with them and turned to me, I ordered beignets for myself, along with a decaf café au lait.

There was another group of street musicians nearby, but their music was a bit more spirited and lively than the sax player's had been. From where I sat, I could also see several teenagers doing a sort of tap-enhanced hip-hop dance to the beat of their music. It was amazing to watch, though soon the crowd that had gathered around was so thick that I could no longer see.

When my order of biegnets came, I took one bite and simply had to close my eyes, it was that good. As I ate I seemed to recall Tom talking about these, insisting that these pastries had to rank in the top three most delicious foods in the world. At that moment, I doubted I would argue with him.

When I had polished off my entire order, I strolled a bit more, eventually ending up back at my hotel. I wished I had a canoe and a waterway so that I could work off the fat and sugar I had just consumed. I considered swimming, but the courtyard was so sedate and quiet that I was afraid a good swim might make too much noise. Finally, back in my suite, I pulled on my bathing suit and then went back outside and slipped silently into the Jacuzzi.

I leaned back and relaxed in the hot, bubbling water, looking up through the trees at the star-filled sky.

*May you love my city as much as I love you,* Tom's note had said. Had he been here right now, instead of thousands of miles away, I would have told him that even though I had only been here a night and a day, I already felt, in a very strange way, as if I had somehow come home.

# Twenty-Eight

The next morning I wore another of my new suits—a gray Anne Klein with a red silk top. Veronica had said that parking at Family HEARTS was a problem, so I left my car in the hotel garage and took a taxi. Once we pulled to a stop in front of the office, however, I was a little embarrassed, as it couldn't have been more than six or seven blocks from the hotel. Next time, I would know to walk.

I paid the driver and then tried the door of the building, which was locked. I was just trying to see inside when Veronica came rushing up behind me.

"Hi, Callie," she said breathlessly. "I'm sorry I'm late. Tucker spilled apple juice all over my pants, so I had to change."

I smiled at her, observing that despite a last-minute clothing change she was still stunning. She used a big, jangling set of keys to unlock the door, motioning for me to step inside. She turned lights on as we came in.

The place was definitely utilitarian, which surprised me. I would have expected someone who dressed and looked like Veronica to have invested a bit more money and effort into her surroundings. Instead, the walls were a scuffed and marred yellow, the furniture was obviously well used, and the whole office gave off a rather tired and worn air.

Still, this was a good sign. Obviously, they weren't wasting money for fancy digs. The last few rooms were a bit better, with what looked like a well-stocked computer lab, and then the phone room, which contained a table with three phones, a television, and a big couch. Veronica's office was at the very back, and it opened through French doors onto a courtyard. She opened those doors now, letting in the morning breeze, and I remarked that there was a similar courtyard at my hotel.

"Oh, honey, in this part of the city everybody's got a courtyard. Didn't you wonder why the buildings are all so close to the street? That's because we tuck our yards out behind us, hidden away, where we can relax in private. I'm just glad it's a cool morning. In an hour or so, I'll have to turn on the air-conditioning."

Workers began wandering into the building, and as the office came to life on a Monday morning, I was able to see, firsthand, the kinds of situations they were dealing with. I could almost feel a checklist in my brain, going down the row and marking items off as they happened. By the time Veronica was ready to sit and talk, there was one volunteer working the phones, another on the computer researching a disease for a family who had just contacted them, and a pharmaceutical representative meeting with someone in the front room about a new drug trial. Through it all, Veronica stayed cool, assigning people to tasks and seeing that things ran smoothly. I was very impressed.

Alone in her office, we were able to get more specific about the full range of services her organization provided. I took notes directly into my laptop, glad to see that I was quickly developing a full picture of the various ways that the company fulfilled their mission statement.

"So what's 'internet weeding'?" I asked, noting that that was one of the services they offered on their brochure.

She smiled, but with a sadness to her expression.

"That's probably one of the most practical services we offer," she said. "Especially in the beginning, when families are first given their diagnosis."

"What is it?"

"It's our way of guiding parents, on the web, to the sites that will do them the most good—and protecting them from the ones that will do the most harm. In this day and age, when a person gets a diagnosis for a rare disorder, one of the first things they will do is run to their computer and go online to find more information about it. Unfortunately, anyone can post anything on the web, you know. My friend Sandy was researching her daughter's disorder when she came across one site that featured a photo on the home page, in vivid color, of a little girl in her casket."

"Oh, no."

"I'm sure the people who created an online memorial to their child meant well, but who would post something like that to the web? I told Sandy to stop searching, that I would do it for her and weed out bad or wrong or maudlin websites and just pass along the ones that were useful. We called it internet weeding, and in those early days, I think it's one of the things that kept her and her husband sane while they struggled to understand their daughter's diagnosis. Sitting down and surfing the web wasn't a hard thing for me to do, and at least I felt like I was helping in some way."

"It makes sense," I said.

"A few years later, when Beth got the diagnosis of JDMS for Maddie, I did the same thing for her. It's funny, but having two friends who both struggle with children who have rare disorders gave me an appreciation for what they go through beyond the scope of simply dealing with an illness. As my husband says, 'If the disease is rare, people just don't care.' Or, at least, people don't get it. These parents feel so lost, watching their kids suffer—and sometimes even die—from disorders that no one has ever even heard of. It's tough. Our organization does what we can."

I typed in a few notes and then asked the question I had been wanting to ask since the day before.

"Can you tell me about Maddie and her condition?" I wanted to know and yet dreaded the story of how such a little girl could be saddled with such a big problem.

Veronica described what had happened to Tom's niece, how Maddie seemed perfectly healthy and normal until one day a few years prior, when a rash popped up on her elbows. Soon, the rash had spread to several other joints, as well as both cheeks. Her doctor prescribed different ointments and creams, but nothing seemed to make the rash go away. Beth noticed that Maddie was increasingly lethargic, sometimes to the point where she couldn't even climb stairs anymore without taking breaks along the way. Fortunately, their pediatrician took all of this into consideration and ordered some extensive blood work. As it turned out, the girl had a myositis disorder, which basically meant that her autoimmune system was malfunctioning, causing her body to attack its own healthy tissue in the muscles.

"She's doing great right now," Veronica said. "In fact, thanks to her meds, she's currently in remission. But the prognosis can be scary. They take it one checkup at a time. The worst part for them is every Friday night, when it's time for Maddie's shot. She gets methotrexate, which is a real wonder drug for keeping the symptoms in check, but it also causes about twelve hours of nausea and vomiting."

"Every week?"

"Pretty much. I've been there when Beth gives her the shot. Maddie just sits there and whimpers, knowing what's coming in the hours ahead. I tell you what, Callie, watching that child suffer like that absolutely breaks my heart. In the face of that kind of ongoing, week-in, week-out misery, if Family HEARTS can provide some hope and support and connection, then it's worth every moment of everything we do."

# Twenty-Nine

Eventually our conversation moved on to other areas of my investigation. Once I felt that Veronica had answered most of my immediate questions, I saved the file in my computer and snapped it shut, telling her that I was thus far very impressed with Family HEARTS and with her.

"You obviously have some real talents in this area," I said.

"Well, thank you," she replied, a slight blush covering her cheeks. "I suppose you could say it was a long and winding road that brought me to my true calling."

"What do you mean?"

"I was a late bloomer, business-wise. First I thought I just wanted to be a wife and mother, and then I went off on a wild tangent and tried to become a model. I finally came to my senses, returned home, and earned my MBA. Now I've come full circle: I'm a businessperson *and* a wife and mother. I'm glad to say I'm quite happy with the way everything in my life turned out."

Unable to resist, I seized the natural segue and asked about her and Tom.

"You were engaged to my boss for a while, weren't you?"

"Tommy?" she asked, her face positively red now. "Another lifetime ago. I'm surprised he even mentioned it."

It had been unprofessional of me to bring it up, but I couldn't help myself.

"Actually," I said, "I asked him one time why he had never married. He said that he had been engaged, but that she broke it off. Then when I was coming here, I learned that the 'she' was you."

"That was all so long ago. A lot of water has passed under the bridge since then."

"You two grew up together?"

"We did. In high school our becoming a couple was sort of a foregone conclusion. Once we were older and engaged, I saw the path all laid out for me and freaked. I *so* wasn't ready for that. It had nothing to do with Tommy, really. It was me. I needed to break away, to see a little bit of the world. To learn what I truly wanted out of life."

"And did you figure it all out?"

She looked away, and I saw something flash in her eyes, an expression I didn't understand.

"It wasn't all smooth sailing," she said. "I went through some painful times."

She turned her focus back to me and forced a smile.

"But, then again, haven't we all? What's important is that now it feels like I have the best of everything—great husband, wonderful son, and a job that's as flexible as I need it to be. Anyway, tell me how else I can help you in this process. Tommy just said that you would be showing up to investigate us, but I didn't get any specifics."

I reached into my briefcase and pulled out a blank three-page form.

"I think we should start with a basic application," I said. "There wasn't one in your packet, but I need it in order to obtain information and get certain permissions. I have to look into a lot of different areas of your business, and this is the best way for me to get started."

"Sure," she said, taking the application from me. "What else do you need?"

I pulled out my checklist and read from it.

"I already have your audit report, mission statement, and board meeting minutes, but I still need salary information on all paid employees, your budgets, any information you can give me on your fundraising practices, and anything you've got about the agency's future plans."

"Not a problem," she said smoothly as I handed her the list, despite the fact that I had asked for an awful lot. "It may take a day or so to pull this all together, though."

"That would be fine," I replied. "I'm sorry to be so exhaustive in my search, but we have certain criteria—"

"Hey, listen," she replied, "if I know anything about Tommy Bennett, it is this: He is a man of integrity. I'm willing to hand over any information he needs."

I liked her attitude. Tom did have integrity, and it was nice to know she was aware of that fact.

Our meeting nearly finished, Veronica invited me to come to her house that night for a Family HEARTS meeting where they would be going over their final plans for their upcoming fundraiser—a dinner, dance, and auction to be held in a plantation home called Grande Terre.

"We do this every year," Veronica said. "In the past few years, it has become a major society event."

She went on about the dress (formal) and the facility (huge and impressive), flipping through a file as she spoke. A moment later she handed me a fat envelope, insisting that if I were still in town by Friday, I should definitely come.

The main item inside the envelope was an off-white invitation, very classy, to the annual Family HEARTS gala, listing the date, time, and location. At the bottom left was information for the RSVP; at the bottom right was the cost, listed as $300 per person or $500 per couple. I let out a soft whistle.

"Expensive," I said.

"Oh, I insist you come as my guest," she replied quickly.

"No, I wasn't talking about myself. The foundation would pay my way. I just meant that's a pretty hefty price to pay for an evening of dinner and dancing. Do you raise much money?"

I looked at the rest of the papers, which included a map to the plantation house and a list of the donations that would be going on the block for the auction. The items were interesting and eclectic, ranging from an antique armoire to a private cooking lesson with one of New Orleans' most well-known chefs.

"Trust me, Callie," she said, leaning forward in her chair. "My daddy taught me this secret years ago: The best way to get rich people to part with their precious money, for the sake of a good cause, is to get them all together and then let them try to outgive each other."

Veronica had to pick up her son from preschool just before noon. She felt bad leaving me to my own devices for lunch, but I told her I would be fine and not to worry. I was glad she had to leave, as it was my intention to use the time to retrieve my car from the hotel parking garage and drive out to Fat City Parcel Service. I just needed to be back here by 2:00, when Beth was coming in to show me their computer system. That was an important meeting for both of my investigations, since, as Tom's sister—not to mention Sparks' ex-wife and a member of the Cipher Five—there were a lot of questions Beth could answer for me, many of them without her even understanding what I was asking.

I set off on foot toward the hotel, weighed down with my laptop case in one hand and my briefcase in the other. I had walked less than a block when suddenly, out of nowhere, a teenager darted toward me and ripped both cases right out of my hands. The force knocked me to the ground, and I landed on my hip with a thud.

"Stop!" I yelled as the kid ran away.

Another man was just getting out of his car right in front of Family HEARTS, and in an instant he seemed to understand what was going on. He started to come to my aid, but I pointed toward the thief, who was just rounding the corner.

"He robbed me!" I said.

The man took off after the fellow, and as soon as I could get to my feet, I kicked off my shoes and ran after both of them. Within two blocks I caught sight of them. I watched, amazed, as my hero reached for a slim pole that was holding up the outside awning of a grocery store. He ripped it out of place and, clutching the end of the pole, swung it forward and somehow swept it across the kid's legs, knocking him down onto the ground. Then he dove for him, tackling him before he could get up. He pinned the young man to the sidewalk, one hand on each arm, and threatened to call the cops.

"No, please," the kid was whimpering by the time I reached them. "You gotta let me go. I'm out on parole. This'll put me back inside for sure."

Looking into the thief's face, I realized that he had the hardened gaze of a criminal, even though he couldn't have been more than 18. The man holding him to the ground looked to be about my age, with broad shoulders and thick, callused hands. I couldn't see his face, but from the way he moved, I could tell he was quite strong.

"You gonna steal from nice ladies again, punk?"

"No, I promise!" the thief cried. "Please let me go."

I was digging in my purse for my cell phone to call the police when, much to my surprise, the man on top simply rolled back on his heels, letting go.

"Thanks, dude," the thief said. Then he stood up and quickly trotted away, leaving my cases on the sidewalk.

I put away the cell phone and picked them up, stunned. I wanted to yell at this guy for letting the fellow go, but if it hadn't been for him, I wouldn't have my things back. With the thief gone and unavailable for questioning, however, I would never know if I had just been the victim of a simple mugging or if he had been hired to rob me specifically.

"Hey now! Hey now!" someone yelled from up the street before the man and I even had a chance to speak.

We both turned to see a woman outside of the grocery store we had passed, red-faced and angry that her awning pole had been ripped from its mounting.

"Oh, I'm in trouble now, me," my helper said to me, his accent odd.

"I'll handle it," I told him.

Together we walked back to the grocery, and I explained what had happened while my rescuer put the pole back in place.

"See?" he said when he was finished. "Good as new. No harm done."

Grudgingly, the shop owner examined his handiwork and then let us go.

We began walking back the way we had come. I thanked the man profusely for his help, asking him where on earth he had learned a maneuver like that.

"From polin' gators," he said, grinning widely. "Not much different, when you get down to it, no."

I looked him in the face to see gorgeous deep blue eyes framed in black lashes. His skin was weathered from the sun, but his teeth were white and straight, his jaw chiseled, his shoulders broad.

"Excuse me?" I asked, returning his smile.

"Polin' gators," he repeated, and then he went on to describe the process of how a man could catch an alligator using two long poles, one with an iron hook on the end. The whole scene felt incongruous to me, but his story was so interesting and his accent so engaging that I let him continue, mentally assessing my physical condition all the while. My hip and elbow were both sore, but otherwise I was okay.

As the man continued his tale of hummocks and claw prints and alligator dens, we walked back to the spot where I had been mugged. My shoes were still there, but now a woman—who looked like a bag lady—was holding them in her hands, examining them closely.

"Oh, *cher*," my friend called to the woman, "them sure look like fine shoes. Would you take five dollar for 'em, yeah?"

The woman eyed us suspiciously, one hand on a battered shopping cart that was filled with crushed aluminum cans.

"Ten dollars and you can have them," she finally rasped.

"Well," the man said to me, nodding. "Pay the lady then."

I started to protest but thought better of it. Instead, I retrieved my wallet and pulled out a ten-dollar bill.

"Nice doing business with you," she said, taking the money and handing me the shoes. She looked down at my bare feet, let out a grunt, and then turned and wheeled her cart away.

"Are you okay?" the man finally thought to ask me. "You look a little shaken."

I ran my fingers through my hair and exhaled slowly.

"I think I'm fine," I said. "Though I just got robbed twice."

"Twice?"

"Yeah, once by that guy, and again just now, when I had to pay ten dollars for my own shoes."

He laughed, the sound deep and guttural.

"Now, who you think need that ten dollar more—her or you?"

I shrugged.

"Her, I guess."

"Okay then," he replied. "Maybe she eat a good lunch today 'cause of your generosity."

When he put it that way, I felt a bit guilty for begrudging her the money. Smiling, I reached down and slipped the shoes onto my feet.

"Speaking of lunch," he said, reaching up to smooth the collar of his blue denim work shirt. "Would you be interested in getting a bite to eat? I promise to protec' you from any and all muggers between here and the nearest restaurant. I'll be a regular Cajun protection service."

"Cajun? Is that what your accent is?"

"Yeah, *cher*. Descended from the Acadians, born and raised in a swamp, I am one hundred percent pure dee Cajun. So how 'bout lunch?"

"I'm sorry," I said, smoothing out my skirt. "I appreciated your help enormously, but I don't even know you."

"Well, then, let me rectify that." He reached up and tipped an imaginary hat. "How do you do? My name's Armand Velette."

Once I recovered from my surprise, I told him my name and accepted his offer to go to lunch, all the while trying to keep my thoughts and emotions from showing on my face. This was Armand Velette, former member of the Cipher Five, and one of the people I had come here to meet and get to know! Though I could have done with a less violent introduction, I knew our meeting this way couldn't have been more fortuitous.

"I probably should clean up a bit first," I said.

He suggested we go inside Family HEARTS so that I could use their restroom.

"I was jus' coming here myself," he said. "I'm sure they wouldn't mind."

I told him I had just come out of Family HEARTS when I got mugged.

"Well, then, you'll have to tell me your connection over lunch," he replied, holding the door open for me. "I been here a lot lately, helping 'em get ready for Friday night's auction."

We went inside and I made a beeline for the bathroom. As I dabbed at a big dirt stain on my skirt with a damp paper towel, I listened to the conversation going on in the next room. It sounded as though he was a real charmer with the ladies, and you could tell they were familiar with him, because I could hear loud giggles and even a squeal.

I finally gave up on the stain, tossed the paper towel in the trash, and turned my attention to my computer and briefcase. After making sure they were locked up tight, I came out of the bathroom and interrupted the flirt-fest to ask one of the volunteers if there was somewhere I could store both items. She suggested Veronica's empty office, so I put the cases in there, trusting that they would remain undisturbed until I returned.

"You ready to go, *cher?*" Armand asked when I came back out.

He opened and held the front door for me as we went, and as he did, I was startled again by his rugged good looks. I realized that I had now met all five members of the Cipher Five: Tom, James Sparks, Beth Sparks, Phillip Wilson, and Armand Velette. Somewhere among the five of them were many of the answers I sought about my husband's death.

# Thirty

Lunch was a very casual affair, a cup of gumbo eaten with a plastic spoon as we strolled through an area called the French Market. Armand was quite funny, and he had a way of saying things just under his breath that made me burst out laughing even as the people around us had no idea what was so funny. Though I was having trouble steering the conversation into any useful direction, we were at least getting along well.

At the far end of the French Market, the roads on either side converged in a "Y," creating a point. In the middle of the point was a statue of a woman on a horse. I read the sign that said it was a monument to Joan of Arc.

"There's 'Joni on a pony,'" Armand said, making me laugh again. "You get a good look at the river yet, *cher?*"

I said that no, I hadn't, and he proceeded to walk me up over a levee to a strolling platform built along the Mississippi River. My first sight of the mighty Mississippi was a surprise, and I suddenly understood why the family had laughed at me over lunch the day before. This river was huge, a swirling brown mass of water filled with tankers and tugs and even a few paddle wheel boats. About a half mile away, a pair of beautiful bridges spanned the river to the far shore.

We sat on a bench in the warm May sunshine and simply enjoyed the view. I was eager to steer our easy chatter to more weighty matters, but then Armand beat me to the punch by asking me what my connection was to Family HEARTS. I had expected him to ask and had been framing my reply during our walk. Now it flowed easily off my tongue, that I was doing a program audit for an independent foundation, which was the truth.

"How about you?" I asked.

"Oh, I'm helping out with their big fundraiser this Friday night. I was just double-checking on some of the details while I was in town."

"You don't live here in New Orleans?"

"Oh, no, *cher*," he said. "I got me a little house down in the bayou. You ever been in a swamp?"

"No, but it must be fascinating."

"You ought to come down," he said. "I'll give you the Armand Velette swamp tour extraordinaire."

"Really?"

"Sure. You ever paddle a canoe, *cher?*"

"A bit," I said, stifling a smile.

"Good then. You should be able to handle a pirogue," he said, pronouncing it *pee-row.*

"What's a pirogue?"

"Kinda like a canoe. You free tomorrow? I gotta go out in the swamp to do some measurements and collect some test samples. You could come wit' me."

I couldn't believe my luck. We set the time, and then he borrowed pen and paper to jot down directions and scribble out a map to his home on the bayou, which he said couldn't always be located via GPS. Though I had missed my midday opportunity to get over to Fat City Parcel Service, at least I had spent that time getting to know another member of the Cipher Five.

It was nearing two o'clock, so I tucked away the information Armand had written out for me and suggested that we head back to Family HEARTS. We parted once we got there, and Armand gestured toward the spot where I had been mugged.

"When you leave here today," he said, "you take a taxi, okay? I won't be around to save you next time."

"Oh, I'll be all right," I said. "I can take care of myself."

He stepped back and tipped his hat again.

"Now don't destroy a fellow's illusions," he said. "There's nothin' I love more than thinkin' I'm indispensable to a pretty lady."

# Thirty-One

Back inside the Family HEARTS building, I nearly walked into two volunteers who were on their way out. They were the women who had been so giggly with Armand, and as soon as I stepped through the door, they started in on me.

"Did you enjoy lunch with the Bayou Babe?" one of them asked.

"We're all in love with Armand!" the other one added, rolling her eyes.

I assured them that it was just a friendly meal, that I had other commitments and wasn't looking to start something up here.

"That's a shame," the first one said. "Because the way he was looking at you, I'm sure he had a different idea."

They said their goodbyes and departed, leaving me to wonder if that was true, if I had somehow led the fellow on. I thought the swamp tour was just a friendly gesture, but if he thought of it as some kind of date, I would need to set him straight right up front.

For now, it was time for my meeting with Beth. I wandered back through the building until I found her in the computer room. Otherwise, the place seemed empty.

We chatted for a few minutes, but she seemed eager to get down to business, so I pulled up a chair and told her I was in her capable hands. She wanted to give me a demonstration of the Family HEARTS computer network, which began with a closer look at their website. It was very impressive, especially the message boards and Listserv archives.

"This is people connecting to people," she said. "Right here, the heart of our program."

We scanned some posts on the various loops, and I could see that it was one long ongoing conversation where people asked questions, shared problems, and offered solutions. Much of it was a mix of simple commiseration and encouragement.

"They know they're not alone," I said softly, reading one of the notes.

"Which is the point," Beth replied. "In my own situation, for example, JDMS is so rare that the closest kid I know who has it lives in Mississippi. But with the internet, we can all be right here for each other all the time. It makes a difference, let me tell you."

She showed me how the network was structured, getting more technical than I would have liked, but I let her keep talking, her excitement building as she went. This was a woman who loved computers. I made notes about all that she showed me, glad that this was yet another area of the Family HEARTS program that seemed well run and effective.

"So what's your computer background?" I asked finally, putting my notes to one side and hoping to move into the areas of my personal investigation. "Have you always done this sort of thing?"

"Sort of. My training is primarily as a user-interface specialist."

"What's that?"

"That's where you take stuff from techies and make it accessible to normal human beings."

"Techies aren't normal?"

"Not the ones I've met!" she said, giggling. "You know what I mean. Their heads are off in the clouds somewhere. I used to take the programs they created and add a user-friendly front end."

"Wow. Did you create any software I would recognize?"

She shrugged.

"Probably not. It was all pretty technical stuff." She rattled off a few software names, none of which I had heard of.

"My brother and I actually worked together on a program for a while, but it was never released. Not officially, at least."

Ah. That was where I wanted to go.

"Is that what Phillip was talking about yesterday at lunch? I thought he said there were five of you working together."

"There were. Tom, me, my husband—well, ex-husband now—Phillip, and Armand, the guy you were just out with. But that was a long time ago, back when the internet was just taking off. We were a bunch of kids, actually, kids who thought they were smarter than they were."

"What do you mean?"

She exhaled slowly, typing some commands into the computer as she spoke.

"Oh, it doesn't matter now," she said finally. "That was eons ago."

I hesitated, my heart pounding. This was the information that I sought, but it didn't sound as though she was going to give it to me. I realized she was probably hesitating not because she didn't want to talk about it, but because it involved past dealings of my own boss, and she might have thought this conversation was inappropriate.

"Tom has told me a little bit about that time in his life," I said finally. "I know about his skills with cryptography, and I know about the FBI investigation. I've just never heard the full story of how everything happened. You know, with your husband and all."

Beth looked at me skeptically.

"Tom talked about this stuff with you?"

"He trusts me," I said. "I ran into an article about him that mentioned the FBI investigation, so he had to give me an explanation."

I didn't add that I "ran into" that article while digging furiously for information about him! She seemed to digest what I had said.

"I'd love to hear the story from your perspective," I added.

That seemed to be enough of a request to get her started. She turned in her seat, taking her hands from the keyboard and resting them in her lap.

"You have to understand that Tom is a cryptologic mathematician," she said softly, echoing what Paul Tyson had told me on the phone. "In the late nineties, he came up with a brilliant theory of secure computer encryption. He didn't have much money back then, but he took out a business loan and hired the rest of us to take his ideas and implement them into software. His ideas worked, and the program we came up with was great. The problems were in the *implications* of that program."

I shifted in my seat, forcing my body language to remain casual. "How so?"

She hesitated for a moment.

"Have you ever heard of the four horsemen of the Infocalypse?"

"The...what?"

"The four horsemen of the Infocalypse: terrorists, organized crime, drug dealers, and pedophiles. Back then, for every hundred people who used cryptology to maintain their privacy or their business security, there might have been one person using encryption to hide an illegal act, especially terrorists, organized crime, drug dealers, and pedophiles. Considering that, the question then becomes, is it worth it? If bad people can use encryption to hide things like terrorist communications, then does that become the price of privacy? It wasn't until we had our working encryption program that we began to understand a fundamental paradox: How can you get an encryption program into the right hands and keep it out of the hands of criminals? You can't! Eventually, that was the question that tore our little group of five apart."

"What happened?" I whispered, hanging on her every word.

She went on to explain that when they finally had the program up and running, Tom began to insist that it couldn't be released until there was sufficient legislation about the use of cryptography. Apparently, the pros and cons of secure encryption were the subject of serious debate among computer experts, businesses, and the government.

"On the one hand," Beth explained, "you've got your businesses and your civil libertarians pushing for strong encryption. On the other hand are the police and other law enforcement agencies pushing to severely restrict encryption. Tom kept insisting there was a third choice, some sort of compromise, that would allow some leverage to both sides of the debate."

"Like what?"

She took off her glasses and cleaned them on the hem of her shirt.

"It's kind of hard to explain. Have you ever heard of key escrow?"

I shook my head.

"Okay, if I want to give someone a secret message, I use a 'key' to encode it, then I send them the message, and they use that same key in reverse to decode it. Right?"

"Yes," I said, remembering that I had watched Tom take a secret code, figure out the key, and then decode it just a few weeks ago.

"Computer encryption works the same way, only there's a lot more back and forth to it and it gets really complicated. But with key escrow, the keys that code and decode the messages aren't just known to the sender and the receiver. They're also given to a third party, who holds them in escrow. No one may see the keys or use them unless the police or the government suspects a crime. Then, kind of like getting a warrant for your house, the cops get a warrant for the keys that are in escrow, they decode your messages, and then the truth is revealed. If the encryption was merely hiding private business, there's no harm done, but if it was being used to hide something illegal, like drug dealing or kiddie porn, then they have the evidence they need to get a conviction."

"Sounds fairly straightforward."

"It has its problems," she said, "particularly with regard to who holds the key in escrow. Let's say I do. What stops me from using it to spy on the person it belongs to or selling it to someone else so that they can use it? It all boils down to who can trust whom, and who watches the ones who are watching. Argh! It's like this endless cycle of what-ifs. We never did come up with a good solution."

"So what happened to the group?"

She returned to her keyboard and began typing again.

"We got mired in the debate. We developed a perfectly usable encryption program, but Tom refused to release it until we could find a way around the question of how to keep it from falling into the wrong hands."

"Why did he create it in the first place if he wasn't going to release it?"

She laughed sardonically.

"Some of the others yelled that exact question to him on a number of occasions. We had some serious arguments."

"And?"

"And Tom admitted that he really hadn't thought that far ahead. You have to understand that it all began as a head game."

"A head game?"

"Secure computer encryption was just a mathematical riddle for Tom, a puzzle to solve. He solved it, all right, and then he rounded up a crack team and paid them to implement his solutions. Once we did, however, he understood the bigger picture and realized that he didn't want to distribute it after all for fear of it ending up in the wrong hands. The finished program was primarily his intellectual property, so without his cooperation, it couldn't be released. He disbanded the company."

"Then what happened?"

"Well, by then I was pregnant with the twins, so I was ready to pull out anyway. Tom moved to California and went in a different direction, still computer-related, of course, but nothing to do with this stuff. As you know, he became successful fairly quickly. No surprise there. Tom's always been outstanding at everything he does."

"What happened to the other members of the team?" I asked.

She shrugged.

"Phillip took a job in his father's import-export business. He's filthy rich now, so no big loss there. Armand gave it up and moved back to the swamps with his family. Now he's involved with environmental protection."

"Environmental protection?"

"He works hard to save the swamps, which from what I can tell involves a mixture of politics, lobbying, public education, and science. He even wrote a book about it, which gets him on talk shows sometimes."

"What about his computer skills?"

"Nowadays he creates computer models for swamp projections. You know, like he can put a part of the swamp up on the screen and show it to you as it is now and then how it's going to look ten, twenty, fifty years from now, all with or without intervention. Armand was always a genius at creating object-oriented frameworks to implement sophisticated numerical algorithms."

"I'll take your word for it," I said, as she had again become way too technical for me. I thought of my conversation with James, where he said that first there were five, then three, then two. "Is that the order in which the group broke up? First you, then Tom, then Phillip, then Armand?"

Beth looked at me oddly, and I'm sure she was wondering why I would ask such a strange question.

"No, actually," she said. "The whole group disbanded at once. Tom called us into his office one day and said he was closing down the company and letting us all go. Considering the conversations we had been having, it didn't exactly come as a surprise to any of us. For security reasons, we had to turn our work over to him—digital files, notes, everything. Once he secured everything, including all copies of the encryption program, he gave us each a severance check and sent us on our way."

"Well, it sounds like everyone pretty much landed on their feet," I said. "What do you think went wrong for your ex-husband?"

I felt a flash of guilt for my dishonesty. If I were a better person, I would come clean with her right now about who I was and how she and I—and he—were connected.

"James," she said, shaking her head. "James couldn't give it up. He had worked so hard on the program only to see it buried in the end. I'm not justifying his actions, but I understand the path he went down that led to them."

"What do you mean?"

"James did the unthinkable. Partly for money, and partly, I think, to get back at Tom. He somehow reconstructed the encryption program and then sold it to a group of terrorists. He put it directly into the hands of the types of people Tom had dreaded the most. James sold us all out for a few million dollars. Who knows what the eventual ramifications of that one simple sale have been—or will be."

I didn't reply, silently willing her to continue.

"He was caught, of course," she said. "We were already divorced by then—and I had no illusions about his character—but that was the final blow. He went to prison for five years. During the course of the FBI's investigation, the rest of us were afraid we might end up in prison as well."

"What about the terrorist group that bought the program? Were they ever caught?"

"Not as far as I know."

"And James acted on his own when he sold the program to them?" I asked, knowing full well that he hadn't—or at least he had claimed to me that he hadn't.

"Yes," she replied. "But the FBI didn't know that. We went through horrible months giving depositions, proving our innocence. Still, poor Tom felt so culpable, especially once the program began circulating on the internet and showing up in all sorts of places he had never meant for it to go."

"Just what he had feared," I said.

She nodded.

"Thanks to James, the program Tom created ended up in the hands of the bad guys after all. As far as Tom is concerned, it was ultimately his fault."

"But it wasn't."

"In a way, Callie, it was. Tom solved the riddle of secure encryption in a way that had never been done before. That encryption was then used to commit crimes. Forever after, he will believe that there is blood on his hands."

# Thirty-Two

Beth gave me a lift back to my hotel after our meeting, and once she had driven away, I walked straight to the parking garage and took out my car. I retraced yesterday's route to the Fat City Parcel Service, glad to see that the parking lot of the small strip mall was nearly deserted. This would be easier for me to pull off if the person behind the counter wasn't busy.

A bell tinkled over the door as I stepped inside. Though the exterior looked old fashioned, the interior was quite up to date, with copiers, printers, computers, and other machines all around the room. I went to the counter and told the woman behind it that I needed to find out who sent a particular package.

"Excuse me?"

"I got a package on Friday that was sent from here, but I don't know who sent it."

I handed her the label, knowing I was taking a big chance. If the package had been reported as missing or stolen, then my inquiry just might get me in a heap of trouble.

The woman adjusted her glasses to read the label and then looked at me in surprise.

"This went to Albany, Georgia," she said.

"I know, but I was driving through New Orleans today, and I thought I would clear up this little mystery while I was here."

She nodded, her glasses sliding down to the end of her nose as she did so. Without another word, she placed the label on the counter and typed in the tracking number. From where I stood, I could see her computer screen at an angle, and I watched it closely for some sort of alert to pop up.

"Okay, I have that information here," she said. "Before I give it to you, I just need to see some ID, Ms. Watts."

My pulse surged.

"Um, Les Watts is my father," I said quickly. "I don't really have any proof of that. My name is different than his."

"I'm sorry, then. The only person I can give this information to is the recipient listed on the mailing address."

"I understand."

Frozen to the spot, I considered my options. I could pull out some money and try to bribe her, but I had a funny feeling that this woman couldn't be bought. Instead, I knew I needed to distract her, and I looked around quickly, making my decision.

"Before I go," I said, "I wonder if you could sell me some bubble wrap? I've got some things in the car that are jingling like crazy, making all kinds of noise."

She looked up to her right, where a huge roll of bubble wrap was mounted on a dispenser over a work area.

"Sure," she said, going over to it, reaching up, and pulling some off. "How much you need?"

I told her that about ten feet should do, so as she pulled and then cut, I leaned casually forward on the counter until I could read the screen. From what I could see, the return address was someone named Pearl Gates at 152 Klegmont Lane in Kenner, Louisiana.

"Here you go," the woman said, handing me the bundle of wrap.

"Thank you," I said earnestly, taking it from her. "How much do I owe you?"

"Don't worry about it," she said. "We go through tons of that stuff here."

Once outside, I had to force myself to walk, not run, to my car. I drove away immediately, my heart suddenly pounding. Maybe that had been a stupid risk to take, but I was glad I had done it. Now I had a name and an address for the origin of the asthma inhaler.

Or so I thought. I drove about 15 minutes to Kenner, and then I tracked down Klegmont Lane. I held my breath as I turned onto the street, which featured a row of identical brick ranch-style homes, each with a carport and a scraggly front yard. The house numbers were on the mailboxes, and I counted off as I drove. When I reached number 152, however, I found nothing but an empty lot.

I drove up and down the street several times to make sure, but there was no question. On one side of the street, Klegmont had a 151 and 153, but on the other side of the street was 150, an empty lot, then 154. There was no house at 152.

Puzzled, I parked and got out, knocking on several doors until an old lady finally answered at 154. She kept the chain on the door, and while a dog barked in the background, she eyed me suspiciously.

"Help you?"

"I'm looking for 152 Klegmont," I said.

"This is 154," she replied, closing the door.

"No, wait," I told her. "That lot next door. Has that always been empty?"

"It has since I lived here."

"And how long is that?"

"Thirty-six years."

I tried not to let my frustration show on my face.

"Do you know if there's another Klegmont Street in Kenner?"

"Not that I know of."

"How about the name Pearl Gates?" I pressed. "Do you know her?"

She surprised me by chuckling.

"Well, not yet," she said, "but I hope to once I cross over."

"Cross over?"

"To the Pearly Gates!" she cackled. "Sorry, hon, but I think somebody's playing a trick on you."

Then she shut the door in my face.

I felt like an idiot. Pearl Gates. Pearly Gates. I had a feeling that was someone's idea of a sick joke.

As I got in my car and drove back toward the French Quarter, my mood grew more and more dark. Pearl Gates. Death. I wasn't sure when I was going to hear from Hydro in Hammond, who was examining the substance inside that inhaler. But when I did, I wouldn't be surprised at all if it turned out to be lethal.

Somebody ought to tell James Sparks to be careful.

# Thirty-Three

Sin is a funny thing sometimes. It can enter into a person's heart so quickly, so easily. So simply. Once there, it lodges like a stick caught in a drain, where leaves and dirt and other detritus catch on the stick and start clogging up the passageway until, after a while, nothing gets through. God starts to seem far away. Isolation sets in.

I knew what I was doing. I knew I needed to get on the phone and call someone and say, "Look, I'm afraid James Sparks' life may be in danger."

Back at the hotel, I even sat with my hand on the telephone for a while, thinking about it, thinking about calling the warden at the prison and leaving an anonymous tip or something.

And yet I didn't want to. I'm not sure why. Maybe because I didn't really know for sure *what* was in that inhaler. Maybe because I didn't want to alert Les Watts to the fact that I was onto him.

Maybe because the man who killed my husband deserved whatever awful thing he had brought onto himself.

That's the other funny thing about sin: Justification becomes an art form. So far in this investigation, I had justified stealing, lying, even suggesting to Gordo that he break the law by bugging. Because of all that sin clogging up my heart, I felt far, far away from God.

But where did it end? Was I really going to sit idly by now while a man's life might be hanging in the balance? Did it make any difference that I felt that man *deserved* to die?

Even in my worst moment, I knew that it didn't. I pictured Sparks' mother, Tilly, and the way she dutifully went to the prison every Sunday to visit her son. Could I be accountable to her for his death? If his death paid a debt to me, who then would pay that debt to her?

Finally, my heart heavy, I called Tom. He was the only resource I could think of who might be able to get a message to Sparks without setting off a big chain of events that would send all of the rats scurrying back into their holes.

Tom and I hadn't spoken since Saturday when I was driving to New Orleans. A lot had happened since then, none of which I was ready to discuss with him. I dialed his number on the scrambled phone, resolving to keep things short and simple.

"Yes?" he said, answering the phone, and just the sound of his voice made my heart quicken a bit.

"It's me."

"Callie?" he gasped. "Are you okay? This is killing me here, not knowing what's going on."

"I need you to do something. It's probably urgent."

"Of course. Anything. Whatever you need."

Without actually admitting that I had stolen it, I explained that I had "come into the possession of" an asthma inhaler I felt certain was meant for Sparks. I was having the inhaler analyzed, but I had a feeling that what was inside might be lethal.

"Sparks needs to know that his life is in danger," I said. "I don't want to tip anyone's hand, but I also can't hold on to this knowledge in case they try to kill him in some other way."

Tom sounded more shocked than I had expected him to be. After all, Sparks had played with fire—why, now, was it any surprise that he was about to get burned?

"But that's all in the past," he said. "Who on earth would want him dead now?"

I really hadn't wanted to get into it, but I ended up telling him about my conversations with Sparks, about his claims that when he sold the program to terrorists, he hadn't been working alone.

"That's a lie!" Tom said angrily. "Of course he was working alone."

"Not according to him. He said he has proof that one of the other members of your group was also involved."

"But we were all exonerated by the FBI."

"James took the fall for somebody, Tom. I don't know who and I don't know why, but he says that he did. I think he's blackmailing someone with the proof he has, and I think they want him dead."

"You have to be wrong," he said. "These were my friends, Callie, they weren't killers. Didn't you say that you're still waiting for an analysis of this thing, this asthma inhaler?"

"Yes. I expect to hear back this week. But in the meantime, I'm starting to get worried."

I explained about the return address, the name of "Pearl Gates." Tom seemed to calm down after that, and I had to admit that upon the retelling it did sound a little silly. Maybe there really was a person named Pearl Gates, and they just accidentally typed her address in wrong.

"Here's what I'll do," he said. "Just to be safe, I'll see that James gets temporarily reassigned to a different facility."

"That'll set off too many warning bells. Can't you just let him know to be careful? Can't you just tell him to watch his back—and his inhaler?"

"He's in a federal prison, Callie. It's not like I can just call him up on the phone."

"You have more contacts than anyone I have ever known," I said. "I'm sure if you set your mind to it, you could find a way to get a message to him in prison."

He agreed, finally, and though I knew he was reluctant to open doors that had long been closed, he also saw that there was no choice.

"How about you?" he asked before hanging up. "Are you all right?"

"I'm okay," I said softly, "I miss you."

I hung up without waiting for his reply. Then I tucked away my emotions and turned my attention to the investigation at hand.

There were still nearly two hours to kill before the meeting at Veronica's house, so I spent them at the table in the hotel, working on the Family HEARTS file. Distraction really was the best medicine sometimes. By 6:50 in the evening, I had crossed off four criteria satisfactorily, determining that the organization served a worthwhile cause, adequately fulfilled their mission statement, was well rated by outside reporting sources, and had a good reputation among their peers. I had also rounded up appropriate salary ranges for nonprofits in the area, so I was ready to make that determination as soon as Veronica gave me all of the paperwork I had requested.

Beth had offered to give me a ride to Veronica's house for the meeting that night, and I took her up on it, knowing that would give me another opportunity to spend some time with her. I waited for her out in front of the hotel, and when she pulled up I was surprised to see that the twins were also in the car. We chatted as Beth drove out of the French Quarter and into a section known as the Garden District.

It was definitely a ritzy area, and Beth pointed out some of the more notable homes as we went. She also filled me in a bit on Phillip and Veronica's situation. She had already told me that Phillip's family had been running a successful import-export business for several generations, but she said that now that he was at the helm of the company, it was more successful than ever.

"Do you think he misses the old days," I asked, "working in computers?"

She laughed.

"Well, let's see. He's now rich, successful, runs a huge company, and has a beautiful wife and son to love. What do you think?"

"Guess not. You know, I think it's interesting that the members of the Cipher Five have stayed friends all these years, considering what you went through way back when. I mean, you said there were so many arguments and things, not to mention the FBI investigation…"

I let my voice trail off. Beth glanced at the twins in the rearview mirror and chose her words carefully.

"Well, not all five," she said. "The one who was incarcerated is definitely out of the picture for all of us. And Tom only comes around a few times a year, so he hasn't exactly maintained all of these relationships. I mean, he sees the others when he's in town, I guess, but usually just in passing."

"Still, that leaves you and Phillip and Armand," I said. "Three friends with a common past."

She shrugged.

"Except when we're getting ready for the fundraisers, I hardly ever see Armand anymore. He doesn't like the city and only comes in when he has to. Phillip and I are fairly close because of our work together on the Family HEARTS network. Plus, his wife is one of my best friends. We all moved on past the friction of the Cipher Five years ago."

She slowed and put on her blinker to turn onto a wide street lined on both sides with big homes and gorgeous, mature oaks.

"Not that it's any of my business," I said, "but what about the, um, extended family of the incarcerated one? Any contact there?"

I was thinking, of course, of Tilly in Georgia and the way she missed her grandchildren. Beth shook her head, glancing again at the kids.

"We were cut off," she said. "Told not to have any contact. So we haven't."

Cut off? Told not to have any contact? Having spoken to Tilly, I knew that wasn't true. So either Beth was lying, Tilly had lied, or James had somehow manipulated them both. With a surge of guilt, I realized I couldn't tell Beth about my conversation with Tilly unless I came clean about a number of other things—and that I wasn't ready to do.

"Told not to have any contact by whom?" I asked.

"The, um, other parent," she replied. "But he was just relaying a message. His mom was very specific about her wishes."

"What are you guys talking about?" Leah asked us.

"A TV show," Beth replied easily.

"That's boring," Maddie said.

"So what are y'all gonna do with Tucker tonight?" Beth asked, changing the subject. "Did you remember to bring Candyland?"

They chattered as we turned into the driveway of a particularly grand home. We got out of the car and headed up the walk, and as we did I was a bit stunned by the opulence. The place was beautiful, with wide white columns and a veranda that spanned the porch. The inside of the home was incredible, with high ceilings and rich, antique furniture in every room. Veronica met us at the door and then led us through her magnificent home to what looked like a family room in the back. There were already about ten people there, and they were working in an assembly line fashion, putting together centerpieces for the fundraiser.

The twins went upstairs to find Tucker, and Beth and I were given places in the assembly line. The end product was a beautiful plant, the pot decorated with multicolored sequin hearts and gold and silver ribbon. My job was to use scissors to curl the ribbon.

As we worked, Veronica called the meeting to order. She sat perched on the arm of her husband's chair, reading from a clipboard, and went through the agenda quickly and efficiently. It sounded as if she had everything under control, from the decorations to the caterer to the band to the auction. After a while I tuned out the discussion and focused on Phillip and Veronica.

They were certainly comfortable together, but it went beyond that. He seemed to draw a sort of energy from her presence, and every time she touched his shoulder or brushed the back of his hand, he leaned into her ever so slightly. As for her, she seemed to look to him for approval, flashing her wide eyes at him now and then, and nodding more assertively when he, too, was nodding. Were I a psychologist assigned the task of analyzing the health of their marriage based on body language, I would definitely give them a passing score.

We finally adjourned the meeting for pizza, but after just one slice Veronica called me aside, leading me to the luxurious master bedroom on the second floor. On the bed were six gorgeous evening gowns.

"My sister dropped these off this afternoon," Veronica said. "Just in case you wanted to borrow something for the ball."

"Borrow something?"

"I didn't think you would have any formal gowns with you."

"No," I said, stepping forward to get a better look. "I left my formal gowns at home."

I was kidding, but she didn't even realize it was a joke.

"I could loan you one of mine, but I'm a size four. I have a feeling you'll do better in my sister's eights. She's a little more muscular, like you."

Why did I suddenly feel like a big, manly hunk of beef standing next to a toothpick? I ignored the insult, but she must have seen my feelings flash across my face.

"I meant that as a compliment," she said quickly. "My sister is a tennis player, so she has that same upper body development you have. I would kill for your biceps. Not to mention your calves."

"Thanks," I said, feeling slightly mollified.

"Do you play tennis, Callie?"

I told her that no, my sport of choice was canoeing.

"But you've got great legs! You didn't get those in a canoe."

I smiled.

"Thanks, Veronica. I've been doing some rock climbing lately, so I guess that helps."

"Rock climbing?" She studied me for a moment, a strange expression now crossing her face. "I understand. Well, why don't you try on these dresses and see if you like anything. Did you meet Mai Li downstairs? She's a seamstress, and she said she'd be willing to come up and fit something to you, if you'd like."

"You brought in a seamstress for me?"

"No, she's one of our volunteers. But when she saw my sister with the dresses and I told her what they were for, she offered to help."

Veronica left me alone with the gowns, and I had to admit that they were very lovely. I locked the door, but before I tried on the dresses, I was tempted to search the room, just to see if I could find something that related to James Sparks—phone bills, FedEx receipts, scribbled notes, whatever. I doubted that anyone would be careless enough to leave anything like that around, however, so I gave up my idea and concentrated on the dresses. But as I pulled up the zipper on a sparkly peach number, my eyes alighted on a row of photo albums on a shelf under the window. I couldn't resist.

The years were stamped in gold leaf on the spine, and so I grabbed the one from the year the Cipher Five was first formed. I flipped through the pages hastily, hoping to find a photo of the whole group. I spotted some pictures of James and Beth and one or two of Phillip, but mostly these were photos of Tom and Veronica. As I had thought, they looked gorgeous together, and it seemed that in every photo they were dressed up at some function.

I put that one back, pulled the next few years, and found more of the same. Eventually, however, the photos changed. There were no more familiar faces except for Veronica's, and from the scenery behind her, I gathered that she was in Europe. One photo showed her sitting with a group of people at a café table. She was wearing sunglasses, looking kind of gaunt but glamorous, like a model. Her arm was hooked through a handsome man's next to her, also in sunglasses. He looked familiar, and I had a feeling he was someone famous, probably a rock star. He sported a dark beard and long black hair, and a cigarette was casually held between two fingers.

A knock at the door startled me, and I quickly put the albums back. I opened the door to see Mai Li, the volunteer from downstairs, who had offered to alter the dress I chose.

"You didn't come down," she said, "so Veronica sent me up."

"I'm sorry. I was just having so much fun trying on these dresses."

"Is this the one you like?" she asked, reaching for the fabric at my waist. "It's a bit wide in the shoulders."

I glanced in the mirror and then back at the dresses on the bed.

"I just can't decide," I hedged. "Maybe you could help me pick."

"Sure."

We settled on a smaller, midnight blue Oscar de la Renta, with modest lace across the bodice and a trim waist that flowed out into ruffles of chiffon all the way to the ground. If I wore it, I would have to get the correct undergarments, not to mention the right kind of shoes, but I thought it would be worth the trouble. The dress was beautiful.

Mai Li said that all it would need was a small tuck at the waist, one simple modification that would give me a perfect fit. She marked the dress and then helped me take it off. As I changed back into my own clothes again, she borrowed needle and thread from Veronica and made the alteration on the spot.

The group had thinned out by the time we came back downstairs, with just Beth, Veronica, and Phillip sitting at the table. In front of them was some paperwork that looked as though it had to do with the auction, but they didn't seem to be talking about that. As we came into the room, in fact, the conversation stopped completely.

"What is it?" I asked after an awkward silence. My heart pounded, wondering if they somehow knew I had gone snooping in their photo albums.

"Nothing," Veronica said quickly. "Callie, Mai Li, would you like some more pizza?"

Mai Li said she had to be going, but I couldn't ignore the odd glances the others were passing between them. As Veronica led Mai Li out, I looked Beth right in the eye.

"Beth?" I asked. "What's going on?"

She busied herself with straightening the papers in front of her.

"Um, we were just talking about…"

"About rock climbing," Phillip said, and then he grinned.

So that was it. I had mentioned the rock climbing to Veronica, and she put two and two together. Tom and I were an item.

Now they knew.

# Thirty-Four

Except for a little bit of good-natured ribbing from Phillip, they let the subject drop. I was glad. I really wasn't comfortable discussing our relationship with Tom's ex-fiancée or his sister.

The girls fell asleep in the car on the way back to my hotel, however, and once they did, Beth seemed eager to talk about it. She told me she was feeling kind of stupid, because she should've guessed it sooner.

"I know my brother," she said softly. "He never tells anybody anything, and yet you seem to know so much about his life and past. I should've figured out that you were more than just an employee."

"I'm sorry I didn't tell you up front," I said. "I was kind of leaving that to him."

"Are you kidding? If you left it up to him, we might never have found out."

"Maybe not."

"Come on. Tom is one of those people you can carry on a full conversation with, and when you're all done you realize you've gathered almost no information about him whatsoever. He's like a master at conversing without really sharing any details."

Man, had she ever hit the nail on the head! I couldn't count the hours Tom and I had spent on the phone before I ever even knew his last name.

"I guess he got that from our father," she added.

"Your father?"

"The king of evasion."

"How so?" I asked, feeling stupid myself now. Truth be told, the only thing I knew about Tom's father was that he had divorced their mother back in the '70s and that he had been only a sporadic presence from then until his death a few years ago.

"Oh, Daddy used to pop in and out of our lives whenever he felt like it. You never knew where he had been or what he had been doing, but no matter how much you asked him about it or talked to him, he would never give you any details. When he passed away a few years ago, Tom and I got his personal effects. You can bet we devoured that stuff like starving children at a banquet."

I felt a surge of sadness, picturing it.

"So, if I may ask," I said, "what had your father been doing all that time? Where had he been?"

She shrugged, turning onto a wide, main street that seemed to lead toward the river.

"Nowhere special. Over the years, Tom and I had built up so many theories—that Daddy had a second family, that he was a secret agent, that he was a fugitive from justice—but in the end it turned out that he had an apartment in Houston, a job selling valves to oil tankers, and an aging girlfriend named Lola. So much for the big mystery."

I looked out at the dark storefronts we were passing. There were small trees planted in flower beds all along the street, each with odd, sparkly decorations among the branches.

"I'm sorry he wasn't there for you," I said. "That must've hurt."

"It hurt worse when we found out there was no real reason for it. At the time he died, we hadn't heard from him in about ten years. There's no excuse for that. We're just lucky our mom is such an amazing person. She was our rock. Still is."

"I look forward to spending more time with her."

Beth glanced at me and then back at the road.

"She doesn't know either?" she asked. She put on her blinker to turn onto a side street, and as she did, I pointed to the trees along the side of the road.

"Sorry to interrupt," I said, "but what's that in the trees? That sparkly stuff?"

She dipped her head to look up and then smiled.

"Mardi Gras beads. This is a main parade route. Beads get stuck in the trees on Canal Street during Mardi Gras and stay there all year."

I also had to smile, just imagining it.

"To answer your question, no. I don't think she knows," I said. "How do you think she'll take it?"

Beth smiled.

"She likes you," she said. "A lot. She told me so yesterday, after lunch."

"That's good. I really liked her too."

And I liked Beth, though I had to wonder how she would react once she found out the connection that existed between me and her, that her ex-husband accidentally killed my husband—and went to prison for it for 16 years! Now that I had come to know her a little better, I was able to separate one from the other. I could only hope that if or when she learned the truth, she wouldn't be angry with me for keeping something of such magnitude to myself.

"Mom's been wishing for a long time that Tom would find a wife and settle down," she said. "I think she'll be thrilled."

"Slow down, Beth," I laughed. "That's getting a little ahead of things."

"But is it serious between you two? I know that's none of my business, but we're all dying to know."

I could feel my face flush, and I was glad the car was dark. We were back in the French Quarter now, and I looked out at the unique buildings, the clusters of tourists, the lights. I could hear music playing in the distance and smell the spices of the local cooking, and for a moment I wished Tom would simply come into town and sweep me off my feet. We could forget the past. We could forget the things that had come between us.

We could make a life here, together. A fresh start for us both.

Beth slowed the car, and I realized we had reached my hotel. She pulled to a stop under the awning.

"Let's just say we have discussed the future," I told her evenly, reaching for the door handle. "What will become of us, though, I'm just not sure."

# Thirty-Five

The next morning dawned hot and sticky. I was disappointed, as this was the day I was headed into the swamp with Armand. I made conversation with the garage attendant while waiting for my car, and he said that the heat and humidity were the norm here, that the last few days—cool and dry—had been the exception.

Still, I was eager to get some time out in the fresh air and was nearly desperate to hold a paddle in my hands and feel the strong pull of the water against my muscles. I didn't care if the temperature reached a hundred by noontime, I was going.

Following Armand's directions, I made my way across New Orleans and then south toward the city of Houma. Once the interstate extension dropped me onto Highway 90, I had about 45 minutes to go. After a while I pulled out Armand's hand-drawn map to find the exit that would lead me into the swamp area he called home. Judging from a few billboards I passed, this was also the way to several plantation homes, including Grande Terre, the location for the upcoming Family HEARTS ball.

It was a fascinating drive. The farther I went, the more exotic the scenery grew. By the time I finally turned at the "dead oak by the deserted strawberry stand," I felt as though I were in a foreign land. The flora and fauna were distinctly swampy. A faded sign announcing "Gator Eggs for Sale" had a big red arrow pointing the way I was going.

The road was made of dirt somewhat "paved" with white shells. Though it was rutted, my trusty SUV handled the bumps well. I had an odd feeling of isolation, and to be safe I called Beth just to tell her where I was. I left a casual-sounding message on her voice mail, saying I wouldn't be coming into Family HEARTS today because I was getting a swamp tour from Armand. I said I hoped that would give her and Veronica more time for pulling the records I needed for my charity investigation, and I would see them in the morning.

I ended the call as I rounded the final curve, which brought me to a grouping of homes out in the middle of nowhere. I slowed to a stop and looked around. I was on a finger of land, and there were homes at about five points around that finger. On Armand's map, he had drawn an "X" on the one to the far left, so I pulled in there. As I came to a stop, the front door opened, and Armand gave me a wave.

I had just opened my car door when a pack of dogs came rushing up from down the street, barking and yelping toward me. I jerked my legs back into the car and slammed the door.

Armand came down the stairs and stepped toward my car, and suddenly I realized where the dogs were headed. They weren't coming after me, they just wanted to greet him. They all jumped up on him, and he fought them off, laughing and finally producing what looked like beef jerky strips from his pocket. He handed the strips out to the dogs, and then they stopped jumping and slowly loped over toward the house.

"I'm so sorry, Callie," he said, opening my car door for me. "I didn't mean for my dogs to scare you like that. I should've thought to tie them up."

"I'm okay," I said, feeling rather embarrassed.

"Anyway, after that terrible beginning, thanks for coming. Did you have any trouble finding the place?"

"No, your directions were great," I said as I pulled my tote bag from the car. "I hope I brought everything I'll need."

"I'm sure you'll be fine. I've got a lunch packed for us."

"Good."

"This is my home," he said, gesturing toward a modest wood house up on stilts and nestled among the trees. There was a pair of sawhorses in the front yard with an oddly shaped boat propped across the top, upside down with several tools littering the top. It looked like a canoe, but the sides were low and the bottom was completely flat.

He pointed to the other stilt-top homes and identified them as well. "Next door, that's Ton Ton—my aunt—and on the end there is the Breaux family. By them is my Big Nanan—my godmother—and Big Parain—my godfather. Their daughter and her husband live next door to them, and they got three kids, them."

Except for the sawhorses, Armand's yard was neat and clean. The other homes here, by contrast, looked like junkyards. Underneath each house was all sorts of detritus among the weeds, most of it water related: crab traps, buoys, floaters, shrimp trawls, broken-down boats. From what I could see, it looked as though behind each house was a dock, with at least two boats tied up. In one yard sat a faded political sign from an election long past. In another, a rope hung down from a massive tree with a dusty black tire hanging at the end.

"I know this might be different than you're used to," Armand said. "But this is home to us."

He led me around the side of his house to his wide back yard and dock. From there, I had a perfect view of the bayou, as striking as any picture postcard.

"That's my view," he said proudly, "every single ding-dong day of the year."

"I live on water too," I told him, smiling. "I can't ever get enough of it."

"A girl after my own heart!" he cried, his blue eyes sparkling in the sun. For a moment, I could see what the women at Family HEARTS had been talking about—this guy was definitely a Bayou Babe.

"So what did I see driving in here?" I asked. "Do you really sell alligator eggs?"

"Yeah, *cher*. We got a breeding pit. You wanna see it?"

"I'm not sure."

Armand threw his head back and laughed.

"Come on," he said, taking my hand. "It's safe."

He held onto my hand as he led me toward a path in the brush, but then once the path widened and we could walk side by side, he didn't let go. I pulled my hand loose myself, thinking I had better set him straight right away.

"Listen, Armand, no offense, but I hope you didn't take this day as a date or anything."

He simply smiled.

"Oh, *cher*, I am never presumptuous. I jus' take every good thing how it comes to me, like the gift of a good sunrise or a bait line filled with catfish."

"Good."

The moment passed, and I was glad I had brought it up. We rounded a curve and came upon a huge wire fence. It was about ten feet tall, with barbed wire along on the top, surrounding a pond that was maybe a quarter of an acre in size. Along the sides of the pond, three gigantic alligators were sunning themselves, and two more were lurking in the shallows.

"Oh my gosh," I whispered. Armand just laughed.

"You wanna go in and feed 'em?" he asked, reaching for the lock on the metal gate.

"No!" I said quickly, stepping back.

"I'm just kidding, *cher*," he said. "You do it over here."

He led me to a set of wooden stairs. Next to them was an old ice chest, and when he opened it up, it stank of spoiled meat. Without hesitating, he reached inside and pulled out a package of chicken from the grocery store, one that was obviously well beyond its sale date.

"Gators like their food rotted," he explained as he opened the package and mounted the steps. Once he was at the top, he walked forward on the wide platform and began tossing the chicken into the shallows of the pond.

Surprisingly, the alligators were slow to respond, but one by one they approached the meat and begin to snap it up.

"We can buy past-date chicken from the grocery store for 'bout five cent a pound," he said. "That's cheaper than raising chickens and killing them ourselves."

Once he had distributed all of the meat, he came down the steps and washed his hands with soap at a nearby faucet. As we walked back up the path toward his home, he explained the whole breeding process, how he harvested the alligator eggs and sold them to a local wholesaler.

"Gator meat is really big in some countries," he said. "I think it's a delicacy in China."

"Aren't you afraid to have that pit so close to your home, though? Don't you worry that the alligators will break loose sometime and go there and eat you?"

Again, he laughed at me.

"Alligators are territorial," he said. "So much so that I bet if you tore that fence down tomorrow, they'd all still be right where they are six months from now. That's their territory now. They don't have a desire to go anywhere else."

As we reached Armand's dock, I put the frightening sight out of my mind and focused on the day ahead.

"Now," he said, all business as we walked out onto the dock, "I wanna take you out in the bayou and show you around, so we got two choices—either my little motorboat, or a pair of pirogues. Pirogues won't take us as far, but it'll get us places the motorboat won't go."

"That's my preference, by far."

"Let's do it, then."

One pirogue was already in the water, so we retrieved a second one from where it was propped up against the house. Together we got in place to lift it: I took the back, and much to my surprise, I realized that the fiberglass craft couldn't have weighed more than 50 pounds.

"It's so light!"

"One of the advantages over a canoe," he said. "Because of its flat bottom, it's a little less stable, but you can take this baby anywhere, even where it's super shallow. As some folk like to say, you can paddle a pirogue on a heavy dew."

We put it into the water next to the other one, and then I told him I needed to make a pit stop before we set off on our journey.

"Oh, of course, I'm sorry. Go up the steps to the back door, there, and down the hall to your left. Second door on the left."

"Thanks."

I really did need to use the bathroom, but I also wanted to get a peek inside of his home as well. While he loaded supplies into the pirogues, I went up the back stairs into the elevated house, my eyes adjusting from the brightness outside to the darkness within.

From what I could tell, the place looked like a typical bachelor's home, with a small stack of dirty dishes in the sink and some books and magazines spread on a cheap wood coffee table next to a comfortable chair in the living room. I found the bathroom easily enough, directly across the hall from what looked like a home office. I was sorely tempted to rifle through his papers just to see if I could find any evidence of contact with Les Watts or James Sparks. But as at Veronica's house, I doubted that anyone would be so careless as to leave such proof lying around.

I heard voices outside, so I peeked from the bathroom window to see that Armand was standing on his little dock and talking to a woman, a spry-looking slender lady in her fifties or sixties. After they finished talking, he came into the house. She, on the other hand, walked to a small shed nearly hidden by the brush at the back of the property next door. When she reached the shed, she did the oddest thing: She carefully looked both ways—as if to make sure she wasn't being observed—before she pushed open the door and quickly slipped inside. Strange.

I could hear Armand in the kitchen, so I washed my hands and then walked up the hall to find him.

"Hey, *cher*, I was just thinking that you need yourself a hat. It's a hot one out there today."

He didn't seem suspicious, so I relaxed a bit. He chose a hat for me from a few that hung on the wall, and then we left.

Getting used to the pirogue wasn't hard. It didn't feel as stable as a canoe, but he was right—it skimmed over the surface of water that couldn't have been more than six inches deep. Incredible!

I sat and used a paddle with my pirogue, but he stood in his, using a pole instead, pushing himself along by pressing it into the muck of the bottom. As we went, he told me about what we were seeing, the grasses and trees that were unique to the swamp. All along the way he stopped to run tests, either gathering water samples or measuring distances between landmarks. I asked what that was about, and he said he was tracking the rising water of the swamp, and the encroachment of salt water from the gulf.

Except for the mosquitoes, the morning spent paddling among the marshy wetlands was one of the most thrilling I had had in a long time. Everything was so lush, so green, so alive. We saw birds and nutria and fish. We passed a great blue heron and a number of snakes—some several feet long!—and, finally, an alligator. This time, however, there was no ten-foot fence between us.

But, just like the ones back at the pit, it was perfectly still, resting in the shallows and watching us go by. Armand didn't seem worried, even though the only thing between us and him was a thin layer of fiberglass.

"He's just catching some rays, takin' his time," Armand said.

I asked him about the day before, when he spoke of "polin'" alligators, and he described the process to me, the old Cajun way of finding a gator in its underwater den and fishing him out.

"Big Parain, he taught me how to do it," he said. "He's the best at it I've ever seen."

Armand spoke with pride, but the thought of a man wrestling an alligator until he could get to the soft part of its head and stick a knife in it gave me the shivers.

Despite my best attempts at manipulating the conversation, I found it impossible to engage him in a discussion about the past and his old computer work with the Cipher Five or James Sparks. Not wanting to seem too transparent, I finally gave up, determined to try again later.

We stopped for lunch at a fishing camp, a little shack on stilts that looked abandoned but had a wide front deck for sitting. We climbed up onto the wood and made ourselves comfortable. Armand opened the cooler that had been in his pirogue and took out the lunch he had prepared for us, thick fried oyster sandwiches on French bread with mayonnaise and lettuce—something I would have called a submarine sandwich but he called a "po-boy." Delicious.

As we ate, he told me about his work, about the quest that drove him, day and night, to save the Louisiana coast.

"It's disappearing, you know," he said. "At a rate of about thirty square miles per year."

"Per *year*?"

He nodded.

"We're losing an area the size of Manhattan every ten months. It's the fastest disappearing landmass on earth. Three million acres, just washing out to sea."

Living in the Chesapeake Bay area myself, I knew of the problems that could beset a coastal area—and I had heard that Louisiana had some big issues—but I had no idea it was that bad. According to Armand, it was caused by the routing and leveeing of the Mississippi River, which prevented the silt and sediment from flowing naturally into these areas and continuously building them up. The oil companies hadn't helped matters by cutting a number of artificial canals directly through the swamp.

"The solution I'm working toward involves artificially diverting the Mississippi through conveyance channels all along the way. It's not ideal, but if we don't do something soon, the consequences will be disastrous."

He went on to list the problems that were presented by the disappearing coast. He talked about the losses of seafood, the oil infrastructure, migratory resting grounds. Most startling of all was the news about hurricanes.

"You know, the marsh acts like a hurricane buffer. Every two point seven miles of marsh can dampen storm surge by a foot."

"I don't understand."

He said that when Hurricane Katrina struck, the category-three storm killed nearly two thousand people and became the costliest natural disaster ever to hit the United States.

"The more the marsh recedes," he continued, "the worse the next hurricane will be. As bad as Katrina was, can you imagine a category-five storm coming here? That would create a flood wall reaching twenty-two feet high! The devastation would be biblical in proportion."

I asked Armand why nothing significant in the way of storm preparation had been done before Katrina, and in reply received a long, involved overview of dirty Louisiana politics. In his opinion, the rebuilding of the city was taking first priority, but swamp restoration had to be done too. Unless the government sent an additional fourteen billions dollars for the project, the problems of the disappearing swamp would continue to compound exponentially.

He also talked about the computer modeling program he had created, which enabled him to manipulate satellite images and project exactly what would happen if they did or didn't do anything to stop the erosion. His jargon became a bit technical, but I was extremely impressed by his intelligence.

After lunch he showed me a canal that had been dug by the oil companies to provide a more direct route to deliver supplies down to the oil rigs in the gulf.

"Nothing wrong with these canals in the beginning," he said, lifting his pole as the current slowly carried us down it, "but now they findin' that the canals are widening all by themselves. One canal, when they dug it, was fifty feet wide. Now it's two thousand. See them dead trees? They used to be on the bank of the canal!"

I looked where he was pointing to see a row of dead trees in the water, a good 30 feet from the current canal bank, stark skeletons against the blue Louisiana sky.

The more we saw, the more despair I felt—and I was new to this swamp. I could only imagine how deeply it hurt the ones who lived here to watch their precious land simply wash away, helpless to do anything about it.

# *Thirty-Six*

Our journey brought us full circle, and we arrived back in familiar territory by sunset without my ever realizing that we had turned around. The swamp was a confusing place, but Armand seemed to know every cypress stump and millet field as if they were road signs. By the end of the day I had counted 15 alligator sightings, along with 12 snakes and a multitude of snapping turtles. The swamp was beautiful, but it was also wild. Armand was sorry that we did not spot any bears or deer. According to him, the swamps were full of all kinds of animals, especially wild boar.

Back at his dock, I was surprised to see a celebration going on, and Armand explained that he had asked his aunt to put together a "crawfish boil and *fais do-do*," a sort of dance party, in my honor. I was a bit humbled until he added that they were always looking for an excuse to party—and that the last one had been a mere ten days ago to celebrate the running of the brown shrimp.

Back on shore I was introduced to Armand's friends and relatives, most of them Cajun. Tables had been set up on the back lawn and topped with newspapers, and there was a gigantic pot boiling on an outdoor cooking fire, filled to the brim with crawfish. Truly, I felt as if I were in a foreign land, since just about everyone over the age of 30 was speaking not English but Cajun French. Three of the people were playing music—one on an accordion, one on a fiddle, and one wearing a sort of washboard which he ran up and down with metal spoons. Armand said the washboard was a *frottior,* which was a common instrument in *zydeco.* I didn't know much about that. I just knew I loved it.

As it turned out, Armand's aunt, whom he introduced as Ton Ton, was the woman I had seen him talking with on the dock earlier. At first glance I thought she was in her sixties, but once we were face-to-face, I realized that she was merely weathered and probably only in her forties. Her skin was deeply tanned and wrinkled, her hands red and gnarled. She treated me oddly, as if she were suspicious of me, and I had to wonder if she was being territorial about her nephew. Certainly, the two of them were close, and as the evening wore on, I learned that she had raised him herself, serving as a mother to her sister's child. According to Armand's godmother, Big Nanan, Armand was their pride and joy. Between his looks, brains, and charm, I didn't find that surprising at all.

Armand eventually rescued me from his family and swept me into a dance. After that I had a series of dance partners, all of them friendly, many of them accidentally stomping on my toes as I tried to learn the Cajun Two-Step.

As I danced I kept thinking about what I had seen that morning, when Armand's aunt had gone into that little shed at the back of her property so suspiciously. Once it was dark, I thought I might be able to slip away from the crowd and take a peek in the shed for myself. People were so wrapped up in the dancing and the conversation that, finally, I seized the opportunity to slip away by pretending I had to get something out of my car.

I walked around the front of the house and opened the car door. Though it was too warm for a sweater, I pulled one on anyway, mostly for the dark coverage it gave my arms. I shut the car door and looked around, but I seemed to be alone and unobserved at the moment.

I quietly backed away from the house, toward the road, until I was well hidden by the darkness. Then I walked as quickly as I could to the far side of the property, skirting along the brush line to get to Ton Ton's backyard.

It was dark—really dark.

Without a full moon I didn't have much to go on, and my terror was that I would walk straight into a snake or an alligator. I could hear all sorts of small rustlings in the bushes, but I kept my eye on the shed's roofline, which was just sticking out from the edge of the brush.

I reached the little building undetected. Once there, I didn't dare go inside, just in case it housed a big alligator or something. Instead, I pressed my face to the window in the door. With the sound of my heart pounding between my ears, I waited for my eyes to adjust. There was something big in there, something metal that just barely glinted in the small amount of light that came in from a hole in the ceiling. I squinted, trying to make out the familiar shape. In a flash I realized what it was, and I almost laughed out loud. It was a still—an old-fashioned, straight out of Prohibition-era, whiskey-making still!

I felt like an idiot.

I hurried silently out of there, retracing my steps across the back lawn and up the road to Armand's driveway. I rejoined the party, ditching the sweater as soon as I got there because of the heat.

After a while I had to admit that I was really enjoying myself. Everyone was so carefree and happy that it put me into a good mood too, despite all that had been going on in the past week. When the crawfish were ready, the people used metal colanders to scoop them out of the water and dump them in giant, steaming heaps on the tables. Once they had cooled a bit, the dancing and the music stopped and everyone dug in, grabbed a pile for themselves, and began to peel and eat.

Armand led me to a spot at one of the tables but then immediately abandoned me to help bring out more drinks. Left to my own devices, I watched how everyone else peeled the crawfish and then tried my best to emulate them. The results were less than impressive, though no one seemed to notice except me. As I struggled with the delectable creatures, I chatted with the man across from me, a grizzled old fellow with no front teeth who delighted in telling me horror stories about past hurricanes. I knew he was exaggerating, but when he claimed to have straddled a tree trunk like a horse and ridden it all the way to Mississippi, even the others began catcalling him.

Eventually, the person sitting next to me got up and left, and Ton Ton slid closer so we could chat. Mostly she talked about Armand, which was good, since the more I could learn about him, the better for my investigation.

"That boy was the smartest thing to ever come out of these swamps," she told me as she peeled a crawfish and popped the meat in her mouth. "He was so bright, nobody knew what to do with him."

She talked about his profound intelligence, saying that his repeated wins in the state science fair during his high school years led to a scholarship at LSU. Once he was there, he completed a double major in only three years—and finished graduate school in another two.

Armand's story sounded similar to James Sparks', that of a child prodigy raised in poverty, his brains carrying him places that others in his situation could only dream of going. The difference between Sparks and Armand, though, was that while Sparks never let go of his desire for great wealth, Armand seemed oblivious to money. That he had eventually given up his career in programming and returned to his roots to fight for the swamp made him an intriguing fellow indeed.

Eventually, Ton Ton seemed to warm up to me, though that could have had more to do with the vast quantity of beer she was consuming rather than my sparkling personality. She saw the difficulty I was having and finally, patiently, taught me how to peel a crawfish. Then she began to regale me with swamp tales of her own—mostly the lessons she had learned at the knee of her grandmother, a Houma Indian and renowned *traiteur*, or healer.

"You got migraines, *cher?*" she asked me. "I can cure dat, me. I can cure most anyting."

I would have been impressed with her homegrown swamp medicine, except that as she talked, I realized that many of her cures involved lighting candles and burning clippings of hair. It sounded like a lot of hocus-pocus to me, and the longer we talked, the more I realized she was as full of baloney as the guy with the hurricane stories. I was relieved when the music started up again and Armand finally pulled me into another dance. I suppose I should have seen it coming, but still I was surprised when the song ended and he suddenly put his hands on each side of my face and planted a kiss right on my lips. At least we were over to one side, in the shadows, where I doubt anyone had seen. Still, my heart raced and not with passion. I was upset.

"Come on, Armand," I said. "That was out of line. I told you this wasn't a date."

"I don't see a ring on your finger, *cher*. No ring, I figure a lady is up for grabs."

Despite the current problems between me and Tom, I wasn't "up for grabs" and doubted I ever would be!

"I have a boyfriend," I said, wondering if, technically, that was still true.

"Oh, come on," he said, stepping closer, "what sort of 'boyfriend' would let you run around down here in the swamps all alone with a fellow that finds you so very beautiful?"

There was a sexy lilt to his voice—and I could imagine this was how he worked his magic with the ladies—but I certainly wasn't interested. I took a step back.

"What sort of boyfriend?" I asked. "You know him, actually."

That stopped him.

"I know him?"

"Tom Bennett," I said, studying his face.

The news seemed to hit him like a bucket of cold water. First, a look of shock crossed his face. Then, much to my surprise, he threw back his head and laughed out loud.

"It figures!" he cried. "It jus' figures. Me and Tom been going for the same girls ever since the day we met."

"You have?"

"Oh, yeah. Sometimes 'cause we was genuinely interested. Other times, just for the competition of it."

"Well, there's no competition here," I said. "I love Tom. I'm not looking for anyone else."

He nodded, running a hand through his hair.

"Okay, I respect that," he said, grinning. "Tom Bennett. How do you like that?"

He seemed to work the concept through in his brain, finally looking at me again and nodding.

"Let's take a walk," he said, reaching for my elbow. "You can catch me up on ol' Tom and how he's doing."

I was feeling a bit overwhelmed by the crowd and glad for a break—and another chance to talk. To get away from the noise, we ended up strolling along the dark road in front of his house. This time the walking was a bit easier because Armand had grabbed a flashlight from his car and shined it on the ground in front of us. We made our way toward the end of the peninsula. As we walked, I told him a few current facts about Tom, that he was living and working in California and that we had met through my job with a foundation. My hope was that eventually I might be able to steer the conversation to the past, to Armand's view of the Cipher Five.

"How did you and Tom meet?" I asked him. "I've heard about the Cipher Five, so I know you worked together at one time."

"Tom gave me my first real job out of grad school," he said. "It was fun, for a while. After the company folded, I did some other computer work, but my heart wasn't in it. I finally gave up programming completely, except for my computer modeling stuff."

"Do you miss it?"

"My work to save the swamp is more important."

"But you're so smart, Armand, so gifted in that area. Don't you ever wish things had turned out differently?"

We walked along with shells crunching beneath our feet. In the distance, I could hear the spirited strains of the zydeco band in Armand's backyard.

"Yeah," he said softly, "sometimes I do wish things had turned out differently. It's a long, bumpy road from idealistic kid to world-weary adult. Older and wiser ain't always the best way to be."

"What about your friends," I asked, "the other members of the Cipher Five? I know you see Beth and Phillip now and then. How about James Sparks?"

I could sense Armand's muscles tighten as he walked beside me. We reached the end of the road, where it petered out in somebody's yard, so we turned around and headed back.

"James was one messed up man," he said finally. "I don't know how much Tom told you, but in the end James stabbed us all in the back. I don't like to think about it now. Too many ramifications that are out of our control."

I knew he was talking about the sale of their encryption program to terrorists, and I realized that maybe Tom wasn't the only one who felt guilty about that.

"Hey, *cher*, take a look," he said, changing the subject. He pointed his light toward the brush on the side of the road—and two pairs of eyes glowed back at us.

"What is that?" I asked, sudden panic showing through in my voice.

"Well, they're not gators, and they're not frogs."

He stepped closer with the light so that we could see the creatures' bodies—only to reveal two cute racoons.

"Hey, that's the stinkin' little night bandits that get into my garbage," he said. "If I had my gun with me, I'd shoot 'em." Instead, he picked up a rock and tossed it at them. They ran away into the night, their striped tails disappearing into the weeds.

When we reached his driveway, I decided it was a good point to call it a night. Though his yard was still full of people, most of them had come on foot or by boat, so my car wasn't blocked in. I mused aloud whether I should go around back and thank his aunt personally for pulling the party together.

"Don't worry about it," he said. "Knowing her, she's face down in the Tabasco by now."

"Face down in the Tabasco?" I laughed.

"Drunk. She likes to party, her."

I didn't tell him that I figured that out myself as soon as I spotted her whiskey still.

I thanked him for the day, for everything he had done to share this beautiful, amazing part of the world with me. To his credit Armand did not make another pass at me. He simply tipped his imaginary cap and thanked me for the pleasure of my company out in the swamp today. As I climbed into my car, he said that he hoped to see me at Friday night's ball—and that if he did, he would appreciate the pleasure of a dance. With a smile, I told him that was fine, as long as it wasn't a slow dance.

"I don't blame you, *cher*," he said, grinning. "One slow dance wit' me, and you'd never think about Tom Bennett again."

Laughing, I drove away into the black night. As I went, the sounds of zydeco fading into the background, I couldn't help feeling that I was leaving some foreign land where they spoke other tongues and ate other foods and danced to a music that was very much their own.

# Thirty-Seven

Back at the hotel, I was just slipping under the covers when my cell phone rang from across the room. I jumped up and grabbed it, wondering who could be ringing me at this hour. As it turned out, it was my PI friend Gordo Koski calling from Albany, Georgia.

"Sorry to call so late," he said, "but you said you wanted to hear from me as soon as I learned anything."

I assured him that it wasn't too late, that I was glad he had called. Bringing the phone back to the bed, I piled up my pillows and sat against them.

"So guess who's my new best friend?" Gordo said.

"Les Watts, the prison guard?"

"One and the same."

"Gordo, I know you're good at what you do, but it's only Tuesday. What are you, some kind of miracle worker?"

He just laughed.

"This guy's pretty friendly, so it hasn't been all that hard. You wanna know what I learned?"

"Please."

"Well, you guessed correctly. Watts is a guard at the prison, but he's also working for someone on the side, someone who isn't local."

"Okay."

"Right now, he's in a bad way. He's in big trouble with his boss, whoever that is."

"Why?"

"Because on Friday afternoon he was supposed to be home waiting on a package, and instead he was off drinking at a local bar. The package either never came or it disappeared once it did, 'cause Federal Express says they delivered it. This has caused a big ruckus. He's really sweating it out."

My heart raced. That was the package I had stolen! Suddenly, I wondered if my simple act of theft might end up costing a man his life.

"Do you think he's in physical danger?" I whispered.

"I don't know, but he's pretty worried. I'm not sure what was supposed to be in the package, but I get the feeling he's some sort of liaison. If I had to take a wild guess, I'd say there's blackmail going on."

"Blackmail?"

"That's just a shot in the dark. But Watts is your go-between, whatever's going on."

*Blackmail.*

If that were the case, then who was Watts a go-between for—and on which end of the transaction was James Sparks? Though I wasn't sure, I had a feeling that he was the one doing the blackmailing.

"Did he say what was supposed to be in the package?"

"Nope. I didn't push it. But he invited me over to his house tomorrow night after work to watch the baseball game. I'll get into it more then."

"Can you look for phone bills while you're there?" I asked. "I'm trying to find out who he's in contact with here in New Orleans."

"I can try," he replied. "I'll call you once I have something more."

We hung up and I fell asleep after that, dreaming of the swamp. In my dream, I was in a canoe without a paddle, just holding onto the sides and letting the current sweep me along. The sky was full of twinkling stars, and then, suddenly, the stars flew down from the sky and began hovering all around me, glowing like eyes in the night.

# Thirty-Eight

The next morning I was back at the Family HEARTS office, where Veronica gave me all of the paperwork I had been waiting for. I needed space to work in, so she offered me a desk in the empty computer room. Once there, I opened my laptop and then began entering some of the information she had given me into my database.

Family HEARTS was looking good. I faxed their audits to Harriet, who was cool to me over the phone but professional enough to do her job anyway. The sad thing was, I knew that even when all of this was over, I could never explain any of it to her. Tom's secrets were my secrets now, and it would always have to be that way.

While Harriet worked on the audits on her end, I crossed off several more criteria myself. The salaries and benefits for employees were right in line with what they should be. I also liked their spending in other areas. I had to get the final determination from Harriet, but as far as I was concerned, the money that flowed through Family HEARTS was being handled responsibly. In fact, the quantity and quality of volunteerism within the organization was so impressive that I made a note to ask Veronica how she did it.

A lot of money that other nonprofits spent on personnel, Family HEARTS was managing to save by using so many volunteers.

Besides the audits that Harriet was working on, that left three final criteria to examine, including their future plans, their methods of fundraising, and their board of directors. I wasn't hungry, so I worked straight through lunch, concentrating on the fundraising first.

From what I could tell, the bulk of the donations that kept Family HEARTS afloat came from four annual events: a ball and auction in the spring, a boating festival in the summer, a golf day in the fall, and a Mardi Gras kickoff party in the winter. Each of these events was coordinated by a different committee, and when I compared the lists from year to year, it seemed like, for the most part, the same folks were handling them each time. That was a good sign, that not only was Veronica hanging onto her best volunteers, but the volunteers were learning and refining the process as they repeated it from year to year. A comparison of the total donation receipts per event showed a steady gain for all four events in the past four years, with the exception of one bad year for the boating festival. When I buzzed Veronica to ask her about it, she explained that a streak of inclement weather had forced them to reschedule three times, resulting in much lower attendance (and donations) than usual. Still, when all was said and done, the board had voted to keep the boating festival because it was a favorite of many, and when the weather cooperated, it was one of their top earners.

Once I had studied all of the data, I was able to conclude that Family HEARTS did, indeed, follow standards of responsible and ethical fundraising. I had asked for a meeting with Veronica at two o'clock, so I closed out my database and went to her office, where we discussed the future plans for the agency. As she described where they hoped to be heading, I had to wonder if maybe Tom would be willing to increase the amount of the grant from the J.O.S.H.U.A. Foundation from $50,000 to much more. Among other things, she wanted to move the agency to a better area—and considering the bad parking, the threadbare building, and the fact that I had been mugged right outside, I didn't blame her. I had a feeling that, with our help, Family HEARTS might be able to purchase a facility outright, something I thought would be prudent for them to do. When I asked Veronica about the successful volunteerism factor here, she launched into a passionate discussion of effective volunteer management.

After we finished I returned to my desk and input the information she had given me, signing off on all but the final two criteria, the audit information and the board of directors. After taking a short break in the courtyard, I came back inside and began studying the last year's board minutes. For a while, I was so engrossed in what I was doing that I forgot there was a larger purpose here, that my reason for coming to Louisiana was not primarily to investigate this charity but to meet the people involved. Fortunately, I was about to kill two birds with one stone, because I had a 4:00 P.M. appointment with Phillip to talk about Family HEARTS' board of directors. In the whole of my investigation of Family HEARTS, that was the only area I was a bit concerned about. Put simply, the board was too big, and from what I could see of the board minutes I had read, they often couldn't make a quorum for the meetings, which was necessary for them to conduct the business of the organization.

I was just getting ready to call a cab for my appointment with Phillip when Veronica offered to drop me off. She was headed home and said it would be on the way.

Traffic was bad, and even though she tried several back streets, we still got stuck simply sitting bumper to bumper. I took advantage of the situation and tried to take the conversation in a personal direction, asking how she and Phillip first met. As it turned out, she and Phillip first became friends when she was engaged to Tom—or "Tommy," as she called him.

"We were all friends," she said. "The Cipher Five were working almost around the clock on their encryption program, so if I wanted to see Tommy, I had no choice but to hang out at his office. I didn't mind. Those were fun days. We were all so idealistic."

"Idealistic?"

"About our futures, about life. We used to sit around sometimes late at night and debate the whole encryption issue."

"Where did everyone stand?"

"Well, I don't claim to understand a lot of it," she said modestly, "but I was around them enough to get the general idea. Beth and I both felt that the government ought to have the right, under certain circumstances, to obtain encryption codes for the protection of the country and its citizens. James and Armand were the exact opposite, adamant that the right to absolute privacy should come above all else. Poor Tommy didn't know what he thought. He just knew there had to be a better way to make it all work."

"How about Phillip? Where did he stand?"

She laughed.

"Phillip cared about the bottom line. Whatever side was going to make more money, that's the side he was on."

Veronica glanced at me, and when she saw the surprised expression on my face, she laughed again.

"What can I say? He's a businessman to the core. That's why he's so successful."

I asked how she went from being Tom's fiancée to Phillip's wife. Though that probably didn't have much to do with my investigation, I really wanted to know.

"Well," she said thoughtfully, resting her hands on the steering wheel, "I already told you, when I thought my future was all sewn up in a nice, tidy little package, I freaked. I left Tommy a Dear John letter and went to Europe to become a model."

"Did you have any success at it?"

"Nah, the competition was too tough. I was disillusioned fairly quickly. I had a…" she hesitated as the car in front of us pulled ahead by several lengths, and she made a turn on a small side street. "I had a very nasty breakup with a boyfriend, lots of baggage there. He wasn't at all who I thought he was."

"That can hurt."

"Well, everything worked out in the end," she said, steering deftly down a narrow lane. "I mean, I wouldn't want to relive that time, but in hindsight it was a real period of growth for me. In the end I came back here, went to Tulane, and got my MBA. I've never looked back."

As she zigzagged our way out of the French Quarter, she went on to describe how it felt when she returned to Louisiana to find that everything had changed.

"I mean, I knew what had been going on here with the FBI and everything," she said, "from talking to Beth and to my mom. But it just hadn't seemed real from so far away."

She said that by the time she moved back in with her parents and started graduate school, the Cipher Five had been dissolved and then investigated by the FBI, James was in prison, Beth was a divorced mom of three-year-old twins, Tom had moved to California, and Armand was back in the swamps. That left Phillip, who was living in New Orleans and working in his family business. He ended up being a friend to Veronica when she didn't have anyone else. Within six months, they were inseparable. Another six months after that, they were engaged.

"I know a lot of people think I married Phillip for his money," she said softly, coming to a stop at a light. "But I didn't. I married him for his sweet spirit, for his good heart. When life starts kicking you around, you learn who your real friends are. Phillip was always someone I could count on."

# Thirty-Nine

Despite the heavy traffic, I made it to my meeting on time. The company was located on the twelfth floor, so I took the elevator, which opened directly into the reception area.

The woman at the desk buzzed Phillip, and he came out to the lobby and greeted me himself. He then led me to his office, an impressive corner room with a massive oak desk placed squarely in front of big windows. A secretary took our requests for coffee and tea, and then I approached the windows to admire the view. Phillip explained what I was seeing in the different landmarks between us and the wide curve of the Mississippi River.

"It's a city of water," he told me, adding that there were more canals here than in Venice, Italy.

"You're kidding."

"Nope. Many of ours are covered, but we've got over 200 miles of canals. Thanks to them, we're sinking. In fact, in some places at a rate of two to four inches per year."

Through the window, he pointed out a building near the river, a structure so large it covered an entire city block. According to him, since that building was first erected back in the 1800s, it had sunk almost three feet.

The secretary showed up with our drinks, so I took the cup of tea from her and sat in the chair across from Phillip's desk as he settled down behind it.

"Armand took me on a tour of the swamp yesterday," I said. "He told me about Katrina and the damage it did and how it could happen again if things don't change."

"He's right. We're on borrowed time. Then again, we always were."

He gave me a brief history of the city, a story of how this location was first chosen by early explorers because it offered an easy portage between the Mississippi River and Lake Ponchartrain. Unfortunately, that also made it an area prone to flooding and disease. Still, for some reason, the city had thrived, and over the years it had been profoundly influenced by all of the different cultural groups that had passed through and settled here. As Phillip talked about the French, the Spanish, the Creoles, the Africans, the Indians, and more, I couldn't help but wish that it were Tom telling me all of this. It was *his* city. I had always thought he would bring me here and introduce me to it himself.

Finally, the chitchat ended and we were ready to get down to business. I expressed my concerns about the board of directors to Phillip, who was a board member himself and had been its first chairman.

"It's a society thing," he admitted. "Some people tend to rack up board positions like they rack up designer suits."

"But your board is bloated now. Once it gets too big, it becomes ineffective. As a businessman, you should know that."

"A horse designed by committee is a donkey," he said, nodding. "You're right, Callie. I hadn't really thought about it before."

I pulled out the paperwork on the board that Veronica had given me, including the list of members and the attendance sheets for the past two years. I had made notes of the ones that ought to go based purely on attendance, which would reduce the board from fifteen members down to seven.

"That's more than half!" he said.

"Seven is about right for an agency this size, though," I said. "A board of between five and seven is all you really need."

We talked about what made a good board for a nonprofit and how it should represent a cross-section of the community that it served.

"Ideally, you should try to have an accountant, a lawyer, a social worker, a therapist, a doctor or a nurse, people like that," I said. "They don't all need to be on the board at all times, but it is good to have them in the rotation. You also need at least one or two people on the receiving end of the equation, people who have children with rare diseases."

"We've got a few," he said. "Plus Irene Bennett, of course, who is a grandmother to one."

Other than the Sunday lunch, I hadn't had any time with Irene this week, and I told Phillip that it might be a good idea for me to meet with her, to get her perspective on the board. Of course, I also had my own personal reasons for wanting to get to know her better, though I didn't tell him that.

He made a few phone calls, arranging for me to meet with several of the board members, including Irene. She was free to see me tomorrow night, though the others preferred tonight. I told him I was flexible, so he set the appointments for me and wrote down the information. The appointment with Irene, he said, included an invitation to dinner at Beth's house.

"So do you think Family HEARTS will be getting a grant from your foundation?" he asked as he handed me the necessary information.

"Well, I don't like to speak prematurely," I replied, tucking my paperwork away in my briefcase, "but everything is looking very good thus far. Veronica's work is especially impressive."

"She's something, isn't she?" he replied proudly, and I realized I might be able to seize this opening to take the conversation where I needed it to go.

"Veronica was telling me a bit about your past together," I said, making myself comfortable. "That's really neat, that you were friends first and then fell in love."

"Oh, that's how it happened for her. I was always in love with Veronica. From the day I met her."

"You mean before she went to Europe? Back when she was engaged to Tom?"

"Yep," he smiled, intertwining his fingers and resting them on his desk. "She used to come down to the office almost every night. We would eat pizza and debate encryption ethics." He laughed. "Doesn't sound very romantic, does it?"

"Not really."

"I thought she was smart and beautiful and capable of so much more in her life than she had planned. I felt bad for Tom when she left, but I couldn't have been happier for her. I never thought the two of them were right for each other anyway, and at least she had broken free from her family's well-laid plans."

I sat back and studied him.

"How about you?" I asked. "You're working in the family business. Didn't you follow your family's well-laid plans?"

"I did it backward," he said. "I thought I wanted to break away and do my own thing. In the end I realized this was my true calling."

"From what I understand, you're very good at what you do."

"Thank you," he said. "I enjoy it."

"So what was your function when you worked for Tom?" I asked.

"I was the network guy. TCP/IP. Hardware."

"Sorry, I'm not very computer literate."

"I took care of the machines themselves," he said. "The computers. I kept them functioning and made sure they could talk to each other."

"Sounds interesting. Do you use those skills nowadays?"

"To an extent. We've got plenty of technicians, of course, but I stick my hand in now and then. When you have an international network, it's a good knowledge base to have."

I thought about that, about him having access to an international network. Did that also give him ties to terrorists?

"Don't you find it interesting that of the Cipher Five, only one of you still works with computers full-time?"

"Who, Tom?"

"Yes."

He shrugged.

"We were kids then, fresh out of school, still finding our way. I don't think it's unusual that we ended up in different fields. Except for James, I think we're all quite happy."

"What about James?" I pressed. "Do any of you ever have any contact with him?"

He shook his head.

"Not since the day he confessed to selling our encryption program to terrorists," he said. "As far as I'm concerned, the sentence he got for that act was far, far too light."

# Forty

My talk with Phillip had been thorough, but I left his office feeling more confused than ever. One question kept pounding through my head: *Did James have a secret accomplice down here?*

I had now talked extensively with every member of the Cipher Five, and I had to admit that I was stumped. They all seemed like lovely people. I had a hard time believing any of them could be involved with someone like Sparks. Then again, if he were blackmailing them, maybe they didn't have any choice.

I checked my voice mail as I left the building, surprised to hear that two calls had come in during my meeting, both from Paul Tyson, the computer hacker in Seattle who had connected me with the kid in Hammond who was analyzing the asthma inhaler. I called Paul back immediately.

"Are you on that scrambled phone of yours?" he asked me.

"No. It's at the hotel—"

"Get it. Then call me back."

He hung up, leaving me standing there on the curb, my heart pounding furiously in my chest. What did he have to tell me?

There were no cabs in the area, so I used my cell phone to call for one. I was back in my hotel room within 15 minutes, my hands shaking as I dialed Paul's number.

"It's me," I said when he answered.

"Girl, are you ever in deep."

"What is it?"

"That inhaler. My boy in Hammond is beside himself. He's ready to call the CIA, the FBI, and anybody else he can think of!"

"Why?" I whispered. "What is it?"

"It's a poison known to be used by terrorists. It's called ricin, and apparently it's an extremely deadly substance. If anyone had taken even a single puff on that inhaler, they would be a goner by now."

"Ricin," I echoed. I had heard of that before. "Is that like anthrax?"

"I don't know. I don't know anything except that you've got to get to Hammond *now* and take that inhaler off that boy's hands. He sounds like he's flipping out."

"Paul, you promised me he was safe."

"What can I tell you, Callie? He thought you were testing for heroin or something. This is a whole different ball game."

"Is he going to set me up? How do I know I won't be arrested the minute I show up there to claim the inhaler?"

"I've got him calmed down for now. But you need to hurry. He wants his money and he wants to be done with this."

"Paul, I—"

"Look, Callie, I don't know what to tell you. Call the kid and set up a time and place now. He's not going to do anything fishy as long as you hurry."

I flipped through my notebook, looking for his telephone number.

"You said you've got him calmed down for now. How?"

"I told him you were FBI."

"FBI?" I asked.

"He said he wanted to call the FBI. So I told him, 'She *is* the FBI, man. It's an internal affairs investigation, which is why she needed to use an outside source.'"

I closed my eyes, feeling myself sinking deeper and deeper into deceit. Still, what choice did I have? Paul had already laid the groundwork. I just needed to keep my mouth shut, pick up the inhaler, and get out of there.

"You'll take care of this?"

"I'm on it, Paul."

My call to the kid I knew as Hydro was tense and brief. I said I had heard from our mutual friend and that I would come to town now and retrieve the inhaler, but that it would take me about an hour and a half to get there. He told me to meet him under the Friendship Oak again, so I agreed, even though my plan was to call him back once I got to Hammond to give him a new place to meet—just in case I was being set up.

I changed into shorts and a T-shirt and put my hair in a small ponytail. I needed to look different than I had the last time I had gone there, not to mention younger. I also grabbed some clothes just in case I wouldn't have time to come back to the hotel before my appointments with the board members.

The drive there felt as though it took forever. As I went, I kept going over different scenarios in my mind for how to make this exchange. The kid had seen my car at our first encounter—a careless mistake I shouldn't have made. Now I could only pray that he hadn't memorized my license plate and turned it over to the FBI.

It wasn't that I didn't think I deserved some sort of punishment for stealing the inhaler in the first place. I knew that I had been wrong to do that, and I was willing to pay the consequences once this investigation was over. My bigger fear now was that I might be arrested as a terrorist or a potential murderer myself for being in possession of this particular substance.

And though I had no doubt that if I were arrested I would be able to sort things out and prove my innocence of any malicious intent, I also could not spare the time, the trouble, nor the hindrance of an arrest. Now that I knew the inhaler contained a deadly chemical, I had incredible leverage with James Sparks. This new knowledge might be the key to get him to talk to me and tell me what I wanted to know. The last thing I needed was to be waylaid by some college kid's overexuberance.

When I got to Hammond, I took a different exit than the one before. This time I made a wide circle and came in from the other direction. That way, if any agents were posted at the expected exit, watching for me, they wouldn't be cued in to my appearance. After I took the second Hammond exit, I stopped off at a thrift store and bought a cheap backpack, hoping I looked young enough to pass as a college student.

Driving slowly through the lovely, very Southern-looking town, I made my way to the campus. I entered it from a different side than before and found a parking spot near a women's dormitory. Once there, I loaded my cell phone and my binoculars into the backpack, slung it over my shoulders, and then jogged down the sidewalk toward the meeting point, passing other students who didn't even give me a second glance. So far, so good. As soon as I saw the Friendship Oak ahead, I jogged toward a nearby building and went inside.

From the sounds in the hall and the signs on the wall, I realized I was in a music building. On the second floor were rooms along the front where I might be able to peek out of the window and look toward the rendezvous point. Unfortunately, all of those rooms were occupied, and from the sounds I heard as I walked by, I had a feeling they were individual practice rooms. Inside were soloists, pianists, and one very talented flute player.

What I really needed was to get to the roof, if there was indoor access to it. From there I would be able to look downward in every direction and see what was really going on. I tried to think logically about where I might find roof access, and I quickly tried several different doors and hallways inside the building, to no avail. Finally, I happened upon an auditorium. It was empty, and my heart raced as I ran down the aisle and up onto the stage. Many theaters had roof access from backstage. Sure enough, it didn't take long to find the metal rungs of a ladder protruding from the wall. Looking up, it was dark, but I gave it a shot anyway, knowing the ladder most likely ended at the roof.

Of course, it was a long climb. As I went I looked neither up nor down but simply straight ahead. When I realized that I was about three stories above the stage and still climbing, I started to get the creeps. But then I used some of the rock climbing techniques Tom had taught me to keep my head clear and my heart rate in line.

I reached the top at last. Squinting in the darkness, I could make out a white square up over my head. I reached up and pushed, and it easily swung free, bathing me in sunlight so bright I had to close my eyes for a minute. I was there. The only problem was that the ladder actually dipped backward in a sort of curve for the last few rungs. If I lost my grip or my footing, I would plummet four stories to the ground!

Still, these were metal rungs. I had done much worse on a sheer rock wall with nothing but tiny crevices for a grip. I felt certain I could handle this.

Focusing on the task at hand, I did it, finally pulling myself through the roof hole and then collapsing backward onto the tar-and-gravel surface, catching my breath. After a few seconds I sat up and looked around, stunned to see that all of my effort had been in vain. The roof was lined on all four sides with a cement wall that must have been seven feet high. I stood and went to the front wall, but there was no way I could see over it, not even if I jumped.

I couldn't believe I had made that climb for no reason!

Desperate, I walked the perimeter and felt a flash of hope when I discovered a small pile of discarded paint cans in a back corner. I carried them to the front, stacked them, and climbed on top of them. It was a bit precarious, but at least I could see over the wall to the Friendship Oak across the street and far below.

I climbed down from the paint cans, got out my binoculars and my cell phone, and then climbed back up. Using the binoculars, I slowly studied all of the cars that were parked around the perimeter, as well as all of the pedestrians in the area. I didn't see anyone who looked suspicious, but I wasn't taking any chances. I dialed the number for Hydro, and when he answered I told him I was so sorry, but I had gotten a flat tire out near the shopping center. Help was on the way, I said, but was there any way he could come and meet me there in the meantime? He reluctantly agreed, so, speaking from memory, I said I was on the left side of the stores, right near the road. He said I was lucky he had brought his car today and not his skateboard.

Once I hung up, I trained the binoculars on the massive tree. After a moment, I saw my purple-haired friend walk out from under it, go to a car, get inside, and drive away.

Now was the moment of truth.

I watched and waited and watched some more, but no one else seemed to spring into action. No cars pulled out and followed him. No people left where they were sitting or standing. The quiet, peaceful campus stayed exactly as it was. He hadn't turned me in.

As quickly as I could, I climbed down from the paint cans, threw my stuff into my backpack, and ran to the hole. Getting started going down was even more terrifying than coming out had been, but I dried my hands on my shirt, gripped the handles, and simply went. Before long, I was back at the level of the stage. I dropped down onto the plank floor and then jogged from the building. I had just burst out into the sunshine when my cell phone rang.

"Pink Panther?" Hydro said. "Where are you?"

"I am so sorry," I said again. "Triple A got there just as I was hanging up the phone, and they changed the tire so quickly I thought I could catch you at the tree. Where are you now?"

"I'm at the mall," he said, sounding exasperated. "Out in front of the shopping center."

"I'll be there in just a minute."

After I hung up, I let out a long, slow breath. Then I ran as quickly as I could back across the campus to my car. From there I easily found the road to the shopping center, where we made the exchange without any trouble. To prevent accidental exposure, he had put the inhaler in a Tupperware container along with a printout about its chemical composition. I took it from him and thanked him for a job well done.

Hydro was sweating, but then, so was I! He seemed both frightened and excited by the whole thing, and as we talked, I felt bad, for
he had bought—hook, line, and sinker—Paul's story about me
being an FBI internal affairs officer. I let him keep that notion.

He even asked me how to go about applying for an FBI job himself. I took my best guess while trying to sound as though I knew
what I was talking about. I suggested that he go to the FBI's website
and said that all of the information he might need would be right
there.

"Can I use you as a reference?" he asked as I climbed into my car.
I looked back at him grimly.

"Sure," I said. "Just tell them the Pink Panther sent you."

# Forty-One

By the time I got back on the interstate, I knew I would be late for my appointments with the Family HEARTS board members that Phillip had set up for me. As I drove I dug out their information and called, rescheduling two of the meetings for Friday. I didn't cancel the third one, because I thought I could still make it. It was at 8:00 P.M. with a woman named Sandy Norris. I seemed to recall Veronica talking about her. She was a friend whose daughter had a rare disorder of some kind.

I dialed Tom's number next, but I was disappointed to get his voice mail. I left a fairly cryptic message, that "the substance had been verified" and that someone had, indeed, been intended for the "pearly gates" just as I had suspected. I hoped that message would lend gravity to the situation on his end, and that Sparks would be kept safe—at least until I could talk to him.

Finally, I called Gordo in Georgia. He didn't answer, so I left a message. While I waited for him to call me back, I thought about what I needed to do. Though I hated the thought of being in possession of the deadly ricin, I was also extremely excited, because the knowledge I had about the contents of the inhaler gave me some incredible leverage with James Sparks. The bottom line was that it was time for Sparks and me to have a confidential conversation, free of the possible electronic surveillance of the federal prison telephone system.

There were only two ways I could accomplish that, however. One was to fly to Georgia and see Sparks in person. The other was to somehow get Gordo into a meeting with Sparks in a private room and have the conversation over a scrambled telephone. I thought the second idea was worth a try.

Gordo called me back 15 minutes later. Before I told him what I needed for him to do, I asked what had happened on his end so far. He said he had managed to sneak a peek at Les Watts' telephone records for the past few months, but there were no long-distance calls on them to Louisiana. He also got a bit more information from Watts about his side job. Apparently, the guard really was just a paid go-between for James Sparks and someone on the outside. Watts delivered messages back and forth and got paid once a month, the amount dependent on how many messages had been exchanged.

Gordo had not been able to get Watts to tell him who the person on the outside was, how he got the messages to this person, or how, where, or when he was paid. I had a feeling that we had already pushed our luck in this matter, and I told Gordo that he didn't need to deal with Watts anymore.

"Good. He was nice at first, but we've run out of things to talk about. Now he's just about the most boring mark I've ever worked. If I have to sit in his living room and listen to his long drawn-out fishing stories one more time, I'll go nuts."

"Well, you may not be so happy when you hear what I need for you to do next."

"Oh, boy. Lay it on me."

I told him I needed for him to have a meeting in the prison with Sparks. "The only way you'll be able to get in to see him is as an attorney," I said. "I'll say you're working for me, which is true, and set it up with the warden. What I need for you to do is get a scrambled cell phone and a nice suit. You're going to have to look the part."

"But I'm not an attorney. I can't pull that off."

"Well, the warden has the right to ask for proof that you are an attorney, but he's not required to. He certainly never asked for anything from me, even though I was ready to give it to him. So chances are he won't ask for anything from you either."

I went on to say that I would request a private conference room from the warden. Once Gordo and Sparks were in there alone, he was to call me on the scrambled phone so that I could talk to Sparks directly.

"Okay, I see a couple problems here," Gordo said. "First off, where am I supposed to get a scrambled cell phone? The Feed and Seed store? I'm in the middle of the boondocks here, Callie."

"Try Albany. It's a fairly good-sized town. I bet you can find a cell phone store or two. Maybe a Radio Shack."

"You paying for the new suit?"

"Of course. Put it on my bill. But no Armani, okay? Try to keep it at a couple hundred. You want to look nice, but you don't want to look too nice."

"One final problem," he said, "and it's a big one. What about Les Watts? Nice suit or not, he's going to recognize me."

"I've been thinking about that. Probably the best we can do is work around his schedule. Do you know what time he gets off tomorrow?"

"Not a clue. I could call him and find out."

"Do that right now, if you don't mind. Ask him what his hours are tomorrow because you want to know if he'd like to go fishing after work."

"Oh, great," he said. "As long as I don't really have to go."

We hung up and I continued driving along the elevated roadway. Five minutes later, Gordo called me back.

"He got the noon to eight P.M. shift," he said. "He wanted to go fishing in the morning, but I said I had to work."

"And you weren't even lying," I replied. "I'll call the prison first thing in the morning and try to set the appointment for nine or ten. You be ready to roll. Right now, you'd better hustle on down to Albany or all the stores will be closed."

"All right, Callie," he said, sounding doubtful. "I hope this works like you think it will."

I felt better after hanging up the phone. I would call the warden tomorrow first thing and request a morning meeting in a private conference room between one of my "associates" and James Sparks. I didn't think there would be any problems there.

All that remained right now was what to do with the inhaler itself. Now that I knew it was filled with a lethal poison, I was very uncomfortable having it in my possession. I tried to think of where I might be able to store it, but every idea I came up with had problems. The in-room safe at the hotel was simply too close for comfort. I needed some other secure location, a place where there was absolutely no chance that anyone else might stumble upon it. A safety deposit box would be ideal, but it was too late in the day to find an open bank. I considered getting a locker at the airport or a bus station or train station, but I was afraid that might somehow endanger others. I needed a less populated spot.

When the elevated road ended and I dipped down onto the regular road, a billboard caught my eye. A "U-Store-It" storage facility was off of the very next exit.

As it turned out, the place was perfect. It was located out in the middle of nowhere, rows and rows of storage rooms with plenty of vacancies. I rented the smallest one they had, a tiny three-by-five climate-controlled room, and bought a big padlock from the man at the desk to keep it secure. Following his directions, I found the room and put the Tupperware container with the inhaler into it.

Having done that, I got back onto the interstate and raced to my appointment with Sandy Norris. I was embarrassed by my appearance, but there wasn't much time to make a switch. I pulled into a gas station and did the best I could, quickly changing into the outfit I had brought along and running a brush through my messy hair. I didn't even bother trying to refresh my makeup. It had been a long day, and at this point all I really wanted was a hot shower and a comfortable bed.

Still, this was an appointment I needed to keep. I was drawing near the end of my Family HEARTS investigation. The sooner I met with some of the board members, the sooner I could wrap it up altogether and focus exclusively on my own investigation.

I checked my image in the mirror and then ran back out to my car. After plugging the address into my GPS, I headed over the Mississippi River Bridge to an area known as Gretna. The house was easy to find, a cute little Victorian-style home on a quiet, dead-end street. I parked out front and made my way to the door, stepping over several toys once I reached the porch.

I rang the bell, hoping this would be a quick and easy appointment and then I could be on my way.

# Forty-Two

Sandy Norris answered the door, an attractive but tired-looking brunette with a rag in one hand and spray bottle of cleaner in the other.

"Perfect timing," she said as I stepped inside. "My husband just took the kids for a walk."

She led me to the kitchen and suggested I sit in the chair at the end of the table.

"We just finished dinner," she said, "so you'll have to excuse me if I clean while we talk."

"No problem."

I would have thought the woman a neat freak for cleaning during a meeting, were it not for the food that seemed to be splattered all over the kitchen. It looked as though a pressure cooker had exploded in there. Besides food all over the table and most of the chairs, there were splatters on the cabinets, counter, the front of the stove, and even on the ceiling.

"Rose is a bit tough at dinnertime," she explained as she ran the rag over the oven. "Food either goes into her mouth or across the room."

I offered to help, but she insisted that I relax, she was used to it. Sure enough, she wiped everything down quickly and efficiently.

"I don't want to rush you," she said as she went, "but we'll only get about fifteen minutes of peace and quiet before they come back, so please don't feel that we have to waste time in idle chitchat."

"Okay," I said, startled but not offended by her bluntness. "I'm here to talk about Family HEARTS, but I suppose we should start with your own situation first, if you don't mind. Maybe you could tell me a little bit about your daughter."

"Sure," she said, pulling out a step ladder from beside the refrigerator, climbing up, and tending to the splatters on the ceiling. "Our daughter Rose has a rare disorder known as mucopolysaccharidosis. I know, that's a mouthful. MPS for short."

"MPS." I repeated.

"Basically," she explained, "MPS is a genetic disorder caused by the body's inability to produce certain enzymes. Rose was born with it, though we didn't even know she had it until she was in school."

"What happened?"

Sandy told me their very sad tale, that her daughter had seemed completely normal until the middle of first grade, when she suddenly started regressing. Rose had been learning how to read, and then she slowly lost that ability. She had been perfectly well behaved, and then all of a sudden she started becoming a bit of a problem child—being hyperactive, throwing tantrums, acting out.

"It's almost like she stopped growing up and started growing down," Sandy said. "Little did we know, that's exactly how the rest of her life was going to play out. Bit by bit, she has lost her use of language, memory, coordination, cognitive function, and so on. At this point, even though she is thirteen, it's more like living with a one-year-old. A very big one-year-old."

"Wow. That must be difficult for all of you."

"We've adapted," she said brusquely, climbing down from the ladder and putting it away. Then she paused, and her expression softened. "Listen," she said, "what Rose gives us in return are enormous hugs and an incredible amount of unconditional love. As hard as it is to live the day to day, it's harder still imagining what our life is going to be like once she's gone."

"What's her prognosis?"

Sandy attacked the dirty table with vigor.

"Most MPS children don't live to see their twenties," she said. "Already, the hyperactivity has calmed down, and her coordination has grown worse. She's not as loud or busy. These are all signs that the disorder has advanced. If I had to take a guess, I'd say we only have a few years left, maybe two or three at the most."

"I'm so sorry," I whispered. I don't know what I had expected to find here, but this wasn't it. I couldn't imagine a more tragic or difficult disorder.

"Anyway," she said, wiping the last of the mess, "can I offer you something to drink, Callie? Iced tea, maybe?"

"That would be fine. Thank you."

She put away her cleaning supplies, washed her hands, and then made two drinks for us in tall plastic cups. As she did, she described a bit more of their daily life. She was so matter-of-fact about it all, but it sounded like a living nightmare to me, from the diapers to the ankle braces to the child's inability to express the simplest needs. Apparently, whether Rose was hungry or cold or wet or in pain, it was up to her parents and siblings to anticipate or discern the problem, because Rose was unable to tell or show them. She could still repeat certain words, Sandy told me, but other than family names, she didn't really know their meanings anymore.

Sandy handed me my tea and invited me into the living room. Once we were there, I saw that it was more like a well-padded playroom. All of the furniture had rounded edges, and there were no knick-knacks on the tables or shelves. A rubber bin held some toys in the corner, and a small TV was mounted near the ceiling, pointing downward toward a big pile of pillows. The walls were decorated with Disney posters, and though the room was clean, there were several big stains in the carpet.

I asked Sandy to tell me how she first became involved with Family HEARTS. She said she was there when the charity was just an idea on paper. Her friend Veronica had always felt a special burden for the needs of families like theirs, families who had children with disorders no one had ever heard of. According to Sandy, Veronica used to talk about the kind of organization that "ought" to exist, and then one day, she decided to bring such a thing into existence herself.

"She drove me crazy at first," Sandy said, "but in a good way. She was always asking 'What do you wish you had?' and 'How much would this help you?' She consulted a number of families and came up with a basic list of services. As the agency has grown, that list has grown as well. Family HEARTS has been invaluable to us from a support standpoint. I also appreciate all of their efforts toward securing research dollars for rare disorders. Really, nobody cares till a star comes down with it."

"What do you mean?"

"I mean that unless some famous person, some celebrity, is diagnosed with your disorder, then you're out of luck. The general population will never hear about it. Donations are minimal. Research dollars are few and far between."

I had never thought of it that way, but it made sense.

"I see that you've been a board member since the beginning," I said, referring to my notes.

"Yes. It's tough getting to the meetings sometimes, but we think it's important. I—"

We were interrupted by the sounds of people. Suddenly, three kids came into the room, followed by a man. I stood and was introduced to them all. Rose had two perfectly healthy siblings, handsome boys who looked to be about eight and ten. The father, Monty, was tall and friendly, with a warm handshake and a ready smile.

And then there was Rose herself. Again, I don't know what I had expected, but this wasn't it. She was a big girl—probably 5'8" and 165 pounds—with large features, dark eyebrows, and a huge, welcoming smile. When we were introduced, she repeated my name, gave me a big hug, and then immediately walked over to my iced tea, picked it up, and drank from it.

"I'm sorry," her mother. "Forgot to warn you. She'll put anything in her mouth she can find."

When Rose had had enough, she surprised me by throwing the half-empty cup across the room. Tea splashed all over the wall and the floor. Much to my surprise, the parents barely reacted at all. While Sandy handed Rose a toy to distract her, her husband retrieved some towels and mopped up the mess.

After that, the boys went up to their rooms to start their homework, and Monty popped a tape in the VCR for Rose. *The Little Mermaid* came to life on the screen overhead, and the big girl plopped down on the pillows to watch it. She remained there all of about ten seconds, and then she was up again, wandering around the room, fiddling with everything she could touch. Sandy pulled out a toddler-level puzzle from under the coffee table, and Rose sat on the floor and put the large wooden pieces into place. As she worked, she babbled to herself.

"One of the hardest things about Rose," her father told me, "is that she can't ever be left alone. We've got safety guards all over the place, dead bolts everywhere, even an alarm on her bedroom door in case she gets up during the night. The biggest danger, of course, is that she might accidentally hurt herself. It's tough, not to mention exhausting."

I had come there to learn about Family HEARTS, but I realized suddenly that this was what it was all about: families, coping the best they could. No matter what services Veronica's agency may or may not have to offer them, at the end of the day they were still very much on their own.

In the face of all of this, some of the questions I had come prepared to ask seemed irrelevant now. I moved through the others fairly quickly, asking Sandy to tell me about the board members and to elaborate on some of the recent board decisions. I told her that I was going to recommend that the board be cut a bit in size, and she agreed that that might be a good idea, that there were several members who hardly ever showed up at all.

"Cakeit!" Rose announced, suddenly standing and going over to Monty. "Woopsie goodle."

She climbed into her father's lap and laid her head against his chest, playing with the button on his front shirt pocket. Despite the fact that she was the size of an adult, he managed to cradle her there like a child. He lovingly kissed her forehead and brushed a lock of hair away from her face. Tears sprang into my eyes, unbidden, at the tender sight. I tried to blink them away, but Sandy saw me.

"It's okay," she said softly, reaching out to put a comforting hand on my arm.

"It's okay," Rose repeated, like a parrot.

Sandy and I shared a sad smile.

"I don't know why this happened to us," she said softly. "But we take the good moments with the bad. These are the cards we were dealt, so to speak, so these are the cards we play."

I wiped away my tears and smiled at her, not surprised to see that there were tears in her eyes as well now.

"Mommy," Rose said, and then she looked at her mother and grinned.

"Yes, baby. I love you," Sandy said.

"I love you," Rose mimicked.

Only God knew whether they were just words or if she still understood what they meant.

# Forty-Three

When I awoke the next morning, my mood was somber. After last night's visit with Rose and her family, I felt changed somehow, as if every single thing in my life had suddenly been put into perspective. Even Bryan's death felt different to me, and I could clearly see the good among the bad for the first time. At least he hadn't suffered. At least I didn't have to watch him slowly waste away before my eyes.

I had given out a lot of grants on Tom's behalf over the past few years, but I doubted there were many that had brought quite the satisfaction to me that this one was going to bring. If we could do anything—anything—to help families like the Norrises, then I was willing to step up to the plate and ask Tom for the biggest grant he was able to give. I thought again about Family HEARTS' mission, to provide Help, Encouragement, Advocacy, Resources, Treatments, and Services to families with children who had rare disorders. Before coming here I hadn't known any such families myself, but between Beth Sparks and Sandy Norris, I had had a taste this week of the struggles they went through. If we could make their lives easier, if we could make their children's disorders more well known, then I would rest assured that I had done the best for them that I could.

That was how I signed off on the report for the J.O.S.H.U.A. Foundation. As far as I was concerned, my investigation of Family HEARTS was complete. The place had passed Harriet's financial audit with flying colors; no surprise there. Now I had a short list of changes to suggest to the board, and if they were willing to comply, then I was hoping I could talk Tom into making his donation much larger than the $50,000 he had first intended.

At 8:00 A.M. sharp, I closed out the file and prepared to call the warden at the prison in Georgia. It was hard to change mental gears back to my own investigation, but as I dialed I forced my brain into the task at hand. I reached the warden easily, and he said that my associate would be allowed a meeting in a private room, no problem. I thanked him and then called Gordo and told him to be there at 10:00 A.M., dressed to kill.

"I didn't have much time to find a decent suit," he replied. "I think I'll just be dressed to maim."

After I was finished talking to him, I decided to take a walk and clear my head. The conversation I was going to have with James Sparks today was going to be different than any conversation he and I had had thus far. This time, I had leverage. This time, he was going to give me answers.

Outside it was muggy and warm. I was glad I had worn sneakers with my slacks as I walked vigorously through the French Quarter, zigzagging my way to the Mississippi River. Once there, I strode alongside it, the murky brown water to my left and the beautiful old city to my right. I passed a giant paddlewheel boat, quiet and still in the morning light, looking perfectly at home on this river amid oil tankers and giant barges. I moved to the right, walking in the shadow of the Jax Brewery and the New Orleans Aquarium. When I reached the ferry landing at Canal Street, I was tempted to take it to the other side just for the scenery, but I didn't know how long the round trip might take. Instead, I turned around, crossed the street, and made my way back through the Quarter toward my hotel. I passed a boutique on the way and paused long enough to go inside and buy a strapless bra and a slip to go with my evening gown for tomorrow night's ball. A few doors down I spotted a pair of shoes that might match the dress and bought them as well.

With a half hour to spare, I was almost to my hotel when I passed a church front with a sign beside the door that said "Visitors Welcome." I hesitated, feeling drawn to go inside.

The door was heavy, and it made a soft whooshing sound as I opened it to reveal a darkly lit entrance room lined with stained-glass windows and glowing pay candles. I stepped onto the marble floor, the door softly swinging shut behind me, and I was caught up in the hushed beauty of the place. Somehow, I could feel the comforting presence of the Lord inside.

Walking forward, I saw there were already several people there, scattered among the wide pews, kneeling and praying. I tried not to rustle my packages as I found a place of my own near the altar. I set my things down next to me and then pulled down the kneeling bench and knelt there, hands clasped together. I closed my eyes.

Truth was, God and I weren't exactly on speaking terms at this moment. At some point during the investigation, it was almost as though a door had closed in my heart, a door of hurt and anger and shame. I thought back now, trying to trace it, and decided the situation began Thursday night at the motel in Albany, when I clutched my pillow and sobbed for all the bad things that had befallen me. Then, the next day, I committed a crime for the sake of my investigation that began a rolling snowball of sins—theft, lies, selfishness. Now, I felt convicted of those things and many more, not the least of which was hypocrisy. Not three weeks ago, I had judged my dear friend Eli for resorting to illegal methods in pursuit of an investigation of his own. I had been shocked to find him in possession of bugging equipment he had no business having for a case he was working on. Now I understood that when the stakes were personal, any of us might also cross the line at any time.

Unable to pray, I opened my eyes and looked up at the altar, where a large plaster Jesus hung in agony from a wooden cross. In my church, the crosses were all shown empty, but at this moment I think I needed this crucifix, the kind that reminded me that all of these sins had already been paid for, long ago, by one Man.

Compared to the sins of some, mine might have seemed minor, but to me they loomed large. Greatest of all, of course, was that I had shut out God. I had denied His grace. I had closed myself to His love.

"I'm sorry," I whispered, the only words I could think of to utter.

I knew that a part of my rejection of God had come not from blaming Him for what had happened in my life, but from not trusting Him in what was yet to happen. I think I had felt safer doing this investigation completely on my own. After all, if I were to trust Him in these matters, then I would have to trust Him regardless of the outcome. And that was hard.

Yet now, in the silence of His house, surrounded by symbols of His deity, it was so simple to let go and give all of it over to Him. *For I know the plans I have for you*, the verse in Jeremiah said, *plans to prosper you and not to harm you, plans to give you hope and a future.* Somehow, trying to take everything into my own hands was a rejection of that verse and of all the promises in the Bible. God held my future in His hands. That was where I needed to place my trust.

I closed my eyes again and asked God to wash away all of my sins. *Make me white as snow, Lord,* I prayed, and as if in response a song came to mind: *Oh! Precious is the flow that makes me white as snow, No other fount I know, nothing but the blood of Jesus.*

Almost as if a dam were breaking inside of me, I thanked Him for that blood, for that sacrifice. Silently, I poured my thoughts out to my Creator, tears of repentance spilling down my cheeks. I thanked God that I didn't have to do anything to receive His forgiveness except to ask for it. The blood He shed on that cross was my absolution.

Finally, knowing that time was running tight, I concluded my prayer and stood. Gathering my belongings, I slipped from the stately building and back out into the morning sunshine, feeling whole for the first time in days. I knew that part of my change of heart had come from last night's meeting with Sandy Norris. Compared with the burden that had been placed on her and her family, mine felt relatively light.

I thought about that as I made my way to my hotel room. Of all the "ignorant" and insensitive things people had said at Bryan's funeral, some of them were nevertheless true.

*At least he didn't suffer.*

*He's with God now.*

*You'll see him again in heaven.*

In light of all that was going on, I needed to add one more oft-expressed thought, especially in these last few minutes before I would speak to James Sparks and learn the truths I sought:

*God never gives us more than we can handle.*

"Oh, God," I whispered as I reached my room. "I really hope that one's true too."

# Forty-Four

The phone rang at 10:15, and even though I was waiting for it, it startled me so much I nearly jumped out of my chair. Hands shaking, I answered it to hear Gordo on the other end of the line.

"Callie?" he said. "It's Gordo. I'm here with James Sparks."

"Any problems getting in?"

"No."

"How's his demeanor?" I asked.

"A little belligerent. You ready to talk to him?"

"Sure," I said. "Give him the phone."

I heard some rustling and then the voice of Sparks.

"The only reason I'm even talking to you," he said, "is because I've been told that my life may be in danger."

"That's correct."

"I have a hard time believing it."

"What would you give to know for sure?" I asked. "What's it worth to you to find out what's really been going on there with your friend Les Watts?"

He exhaled slowly.

"I don't know," he said finally. "What do you want?"

"I want what I've always wanted," I said. "The truth about my husband's death."

He was quiet for so long that I was afraid he had hung up on me.

"James?" I said finally. "You still there?"

"You tell me what you know," he said, "and then we'll see."

It was a gamble, my going first. But since a man's life currently hung in the balance, I knew he had me. I had to tell him about the ricin either way.

Plainly and directly, I talked about the asthma inhaler that I took from Les Watts' carport. I said that it was a simple FedEx package with no note, addressed to Watts and sent from a nonexistent address in New Orleans. Inside the package was a yellow asthma inhaler that looked just like the one Sparks regularly used—except I had had this one chemically analyzed, and inside was a deadly poison known as ricin.

"Ricin?" he said. "What's that?"

"I don't know a lot about it," I replied. "But if I hadn't taken that inhaler, and it had made its way into your hands, you would be dead by now."

I wished I could see his face. He was quiet for a long time and when he spoke he sounded utterly defeated.

"I didn't think it would come to this," he said softly.

"Who is it, James?"

"It was just about money. I can't believe—"

He stopped himself. The line was silent between us, so finally I spoke.

"At this point," I said, "I can do whatever you think is best. I can turn this over to the police, I can bring in the FBI, I can do whatever it will take to save your life. Les Watts can be arrested. If you won't tell where that inhaler came from, maybe he will."

"Les Watts doesn't have a clue who's at the other end of those communications. He uses a dead drop."

I knew that a dead drop offered a way for people to communicate without ever having to meet face-to-face; an item would be left at a predesignated spot by one person and then picked up from there later by the other. Chances are, Sparks was telling the truth and Watts really couldn't reveal the source.

"Who sent it, James?"

"I don't think that's relevant to you, Mrs. Webber. But, by the way, thanks for saving my life. I guess if you're going to turn that inhaler over to the proper authorities, you'd do best to contact the NSA. As soon as possible, actually."

"I'll do it the moment we hang up," I said, my stomach clenching. I didn't know what would happen to Sparks from here, but as soon as I reported what I knew, he would become, yet again, the NSA's problem—for whatever that was worth. "Right now, tell me about my husband's death, James. I think I have offered a fair trade."

"Fine. I'll tell you what I can."

I held my breath and waited.

"As you know," he began, "four years ago I was in prison at Keeplerville, serving out my sentence for violating export restrictions. I had just eight months to go and I would be a free man. Then one day I was transported out of there with no explanation and brought to a house in Virginia, way out in the country, where the NSA was waiting for me."

"Including Tom Bennett?"

"Especially Tom Bennett. They explained that there was a... national crisis, shall we say, looming on the horizon. They needed my particular expertise. In exchange they were offering me my freedom and something more: Break the code and get my record completely expunged. I would walk away a free man with no history. I would be able to make a new start."

"Why there?"

"Secluded location, fairly close to D.C., I guess."

"What was the crisis?"

"Can't tell you that. But the situation required the breaking of the very code I had helped to create. The NSA had already been trying to break it for two months, but they had gotten nowhere. Tom Bennett had gotten nowhere. Do you understand that? The great water walker himself could not break this code."

"But he thought you could?"

Sparks laughed.

"Not the usual way," he said. "He remembered my work with the key escrow problem. He thought I might have built in a back door when we originally designed it. After studying the code extensively, he was pretty convinced the back door was still there."

"So you agreed to give them the back door in exchange for your freedom."

"Well, yeah. But it wasn't that simple. Like I told you before, I hadn't been working alone. During my incarceration, the back door had been changed."

"Changed?"

"My...colleague...on the outside had altered it somewhat. I made the deal for my freedom with the NSA, but once I got in front of the computer and started working, I saw that I wouldn't be able to give the NSA what they had bargained for. All I needed was to make a phone call and I would have it, but of course our location was so secure and isolated, there were no phones."

"No phones?"

"We had an internal network between the computers set up in that house, but no communication with the outside. The only way to get messages in or out was through an NSA pouch. I knew I couldn't go that route because my person on the outside would be caught."

"Why were you protecting them?"

"Why do you think?"

My mind raced. Love? Money? Blackmail?

"I think you were blackmailing them," I said. "I think you took the fall for selling the encryption program to the terrorists all by yourself because you were the only one that the FBI had absolute proof on. I think you offered this person your silence in exchange for money. I think that money has been accruing somewhere for you since you went to prison the first time."

And if that were true, I realized, then the colleague in question would have to be Phillip Wilson. After all, who else of the original team had any real money, other than Tom?

"You are one sharp lady, Mrs. Webber," Sparks said. "You ought to be a detective or something."

"Is it Phillip Wilson?" I whispered.

"Phillip Wilson couldn't program his way out of a hole in a bag," Sparks said derisively. He didn't, however, deny it. "It doesn't matter who the other person is. I needed to talk to them, and there wasn't any way to do that. I stalled for a few days, but I knew my time was running short."

I closed my eyes, trying to picture it all in my mind. While Bryan and our friends and I had been making our way to the river and setting up camp, not two miles away Tom Bennett and a team from the NSA had been holed up in that isolated vacation rental house, trying to break a secure encryption code and avert a national crisis. Unbelievable!

"So what happened?" I asked.

"I bided my time, behaved myself. Security got a little lax. No one thought of me as a real flight risk, you see, since they all knew I was about to go free. One afternoon I found my opportunity and took it. I knew there was a boat down in the boathouse, and I slipped away. All I was doing was going to a phone. All I was doing was going to get a little information, and then I was going to slip back into the house and do what they had brought me there to do. No one would ever even know I had been gone."

"Except for what happened in that boat."

"Yeah. Just as I was going for the phone, some fat old guy tackles me and tells me I murdered someone. I never saw your husband in the water. I swear, I never knew I hit anybody."

And all the pieces of the puzzle began to slide into place. When he was arrested, Sparks hadn't told the police his name or anything about himself. Stuck in an impossible situation, he made his one phone call to the NSA and then simply remained mum while wheels quickly spun all around him. The NSA removed his information from the police computers and then fabricated a different identity for him, one that explained his presence there on the river as a drunken boat driver with a long history of priors. When Officer Robinson ran Sparks' prints the second time, the record that came up on the screen was the fictional one. All of the information there had been bogus, as were the "facts" Sparks gave to my lawyer in his depositions.

"If you weren't convicted of involuntary manslaughter," I said, "then exactly what charge are you serving time for now?"

"Felony murder. I caused an accidental death while in the commission of a felony."

"The felony being escape?"

"Yes. I killed your husband while 'escaping' from custody. That left me faced with a long sentence in a maximum security prison."

"So how is it that you're now serving sixteen years in minimum security?"

"How do you think?" he asked. "When all was said and done, the NSA still needed my back door. Of course, by the time I was able to negotiate a new deal with the NSA, I had gotten a message out to my partner in crime, and I had obtained the proper code. My complete freedom was no longer an option they could offer me, of course, but they did the best they could. A shorter sentence, easy time, all in a prison within driving distance of my sweet mother. And, oh, by the way, the code I gave them in the end actually worked. This scum bag who killed your husband is also the hero who helped to avert a national crisis. Not that anyone else can ever know that, of course."

I was scribbling notes furiously as he talked. Some hero. It was his dirty dealings with terrorists that probably created the national crisis in the first place.

"Why was your partner in crime willing to help you at that point and give you the changed code?"

"Could be the proof I have of that person's involvement in the original deal."

"What proof?"

"That's none of your business. But don't worry, it's out there."

"Fine," I said. "There's just one thing I don't understand. Why does Tom Bennett hold himself responsible for the death of my husband? You're the one who was driving the boat."

He mulled that one over for a few minutes.

"A couple reasons, I guess. First of all, it was the code *he* helped create that got into the wrong hands and put this country in danger."

"What else?"

"When he tried to crack the code, he couldn't do it. He failed there."

"What else?"

"He was the one who insisted that my presence was required for breaking that code. He talked the NSA into having me released from Keeplerville into their custody."

"You mean, it's because of Tom that you were there at all?"

"Yep. It's also because of Tom that I was able to escape."

My pulse quickened.

"How?" I whispered. "What happened?"

"I duped him," he said. "He was in that house around the clock, but the guards made a shift change every eight hours or so. Like I said, things got lax. One guard in particular would sit out on the front porch and fall asleep. I knew that was their weakest link. I figured if I could get Tom out of the house during that guard's shift, then I might just get lucky and be able to slip away and make my phone call."

"You tricked Tom into leaving? How?"

"Well, see, he and I shared a history, you know. I was married to his sister. I knew what made both of them tick. I knew his one area of weakness."

"And what was that?"

"His father. I wrote a note to Tom, ostensibly from Daddy, saying he would be changing planes at Dulles the next day at a specific time, and that he hoped his son would come to meet him there, because he had something extremely important to tell him about the past. Brilliant of me, don't you think?"

"I don't understand," I said. "Tom's father was dead by then, wasn't he?"

"No, he was still alive. He didn't pass away until about a year later."

"Go on."

"Well, I slipped the note into the NSA pouch and Tom never knew it hadn't come in from the outside. Like clockwork, when the time came, Tom simply up and left me alone there with the guard. Tom was gone for hours on a wild goose chase to the airport, all to no avail. By the time he got back to the house in Virginia, of course, everything had changed."

"Changed?"

"I was in the local jail. The NSA was going nuts. And, I'm sorry to say, your husband was dead."

# Forty-Five

I needed to think.

Once my phone call with James Sparks had been concluded, I knew that more than anything I needed to get away and clear my mind. I told Gordo to call me back as soon as he was out of there, and while I waited for that to happen, I did what I had said I would do: I called Tom, so that he could alert the NSA to the full reality of the situation.

He sounded rushed and distracted when he answered, and I was glad. I wasn't yet ready to talk about all that I had learned.

"This'll just take a second," I told him.

"Good, 'cause I'm about to board a plane for D.C. I got your message last night about the substance, so I'm on my way to an emergency conference at…um…headquarters."

"NSA headquarters?"

"Yes. I've been thinking a lot about what you said, about Sparks' claims that there was some…collusion…between him and someone else. If that's really the case—and it's looking fairly obvious that it is— then it's time to turn this whole thing over to the authorities. I know that sort of messes up your agenda, but I don't see that we have any choice."

"Actually, that's why I'm calling. I thought you'd like to know that the substance inside the inhaler is ricin. I don't know anything about it, but it's supposed to be lethal. I agree that it's time to bring in the NSA."

"Where is the inhaler now?"

"Locked up in a climate-controlled storage facility out in the middle of nowhere. I wasn't comfortable having it around."

"You did the right thing. The NSA will take it from here. I've already had some conversations. While they need to keep the man safe, they're also interested in letting the situation play itself out a little bit—though in a controlled fashion, if you know what I mean."

"You're going to track the prison guard and see who he's working for?"

"Exactly."

"Well, for what it's worth, he uses a dead drop. It might not be that simple."

"Duly noted. We'll also need to get that inhaler from you to have it analyzed for fingerprints. Someone will be in touch. I'm sorry, but they'll also need to question you about your involvement. Just be honest with them."

"I understand."

In the background over the phone, I could hear an announcement from the loudspeaker.

"Final call," Tom said. "I have to go."

"Tom, I—"

"Look, I don't know any other way to say this, Callie. I'm sorry, but I think once the NSA is finished meeting with you, you'll need to pack up and go home."

"Go home?"

"Just drop your investigations and go home. Considering all that's happened, I don't think you're safe there. We'll handle it from here. I'll be in touch."

"But—"

"I have to go. I'll call you later. I love you."

Then he hung up the phone. Before I could even process all that he had said, the phone rang again.

"Tom?"

"No, it's Gordo. I'm outta there and already on the highway. That was one doozy of a phone call, huh? I hope it gave you the information you needed."

"And then some," I replied. I thanked Gordo profusely for all of his help this week. "You understand that every single thing you heard in there today was probably classified information you can never divulge to anyone."

"Are you kidding me?" Gordo said. "If you knew some of the things I've learned in my years in this business, your head would spin. I won't breathe a word to a soul. I never do."

"Good. I knew I could trust you."

I told him that his work there was finished and that he was free to go home.

"You'll get my bill," he said. "And it won't be cheap."

"You're worth every penny, Gordo. You always are."

After I hung up, I grabbed my tote bag and my room key, and then I went to the front desk and asked if there was anywhere in all of this city that a girl might rent a canoe. I thought if I didn't get some space and a way to think things through, I might explode!

A half hour later I was on the water of Bayou St. John, a sort of canal that wound its way through an area known as Mid-City. There were few crafts on the water, but the banks were bustling with activity, mostly walkers and bikers taking advantage of the wide sidewalks that lined the waterway, which was shaded by huge oaks and flanked with stately old homes. I would have preferred a more isolated place for canoeing, something more like my river back home, but this was probably for the best anyway. I didn't know if I was in any personal danger, but isolating myself out in some quiet, hidden river somewhere really wouldn't have been wise or prudent. This very visible spot was a much better choice.

And, oh, did the paddle feel right in my hands and the sun feel good on my face! I gave it my all, stroking vigorously in the muggy noontime hour, racing down the canal through what had to be one of the most architecturally and culturally interesting cities I had ever visited. Tom had hoped I would love it here, and I did. I could think of nothing more perfect than a future that included this place.

But what of that future?

The truths that had been hidden from me, the truths that I had so desperately sought, were all laid out on the table now. While I still didn't know the full story of James Sparks nor who his accomplice was, that really had nothing to do with me or with Bryan's death. The facts I needed in order to make some decision of forgiveness about Tom had all been provided.

Now that I knew the whole truth, all I could think was: Did he really think these were things I couldn't forgive?

Tom was hard on himself, much harder than I thought I had the right to be. In my mind, I went through the list of what he had done wrong that led to the death of my husband.

*Tom created a secure computer encryption program.*

Could I blame him for being smart, for taking his ideas and making them a reality? As Beth had said, it simply started as a puzzle for him. Once he understood the implications of that puzzle, he halted everything despite the personal cost, both literally and figuratively. It wasn't his fault that the program had made its way into the wrong hands. That code was sold to terrorists by James Sparks. But at the time, Tom had already realized the danger potential of the program and had disbanded the company. He couldn't have known what Sparks would do.

*When Tom tried to crack the code, he couldn't do it.*

He was still the brilliant Tom Bennett. He had still done wonders with mathematics and code breaking. That he couldn't break his *own* code was really a testament to his genius. If he couldn't do it, no one could. I couldn't fault him for that.

*Tom was the one who insisted that James Sparks' presence was required for breaking the code. He talked the NSA into having Sparks released from Keeplerville prison and into their custody.*

Again, who was I to judge? I didn't know anything about the national crisis that sparked that need, but I could only assume it was something extremely dire. And while I hated the secrecy that surrounded Tom's work, and I would have given anything to know what the crisis was that had resulted in my husband's death, that was the nature of national security. Who was I to judge the decision to pull Sparks out of prison?

*Tom's desire to connect with his father had caused him to commit the careless and selfish act of leaving the house that day, ultimately allowing Sparks to escape in the boat.*

I had a feeling that that was the element of this whole thing that Tom most blamed himself for. The brilliant mathematician had been easily duped because the trick Sparks used—the fake note supposedly from Tom's father—tapped into the one unsettled, uncertain part of himself that was vulnerable for exploiting.

And while it bothered me a little that Tom had never shared with me his feelings about his father or the sad past that bound them together, I also couldn't blame him for making one stupid decision. He was human. He had made a mistake. When I pictured him reading that note and leaving the house despite the fact that he had a responsibility to stay there, I didn't feel anger. I just felt sad— sad for a man who wanted nothing more than to connect with his dad and to solve the mysteries of his own past. This, I knew, was the act he had thought I wouldn't be able to forgive.

More than anything, I wanted to go to him now. I wanted to take him in my arms and tell him that now that I knew everything, I did not hold him to blame for Bryan's death. Bryan died from a difficult and complicated set of circumstances. Yes, Tom had been a part of those circumstances, but I didn't find his actions unforgivable.

I looked up at the sky, at the vivid blue fringed with clouds, and suddenly my heart soared. I finally knew the truth, and while it was very tragic, it was also something I could live with.

For better or for worse, I knew I could live with it for the rest of my life.

# Forty-Six

When I arrived back at the hotel, I wasn't surprised to see two men sitting outside my door. The courtyard area was deceptively peaceful, but I knew they hadn't come here to enjoy trailing ivy and twittering birds.

"Mrs. Webber?" one of them said softly as they both stood.

"Yes."

"I'm Brett Devlin. This is Chester LaForest. NSA. Do you mind waiting a moment while we make a phone call to verify?"

I nodded and then simply stood there as he pulled out a phone and dialed.

"Janine McDowell, please," he said.

For some reason, that name sounded familiar.

"Janine, Brett Devlin here. We're ready. Can you put us through? Thank you."

He put one hand over the mouthpiece and spoke to me.

"Mr. Bennett's on an airplane right now. We have to do this through the FAA."

The FAA. Of course. Janine McDowell was Tom's contact there. I had met her last fall, a gorgeous blonde who sought me out in an airport to deliver a message personally to me from Tom.

"Thank you. Mr. Bennett? It's Brett Devlin. How are you, sir? Good. Bravo six niner alpha bravo. Yes, sir."

He passed the phone to the other agent.

"Chester LaForest here. Thank you, sir. Yes." He smiled. "It was a girl. Eight pounds, nine ounces. Thank you. Charlie zero zero bravo delta. Thank you."

He handed me the phone. I took it and spoke hesitantly into the receiver.

"Tom?"

"Hey, Callie. It's me. You're there with Agents Devlin and LaForest."

"That's what they tell me."

"They're good guys. You can talk with them and tell them anything they need to know."

I turned away from the two agents and lowered my voice. "This isn't exactly easy for me, Tom. As you and I have discussed, there are things I've done in this investigation I'm not exactly proud of."

He took a deep breath and blew it out slowly. "I know, and they know that too. I've already given them a brief overview of the situation. Just remember that there are far more important things going on than a few misdemeanors and bad choices. Because of that inhaler, this has literally become a matter of life-and-death."

"Do you think they will arrest me? After all, I did steal a delivery from someone's front porch. I'm not sure if that's a misdemeanor or not, but—"

"I assure you, Callie, that right now they have much bigger fish to fry. I requested these two specifically. They understand what's important here—and what isn't."

I nodded, suddenly understanding what he *wasn't* saying.

"Callie," he added, his voice suddenly husky, "I promise you that you can trust me on this."

"I know," I whispered. "I know I can."

Opening my eyes and glancing at the two men who waited nearby, I found myself wishing our conversation didn't have to end here. I wanted to say more. I wanted so badly to blurt out, *Tom, it's okay. I forgive you!* But the situation wasn't right. We said goodbye, and I handed the phone back to Agent Devlin, who concluded the call and hung up.

"Would you like to come in?" I asked, gesturing toward my room.

"Actually, we need to go for a ride. First stop is a storage facility, I believe, and then we'd like to head over to our branch office."

"Of course," I said. "Can you wait a minute while I change? You can come in."

"We'll wait out here, thank you."

They sat back down in their chairs as I let myself into my room. While they waited, I quickly freshened up and changed into black slacks and a cream-colored shirt. I gathered my things—briefcase, computer, key to the storage unit. Then I rejoined them outside and locked the door.

"Okay, gentlemen, I'm all yours."

And gentlemen they were. They held the door for me at their car, spoke politely to me on the drive, and treated me with an air of respect throughout the whole process of retrieving the inhaler and driving to their office. Besides the fact that they were nice guys, I had a feeling they had been told to handle me with kid gloves because of my relationship with Tom.

The NSA facility was not labeled as such. It was just a nondescript building in the Central Business District, quiet on the outside but bustling with activity on the inside. After going past several clearance points, I was taken to an interrogation room lined with one-way mirrors. They brought me coffee and tried to make things as comfortable as possible, but I knew I was being recorded, observed, and no telling what else. For all I knew, the chair I was in was collecting my body temperature and heart rate.

The two men sat down across from me and asked me to recount for them, as thoroughly as I could, all that I had done and discovered in the last week with regard to James Sparks. Though I left out a few key points (the fact that Tom wanted me to investigate and the phone he had slipped me), I was generally honest.

I described for them my visit to Virginia, where I found all sorts of discrepancies between the "facts" of the matter and the truth. I told them about locating Sparks and then going to the prison and talking with him, and the odd way he seemed to be using me to get some response out of the guard. My face red, I told them about going to the guard's house and stealing from his carport the FedEx envelope. Much to my relief, it didn't seem as though anything official would come of that crime because Les Watts hadn't reported the theft to the police, and it was doubtful that he would press charges against me once he was in custody. Considering what had been inside that envelope, he would more than likely deny that something like that might even have been intended for him at all.

The fact that I had broken the chain of evidence was fairly significant, but I reminded them that at least by doing so I had probably saved a man's life. In a way, I realized, I had saved two lives because the theft had also prevented Les Watts from committing murder and probably ending up with a death sentence—or, at the very least, life in prison.

I wouldn't give up the name or location of the person who analyzed the substance for me, and they weren't happy about that. But I had my limits, and one of them was that I never, ever gave up a source to whom I had promised confidentiality. Of course, Hydro's fingerprints were probably all over the envelope and the inhaler, but as long as the kid had no past history of a crime, his name wouldn't pop up in any database when they ran those prints.

We ended by going over, in detail, my conversation with Sparks on the phone yesterday. In that situation I hadn't promised him confidentiality at all, but merely a trade—my information in exchange for his—and so I felt free to recount the entire conversation, almost word for word. These agents seemed particularly interested in the whole "going to make a phone call" element of the day Bryan was killed. From what I could gather, no one at the NSA had ever understood why Sparks had been trying to escape that day. The explanation of the changed code and the need for some outside communication by him to this nameless, faceless contact seemed to make a lot of sense.

But it also left the door wide open for speculation. Who was the person he was working with on the outside? We went through each of the Cipher Five, and on the one hand, they each seemed culpable, and on the other hand, none of them seemed like a logical suspect. As we talked I realized that the real culprit could have been *none* of the Cipher Five but instead some member of al-Sharif, the terrorist group. It was confusing, to say the least. Regardless, the NSA had the resources and personnel to take things far beyond where I had been able to go, and I wished them well.

As my interrogation was primarily a one-way conversation, they didn't tell me much about how they were going to solve these riddles. But I knew enough to understand that Les Watts was the key to everything. I had a feeling the poor man was now under total sur-veillance—and that the moment he attempted to communicate with anyone regarding Sparks, the walls of justice would slam down around him like a cage. Of course, if the person who had sent the inhaler was smart, he or she would know the feds were onto them now, and they would lay low for a while, not saying or doing a thing.

Then there was Sparks himself. Soon the pressure would be on him to reveal the name of the person he was blackmailing. I could only imagine what sort of "deal" he might wrangle with the NSA this time in exchange for that information.

I did wonder why, after all of this time, the attempt on Sparks' life had just happened to come this past week. Then, in a flash, it hit me: It was because of *me* that it happened when it did. When I showed up at the prison last Thursday—exactly one week ago today— Sparks had been dumbfounded to see me. But by the next day, when I returned to the prison at his invitation, his whole demeanor had changed. I told the NSA agents that Sparks must have gotten a mes-sage to his outside people as soon as I left the first time, telling them about me and turning up the heat on whatever ongoing blackmail relationship they had. They must have resisted, because when he and I met the next day, he had really pushed the envelope on giving me pertinent facts before the guard stepped in and halted the conversation. Sparks had thought he could use me as leverage, but whoever was on the outside was willing to kill him now rather than risk what a loose cannon like Sparks might say or do.

They had acted quickly, too, sending out the ricin-enhanced inhaler the very day they got his communication. That led me to believe that killing Sparks was something they had at least been prepared to do all along. His conversation with me was probably the final straw that forced them to try and make that idea a reality.

It was late afternoon by the time the agents finally finished my interrogation. They thanked me for my help and delivered me back to my hotel. I was exhausted and wanted nothing more than to take a nap. But I had a dinner appointment with Irene Bennett, and nothing was going to make me miss that. I tried calling Tom but got only his voice mail. I didn't leave a message.

I had a few minutes to spare, so after I was completely ready to go, I simply laid down on the bed with a cool washcloth over my eyes and blanked out my swirling mind. It didn't do a lot for my mascara, but at least I felt a little refreshed by the time I got up. I touched up my makeup and then left, strolling to a nearby gift shop before claiming my car. I bought a box of pecan pralines for Beth and Irene, and two cute little dolls for the girls. Then I took my car out of the hotel parking and once again made the drive that put me onto the Causeway out over the lake. As I drove, I tried to think of what I hoped to accomplish tonight.

My Family HEARTS investigation was sort of on hold, not to mention possibly irrelevant once we got to the bottom of who was being blackmailed by Sparks. If someone involved with the charity was the culprit, I couldn't see the grant going through at all. Still, that had never been my real reason for meeting with Irene in the first place. No, I was coming there to get to know my potential mother-in-law. Now that I had unearthed all the facts on Tom and knew I could forgive him, the vague possibility had become a legitimate reality.

# Forty-Seven

Once I reached the North Shore of Lake Ponchartrain, I drove to Beth's suburban home, surprised to find that she lived in a well-to-do neighborhood. I drove past opulent houses and wide, expansive lawns until I reached the one I was looking for.

Leah met me at the door, and she squealed over the dolls I had brought for her and Maddie. Irene also came to greet me, warmly thanking me for the box of pralines. Beth waved to me from the dining room, where she was setting the table. A light orange cat darted out from under a chair and ran up the stairs.

"Mrs. Webber, you wanna come see our Barbies?" Leah asked enthusiastically, taking my hand.

I glanced at Irene, feeling a bit nervous as I didn't know whether Beth had told her about me and Tom or not.

"Go ahead, Callie," Irene said, "if you don't mind. We'll eat in about fifteen minutes."

I let Leah lead me upstairs, past several bedrooms to a large playroom at the end of the hall. Maddie was there, sprawled on the floor and surrounded by enough Barbies and Barbie furniture to fill an entire Toys-R-Us. She smiled when she saw me, but she also looked very tired, and I remembered that fatigue was one of the effects of her disorder.

"Wow," I said, coming into the room, "what is this, a toy store?"

"Uncle Tommy gave most of them to us. Every time he comes, he brings us more stuff."

Suddenly the little dolls I had picked up for them paled by comparison. You wouldn't have known it, though, by the way they quickly incorporated them into the game. As Leah showed me the various clothes, furniture, and houses that they already owned, Maddie thought up a scenario that would introduce the new dolls to the story they had going.

I sat on the floor with them, and soon the three of us were playing Barbies, the cat watching us from his perch on the windowsill. It had been a while since I had hung out with eight-year-old girls, but they were delightful, and the story they came up with about a secret princess hidden in the dungeon of a mighty castle was a familiar one. We were just introducing a dragon slayer into the mix when Beth appeared in the doorway.

"Okay," she said. "Dinner's ready."

Reluctantly, we put away our toys and joined the grown-ups downstairs.

Dinner was as pleasant as it had been the other day at the restaurant, though I couldn't help feeling as though the tables had turned a bit. Now, instead of me being there to check them out, it felt as though they were checking out me. Had they known the extent of my relationship with Tom or the turn it was about to take as soon as I could speak with him from my heart, they might have been even more curious. As it was, they asked an awful lot about me, my life, and my past. I said that I had been married before but that I was a widow now, and I had no children of my own. I wondered how they would feel if they knew the whole truth. The situation was complicated, and I didn't think it was my place to enlighten them.

After a delicious Southern dinner of fried catfish, green beans, grits, and cornbread, Irene and I moved into the living room as

Beth and the girls said their goodnights. I was touched by the way both children asked for a hug from me before going up.

"Are you in love with my Uncle Tommy?" Leah asked after she hugged me. I was trying to frame an appropriate reply when she added, "Or do you just love his money?"

"Leah!" Beth cried.

"Well, you're the one who said it," Leah replied to her mother.

"I just said that Tom has to be careful because sometimes a man's wealth can be a very attractive thing. If you're rich, not everyone who loves you loves you for the right reason."

"But you were talking about her," Leah insisted, pointing to me. If she were younger, I would have thought this was a case of a child's innocence creating a foot-in-mouth moment for her mother. But Leah knew better, and there was nothing innocent about her right now. The troublemaking glint in her eye said it all.

I glanced at Beth, whose face burned vivid red, as did Irene's. The only one who wasn't blushing was me.

"Leah," I said sternly, "I'm surprised at you. You shouldn't ever repeat publicly the things your mother told you in private. It's rude, and I think you know better."

"I'm sorry," the kid mumbled, her eyes cast down to the ground.

"Thank you, but I'm not the one you owe an apology to, am I?" Her little eyes filled with tears. She looked up at her mother.

"I'm sorry, Mommy!" she said, throwing her arms around her.

Beth gave her daughter a hug and then looked at me curiously over Leah's shoulder.

"Good," I said. "Now that that's done, I don't mind answering your question. Why don't you sit down for a minute."

Leah seized the moment and plopped on the floor in front of me. In a way, I was glad this had come up. Loving a rich man was always going to be suspect, even when it was genuine. We might as well address the issue that was on everyone's mind.

"Leah, I'm going to tell you a little story."

"Okay."

I glanced at Maddie, who had planted herself on the stairs.

"You can join us if you want, Maddie."

"I'm okay. I can listen from here."

I took a deep breath and then exhaled, silently asking God for wisdom.

"A long time ago, when I was just a teenager," I said, "I fell in love with a guy named Bryan Webber. He was everything I ever wanted in my life. He was sweet and good-hearted. He loved God. He treated me with kindness and respect. He was funny. He was smart. He was handsome. He was my dream come true."

"Was he rich?"

"He was only sixteen," I said, smiling. "I suppose he might've become rich one day, if he'd really wanted to. Bryan and I fell in love. Eventually, we grew up and got married. We were very, very happy together. Then one day, in a terrible accident, Bryan died."

"Died?" asked Leah.

"That's so sad," Maddie said from the stairwell, her eyes wide.

"It was very sad," I replied. "I cried so hard I didn't think I would ever stop crying. Have you ever been that sad?"

"I cried like that when our cat Misty died," Leah said.

"Me too," Maddie echoed. "Now we have Muffin."

"I was so sad," I continued, "I didn't even want to talk to anybody. I got a lot of money from my insurance, so I used some of it to buy a new house far away from home, way out in the woods beside a river. I didn't want anybody to bother me."

"You must've been *really* sad."

"I was. I knew I would never love anyone again as much as I loved Bryan Webber. For a long time I wished I had died too."

"I bet you were lonely," Maddie said.

"I was lonely. But then, after a while, I got a new job and I started to make some friends. I got to know your Uncle Tommy, just as a friend. And you know what happened?"

"What?" Leah asked, her attention rapt.

"I realized that he was sweet and good-hearted. He loved God. He treated me with kindness and respect. He was funny, he was smart, and he was handsome."

"Just like Bryan!"

"Except he wasn't *just* like Bryan. He was very different, in fact. But for some reason, Tom fell in love with me. And though it was really, really scary for me, I finally had to admit that I loved him too."

"Why was that scary for you?" Maddie asked.

"Because she was afraid he might die too, stupid!" Leah responded.

"Not just that," I said. "When you love something and then you lose it, it's hard to love again. It's about trust. It's about letting God be in control of your life instead of you. Do you understand?"

Leah nodded solemnly.

"Let me ask you a question," I continued. "Do you like it when your Uncle Tommy comes for a visit?"

"Yes!" both girls said emphatically.

"Do you like the Barbies he brings to you when he comes?"

"Yes!"

"If he didn't bring anything, would you still be glad to see him?"

"Yes!"

"Why?"

They looked at each other and then looked back at me.

"Because he's fun."

"Because he plays with us."

"Because he makes corny jokes."

"Because he takes us places."

"But what about all of his money?" I pressed. "Isn't that why you love him?"

"No," Leah said, leaning back on her arms. "We don't love him for his money."

"Well, neither do I," I said. "Now, I'll admit, his money lets us do fun things. His money makes me feel good because sometimes I get to give it away to special places."

"Like Family HEARTS?"

"Like Family HEARTS. But money is one thing. Love is something else entirely. I don't ever want you to doubt this: I love your Uncle Tommy because of who he is, because of what's inside of him. His money has *nothing* to do with it."

My words settled into the air around us, and all was silent until Maddie spoke.

"I wish he would show up on a white horse and sweep you away to a magical castle," she said dreamily. "And you could be a beautiful princess."

I glanced at Irene, who seemed touched by all I had said, and then I looked back at Maddie.

"I don't need the horse or the castle," I said, smiling. "I'm happy with just Tom. He's my handsome prince."

That seemed to satisfy them all. Beth quietly thanked me and then, without any further conversation, she stood and began ushering Leah toward the stairs. Irene waited until they were gone before speaking.

"Thank you, Callie," she said softly. "You managed to settle some doubts and toss in a little well-needed discipline all in one fell swoop."

"Good. I hope I wasn't out of bounds there at the beginning."

"Not at all. Leah's a little pistol. Her mother is the first to admit it."

I settled back into the couch, feeling much more comfortable now that everything was out in the open.

"Would I be correct to assume that things are fairly serious between you and my son?"

Now it was my turn to blush.

"I'm sorry he didn't tell you," I replied. "Being his employee makes it kind of complicated. We have kept things very discreet."

*Not to mention, my husband was killed by James Sparks—your ex-son-in-law and the father of your granddaughters...*

"My son is a very private person," she said. "I'm sure he'll share it with me when he feels ready."

"I'm sure he will."

She shifted in her seat, hands clasped delicately in her lap.

"So are you ready for tomorrow night's ball?" she asked, gracefully changing the subject. "I understand you're borrowing a gown."

"Yes, from Veronica's sister. It's gorgeous. I picked up some shoes to go with it this morning."

"How about your mask?"

"My mask?"

"It's a masked ball," she said. "Didn't anyone tell you? Here's the one Beth will be wearing." She stood and hobbled over to a nearby table and picked up a gorgeous, sparkling Mardi Gras mask covered in jewels and topped with feathers. She handed it to me. "It's a family heirloom."

"It's beautiful," I said, holding the mask under the light to study it more closely. It was also valuable. What I had thought were rhinestones were actually, I saw upon closer inspection, semi-precious gemstones.

"I'm sure we have one you could use," she said. "Though, of course, nothing this elaborate. Let me take a look."

She disappeared into the kitchen and came back a few minutes later with a large shoebox. Inside were beads, doubloons, and several masks.

"I'm sorry that this is all we have," she said, pulling them out one by one. "They're just throwaways. You wouldn't even have to give it back."

"Are you sure?"

"Oh, absolutely."

I looked through them until I found one all in silver that I thought would match my shoes. It was made of plastic covered with a shimmery fabric and trimmed in sequins, and when I put it on and looked in the mirror, I thought it looked nice. I told Irene it would do just fine.

"Well, good," she said. "I'm so glad I could help."

As she put the box away, I thought about how very much I liked her. There was a sweetness about her that made me want to curl my legs up under myself and tell her my deepest secrets.

Instead, she rejoined me on the couch and we talked about superficial things, moving eventually into my questions about Family HEARTS and discussing the difficulty her family faced in dealing with a rare disorder. I told her of my visit to the Norris' house last night and how profoundly I had been impacted by it.

"That is one extremely impressive family," she said. "Considering what they go through, I cannot imagine how they cope. Sandy has been a huge inspiration for Beth."

Speaking of Beth, she came down the stairs dressed in shorts, a T-shirt, and sneakers.

"I'm going for a run," she said to her mother. "The girls are doing their reading and then I'll be back to tuck them in."

"All right, dear."

"Callie," Beth said, "if you leave before I get back, it was good seeing you again. Nothing personal from earlier, huh?"

"I have a brother too," I said, smiling. "I know how it is."

She left, and then it seemed to be a good time for me to be leaving as well.

"Before you go, Callie," Irene said, "maybe you'd like to see a few pictures."

"Pictures?"

"Of Tom. As a boy. Beth has some of our old photo albums here."

That was an offer too good to resist! As it turned out, I ended up staying another hour and a half, sitting side by side on the couch with Irene, looking at old family photos, and hearing stories about Tom's boyhood. Though I was sure he would have died to know he was the hot topic of discussion, I had a whole lot of fun, and I gained some valuable insights into his character as well.

I finally called it a night after the last photo album. It was late, and I still had to get back across the Causeway to the city. Beth had already come back from her jog and gone to bed, so Irene walked me to the door by herself and surprised me by giving me a hug goodbye.

"Thank you, Callie," she said. "I hope this was just the first of many times we can share together."

"Thank you, Irene," I replied. "That means more to me than you could ever know."

# Forty-Eight

The night was dark, and my wheels made a steady thump, thump, thump on the ridges of the Causeway. Traffic was light and I had the urge to speed up a bit, but I had seen a number of police cars on the drive over, and I had a feeling this long bridge was probably one big, extended speed trap.

Instead, I simply let myself be lulled by the rhythm of the sounds the car was making. There was a slight drizzle outside, and between the thump of the tires and the swish of the windshield wipers, the effect was nearly hypnotic.

Until I heard the hiss.

I thought I had blown out a tire at first. It sounded like that, like the shooting of compressed air. It was closer than that, though, and a moment later I reached for the interior light to see if I had left a soda can on the floor that had sprung a leak. Instead, when I flipped on the light, I spied a giant snake, slithering out from under the seat between my legs. It was hissing.

I slammed on the brakes so hard I nearly spun out. With a giant screech, I came to a stop, slammed the gear into park, and then jumped out of the vehicle. I was lucky there were no other cars passing at that moment, or I would have been killed. I fell onto the center lane, unable to stop myself from screaming. Afraid I would be run down, I scrambled up and then ran further to the middle, where there was a turn-around lane.

The snake was still in my car, and suddenly it didn't matter where I was stepping, it felt as though there were snakes everywhere. I looked all around on the ground, thoroughly rattled by long, thin strips of discarded tires. Everything looked like a snake—including the real snake in my car, which I could still see by taking a few steps back toward it. It had slithered onto the brake pedal and was resting there, its neck coiled, its head erect.

Frantic, I looked in both directions, my heart nearly pounding out of my chest. There were cars in the distance both ways, and though I wanted simply to run away and hide, I realized that if another car came upon my car too quickly, there might be a terrible accident.

Steeling my nerve, I ran back the way I had come, waving broadly to the next car that came by. Though they did not stop, they slowed down enough to veer around my vehicle.

The next car that passed did the same, but finally someone coming from the opposite direction pulled over into the turn-around lane. Much to my relief, I saw that it was a police car.

"Officer, help me," I said, running toward him.

"That your vehicle, ma'am?" he said.

"Yes."

"I'm afraid you'll have to pull it over here as quickly as possible, if you can."

"I can't!" I cried. "There's a giant snake inside!"

He looked shocked, but he sprang into action nevertheless. He maneuvered his car across the lane and behind mine and then turned on his flashing lights. Quickly, he hopped out of his car and then ran along behind it, dropping lit flares for another 50 feet or so.

Finally, he ran back to where I was waiting, on the crossover lane.

"Are you all right, ma'am?"

I looked down to see that my knees were scraped up and bloody from my fall on the road.

"I wasn't bitten," I said, trying to get myself under control. "I was just driving along and then I heard something hissing, and when I turned on the light, there was a big snake in the car by my feet! It was horrible!"

He placed a warm hand on my arm and looked me in the eyes.

"I'm going to radio for help," he said. "Are you sure you didn't get bitten?"

"Yes, I'm sure."

"You gonna be all right for a minute?"

"Yes."

I clutched my arms around myself, shivering despite the nighttime heat. I realized that in the drizzle my hair had gotten all wet.

After he finished on the radio, he invited me to sit in the police car where it was dry, but I resisted. All I could see were snakes under every seat.

"We'll just wait here a few minutes," he said. "I got another vehicle responding, and they're gonna bring a loop."

"A loop?"

"It's a tool to get the snake out."

I closed my eyes, swallowing hard.

"I can't believe there was a snake in my car," I said.

"Oh, this ain't the first time I've seen this," he replied. "People leave their windows open around here, don't think twice about it, and next thing you know a whole family of water moccasins has moved right in."

"A whole family?"

"You know what I mean. You're gonna be fine."

I felt better once the other unit had responded. One of its officers had brought a long metal pole with a hook at the end, and it took him a while, but eventually he was able to reach into my car with the pole and loop it around the snake. He jerked it back, pulling the snake out, and we were all shocked to see that it was about five feet long.

"Probably just a kingsnake," one of the cops said, whistling. "Sure is a big one."

"Is it poisonous?" I asked.

"No, but it can bite, and, man, does that hurt."

The officer with the pole surprised me by simply walking to the railing and dropping the snake overboard, into the lake. I ran to the side in time to see it slithering away in the black water.

The cops thought that would be the end of things, but I was insistent that they conduct a thorough search of my vehicle. They used flashlights to look under seats, in the glove compartment, and everywhere else a reptile might choose to hide.

"Looks like that's it," one of them said. "There was only that one."

They took some information from me for their report and sent me on my way. By the time I made it across the lake, to the French Quarter and the hotel, I was violently trembling. After I checked the car with the valet, I sought out the bell captain and explained what had happened. He could tell I was thoroughly spooked, and after grabbing the hotel's first aid kit, he insisted on coming with me to my room to check every nook and cranny to make sure it was safe.

It was. Finally, I took some antiseptic ointment and bandages from the first aid kit, tipped him well, and then locked, bolted, and blocked the door. I ran a bath and climbed in, picking gravel out of my scraped knees while I waited for the hot water to fill.

A snake.

In my car.

I had no doubt it had been put there on purpose.

After my bath, feeling much more calm, I bandaged my cuts, dressed in my nightgown, climbed into the bed, and then called Tom on the secure phone. Though it was late, I could tell he wasn't alone. I could hear other voices in the background. Trying to keep myself from sounding too upset, I explained what had happened.

Tom was astounded and angry. After he listened to my full story, he put me on hold for a moment and then came back on the line to tell me they were contacting the NSA branch office in New Orleans. He had a feeling they would want to come right over to retrieve my car and search it for evidence.

"I'll send Jacques to your room to get your car key so you don't have to be bothered. You can pick it up at the front desk in the morning, when you check out."

"I'm not checking out."

"Yes, you are. If I can't convince you, then the snake should. You're not safe there, Callie. You know too much. The NSA needs some time to bring this investigation to a close, but your job is done. You can leave now."

"We'll see," I said. I closed my eyes, exhaling slowly. "Tom, I hate to say this because I know she's your sister, but the most logical culprit here is Beth. She went out for a jog while I was there, and then a snake turned up in my car? Who else could it be?"

"I understand what you're saying," he replied, "and I'd be willing to consider it if not for the fact that we're talking about a snake. Beth *hates* snakes, Callie. She wouldn't touch one for a million—no, for a trillion dollars. This had to have been done by someone who isn't afraid of reptiles."

Callie thought for a moment. "So who are you thinking of? Armand?

"Yeah. He must have come to Beth's house and put that snake in your car. The swamps are full of snakes, and the man is a natural around reptiles."

"You're probably right."

I felt a wave of relief that we had discovered Sparks' accomplice, followed by a surge of sadness that it had ended up being Armand. He was an unusual man, but also so very full of life. And I couldn't help but like anyone who was as at home on the water as he was.

"I'm sorry, Tom," I added. "I know he was your friend."

"Well, so was James once upon a time, and look where he ended up. Truly, nothing could surprise me anymore."

# Forty-Nine

A half hour later, the bell captain had retrieved my car key and my bandaged knees were really starting to smart. I was thinking that perhaps I should try to get some sleep when the phone rang. It was Tom again.

"Hey."

"Turn on the TV," he said, his voice sounding strained.

"What?"

"Turn on the TV," he repeated, naming the station he wanted me to find. I reached into the bedside drawer for the remote and then held it out toward the television and flipped through the channels until I had reached the correct one.

"It's a car commercial," I said.

"Keep watching."

We waited for the show to come back on, the line silent between us. I so wanted to talk to him about us, but now didn't seem like the right moment, especially because he still wasn't alone. I wondered if we would have that "right moment" before this investigation was wrapped up.

The commercial ended and then the camera went to a close-up of a man with silver hair and blue eyes.

"Welcome back to *Late Night with Donald Mason Live*," he said. "We're talking with Armand Velette, author of *A Louisiana Guide to the Disappearing Coastline*. Armand, you're saying that the disappearing coastline isn't just Louisiana's problem, it's everybody's problem?"

The camera pulled back to reveal Armand sitting there across from the host, looking handsome in a dark suit, his eyes twinkling in the bright studio lights.

"That's right, Donald," Armand said. "For starters, did you know that Coastal Louisiana, by itself, accounts for thirty percent of this country's annual seafood harvest? Thirty percent! What's this country gonna do without that?"

I turned the sound down a bit and spoke into the phone.

"What is this?" I said.

"It's what it looks like," Tom replied. "Armand is on a live TV talk show."

"I don't understand. I thought this was the sort of thing he did all the time."

"The operative word here is *live*, Callie. We checked. It's happening right now, even as we are watching. They film in Houston. According to the producer, Armand has been there at the studio since six o'clock this evening."

I closed my eyes, understanding that that now ruled him out as a suspect with the snake, at least as far as putting it there in my car himself. Of course, he could have had someone else do it for him, but, then again, how would he even have known where I was going to be tonight?

My mind turned again to thoughts of Beth. Who was to say what she'd really been doing when she'd gone out earlier? She had known I would be there visiting and could have had prepared ahead of time, maybe had the snake waiting in a bucket somewhere or something. I hated to have to bring it up again, but I had no choice.

"I still say Beth could have done it," I told him softly. "She was outside tonight for a long enough period of time, anyway."

The moment was awkward.

"I'm here with the NSA," Tom said finally, his voice noncommittal. "She's already on their short list. If Phillip knew you were going to be there, it could've been him too."

"He knew," I said. "In fact, he's the one who made the appointment for me with your mother."

"Ah. Well, then we're back where we started, aren't we?"

Even as thoughts were swirling in my head, Tom wrapped up the call, telling me again to check out and head home in the morning. I didn't make any promises. We hung up and then I sat there, knees hurting, heart hurting. I missed him! I wanted to be with him. Most of all I wanted him to know that nothing stood between us now.

Thinking that I wouldn't be able to sleep, I turned up the television and watched the rest of the show. Armand was funny and articulate and handsome, the perfect spokesman for protecting the swamp. I pictured him in that environment, tossing food to alligators, moving so naturally among the passing wildlife, and I had to wonder suddenly if the snake in my car tonight had been put there specifically to frame him. Did one of the others want us to think it was Armand? If so, they made a big mistake by not doing their homework to make sure he didn't have an alibi.

So which one was it, Beth or Phillip—or *both?* My mind racing, I thought about calling Paul Tyson in Seattle to get financial profiles of Beth Sparks and Phillip Wilson. But Paul and I had already had a conversation last week where I asked him all about encryption programs and the Cipher Five. I really didn't think it would be prudent to clue him in now on the specifics of who or what I was really investigating.

I climbed out of bed and went to my computer. The best I could do was an internet search for assets, using the investigative databases to which I subscribed. Though I was tired, I soon got into it, finally turning up some real estate sales and purchases for Phillip, as well as several other indications that the man was quite well off. I already knew he was rich, though, so I concentrated on Beth, deeply concerned when I finally came across an enormous amount of stock holdings in her name. As I studied the list of companies, I couldn't think of any common denominator between them— except that they were good, solid investments, by and large.

Yet Beth was a full-time mom, with only some minimal, part-time computer work on the side. How was it that she was so rich? And if Sparks were blackmailing her, then wouldn't the money be paying *out* and not *in*? My mind wrapped around that thought, including the possibility that Beth and her ex-husband were working together to blackmail Phillip. But if that were the case, I wondered, then how could Beth and Phillip still be such good friends—unless he wasn't aware that she was working through James to take his money. Was that it?

I finally gave up. I turned off the light and got under the covers again, feeling utterly confused and frustrated. I could only hope that somehow God would show me some clarity in the midst of this muddle. It took a long time for me to fall asleep, but at least once I did, I slept deeply.

I awoke after 9:00 A.M., much to my surprise. And though my knees still hurt, my hands were fine, no longer even red. I thought about the day ahead of me, mentally planning out the schedule between now and the ball tonight. For my own safety, Tom wanted me to go home as soon as possible, but I was determined to extend my stay here until tomorrow.

There was no real reason for me to stick around other than plain stubbornness. I had come to New Orleans for two reasons— to get to the bottom about Tom's involvement in my husband's death and to conduct a charity investigation of Family HEARTS. I had found out the truth about Tom, and for all intents and purposes, my charity investigation was nearly finished as well. But all of my digging around about the past had set off certain events, not the least of which was the attempted murder of James Sparks. Now it felt as though I was peculiarly positioned to bring about some answers to the questions my investigations had raised.

Tonight at the ball I would be able to observe Armand, Beth, and Phillip all in one place together. If I could somehow use my access to turn up just a bit of information about James Sparks' silent accomplice, then at least I could leave town feeling as though I had done all that I could here. This extra day would also allow me to fulfill my appointments with two of the board members of Family HEARTS and then close out that investigation completely.

I promised myself I would leave in the morning and go home, whether I made any progress today or not. If I left early Saturday morning, I could drive all night and get to D.C. by Sunday afternoon. Tom would still be there. Somehow, we would steal away some time alone where I could tell him all that I learned and all that I had been thinking. I knew he was absorbed with the new investigation of the Cipher Five, but I didn't think he would mind being dragged away for an hour or so once he heard what I had to say.

My meeting with the two board members of Family HEARTS was scheduled for noon at a home in the Garden District, so I decided to have breakfast out and then take a streetcar there.

I dressed in another of my new suits and then set off on foot into the warm and humid morning, doubling back a few times to make sure no one was following me. Feeling secure, I chose a lovely restaurant and was seated in a center courtyard at a small table next to a fountain. I ordered eggs Benedict and then sat back with my café au lait and soaked up the ambiance while I waited for my food to come. How I wished Tom were with me! I knew New Orleans was often referred to as the "Big Easy," and now that I had been here a while, I understood why. At least in the French Quarter, there was something so very laid back about it, so utterly unconcerned with the usual rhythms of a busy city's work week. I loved it. In fact, the only problem with this place was all of the food. It was so good that I had a feeling if I lived here, I would have to double my workout schedule just to keep up.

After breakfast my adventure on the streetcar was immensely pleasurable. I sat by a window and watched, rapt, as we rode up St. Charles Avenue past one beautiful home after another. I got off at my stop and then walked a half a block to the home I was looking for. It wasn't as large as some of its neighbors, but it was richly appointed inside and quite beautiful.

It hadn't dawned on me that my meeting would include lunch, but soon I was seated at a long table where several courses were served up, one after the other, by a silent and dour-looking butler. Not wanting to seem rude, I ate as much as I could, picking at the rest, and feeling as though I were going to explode. The two women I had come to meet were good friends with each other, both in their seventies, with expensive coiffures and somewhat affected manners. But they were sweet and very interested in the foundation and very proprietary about Family HEARTS. I got the impression that they served on a number of different boards and that they took their charity work *very* seriously. They answered all of my questions, and when we were finished, they said that they hoped to see me at the ball tonight.

Back at my hotel, I entered all of the information they had given me and then sat back and studied the full picture of Family HEARTS. I had received responses from most of my sources, and the few that had had dealings with Family HEARTS gave the organization hearty endorsements. With a few minor adjustments on their part, the charity would pass my investigation on all counts. I closed out the file, knowing that if this were a normal case, it would now be time for me to write out my recommendations and then cut them a check. But this case wasn't normal, and while I could say without reservation that the charity was a good one, I knew we couldn't hand over any money to them until these other, seemingly unrelated questions were answered. Was Phillip a criminal? Was Veronica involved somehow? Until we knew for sure, there wouldn't be any money given from the J.O.S.H.U.A. Foundation to Family HEARTS.

Putting that out of my mind for now, I went online to do a bit of research. I wanted to know more about ricin, the poison that had been in the inhaler. What I learned was that ricin, a by-product of the castor bean plant, was an incredibly deadly substance. Apparently, just one gram of ricin was 6000 times more poisonous than cyanide and 12,000 times more poisonous than rattlesnake venom. It would take only one millionth of an ounce to kill a man—yet the death wouldn't be instantaneous. From what I could tell, symptoms wouldn't even show up until 18 to 24 hours after exposure, with death resulting anywhere from 12 to 54 hours after that.

I found some pictures of the plant, and the shiny seeds looked to be about the size of pinto beans, each very pretty, with delicate designs of brown and black and white on their hard shells. The beans were deceptively beautiful, however, because they provided one of the most potent cytotoxins in nature—a cytotoxin which could be derived through several processes, including simple distillation.

Of course, castor oil was taken from the same source, and that was a useful product found in lubricants, paints, plastics, shampoo, cosmetics, and more. Apparently, however, because of the dangers of ricin poisoning, not much castor oil was produced in the United States anymore. Even workers who processed it safely were prone to developing allergic sensitivities, ranging from contact dermatitis to asthma to anaphylactic shock.

The thought that frightened me the most, though, was when I considered the danger of ricin dust in the hands of terrorists. Because castor bean plants were fairly common worldwide—and the toxin somewhat easily produced—the potential for ricin to be used in chemical warfare was staggering. As I looked at website after website, I felt myself growing increasingly anxious. If such a potent poison were released into the general population, we would all be dead of acute hypoxic respiratory failure within days.

With a shudder I finally signed off and went to prayer. I asked God for protection, not just for myself but for my entire country. In such unstable times, I could only pray that the Lord would keep His benevolent hand upon all of us and keep us safe. I also prayed for wisdom and discernment for the NSA agents who were working to crack this case. Finally, I prayed that Tom would stay safe until we could be reunited.

When my prayer was finished, I went outside for a breath of fresh air. The sun was hot, and a number of people were lounging around the pool. I would have loved to go for a dip myself, but there wasn't time. I would need to start getting ready for the ball soon. First, however, I went back inside my room, sat down, and dialed the phone number of my friend and mentor Eli Gold.

We had a good talk. Things had been somewhat contentious between us since the conversation I had overheard between Eli and Tom in the hospital in Florida, when I first realized that Tom was somehow connected to Bryan's death. Now I apologized for all I had said and done in my desperate pursuit for answers. I told Eli that, above all else, I wanted him to get better. Still healing from a gunshot wound, he promised me that he would focus fully on his recovery now that he and I had made our peace.

I asked him if he would mind verifying for me the truths that I had uncovered about Tom and James Sparks. One by one, I went down the list of reasons that Tom felt culpable in Bryan's death. Eli confirmed all of them.

"Is that everything?" I asked. "Is there anything else I don't know?"

"No, Callie," Eli replied. "I believe you have unearthed it all. I always knew you could."

"Everything except how the J.O.S.H.U.A. Foundation came to be," I said. "All I know is that somehow it was created with me in mind."

"It was my idea, actually," Eli surprised me by saying. "Now that you know everything else, I guess I can tell you how it happened."

He went on to describe his own investigation into my husband's death, which he conducted the summer that Bryan died. Unbeknownst to me, Eli had had questions about the boating accident from day one, as certain things simply didn't add up for him. He had taken it upon himself to seek out some answers, and slowly his investigation led him to James Sparks and Tom Bennett. Because Eli was a former NSA agent himself, he was able to get confirmation on certain facts, and in the end he became acquainted with Tom personally.

Eli liked Tom a lot, and he believed him to be a true man of character. They had some long conversations where Tom expressed extreme remorse over the death of the man in the water—and the widow who had been left behind.

"He told me once," Eli said, "that ever since the accident, he was just one soul hoping for ultimate absolution."

"Absolution?"

"He needed to find a way, somehow, to pay for his sin."

"We don't pay for our own sin, Eli. Jesus died on the cross to take care of all that."

"I know," Eli replied, "and Tom knew too. He just couldn't shake his own sense of responsibility in ruining your life. He didn't know you, of course, but he still felt bound to you. What made it so hard for him, I think, was that he could never go to you and tell you what had really happened, or how sorry he was that it had all taken place on his watch."

"I understand," I whispered, surprised at the tears that sprang into my own eyes—tears of pity for Tom and his sense of guilt in the matter. I could almost picture him agonizing over me and my pain. He was just that kind of person.

"Of course, Callie, while I was doing the investigation and getting to know Tom, you were slipping deeper and deeper into depression. Finally, I thought of a way that Tom could repay his debt to you. He wanted absolution? I told him that maybe he could find it by giving to others—and that that would start by offering you a job that would pull you out of your despair and offer *you* a way to give to others as well."

I closed my eyes, picturing it all. My beloved Eli had somehow engineered a path to healing for Tom and for me in one fell swoop. And though a part of me probably should have been mad at Eli for being so manipulative, I knew there was only love in his efforts. I thanked him, from the bottom of my heart, for doing what he thought was right, for suggesting the formation of a foundation and convincing me to pull out of my own grief and step into a job that fit me like a glove.

# Fifty

By 5:00 P.M. I was in the car and on my way to the plantation house where the ball was to be held. My hair and makeup had turned out well, and when I slipped on the beautiful gown, I felt a bit like Cinderella. Shimmery stockings, new shoes, and the silver mask made my look complete. Now as I drove, the mask was on the seat beside me, and I could only hope that an hour and a half in the car wouldn't wrinkle the gown too badly.

Traffic was heavy, but once I got through the city, I made good time. Following the signs to Grande Terre, I drove down several long, winding roads until I reached the main entrance.

There were already a number of cars there, and as I turned onto the long lane that led to the house, a man in a bright orange vest waved me toward the valet parking area. Instead, I waved him off and found a spot myself, parked the car, and checked my image in the mirror on my visor. As I was freshening my lipstick, I noticed several couples walking into the house. The women looked elegant in gowns even fancier than mine, and the men all wore tuxedoes. On their faces were Mardi Gras masks, which reminded me to put on my own.

The plantation grounds were beautiful, full of massive, graceful oak trees dripping in moss, the walkways lined with azaleas. I walked up the front steps and into the home, showing my invitation to a man at the door. He checked my name off of a list and then welcomed me inside.

To the lilting sounds of a string quartet, I strolled through the first few rooms of the home. They had been restored to the period, with sturdy antique furniture and some impressive paintings on the walls. Allowing myself to flow with the crowd, I came to the ballroom, which was attached to the house via a long, grand hallway. Emerging from the other end, I found myself in a stunning space lined with tall windows and high ceilings that were as gilded as those in a palace.

Someone handed me a copy of the auction list, and I found an empty seat at a table in a corner. Others drifted my way and sat at the same table, some making polite conversation. I found it a little awkward to talk from behind a mask, but I didn't take it off since everyone else was still wearing theirs.

Out of curiosity I read the auction list, astounded again by some of the offerings. Some incredibly valuable items had been added since the other day, including an original Degas and a trip for two to Tahiti. There were also a number of celebrity items, from a personal training session with a famous fitness guru to a five-song private concert by Harry Connick Jr. Everyone at my table talked about the list, what they planned to bid on, and what they thought would sell high. My very favorite listing was an MDM 1.3-m McGraw Hill telescope, used previously in the Kitt Peak National Observatory in Tucson, Arizona. Before his death, Bryan had been an avid astronomy buff, and something like that would have thrilled him no end. I couldn't imagine how much it might sell for.

Soon waiters began circulating with drinks and hors d'oeuvres. I sipped a ginger ale and watched the room slowly fill up with people. I saw Beth and Irene come in, and even from across the room the family mask that Beth wore simply glistened. I waved them over and they gladly joined me, greeting other people all along the way.

Finally, Veronica appeared at the front of the room, looking stunning in a vivid red gown, her lipstick a perfect match to her dress. She thanked everyone for coming, outlined the events of the evening, and then introduced the auctioneer. He took the microphone and warmed up the crowd with a rousing comedy routine. Then the auction began, and I saw that Veronica had been right: These people were determined to outdo each other.

The prices soon skyrocketed into the thousands, and by the time the telescope came up on the block, the bidding started at $5000. The final price was well over $10,000, sold to someone at the front of the room.

Once the auction was finished, the masks came off for the meal and the fabulous dinner began, five courses that I barely ate, as I was still full from my double lunch! As I picked at my food, I discreetly searched the crowd for Armand and Phillip and anyone else I might know. Beth seemed quiet, but Irene was particularly chatty, and the meal time flew by.

After dessert I excused myself and made my way outside for some fresh air, but everywhere I went were clusters of people smoking. I started to walk beyond the group of smokers to the formal gardens, but it was dark out there and I didn't think that would be wise.

Back inside, I found that the food had all been cleared away and the band was just starting up. All of the guests had put their masks back on, and the room had the look of an eighteenth-century Viennese ball. Fortunately, Bryan had taught me some ballroom dancing early in our marriage, so I held my own when I was asked to dance several times by polite men with fancy masks and charming Southern accents. Though I didn't mind dancing with them, one didn't want to let me go when the song was over. He had just cornered me and launched into a long, involved tale about the history of his family's Mardi Gras krewe when Armand surprised me by interrupting us.

"Oh, *cher*, where is that dance you promised me?"

He looked handsome in a tuxedo, his mask of the simple black "Lone Ranger" variety. True to his word, he was as adept at ballroom dancing as he had been at the Cajun Two-Step. He gripped me firmly, guiding me around on the floor as my beautiful dress swirled along behind me.

"I guess I should feel privileged to be in the presence of a television star," I told him as we danced.

"A television star?"

"I saw you last night. You were very impressive."

He grinned.

"You caught me on Donald Mason's show?"

"Yes. You have a real screen presence, Armand. You should do as much TV as you can."

"Oh, I try. I'll do anything to spread the word."

He pulled me closer and continued the dance. When the song was over, he brought me to his table so that I could say hello to his aunt. Though she wasn't exactly "high society," she didn't look all that out of place in a simple gray floor-length dress, with black, elbow-length gloves and her hair in a home-done up-do. In front of her was a glass of champagne, and she was just giggly enough that it seemed as if it had already gone to her head. I chatted with them both for a minute or so and then seized the opportunity to break away when I spotted Phillip and Veronica.

"Callie!" Veronica said, giving me a big hug. "Where've you been? I've been looking for you all night."

"I'm over on the side, in the back," I said. "With Beth and Irene."

"Well, what do you think of our little ball?"

"Your little ball is a big cash cow!" I replied, and we both laughed. "Very well done."

"Did you bid on anything?" she asked.

"No, it was too rich for my blood. But it was fun to watch."

We chatted for a while, and I slowly realized that while this evening was certainly pleasant enough, it wasn't going to be of any value to my investigation. I had hoped to observe the members of the Cipher Five interacting with each other, but it was simply too crowded and too chaotic for that. After a few more dances with complete strangers, I considered going home. I wondered if there might be a security guard or a traffic director outside who would be willing to go with me to my car to check for snakes.

I was on my last dance when yet another man cut in. I started to beg off, but then the song changed and the moment passed. This would be my final dance, I decided, and then I would definitely call it a night.

The music moved into a familiar tune, and soon I realized that it was my song with Tom, the song we considered "ours." My heart literally ached for him, and I wondered briefly if I should drive straight to the New Orleans airport and catch the next plane to D.C. I smiled to myself, picturing how absurd I would look getting on an airplane in a formal gown.

"Is something funny?" my dance partner asked. "You're smiling."

I started to reply, but then my breath caught in my throat.

The man wearing the mask in front of me, the man who was leading me so skillfully around the room in a dance, was *Tom!*

"Shhh," he whispered. "Don't let anyone else know, Callie. Let's just dance our way to the exit."

We did just that, and I don't think I could have spoken at that moment even if I had wanted to. At the edge of the dance floor we turned and walked to the door, stepping outside past the smokers and toward a gazebo around the corner. The pathway was lighted, and as we went, a surreal sort of quiet came over us.

"You know," he said softly, taking my hand in his, "I was sure you wouldn't go home today. So I figured the only way to keep you safe was to come here and protect you myself."

"For the rest of our lives," I finally managed to say, "are you always going to keep showing up and surprising me?"

We reached the gazebo and stepped inside. Pulling off our masks, we moved into a long, fierce hug. Tom was here! He was with me! For the first time in days, I felt complete.

There was a bench along the interior wall, so we sat, side by side, hands clasped, fingers entwined. I had so much to tell him, but before I could even begin, he spoke.

"Callie, I don't know what you've managed to find out about my involvement with Bryan's death, but I can't stand this anymore. I'm here to make a plea for our relationship, for us, regardless of whatever secrets still remain."

"I don't know if any secrets do remain," I said. "Let me tell you what I've learned."

There, to the gentle accompaniment of chirping crickets and music playing softly in the distance, I told him everything I had found out about that fateful day when Bryan was killed. One by one, I went down the list, revealing what I knew and how I felt about it. I said that as far as I was aware, the only mystery that still remained was the nature of the national crisis that had brought them to that vacation house in the first place.

"But I can live without knowing that," I said. "Just tell me, Tom, is everything else all there was?"

"Yes, Callie, but isn't that enough?"

"Oh, Tom, there is absolutely nothing there that I cannot forgive."

"Callie, do you understand what you're saying? *I'm* the one who got James out of prison. *I'm* the one who insisted he had to be there, even though he was a flight risk, even though the NSA was convinced he still had an accomplice on the outside. I took full responsibility for him, and then *I'm* the one who dropped that responsibility and left town. If not for me, it never would've happened."

I reached up and touched his cheek, his jaw strong and handsome in the moonlight. His eyes were filled with guilt and pain.

"I forgive you, Tom. For everything. I love you."

He let out a soft moan and wrapped his arms around me, pulling me so tightly against him that I could hardly breathe. In his muscles, I could feel four years' worth of self-judgement simply melt away. There was no longer any need for regret. There was no longer any need for guilt.

"Just one soul hoping for ultimate absolution," he said, his lips against my hair. "That's what I've been ever since it happened."

I nodded. Eli had told me the same thing earlier.

As we sat there together in the darkness, it clicked for me.

J.O.S.H.U.A.

The J.O.S.H.U.A. Foundation.

Just One Soul Hoping for Ultimate Absolution.

My heart nearly breaking for the sake of his past pain, I put my hands on either side of his face.

"J.O.S.H.U.A.," I whispered, looking into his eyes. "I understand."

I kissed him then, a sweet, long kiss that seemed to go on forever. It was a kiss of love.

It was my kiss of forgiveness.

# Fifty-One

Though Tom didn't really want to speak with anyone else or let them know he was there, I couldn't leave without saying goodbye to Veronica, not to mention Beth and Irene. So while he waited just outside the door, I went into the ballroom and sought out all three of them and told them goodbye. My words met with mild protestations, but I said that I had had a long day and that I wanted to make the drive back to New Orleans before I got too sleepy.

I found Tom outside where I had left him, though now he was on his cell phone, and it sounded as though he was touching base with the NSA. As I waited for him to conclude the call, I peered back at the festivities inside. Looking through the window was like looking at a photograph, and I watched as Veronica walked to her table and sat. She pulled off her mask and then tucked her hand in Phillip's elbow, and for a moment her pose reminded me of one of the photos in her album, the one with her at a European coffee shop, hanging onto the arm of a rock star.

I hadn't remembered who the rock star was, but now as I looked at her, her eyes shining, her expression blank, my heart suddenly started pounding. As soon as Tom got off the phone, I grabbed his arm and told him we needed to get to my car.

"What's the matter?"

"I have to check something."

Together, we made our way through the main house and out the front door. I led him to my car and pulled out my laptop. I opened it right there, powered it up, and went to the folder where I had saved the downloads of the news reports about the original sale of the encryption program to terrorists. I pulled up the page that showed the photos of the six members of the al-Sharif terrorist cell. There on the bottom row, left column, was the same man I had seen in a photo with Veronica. Now I knew why he had looked familiar: It wasn't because he was a celebrity; it was because he was one of the terrorists!

"I looked in Veronica's photo album," I said to Tom breathlessly, "from when she lived in Europe. She has a photograph of herself sitting at a restaurant with this man!"

He opened his mouth to reply, but before he could say a word, we both heard a noise from the parking lot. It sounded like a woman singing, and we turned to see Armand's aunt weaving her way down the rows of cars.

"Miz Velette?" Tom asked, stepping toward her. "What's the matter?"

She looked at us, bleary eyed, and I saw that in her hand was a set of car keys.

"Goin' home," she said. "My feet hurt."

"You driving?" Tom asked. "What about Armand?"

"He's got his pickup truck. Besides, he's chatting up some little tootsie inside." She seemed to locate her car and tried unsuccessfully to put the key in the lock.

"Listen, you can't be driving in this condition," Tom said. "We'll take you home."

"What about my car?" she slurred.

"Your house isn't that far up the road. We'll come back and find Armand and give him the keys. He can drive it home later."

She considered his proposal and then finally turned and focused in on him.

"Tom?" she asked, squinting at him. "Tom Bennett?"

"Yes, ma'am, it's me. I'm gonna run you home, okay?"

"Okay. How you been, *cher?*"

"Just fine, thanks."

While I stood there with her, Tom put my computer in the car, and then he jogged down to the other end of the row and retrieved his vehicle.

"Here we go," he said a minute later as he pulled his rental car to a stop in front of us. I helped Ton Ton into the backseat, where she promptly passed out. I could only hope she wouldn't end up being sick on the clean carpet.

Tom pulled out onto the highway, the twin headbeams of his vehicle cutting a bright swath through a dark night. He knew the way to Ton Ton's house, and as she snored from the back, we spoke softly in the front.

"That information you just gave me," he said, obviously referring to Veronica and her connection with the terrorist, "was already a known factor."

"A known factor? Known by whom?"

"By all of us." He glanced back at the sleeping woman and lowered his voice further. "When the arrest was made in the first crime," he said, meaning when James Sparks was caught selling the encryption program to terrorists, "Veronica immediately came forward. There was no intentional collusion on her part. She just unfortunately talked about things she shouldn't have to the wrong people."

"I don't understand."

"At the time she left me and went off to Europe, my company was still up and running, though it was getting near the end. She made friends over there and talked about the frustrations of this 'exciting encryption program' that might never see the light of day, one that her friends had developed over in the U.S. Soon, this guy, Habib, got word, and he started cozying up to her to get more information. She didn't know he was a terrorist; she just thought he was a friend.

Within a few weeks, he had names, location, personality descriptions, everything. He came to America and sought out James Sparks, the one they thought was most likely to be bought."

"Loose lips sink ships," I said.

"Veronica had a hard time of it. She was fully investigated and her life was turned upside down. I'm ashamed to admit it, but the only one of us who was still willing even to talk to her when all was said and done was Phillip. He had always loved her, you know, and I think he believed in her when the rest of us still had our doubts."

"Do you have doubts now?"

"Absolutely none. I've seen the transcripts and studied the evidence. She was used, yes, but it wasn't intentional. Still, she carries a lot of guilt around. It doesn't surprise me that, like me, she ended up being involved in the nonprofit sector. It's a way to give back, you know. To make amends."

Tom put on his blinker and turned at the deserted strawberry stand.

"So who does that leave, Tom? Who was Sparks' accomplice in all of this?"

"Callie, I just keep thinking that the key lies with whoever could've reconstructed that encryption program. When we disbanded the company, I saw that all copies of the program were destroyed except one, except mine. I never did quite comprehend how Sparks was able to rebuild it. It is only in the last few days that I have started thinking in terms of the program itself. I think Sparks didn't want an accomplice, but he had no choice. He must've somehow been able to merge the fragments of the program that he had with another member's fragments, building it back together into one complete whole. If that were the case, then Phillip is ruled out as a suspect. He was a hardware guy, not a programmer."

"So that leaves Armand," I whispered. "Or Beth."

We pulled into the driveway of Ton Ton's house, and Tom left the motor running as we got out. Immediately, the dogs at Armand's started barking, but I could see in the dim porch light that they were tied up safely to a tree.

I turned my attention to Ton Ton. The woman was dead weight, and even though she was wiry and petite, getting her out of the car wasn't going to be easy.

"This poor soul," I said, struggling to pull her up into a sitting position by her hands. Her long black gloves slipped off, so I set them down and tried again. "I think she needs to find a good AA program. Do you know she has a big old whiskey still in her backyard?"

Tom opened the other door to try from that side. He put both hands under her arms, and pulled. As he did, I let go of her hands. They flopped down, lifeless, against her simple gray dress, and in the light of the car I couldn't help thinking how oddly red they were. The palms were inflamed and angry, as if covered in a rash.

Or contact dermatitis.

I stood up straight and looked at Tom, my eyes wide. He was holding her up and trying to lift her so that he could carry her.

All at once I had a disturbing thought. Her hands. The still. What if it wasn't being used to make alcohol?

What if it was being used to distill castor beans into ricin?

Suddenly, we were blinded by the lights of a truck racing into the driveway. As it screeched to a stop, the beams trained directly on us, Ton Ton stood up straight, pulled herself loose from the surprised Tom, and deftly stepped away. Before we knew what had happened, she had reached down toward her ankle and whipped out a knife. She held it up, ready to strike.

"No, Ton Ton, what are you doing?" Armand said as he climbed from the truck. "Put it away!"

The dogs went crazy next door, barking wildly, straining against their ropes to get free. My heart pounded. I forced myself to focus.

"They're going to ruin everything," she said to Armand. "Can't you see that? All your work, all you've accomplished—they're going to take that away from you."

Armand looked at us desperately, and in his face I saw clearly fear, then guilt, then something like resignation.

"I always had a feeling there might come a time..." he began and then stopped and shook his head.

"What, Armand?" Tom asked.

"The encryption program. I knew I couldn't milk it forever. But I thought at least I would be able to finish what I started."

Tom shook his head sadly. "Armand, you're the one?" he asked, sounding genuinely wounded. "You were James' accomplice? But why?"

"James needed my piece of the puzzle, so I gave it to him. I didn't know he was gonna get me on tape incriminating myself. And I sure didn't know he was gonna turn around and sell the program to terrorists."

"What did you *think* he was going to do with it?" Tom demanded.

"What I've done with it since then," Armand replied. "Sell it to businesses. Donate it to government institutions. I still have the keys, you see. Everyone thinks their encryption is secure, and it is. Except from me. I can read anything I want to."

My mind raced, wondering how I could have read this man so wrong. Unlike the greedy Sparks, money seemed the last thing Armand was interested in. I thought about that, and then suddenly understanding filled my brain.

"Your work with the swamps," I said to Armand. "With the legislature. That's your driving force."

"Listen, *cher*, the only way to fight dirty politics is with something even dirtier. Between the money I make selling company information and the secrets I learn spying on government communications, I've been able to do a lot toward protecting my bayou. To me, that's all that matters."

I looked at Ton Ton, who still stood at the ready, the knife glinting in the darkness. I didn't even have to ask her motivations. I felt sure she was willing to do whatever she could to protect Armand—including using her knowledge of swamp medicine to whip up a deadly poison of ricin and inject it into an inhaler.

"Do you know that your aunt tried to kill James Sparks?" I said.

Armand looked at Ton Ton in despair.

"No," he said.

"I told you he couldn't be trusted," she said. "I told you the day would come when we would have to use Watts for more than just delivering messages."

"But to kill him?"

"Armand," Ton Ton said, "you honored your part of the agreement. James doesn't understand that what you're doing is more important than money."

"What agreement?" asked Tom.

Armand hesitated and then exhaled slowly.

"When James got caught on film by the FBI, selling to the terrorists," Armand explained, "he was gonna turn me in, but I gave him a better alternative. I told him that if he kept silent about my involvement, I would be able to make things happen on the outside, so that by the time he got out of prison, there would be some money waiting for him. Big money. We set up a numbered bank account overseas, and half of all my profits goes in there for him. He's worth a couple million dollars by now."

"Money he doesn't deserve," Ton Ton said. "James was supposed to keep his mouth shut. Then *she* shows up, and before you know it, he thinks he can dictate to us, thinks he can use *her* to get more money out of us. It makes me sick. I just did what I had to do. I'm still doing what I have to do."

Tom and I looked at each other, eyes wide. My biggest fear was that he might try and do something brave so that I could escape. I had to keep that from happening, had to keep them talking until I could figure a way out of this where no one would get hurt.

"So when James was in that house in Virginia four years ago," I asked Armand, "the phone call he needed to make was to you?"

"Yeah, *cher*. I had made some modifications to the program. I didn't know that he would need to use the program himself or I wouldn't have done it. As it is, once he had that boating accident, everything changed. When he found himself facing sixteen years, he started upping the ante with me."

"James is always wanting money, more money, all the time," Ton Ton added. "He doesn't understand there are more important things going on here. The swamp is disappearing out from under our feet!"

"So let me ask you a question, Armand," I said. "The day we met, outside of Family HEARTS, when I was mugged—"

"You were mugged?" Tom asked.

Armand looked embarrassed.

"Yeah, that was Ton Ton's idea. I paid some kid twenty bucks to steal your purse and let me catch him. I needed a way to get you to trust me. I had to get close to you, to see what you knew."

"She knows plenty," Ton Ton said. "She's got to go. So does he."

She crouched a bit, focused in on Tom, ready to pounce with the knife. My pulse surged.

"Ton Ton, *you* put that kingsnake in my car."

"That wasn't no kingsnake, *cher*," she said. "That was a canebrake. If it'd bit you, you'd be dead."

"What did you do?" Armand demanded of his aunt.

"I drove up to the hotel yesterday and put a snake in Callie's car. I thought she woulda been bitten and killed—and no one would ever have known it wasn't an accident."

I shuddered, realizing that the snake had been in the car with me all the way to Beth's house and halfway back again before it showed itself.

"Ton Ton," Armand said. "Put down the knife."

Without waiting for her reply, he walked back to his truck and reached inside. When he reemerged, he was holding a shotgun. I thought he was going to point it at her, but instead he trained it on us.

"Go ahead, Ton Ton," he said sadly, still looking at us. "Put your knife down. I don't want you getting hurt."

"Armand?" Tom said, taking a step back. "You're my friend."

Armand shrugged.

"But she's family," he said simply. "And in a way, she's right. Our fight for the swamp must go on, whatever the cost. Think of it like a war. The two of you will just be casualties of war."

Much to my amazement, as we stood there under the barrel of Armand's gun, he and his aunt debated about the most logical way for Tom and me to die. They even talked about using the ricin, but Ton Ton said that sort of death wasn't fast enough.

"They've got to disappear," she said. "Now. Tonight. Just shoot 'em and we'll sink their bodies out in the swamp."

My mind raced to think of some way out.

"Too risky getting them out there," he said. "I've got a better idea."

With the gun he motioned for us to start walking. Quickly, I realized where he was leading us.

"Not the alligator pit," I whispered.

"Look at it this way," Armand said as we walked. "At least you won't be eaten alive. Alligators like their food rotted. They'll just drown you and then pin your body up under a log. In a few days, when you start to decompose, that's when they'll finish you off."

"Thanks, Armand. That comes as a great comfort to me."

I had to act, whether it got me shot or not. As we walked across Armand's lawn to get to the trail that would lead to the pit, I knew I had one good option. I could only hope that Tom would be fast enough to react. Glancing at the upside-down pirogue on the sawhorses, I thought I could see that a few tools were still scattered across the top as they had been the other day. Without hesitating, I took a chance at what I knew was my only choice. Turning, I ran and dove for those tools, grabbing a hatchet and then hitting the ground and rolling toward the dogs, counting on the fact that he wouldn't risk shooting toward them. By the time I held the hatchet up over my head and looked up at Armand, he had his arm gripped around Tom's neck, the rifle pointed awkwardly at Tom's head.

"Put it down, Callie," Armand said. "What do you think you can do, throw it all the way over here?"

"No," I said, trying to catch my breath. "I guess not."

As hard as I could, I slammed the hatchet toward the ground, cutting the rope that kept the dogs bound to the tree. In a flash, they were free, running to Armand and jumping up against him.

"Run, Tom!" I screamed. "Run!"

From the corner of my eye, as I took off myself, I could see Tom also break free and run. We both ran under the house and into the backyard, not even stopping when we reached the water.

Together, we untied the pirogue that was there at the dock, jumped in, and pushed out. We couldn't get it to go fast enough, though, and soon we were being peppered with gunfire. A bullet hit the back of the boat, and it quickly began to fill with water.

"Get out and run," I said to Tom. "It's not deep here."

We leaped into the water and tried to run, our feet sucked deeply into the mud.

"Forget running. We'll have to swim," Tom cried.

Together we did what we could, half swimming, half running, until the bottom dropped out and we were in open water.

"He's coming," Tom said, pointing to a light near Armand's dock.

I could hear a boat motor quickly advancing toward us.

"We'll have to go under," I whispered. "Stay down as long as you can and don't let out any bubbles!"

Without waiting for a reply, I sucked in a deep breath and did a surface dive, cringing as my face eventually touched the mud of the swampy bottom. Though I hated feeling around down there, I was able to dig out a root, which I held on to tightly to keep myself at the bottom. With my other hand, I grabbed at Tom's arm and pulled it to the root as well, and then I struggled to pin my full skirt against my legs.

I didn't want to open my eyes in the filthy water, but I had to look up. As I did, all I could see was a spotlight moving across the surface, about eight feet up. The light swept on ahead, and then the loud motor passed directly over us. The boat was moving slowly, the light sweeping side to side. I was desperately in need of air, and once it was about 20 feet ahead of us, I patted Tom on the shoulder and then let go of the root to shoot toward the surface.

Careful not to make too much noise, I found myself gasping for air nevertheless. Tom surfaced beside me and did the same.

"Come on now, Callie," Armand was saying loudly from the boat, calling out into the darkness. "You know you can't get outta here alive. You'll get bit by a snake, eaten by an alligator, no telling what."

I looked at Tom, but neither of us could think of what to do next. With Ton Ton standing on the dock, holding onto a gun and shining her own light out on the water, the only choice was to get into the waterway, past Armand.

"Maybe we can overpower him in the boat," Tom whispered.

"He's got that rifle," I said.

"What about the neighbors?"

I glanced at the other houses on the peninsula, where lights were starting to come on from all the noise.

"They're his family," I said. "Which means they're probably going to believe whatever he tells them. I think we're out of luck there."

Suddenly, the spotlight on the boat started sweeping toward us. Clutching hands, we ducked under the water, staying down until it had swept past. The whine of the boat engine changed, and I realized it was turning around to head back this way again.

After a quick gasp of air from the surface, we dove back down again, clutching in the mud for the root. I couldn't find anything to hold on to, but my long gown was now so weighted down, it was almost like wearing a weight belt. I could only hope Tom's tuxedo and shoes were serving the same purpose.

As soon as the boat passed by, the shrill roar of the spinning blades overhead, I tugged on Tom's arm, pulling him forward. I knew that Armand would go up and down this same little channel all night, if need be, to find us. We needed to seize the opportunity to slip away while we could.

Surfacing carefully for air and to get our bearings, we worked our way up the channel to where it met with a larger waterway. It wouldn't be long before Armand came out that far and started looking for us there, so I knew we needed to hurry.

"There's dry land," Tom whispered, pointing to a far bank. "We might do better there, on foot."

I shook my head.

"Armand's a tracker," I said. "He would find our trail. We've got to stay in the water for as long as possible."

Once we rounded the bend, at least we were out of the possible line of sight from the peninsula and its channel. We started swimming on top of the water rather than under, though with all of the muck and mire, it was slow going.

Ahead, I spotted a dark shape in the water. Afraid that it was an alligator, I wanted to give it a wide berth. On the other hand, if it were a log, it might save us. I pointed it out to Tom and he stared hard in the darkness, convinced in the end that it was a log.

We inched our way closer until we were sure, then we swam to it and grabbed hold. At his insistence I pulled myself onto the log and straddled it, while he stayed in the water and hung onto the end. The balance was tricky, and after a moment I rolled right off.

We tried different variations of the same, but it was no use.

"We need two logs," I said. "Bound together. That would work."

Holding on the one log we already had, we paddled and kicked into the darkness, farther and farther from the sounds and lights back near Armand's. I didn't even want to think about being hopelessly lost in the swamps—but the unknown elements there were still a safer bet than the gun that waited for us closer to shore.

We paddled toward a stand of trees out in the water, and I recognized them as the dead trunks Armand had shown me on my tour. Cringing at the thought of snakes or spiders making their homes among the wood, we pressed at each of the trees until Tom identified a slim one that was loose and ready to snap. Hoping it wouldn't make too much noise, we worked together to pull it down. As it fell into the water, it pulled a second tiny tree with it. They hit the water, sank, and then sprang back up and floated there.

"Do you think he heard that?" I asked.

"We'll know in a minute," Tom replied.

Luckily, the sound of Armand's boat motor did not seem to be coming any closer. As quickly as we could, Tom and I lashed the three logs together. We used his cummerbund for the front of the raft, and strips of material torn from my skirt for the middle and back.

"I bet Veronica's sister will never loan me a dress again," I muttered as I ripped off another piece.

But our miniscule raft worked. We were able to climb aboard and kneel there, me in front and him in back, using sticks to pole ourselves forward. From what I could recall, if we could pass through a narrow, shallow area lined with millet grass nearby, then we would end up in the wide oil passage canal. There wasn't much current where we were now, but I had a feeling if we could get to that canal, we would be quickly carried out with the tide.

By the time we finally made it, we could hear several motor boats on the water behind us. Armand must have roused his family members to help in his pursuit. For a brief moment, I hoped that maybe these were cops or NSA agents come to rescue us. But then I could hear the unique *patois* of Cajun French being shouted back and forth, and I knew we were out of luck.

Still, they hadn't seemed to spot us yet. As we poled through the millet, we finally broke free to the other side. Sure enough, we were at the canal.

We gave it one last big heave and then pulled our sticks out of the water and collapsed into each other, letting the strong current grab hold of us and do its work. I wasn't sure where we were going to end up, but at least we would get there fast.

I opened my eyes and looked up at the brilliant, starry sky, grateful that the commotion of the Cajuns was well behind us. Tom said a prayer softly aloud for our safety, and then we simply floated into the night, holding onto each other as we went.

# Fifty-Two

The mosquitoes were the worst part. As the minutes turned into hours, it felt as though we were being eaten alive. The bugs seemed to abate somewhat with the daylight, but then, as the sun crept higher in the sky and the morning turned humid and hot, we both began to grow unbearably thirsty. All I could think about was how badly I wanted to take a scoop of water and simply drink it. Tom and I had talked about it, though, and we knew that would be too risky. Surely somehow, soon, we would run across some sign of civilization and be saved.

In truth, floating down a wide Louisiana canal on a hastily made impromptu raft could have been worse. At least we were together. At least the raft had held up. At least neither one of us had been injured beyond some minor scrapes and bruises. As we floated, we talked about what we would do as soon as we managed to get out of there. We didn't talk about the danger of being swept past all land and out into the Gulf of Mexico. Surely, the mouth of this canal would have enough boat traffic that someone would spot us and that wouldn't happen.

Several times we considered paddling to the bank and trying to make our way out of the swamp on foot. But there were no signs of civilization anywhere along here. We both agreed we were probably better off staying in the water for now.

In the early morning hours, we spotted almost all of the wildlife that I had missed on my tour with Armand. We saw a small brown bear and all kinds of mammals and plenty of snakes and birds and deer. Finally, as we rounded a bend, a loud crashing sound from the shore startled us, and we looked up to see a wild boar running after a scampering nutria.

Tom put his hands on my shoulders, gently kneading the muscles, and then he wrapped his arms around me from behind and simply held me. I closed my eyes, thinking how very much I loved him, how he was all I really needed in this world.

"Hey, Callie?" he said gently.

"Yes?"

"I have a question for you."

"Okay."

"Maybe it's not the right time. I don't have a ring with me. And I'm sure I've looked better. But I hope you don't mind if I ask it anyway."

I sat up and turned so that I could see his face.

"Ask," I whispered, my pulse surging.

"Callie," he said, looking me deeply in the eyes. "When we get out of this mess, will you marry me?"

I put a hand to my mouth. My mind, my heart, my soul were so full that for a moment, I couldn't even speak.

"Oh, Tom," I said finally, tears of joy filling my eyes. I thought about all we had been through and all that lay ahead of us, and the only thing I knew for certain was that I wanted to spend the rest of my life with this man.

Before I could say yes, though, his eyes suddenly widened, and he reached up, grabbed my shoulders, and threw me off the raft and into the water.

"Watch out!" he screamed, jumping in after me.

I turned to look behind me and saw a giant barge nearly upon us. The massive vessel was so huge that all we could do was swim toward the side of the canal as quickly as possible. The barge's passage was nearly silent except for the dull thud of the engines, and though we screamed as we swam, no one seemed to hear us.

*At least Tom made it,* I thought as I slipped under, pulled backward by the boat's strong current. Almost as if in slow motion, I knew what would happen now. I would be sucked into the engine and cut into a million pieces.

Then I felt Tom's hand, tugging mine, pulling me, fighting the current. I kicked as hard as I could along with him, out of air but still underwater. He pulled me farther, and then suddenly the sucking current released me, and I burst through to the surface. With great gasps I caught my breath and found my footing and allowed Tom to half drag me to safety on the shore. We collapsed there in swampy mud, breathing heavily, the waves of the ship's wake splashing up to our chins.

Once it had subsided, we could see our raft, splintered into six different pieces out on the water. I looked at it and then looked at Tom, knowing he had just saved my life. I threw my arms around him, both of us silent and shivering from the horror that had just nearly overtaken us. When I finally found my voice, it was to thank him for pulling me to safety.

"Are you folks okay?"

We turned to see a grizzled old man, looking down at us from the solid ground of the shore. He wore hip waders and carried a big fishing pole in one hand and a tackle box in the other.

"I heard screaming," he added, looking at us and our odd garb warily. "Did y'all fall off that barge?"

"We need some help," Tom said as we stood shakily and stepped up onto the bank. "Is there any way you could get us to a telephone?"

"Ain't got no phone lines out this far," the man replied. Tom and I looked at each other in despair until the man added, "Would my two-way satellite radio do?"

# Fifty-Three

In the end, the NSA sent a helicopter down to get us. They brought us to a hospital in New Orleans, where we were both treated for mild dehydration and released. After taking showers and putting on some borrowed scrubs, we were brought to the NSA office. They assured us that they were retreiving our vehicles and that they would send an agent for some clothes of our own. After that, one of the agents updated us on all that had happened during the night.

Armand and his aunt were now in jail, arrested on a number of charges, not the least of which was the attempted murder of the two of us. Apparently, it was thanks to Veronica and Phillip that things came together as they did. When all was said and done and the ball was over, only two cars had remained in the parking area at Grande Terre last night: mine and Ton Ton's. Veronica had spotted Tom incognito at the ball, so she had a feeling I had left with him. But she didn't understand why Ton Ton's car was still there, so they had made an obligatory phone call to the local police, just to have them go over to Ton Ton's and make sure all was well. Knowing the woman's history of overzealous imbibing, they were afraid she might have gotten drunk at the ball and tried to walk home.

Of course, by the time the police arrived out on the little peninsula, the swamp was full of Cajuns in boats brandishing shotguns. Chaos had ensued, but the NSA caught wind of it over the police radio and quickly stepped in and took over. They seized Armand and his aunt, but the agents had had to wait until daylight to begin conducting a swamp search for us from the air. Now they realized that they hadn't even been looking in the area where we finally turned up. No one could believe we had managed to float that far.

This morning, learning about all that had happened here, James Sparks had wrangled another plea bargain that involved giving up the proof he held on Armand. Much to everyone's surprise, the audiotape was in a waterproof lockbox at the bottom of Armand's alligator pit! Years before, during the FBI investigation, Sparks had needed a secure hiding place where he knew no human would ever find it, and though his original intention was to bury it somewhere out in the swamps, he got a last-minute inspiration to toss it into the pit instead. All this time Armand had been blackmailed by Sparks' proof, never knowing that that proof was right there under his nose, on his own property.

Tom and I were each fully debriefed on our own, and when my session was over I was led into a room where the clothes I had requested from the hotel were waiting for me. I got dressed and returned to the hallway, where I was reunited with Tom. He looked much better, and he said that the NSA had retrieved both of our cars and they were parked outside. An agent asked us to wait in a pair of chairs. Exhausted, we simply sat there, side by side, with our eyes closed.

Soon, though, the mood in the building seemed to change. People were walking more quickly, whispering among themselves. A sort of hushed excitement radiated through the air.

"I wonder what's going on?" I whispered.

"I think there's one more person they want us to see," Tom replied cryptically.

I was about to respond when Agent Devlin showed up to escort us downstairs and out to a waiting car. Tom seemed quietly confident, so I followed his lead and got inside without asking for an explanation.

We drove onto Interstate 10, toward Slidell, but before crossing the lake we got off again and turned at a sign that indicated the New Orleans Lakefront Airport. As we drew closer, we came upon a roadblock, where Devlin pulled the vehicle to a stop, showed some ID, and was allowed to pass through. There were no other cars on the street as we made our way into the airport, which also seemed deserted.

"It's so small," I whispered to Tom.

"This is just the Lakefront Airport," he replied. "New Orleans International is on the other side of town."

"Oh."

We drove right onto the tarmac and came around a building, and there in front of us was a sight I had never expected to see in my lifetime, at least not up close: Air Force One.

The airplane of the president.

I looked at Tom, who had a slight smile on his lips.

"What's going on?" I asked as we pulled to a stop.

"From what I understand," he replied, "the president decided to make a little stopover here on his way to Mexico for a summit meeting."

The doors were opened for us and we climbed out. Devlin gestured toward the airplane stairs, and so up we went. My heart pounded as I mounted them, and at the top of the steps another man greeted us and then led us to a room down a narrow hallway. We stepped inside and the door shut behind us. There, sitting at the end of a long table, was the president of the United States of America.

"Tom!" he said, rising to greet us. He stepped forward to shake Tom's hand and then turned his attention to me. "And you must be Callie Webber," he added, shaking my hand as well, and then he laughed. "From the look on your face, I guess you could say you're a tad surprised to find yourself here."

I cleared my throat and swallowed hard.

"Yes, sir," I finally uttered.

"How are you?" Tom asked stiffly.

"Can't complain," the president replied. "Why don't we have a seat?"

He gestured toward a grouping of chairs at the end of the room. Feeling as though I were in some surreal otherworld, I walked toward the chairs and sat, Tom on my left, the president at an angle to my right.

"We don't have a lot of time," the president said, "so I guess I'd better cut to the chase. I have something to tell you, Tom, and I decided to bring Callie—may I call you Callie?"

"Of course."

"I decided to bring Callie in on this as well. You may be bound by a confidentiality agreement, Tom, but I'm free to speak about this matter as I deem necessary."

I swallowed hard, wondering if I still looked as dumbfounded as I felt.

"You might like to know, Callie, that a few weeks ago, young Tom here came to me and asked for special permission to amend his confidentiality agreement with the NSA. Apparently, he wanted you to know all the facts surrounding that terrible day your husband was killed."

I nodded. Tom had told me he had "pulled every string" that he could and "exhausted every option" in his attempt to get around that agreement. Now I understood that he hadn't been exaggerating. In his pursuit for permission, he had appealed to the highest office in the nation.

"At the time," the president continued, "I was not able to grant that request. From what I understand, when he told you that his request had been denied, you simply conducted an investigation on your own and uncovered most of those facts anyway."

"That's true."

"Quite impressive, especially since you also helped put a few more criminals in jail and bring closure to a long-outstanding FBI investigation. Good job."

"Thank you, sir."

"We have several agencies that could use your type of skills, by the way," he added. "CIA, FBI, just name it. If you ever want to do some consulting…"

I glanced at Tom, who was grinning at me proudly.

"Thank you, sir," I said, turning back to the president. "I'll keep that in mind."

"Well, then, let's move on. Tom, there is one bit of information that even you never had, and I think the time has come to fill you in on it. This is FYEO and will never leave this room. Do you agree?"

"FYEO?" I asked.

"For Your Ears Only," Tom told me. "Yes, I agree."

The president turned his gaze to me.

"I agree also, sir. My lips are sealed."

"Good," the president said, settling back in his chair. "Now, Tom, I understand that you feel fully responsible for the death of Callie's husband, but I want you to know that that isn't the case. The fault does not lie with you."

Tom shifted in his seat.

"I'm afraid I don't understand," Tom said.

"Son, when you were trying to crack that code four years ago, you said that you needed James Sparks' help in order to do it. Through a lot of maneuvering, you managed to get him released into your custody at that house. He subsequently made a run for it and ended up killing an innocent man. The truth is, there was more going on there than even you knew about. Now that his accomplice has been caught, you can know the whole truth."

"Sir?"

"All along, the FBI was aware that Sparks had an accomplice when he sold your code to the terrorists—they just didn't know who the accomplice was. When arrangements were made for Sparks to go to that house, the FBI had great hopes that Sparks might seize the opportunity to contact that accomplice. We weren't sure how or when he would make that attempt, but you were all under full surveillance. Agents were stationed at several nearby houses as well as all along that river. We told you that security was light because Sparks was not assumed to be a flight risk. In truth, we knew he would try to slip away for that call. We wanted him to."

I looked at Tom, whose face was pale.

"Think about it," the president continued. "One guard per shift—and one of them prone to falling asleep? The keys to the cars and the boat, right there on the kitchen counter, accessible? We even had the guards talk about 'the nearest pay phone' being at the Docksider Grill. That phone was tapped and ready. The one thing that none of us expected was that Sparks would accidentally kill a man on his way there."

Tom stiffened next to me, and I could only imagine the range of emotions that was coursing through his veins. Shock. Confusion. Anger. I knew, as I had recently gone through all of them myself. I wanted to reach out and take his hand, but I wasn't sure if that would be appropriate in the presence of the president.

"Callie," the president said, turning to me. "You cannot know how sorry I am about the way things turned out, but you have to know that *none* of it was Tom's fault."

This time, I did reach out and take Tom's hand, squeezing it.

"I forgave him anyway," I said. "But thank you for telling us, sir. I'm sure that is a huge burden off Tom's shoulders."

The president leaned back in his chair, crossing one leg over the other.

"You know," he said to both of us, "Harry Truman used to keep a little sign on his desk. It said 'The Buck Stops Here.' This is why I brought the two of you here today. The responsibility of Bryan Webber's death doesn't lie on your shoulders, Tom. As this nation's leader—and the one who ultimately approved the FBI's plan—it lies squarely on mine. Tom, Callie, truly, with regard to Bryan Webber's death, the buck stops *here*."

Tom remained quiet as we wrapped up our meeting. When the president stood and thanked us for coming, I steeled my nerve and seized the opportunity to ask the one question I knew would hover in the back of my mind for the rest of my life. *File it under nothing ventured, nothing gained,* I thought, and then I spoke.

"Mr. President," I said, "before we go, I have one more question, one more mystery about this whole thing that I have not been able to solve—and I doubt I ever will, unless I hear it straight from your lips."

The president nodded, looking amused.

"Well, go ahead," he said. "Ask me."

"My husband's death was a senseless accident. But it would help me enormously to understand the larger scope behind the whole sequence of events that caused it. Sir, what was the national crisis that brought Tom and Sparks to that house in the first place? Why did they so desperately need to crack that code?"

The president shook his head.

"I'm sorry, I—"

"Don't you think you owe her that?" Tom said suddenly. Then he added, more respectfully, "Don't you think you owe it to me to tell her?"

The man looked at Tom, seemed to consider our request, and then finally exhaled.

"Sit back down," he said, and so we did. "Now this is *really* FYEO."

"Yes, sir," I whispered, heart pounding.

"Callie, about four and a half years ago," he said, "our intelligence forces uncovered some disturbing information. A certain T-Seven country had begun vaccinating their soldiers for smallpox. You can imagine the implications."

"Sir?"

"Smallpox has been eradicated off the face of the earth," he said. "In fact, the virus is safely contained under maximum security in only two places: We have it at the CDC in Atlanta, and the Russians have it at their similar facility over there. But somehow, based on the information we were being given, this other country had gotten hold of it too. The fact that they were inoculating their soldiers made us very nervous indeed."

"I see."

"As it turned out, much of their communications were encrypted with the program designed by Tom and his colleagues.

There came a point where we knew we had to break that encryption if we were to learn the nature of their plans. Tom was brought in, and when he couldn't break the code alone, James Sparks was rounded up as well. Eventually, they did break that code and we were able to stop the unimaginable from happening."

I sat back in my chair, stunned. Though I knew Tom's work with the NSA was important, I had never understood the situation to be of quite this magnitude.

"You know," the president said, "we don't even give smallpox vaccinations in this country anymore. If this enemy of our nation had managed to introduce the virus into the general population, the results would've been devastating. From what our scientists tell me, one man with this virus can infect another thirty people before he even knows he has it. And it would increase exponentially from there. Just catastrophic."

"Wow."

"In a way, Callie," the president continued, "your husband was an unfortunate casualty in our fight against terrorism. Tom's efforts helped save the world, even though no one outside of those directly involved—and now you, of course—can ever know."

I looked at Tom, who smiled at me humbly before dropping his gaze. He was already my hero.

Now I knew he was my country's unsung hero as well.

# Fifty-Four

After a final thanks and farewell to the president, Tom and I were delivered back to the NSA office and released. Our cars were there, and so we dropped mine at the hotel, got into Tom's car, and drove to his sister's house on the North Shore. He had called ahead, knowing that the story of Armand's arrest was all over the news and that they would be wanting a full explanation. On the way there, we constructed our story, a mix of truths, half-truths, and blatant omissions. Tom's family knew nothing of his real work, of the silent service he provided to his country. I understood now that with the NSA, you did what you had to do but kept it to yourself, all for the greater good.

I asked Tom about Beth's stock holdings, about how a woman with only a part-time job could be worth so much money. He explained that some of her early computer work, right out of college, had been for a few high tech start-up companies that paid heavily in options to make up for meager salaries. Fortunately for Beth, she had sensed the unstable nature of the dot com market and had cashed in before the crash, converting her holdings to more tangible, long-term investments.

"You bought her house for her, didn't you?" I asked.

"Yes," Tom said, "and I have supported her financially over the years so that she could continue to be a full-time mom even after her divorce. I wouldn't let her touch her stocks. That's for her future. I'm taking care of her present—at least until the girls are grown."

I reached over and slipped my hand into his, squeezing tightly.

"You're a good, good man," I said.

When we arrived to Beth's house, she and Irene and Veronica and Phillip were all waiting for us, confused and anxious. While the twins entertained little Tucker on the swing set out back, the adults sat in the living room and Tom laid out our modified version of things. If there seemed to be holes in our story, they didn't catch them, at least not at first. Finally, though, Beth looked at me and asked, straight out, what my connection was to all of this beyond my relationship with Tom.

I glanced at him and answered as honestly as I could. I said that a few years ago, when James was out of prison (not exactly a lie), he was staying in a vacation home in Virginia (true), and he went for a drive in a speed boat that he didn't know how to control. He ended up accidentally killing my husband, Bryan. I said that it wasn't until Tom and I began dating that I realized that this awful connection even existed between me and Tom and James. What I didn't add was that *Tom* knew of the connection all along—and that, in fact, it was the reason he created his foundation and hired me in the first place.

"It was difficult to understand at first," I said, "but now that all of the facts have come to light, we have decided to put it behind us. Beth, I hope this isn't something that will come between you and me either."

"That my ex-husband accidentally killed your husband?" she said, the shock evident on her face. "Callie, I'm so sorry. But I can move past it if you can."

I told her about my meeting with James' mother, Tilly, in Georgia and how the woman had cried over how badly she missed the twins. Beth got tears in her eyes as she understood that their estrangement was indeed her ex-husband's doing. She decided to contact Tilly as soon as possible and attempt to mend that relationship.

And that was basically how the conversation ended. Veronica was the most truthful when she sat back and said, "Well, I don't know about the rest of you, but as sad as I am about Armand, I'm also kind of relieved. The FBI's case always seemed so unfinished and incomplete. Now I think we finally have closure."

Everyone agreed, nodding. Then Leah burst into the house from the back door.

"Uncle Tommy!" she said, grabbing hold of his hand. "I want you to know something!"

He put his arm around her and gave her his full attention.

"What's that, honey?" he asked.

"Even though you didn't bring us any Barbies this time, we love you anyway." She smiled proudly at me, to show that she had learned her lesson well.

"Who says I didn't bring Barbies?" Tom asked. "Did you take a look in my trunk yet?"

She squealed and ran back outside to get Maddie, who also squealed. Tom took the twins out to the car, Phillip went out back to see after Tucker, and Beth and Veronica headed to the kitchen to start cooking up dinner for the whole clan. That left me and Irene standing in the living room together. She took an uneven step toward me and then gave me a long hug.

"You are a dear woman," she said, pulling back to wipe tears from her eyes. "I believe my son is one lucky man."

"Oh, no, ma'am," I replied. "I'm the fortunate one."

Veronica also must have felt quite blessed when, an hour later, Tom and I presented her with a check to Family HEARTS for one million dollars. As I gave my usual spiel, she and Phillip hugged each other, knowing that their biggest dreams for their charity could now become a reality.

There came a point, later in the evening, when we were all outside. Tom was manning steaks at the grill, the other adults were sitting around on the patio, chatting, and Leah and Tucker were digging in the sandbox. I was at the swing set, pushing Maddie. I was exhausted but happy, thinking that this was one of those golden moments I would love to be able to freeze and save for posterity. There was something so utterly domestic and normal about it. Tom and I could do with a lot more normalcy in our lives.

"Hey, Callie," he called to me across the yard. I looked over at him. "Hmm?"

"I just realized that I asked you something this morning, and you never gave me an answer."

My heart started pounding in relief. All day I had been afraid that his proposal was some eleventh-hour-if-we're-going-to-die-anyway-I-might-as-well-ask-you sort of thing. Now I stepped away from the swings as everyone stopped talking, their eyes suddenly on us.

"I'm sorry," I called back to him. "Could you repeat the question?"

Grinning, he put down the spatula and stepped around the grill, off the patio, and onto the grass, where he got down on one knee. From his pocket, he produced a small velvet box, which he opened to reveal a not-small-at-all diamond ring.

"Callie Webber," he said, "will you marry me?"

The children gasped.

"It's just like Prince Charming!" Maddie cried breathlessly.

I stepped forward, crossing the lawn until I was directly in front of him. I thought of all we had been through and all that was yet to come. Somehow, God had seen fit to bless me with true love twice in one lifetime. I didn't know what I had done to deserve it. I just knew that with every fiber of my being I wanted to be Tom's wife.

Tears filling my eyes, I reached down for his free hand and pulled him up onto his feet. Looking up at him, my heart was so full of emotion that I had trouble finding my voice.

"Yes," I said softly. Then I said it again, more loudly this time. "Yes!"

# Epilogue

"Are you ready, honey?"

I glanced up to see my father in the doorway, looking stiff and uncomfortable in his tuxedo. He tugged at his collar with one finger, his face bright red.

"You okay, Daddy?"

"Just nervous," he replied. "You know I don't like being up in front of people."

"Nervous, nothing," my mother said. "His sunburn's hurting."

"Tom told you to wear sunscreen," I chided him. "You should've known better."

Yesterday, to get the men out of our hair while we made the final preparations for the wedding, Tom had taken all of them deep-sea fishing in the Atlantic. They had come home with 36 tuna, one marlin, and several bright-red fishermen. Thank goodness, the groom wasn't one of them.

My mother lifted my hat from its stand, carefully placed it on my head, and bobby-pinned it into place. I had grown out my hair a bit for the wedding, and now it framed my face in soft waves, the perfect compliment to the hat. The whole suit looked perfect, in fact, a cream-colored silk couture Vera Wang with pearl-and-diamond buttons. Tom's gift to me.

Tom had given me a lot of gifts lately, including the biggest suprise of all: our very own mini yacht! Tonight, we would set sail for a two-week honeymoon through the Caribbean, after which we would settle into our new home in Maryland, about ten miles from NSA headquarters, where Tom was now based. I would continue my job with the foundation—at least until we started a family—only now it would be our money I was giving away instead of just Tom's.

Though we had decided to embrace suburbia, we were keeping my house on the Eastern Shore, where we hoped to spend many weekends. Between the two of us, we also owned a condo in California, a mountain cabin in North Carolina, and an apartment in downtown D.C.—not to mention numerous real estate holdings in Louisiana. I didn't think we would lack for places to visit any time soon.

Now, however, it was time to be married in my church's seaside prayer garden, in front of our dearest friends and relatives. Harriet was my maid of honor, and she rushed into the room to announce that there was something wrong with the musicians. Instead of an elegant orchestra playing classical music, they had launched into a jazzy blues version—complete with harmonica—of "Blessed Assurance."

"That's what you get when you marry a Louisiana boy," I said, smiling. "I let him pick the music."

I stood and turned to face Harriet and my parents. Almost instantly, my mother's eyes filled with tears, my father started clearing his throat, and Harriet let out a long, slow breath.

"Come on, guys," I said. "Do I look that bad?"

"On the contrary," Harriet said. "You look prettier than a butterfly on a daisy in a lily patch."

"I'll take that as a compliment."

My mother handed me my bouquet, and then the four of us left the church and strolled along the walkway to the prayer garden. It was a beautiful fall day, warm and sunny, the leaves just starting to turn. Our guests were seated in chairs with a full view of the water, and soon Pastor George would take his place under an ivy-covered trellis and pronounce Tom and me husband and wife.

For now, I stood behind a row of rose bushes, waiting for the song to end and the wedding to begin. Harriet also waited, but she kept peeking at the crowd through the bushes, pointing out people we knew. So many had come here today, and I was touched by their presence. I was especially happy to have Eli and Stella here. He had lost some weight since his gunshot wound in the spring, but otherwise he seemed none the worse for wear.

Tom's mother appeared from the other direction on Phillip's arm, also walking more smoothly than she had even several months ago. In the past few days, Tom's mother and my mother had become fast friends. Now they both marveled at each others' beautiful dresses and then turned their attentions to mine. Irene hugged me, and then she held out a small box.

"Here's your something old," she whispered, "It was my grandmother's. I want you to have it."

I opened the box to see a beautiful pearl bracelet. I thanked her and slipped it on my wrist, where it was the perfect accent to the buttons on my suit.

"Oh, I almost forgot. Here's blue," Harriet said, reaching into her pocket. She pulled out an outrageous blue garter, trimmed with rhinestones and feathers.

"No way," I said, laughing.

"Oh, honey," she replied. "I simply insist. Let Tom find it later, to kick off the honeymoon."

Face burning, I let her hold out her skirt to block the view while I discreetly slipped the garter over my ankle and halfway up my thigh, where it would be hidden by my dress.

"You need something borrowed," my mother said. "How about a handkerchief?"

I accepted the lace hanky that she proffered and tucked it against the handle of my bouquet, hoping I wouldn't need it during the ceremony.

That left something new. I supposed my outfit would do. The twins came next, each holding one of Beth's hands, prancing daintily up the path in their flower girl frocks. They looked like little angels. At last night's rehearsal dinner, we had given them bride and groom dolls, and ever since they had been deeply involved in their own little pretend world.

Beth kissed my cheek, showed the girls where to stand until it was time to go forward, and then took the usher's arm and headed up the aisle to find her seat. The song ended and then the band toned things down and launched into the more traditional tune of Pachelbel's "Canon in D."

"Oh, thank goodness," Harriet whispered. "As much as I love dancin', I didn't want to have to do the St. Louis Strut up the aisle!"

My brother, Michael, appeared then, ready to escort my mother to her seat. Phillip and Irene went first, then Michael gave me a brotherly little wink and a wave, took my mom's arm, and went. Harriet squeezed my hand and took her place behind the twins at the entrance of the garden. That left me and my father. I slipped my hand into the crook of his elbow and we got in line behind Harriet. I started to say something to him, but one glance at his face told me that he was pretty choked up already.

Ahead of us I could see the backs of everyone's heads and the pastor taking his place up front. Then Tom and his best friend, his minister from California, came in and stood there as well. Even from where I was standing, Tom looked more handsome than I had ever seen him.

It was time to meet my groom at the altar and become his wife.

As the song entered the final stanza, the twins started their long walk up the aisle, followed by Harriet. My dad and I waited, and as we did, I could already feel tears welling up in my eyes. Blinking them back, I glanced down at the bouquet in my hands, in which I had placed a single white rose, in honor of Bryan.

I had loved him. Oh, how I had loved him!

But now it was time to start anew. This morning, I had received a beautiful delivery of flowers from Bryan's parents, Dean and Natalie Webber, with a note wishing Tom and me the best on our special day and thanking us for the magnificent telescope that had been donated in Bryan's memory to his childhood school.

"We know the donation was made anonymously," Natalie's note said, "but the brass dedication plate finally arrived last week, and the order slip had Tom's name on it."

Tom had never even told me that he was the one who won the bid on the telescope at the Family HEARTS auction—nor that he had donated it to Bryan's old school. That was just like him, to do the perfect thing and never even expect an acknowledgment.

The canon ended and the bridal march began. The people stood and turned to look back at us, smiling. As my dad and I started up the aisle, my mind was suddenly filled with a snippet of a familiar psalm: *He put a new song in my mouth...*

That was my "something new," I realized. A new *song*. Somehow, through all the pain and the loss, God had chosen to bless me yet again. My father gave me away and I took Tom's arm and looked into his eyes. As I did, I saw reflected there all the love I would ever need for the rest of my life.

"Dearly Beloved," the pastor said. "We are gathered here today to join this man and this woman in holy matrimony."

It had been a long road to get where I was right now. But all along the way, God had been there, holding me up, carrying me through, loving me. Now He was about to become the center of a union, the third strand in a cord that would not be broken.

"Thank You, Lord," I whispered softly as a prayer.

Then I started the next great adventure of my life.

# Other Books
# by Mindy Starns Clark

### The Million Dollar Mysteries
A Penny for Your Thoughts
Don't Take Any Wooden Nickels
A Dime a Dozen
A Quarter for a Kiss
The Buck Stops Here

### A Smart Chick Mystery
The Trouble with Tulip
Blind Dates Can Be Murder
Elementary, My Dear Watkins

### Standalone Mysteries
Whispers of the Bayou
Shadows of Lancaster County
Under the Cajun Moon
Secrets of Harmony Grove

### Contemporary Fiction
The Amish Midwife *(cowritten with Leslie Gould)*
The Amish Nanny *(cowritten with Leslie Gould)*

### Nonfiction
The House That Cleans Itself
A Pocket Guide to Amish Life

### Gift Book
Simple Joys of the Amish Life
*(cowritten with Georgia Varozza
and illustrated by Laurie Snow Hein)*

# ECHOES OF THE TITANIC

**What lies echo from the night *Titanic* sank?**

Kelsey Tate's great-grandmother Adele endured the sinking of *Titanic* and made it safely to America, where she not only survived but thrived. Several generations later, Kelsey is a rising star at Brennan & Tate, the firm Adele helped to establish 100 years ago.

Now facing a hostile takeover, the firm's origins are challenged when new facts emerge about Adele's actions on *Titanic*'s last night. Kelsey tries to defend the company and the great-grandmother she has long admired, but the stakes are raised when someone close to her is found dead—and the police won't say if it's suicide or murder.

Forced to seek help from Cole Thornton, a man Kelsey once loved—and lost, thanks to her success-at-all-costs mentality—she pursues mysteries both past and present. Aided by Cole and strengthened by the faith she had all but forgotten in her climb up the corporate ladder, Kelsey races the clock to defend her family legacy, her livelihood, and ultimately her life.

∽

This thrilling new mystery combines a fascinating tale of modern-day corporate intrigue with the deeply moving story of *Titanic*'s fateful voyage.

## Whispers of the Bayou

*What mysteries lie hidden beside the dark water of the bayou?*

Swept away from Louisiana bayou country as a child, Miranda Miller is a woman without a past. She has a husband and child of her own and a fulfilling job in a Manhattan museum, but she also has questions—about the tragedy that cut her off from family and caused her to be sent away, and about those first five years that were erased from her memory entirely.

Summoned to the bedside of Willy Pedreaux, the old caretaker of her grandparents' antebellum estate, Miranda goes back for the first time, hoping to learn the truths of her past and receive her rightful inheritance. But Willy's premature death plunges Miranda into a nightmare of buried secrets, priceless treasure, and unknown enemies.

Follow one woman's search through the hidden rooms of a bayou mansion, the enigmatic snares of an ancient myth, and the all-consuming quest for a heart open enough for love—and for God.

## Under the Cajun Moon

### *What secrets can be found by the light of the Cajun moon?*

New Orleans may be the "Big Easy," but nothing about it was ever easy for international business etiquette expert Chloe Ledet. She moved away years ago, leaving her parents and their famous French Quarter restaurant behind. But when she hears that her father has been shot, she races home to be by his side and to handle his affairs—only to learn a long-hidden secret that changes everything she knew to be true about herself and her family.

Framed for murder, Chloe and a handsome Cajun stranger must search for a hidden treasure, one whose roots weave through the very history of Louisiana itself. But can Chloe depend on the mysterious man leading her on this cat-and-mouse chase into the heart of Cajun country? Or by trusting him, has she gone from the frying pan into the fire?

Following up on her bestselling Gothic thriller, *Whispers of the Bayou,* and Amish romantic suspense, *Shadows of Lancaster County,* Mindy Starns Clark offers another exciting standalone novel, one full of Cajun mystery, hidden dangers, and the glow of God's unending grace.

## Shadows of Lancaster County

### *What Shadows Darken the Quiet Valleys of Amish Country?*

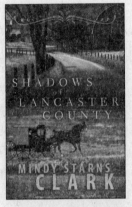

Anna Bailey thought she left the tragedies of the past behind when she took on a new identity and moved from Pennsylvania to California. But now that her brother has vanished and his wife is crying out for help, Anna knows she has no choice but to come out of hiding, go home, and find him. Back in Lancaster County, Anna follows the high-tech trail her brother left behind, a trail that leads from the simple world of Amish farming to the cutting edge of DNA research and gene therapy.

During the course of her pursuit, Anna soon realizes that she has something others want, something worth killing for. In a world where nothing is as it seems, Anna seeks to protect herself, find her brother, and keep a rein on her heart despite the sudden reappearance of Reed Thornton, the only man she has ever loved.

Following up on her extremely popular gothic thriller, *Whispers of the Bayou*, Mindy Starns Clark offers another suspenseful standalone mystery, one full of Amish simplicity, dark shadows, and the light of God's amazing grace.

## SECRETS OF HARMONY GROVE

### *What Secrets Lurk Deep Inside Harmony Grove?*

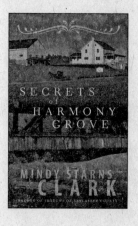

Philadelphia advertising executive Sienna Collins learns she is under investigation by the federal government for crimes she knows nothing about. Suspecting the matter has something to do with one of her investments, the Harmony Grove Bed & Breakfast in Lancaster County, she heads there only to find her ex-boyfriend dead and the manager of the B and B unconscious. As Sienna's life and livelihood spin wildly out of control, she begins to doubt everyone around her, even the handsome detective assigned to the case.

As Sienna searches for the truth and tries to clear her name, she is forced to depend on the faith of her childhood, the wisdom of the Amish, and the insight of the man she has recently begun dating. She'll need all the help she can get, because the secrets she uncovers in Harmony Grove are threatening not just her bed-and-breakfast, but also her credibility, her beliefs, and ultimately her life.

Following up on her bestselling Amish romantic suspense, *Shadows of Lancaster County,* Mindy Starns Clark returns to Pennsylvania to offer another exciting standalone novel, one full of mystery, hidden dangers, and the life-giving truth of God's forgiveness and grace.

To learn more about books by Mindy Starns Clark
and to read sample chapters, log on to our website:

**www.harvesthousepublishers.com**

HARVEST HOUSE PUBLISHERS

EUGENE, OREGON